REALMS OF EDENOCHT

Descendants and Heirs

Realms of Edenocht Descendants and Heirs

D.S. JOHNSON

A Young Adult Fantasy Fiction Action Adventure Novel

DS JOHNSON
2019

First Printing: 2019

ISBN 978-1-7339333-6-0

Illustrator -DS Johnson

Rosecrest Printing
Herriman, Utah 84096
www.dsjohnsonbooks.com

Dedication

To my amazing husband who is forever by my side and is my reason for everything.
To my family and friends who love to play and have fun in life.
To Shaz, Serin, Riddick, Ladtwig, Turkill and now Amirra whom tell their story to me in so many ways.
To my fans and readers who give me the reasons to forge ahead even when it seems like a good time to quit.
To the universe that says, 'there's still more out there, so keep exploring'.

Let's imagine together!

Contents

Realms of Edenocht

Demise of the Rangers

105 Rotations before The End of the Realms

Thirteen heavily armed and highly trained members of the Queen's secret forces sat quietly in a circle. Some sat facing the fire and some with their backs to it watched the distance. The fire's crackles and pops echoed against the cool night. Amber lit shadows danced on their emotionless faces as the fire consumed the dry wood. The three moons peeked through drifting clouds, occasionally shining the purple haze onto the thick forest. A sturdy red-haired mercenary with his back to the flames sat up tall and cocked his head to one side. Almost in unison, the others responded and rested their hands on their weapons and waited.

"Yannick, behind you," Graylon whispered from across the circle.

Yannick slowly stood and pulled his sword from its sheath. He scanned the surroundings as he turned slowly from the fire. A pair of dark eyes pierced through the darkness. The other warriors followed with exactness. The entire circle of men, however, was surrounded by figures garbed in deep-red cloaks which stood in the shadows.

"Blast!" cursed another Ranger.

Graylon gripped his sword with fury and stepped toward the Velshari. A chilly breeze blew through the trees and swirled around them as though with a purpose. Bright lights flashed as electric bolts sizzled through the air. Several Velshari fell as the Rangers deflected the elements of lightning with their unique magic resistant swords. The mercenaries were no strangers to battling Gavin Rhill's forces of magic users. Their enchanted blades could resist most types of magic and were exceptionally light and easy to maneuver.

Runemagic was tailored to each weapon which added extra strength, wit or intelligence for each Ranger's specific fighting styles, strengths, and weaknesses. It hadn't been but a few minutes that the Rangers had sent many of the Velshari to the next life, and normally, these elite Rangers could fight for days, but they found themselves out of breath and sweating. As many of the Velshari they killed, there were that many more that emerged from the darkness. It was becoming harder and harder to even raise their swords. Before too long, they were leaning onto their swords for support.

"What's happening?" Yannick asked.

"I don't know," Graylon said through heavily labored breaths.

A loud crack and a sucking noise echoed around the small clearing as each Ranger fell, completely drained as their last bit of strength was sucked from their bodies.

Bringald struggled to stand but fell back onto his hands and knees. A tall man made his way through the hooded figures, each one bowing as they parted. The man stopped in front of Bringald and smiled under his oversized hood. Bringald tried to search the forest for the young boy he had rescued without giving up the boy, but he couldn't see him anywhere and he sighed a breath of relief. The Velshari took this as defeat and cackled into the night.

"This is not a surrender, Ar-te-bus, you scum," Bringald yelled.

"Then what is it?" the man asked, his tone gleefully eerie.

Bringald closed his eyes and tried to bring as much energy from his core to his limbs, but there was nothing. The shadow magic was too strong, and it had overpowered him completely. Bringald heard a scuffle from the forest and yelled in his mind at Reinholt to stop and be still. Reinholt heard his teacher and hid behind a tree. He peered around the rough bark at the deep red cloaks of the Velshari. They had swords in one hand and an electrifying crackle sitting in the palms of their other hand.

Reinholt's eleven-year-old frame froze, and he couldn't move. A deep pit grew in his stomach, and he wanted to wretch. It was happening again, and this was all his fault. If he hadn't spent so much time with that stupid color-changing lizard he found perched on a rock. If he had gotten the wood like he was told, they wouldn't have had to wait for him, and they would have been able to escape the Velshari.

He peeked through his fingers. He didn't want to watch, but he needed to see who it was. A face, a mark, anything. Reinholt's first lesson with The Ranger's leader, Bringald had been to pay attention to detail quickly and accurately.

Reinholt noted the leader of the Velshari standing with his hands clasped under his cloak, which hung loosely on his body. A small amulet hung around his neck and rested above his navel. Reinholt studied diligently from his distance. The shiny metal gleamed faintly, but enough for him to see the shape of the serpent-like lizard that encircled some rune markings.

Another Velshari gripped Yannick by the hair and yanked his head backward. The force nearly knocked Yannick backward, and Yannick spat in the Velshari's face. The Velshari pulled up his sword and brought it down with speed. The blade sliced through the bone and tissues of Yannick's neck. The Velshari held up Yannick's head, and the crowd cheered. He flung the head into the fire and moved to Graylon. Reinholt's eyes filled with angry tears. He wanted to yell the same words he yelled the night the gryphton's attacked his clan, but he was afraid it would kill his new friends. Maybe they would find a way to get out of this mess. Maybe they wouldn't leave him too. He clenched his jaw together so tightly it hurt.

Graylon lifted his head and spat into the executioner's face before he, too, was executed. Each elite fighter lifted their heads to investigate their killer's face. It was a sign of strength and courage. A warrior's death. The Velshari executioner then moved to Bringald, but the leader held his hand up. The executioner stepped back.

"How did you know it was me?" Ar-te-bus asked.

"Your joking, who else is obsessed with ending my life?" Bringald growled through clenched teeth.

"Then why didn't you try to escape? Oh yes, because you couldn't. Because I am more powerful than you," he sneered and let out another loud cackle.

"You will not win," Bringald said.

"Oh, that is where you are wrong, Bringald, I already have. While you, and your pathetic band of Rangers, have been traipsing about the countryside, I have made allegiance with your precious Queen. She doesn't know it yet, but she is mine, and I *will* take her magic. I *will* have eternal life, and *nothing* you can do will change that." Ar-te-bus sneered.

"How did you find us?" Bringald asked.

"I secretly placed a tracking spell on the amulet the Queen gave you at your last meeting in Srinna Vossa. I have been watching you for over a rotation," Ar-te-bus said.

Bringald's brows raised. He needed to tell Queen Ambrosia what Ar-te-bus was up to.

"That may be so, but there is another," Bringald said.

"Another what?" Ar-te-bus's eyebrow rose slightly.

"Another who seeks to destroy you, and he is one of you."

"Preposterous. My followers swear by magic allegiance. They would die before betraying me. You are reaching for anything you can to spare your life, but it won't work."

"Yet, there is. I have seen it in an Omen. Nothing can be done about that," Bringald said.

Ar-te-bus sneered, narrowed his eyes and gazed into the distance as if he were looking for someone in his head. He smacked Bringald with the back of his ring studded hand, sending blood spatter from Bringald's lip.

"We shall see about that," Ar-te-bus said.

"You cannot take one's magic, it has to be given, and I do not give you my magic." Bringald said spitting blood to the ground, "None of my men did. This will be all for naught but to revel in old jealousies. You know she picked me, and that is why you hate me, and hunt me, nothing more."

"That's a lie!" Ar-te-bus yelled.

A satisfying grin came to Bringald's lips. His eyes wide, he was not afraid to die, he honored it. To die in the service of others was held at the highest level for a Ranger. He did, however, fear for the lad. There was so much talent in him. It was truly rare to find one with his abilities. Bringald sensed the boy's fear from the shadows.

"I will have you know also, there is a young one that will destroy you, and take on my revenge," Bringald said.

Reinholt was certain he was talking to him, and he knew he had to speak the words of destruction. He took a step out from behind the tree, but a cold dark shadow gripped his shoulder. Reinholt froze, then he looked up. Yannick's face emerged from the sifting mist. Yannick shook his head, and Reinholt slipped back behind the tree. Ar-te-bus's eyes narrowed, his brows furrowed with fury, and his lips pursed together. He took the amulet and put it on Bringald's forehead. A bright light flashed in the darkness. Reinholt heard the brush crumble underneath the body of his trainer. Tears flowed down his cheeks, his blood boiled underneath and his heart pounded in his chest, he wanted to run but his legs were frozen in place.

"Reinholt, RUN!" exclaimed a voice standing next to him.

Blurrily, he looked up at Bringald's ghost standing next to him. Bringald looked into his eyes. A fatherly look peered at him, but they were also filled with urgency. His arm stretched out and pointed deep into the forest. Reinholt turned on his heel and darted off in the direction he was told. This time his body responded with exactness.

Reinholt could hardly see as the darkness encompassed the countryside. Small skiffs of mist floated along the uneven ground, leaving it difficult to run. He jumped over fallen trees and slipped under bushes. From the corner of his eyes, he noticed the ghosts of the Rangers. They were running next to him, and formed a circle around him, shielding him from the view of the Velshari in case they may have seen him and were chasing him. He ran between sizeable thorn bushes that filled the empty spaces between the large birch trees and scattered waslick trees. He winced at the pain as the thorns tore through his clothes and skin.

The Forest of Madness was not a gentle place to casually find refuge from everyday life. Most people avoided it like the plague. The dangers were too horrifying, and no one dared. Many scary stories were told to children to keep them from ever going in there. Reinholt ran as fast as his little legs carried him. His heart pounded in his chest, both from fear, and the loss of his new friends.

His chest ached. He felt like he had been running for hours. Every time he wanted to stop, one of the ghosts would yell for him to keep going. He didn't understand why or how he could see them, but he wasn't complaining. They were taking him somewhere specific, but where he could tell. The trees had now been replaced with robust rocks and boulders that blocked his path. He gripped the rough surface and kicked off the soggy ground, but he couldn't hold his grip and slipped back down. The jagged rocks ripped through his fingers and shins. He cried out as he fell to the ground.

"You must keep going, young one," Graylon said.

"I can't, it's too hard."

He showed his fingers, ripped and torn from the sharpness of the rocks. He clenched them tightly to stifle the pain, but it didn't help. The ghosts hurried him along as the deep mahogany purple hues of the night sky faded as the three moons passed overhead on their way into day. Light now gave more detail to his surroundings and Reinholt observed as much as possible, still practicing his first lesson. He noticed small bugs and critters, as well as colors and sounds.

He tried diligently to commit as much of it to memory, stretching the capabilities of his mind. Bringald had told him *to be truly magnificent. He had to stretch his mind to comprehend all things*. Now, with him gone, he wanted more than ever to please him. He found a section of rock which had been carved into steps and scaled them to the top. He kept stumbling and having to catch himself.

"Can we stop now? I am so tired, and hungry, my legs hurt, and my chest is about to give out."

"Soon young one, soon." Yannick's ghost said in a whoosh like sound.

Reinholt questioned if, to others, their voices sounded like the wind howling. After three more boulders and a small ravine, they stopped next to a babbling brook.

"The boy needs to eat and sleep. He needs to tend to his wounds." Grigore, a darker-haired blonde said.

"We'll make camp over the next ridge," Yannick said.

The ghosts nodded. Reinholt had just met them and hadn't learned all their names yet. He wondered where Bringald was. He could see all the others, and he had seen him the night before, but he wasn't there now.

"Bringald is tending to other matters, but he will meet us at Hammerstead," Yannick said.

Reinholt nodded, but then realized he hadn't spoken. He thought to himself, *how did they know what I was thinking.*

"Bringald brought you into our band of brotherhood. We are brother's now young lad, and now that we are on the other side of the barrier, we are not limited by our physical ears. We can hear all your thoughts."

"Oh," Reinholt said, blushing.

A small babbling brook popped out from a pile of rocks just past the ravine.

"Drink, we still have a long way to go, but now we can walk," Graylon said.

Graylon's long blonde hair was like Bringald's, but he was taller and not as bulky. Reinholt drank eagerly and swooshed his hands around to soothe the pain each time he dipped them in for more. It was good to have the ice-cold water penetrate his body each time he swallowed. The cold gave his hands relief too. He slipped his worn shoes off and dipped his bruised toes into the cold water. A shiver ran through his body as the cold soothed the painful blisters but stung his skin. Several minutes later, he found a small rock and sat down. He crossed his arms over his bent knees and laid his head into the crease of his elbow. His eyes sagged until they closed.

Reinholt thought back to when he first met Bringald. Bringald was traveling alone on his way back to the Rangers, through the nether region, when he came upon a small encampment. He approached the tiny huts discreetly, not knowing who occupied them. He had been here before and there had never been anyone dumb enough to live there because of the wild animals that roamed the region. There had also been reports that the gryphton realm had somehow broken the barrier, which is what Bringald had been sent to investigate. The gryphtons were an intelligent creature with the head of an eagle, chest of a human, and legs of a lion. They were meat-eating and were reported as poaching the wild animals, which in itself wasn't a bad thing. It was, however, that they weren't supposed to be in the realm and if there was a rift or tear, they needed to fix it so that other issues wouldn't surface.

A small fire, left in the center of the huts, sizzled and smoldered. It had been unattended for a while and there were no signs of anyone. Bringald heard a rustling from one of the huts a few lengths ahead. He quietly made his way around several piles of ash and soot. He had never seen this before. In all his rotations, over three hundred, this was something that baffled him. He drew his sword from under his traveling cloak and opened the flap that covered the doorway. There was a scuffle toward the back with a sniffle, that of a child.

"It's alright lad, I won't hurt you. What happened here, and where are your people?" a soft deep voice came.

"I don't know," Reinholt replied as he choked with tears.

Bringald put his sword away and knelt on his haunches at the doorway.

"What is your name lad?"

"Reinholt," he answered softly.

"I am Bringald. Maybe I can help you find your parents."

"No, they are dead, I killed them."

"You killed them? How so?"

"The beasts attacked. Some carried off some of the women, and others fought with the men. I am the only child, so I ran and hid. But when I saw the beast kill my father, I ran out of the bushes and yelled at them. Then they all burst into flames and burned to ashes."

Bringald had never heard of this before, but he had seen the ash piles, so he guessed it to be so.

"I am sure it wasn't your fault. I bet it was just a coincidence."

"No, it wasn't." sniffled the boy, "I said the old words and then it happened."

"Old words, like what?"

"I can't, no, I won't say it again."

"Tell me one word?" Bringald nudged.

"Alright," he began to say the first word he remembered.

"I see." Bringald interrupted, "No need to finish."

"You know what it is?" Reinholt asked, shifting in the hut.

"Yes son, can I ask you where you heard these words?"

"I don't know, I never heard them from anyone, they just come into my head," he replied.

Reinholt covered his ears. He shook his head, trying to remove the images out of his mind.

"Come out and I will tell you what happened."

Bringald put out his glove covered hand to the boy. The boy reached for his hand and climbed out of the hut. It was the first time he had seen his tiny homestead since the day before.

"Are you hungry?"

"Yes, starving," he said.

Reinholt wrung his hands together nervously.

"You'll be alright," Bringald said.

He handed him a piece of dried meat from his side pouch. The boy scarfed it down, hardly chewing.

"Now, let me ask you, do you see certain colors around my body?"

"Um-hum," Reinholt muttered, gnawing at the last segment of meat.

"What colors do you see?"

"All of them, even black."

"How long have you seen colors on people?"

"As long as I can remember."

"I see," Bringald stroked his scruffy beard and tapped his finger on his chin. "Where are you from?"

"Dunno, we move all the time, never lived anywhere for too long."

"And your father, mother?"

"Just father, mother died when I was a baby. Father said I was too much for her at birth."

"You have a birthmark?"

Reinholt looked up, surprised. He gulped down the last bite and studied the man's eyes. He beheld the colors dance around him. His father had instructed him to never talk of his birthmark. How did this man know about it? He concluded that the stranger already knew, so Reinholt slowly lifted his shirt, revealing a small red mark under his left arm.

"Well, Reinholt, you are a chosen son of the Rangers. You have been born here to help our world rid it of the evil that is taking over." Bringald removed his glove and raised his arm and showed the child the same mark, "There is much for you to learn and much I hope to learn from you. But for now, let's take you out of here and somewhere safer," Bringald said.

He searched around for a pack to put the boy's things in.

"Rangers?"

"We have plenty of time. Let's work on getting your stuff and see if we can gather the last of the supplies. Go gather your things and put them in a satchel, we need to be quick."

Reinholt returned to his hut and scurried around. He threw all he thought of into a satchel. As he brushed through the scattered mess, a bronze metallic shape stood out from under a blanket. The small amulet glowed a rusty red. He moved the blanket out of the way. His eyes squinted sharply as he stared at it. It was the same as his birthmark. Gingerly, he picked it up and rubbed his skinny finger over it. A tingle surged through his finger and into his hand. It coursed through his body. He had never had this sensation before.

"Are you ready, boy?" Bringald called gruffly.

Reinholt crammed it into his pocket and grabbed his satchel. It was almost too heavy for him to carry, but he had done it many times before and was surprisingly strong for his skinny little frame. Reinholt struggled to keep up with Bringald's strides.

"Come, time to go," Graylon said, jarring Reinholt from his memories.

His voice echoed a slight sense of urgency. Reinholt sat up and rubbed the sleep from his eyes. He jumped up but was reminded that his entire body ached.

"Did I fall asleep?"

"For a little bit, young one," Grigore said.

"I'm sorry."

"No need, but now we must keep moving."

Reinholt followed the ghosts farther up the mountain. The sun brightened the sky as they moved higher and higher. A soft, gentle glow settled on the peaks behind him as it finally crested the horizon. In the distance, he found tiny little islands floating in the sky. He tried to take a good look, but he stumbled over a tree root. He caught himself with a branch and was surprised to feel his stomach lurch and he felt off-balance as he observed the beasts in the grasslands below, the extreme birds of prey leaping into the sky from the peaks above, and the smells of morning dew and fresh berries.

"How long will it take to get there? Not that I'm complaining."

The ghosts chuckled.

"Two days' journey if we keep this pace."

Reinholt sagged a little under the news, but decided to put forth his best effort. The sleep had done him a little good, but he still felt like he could sleep for a week. The dread that his journey would only become harder as the days passed became clear. The small band of elite warriors was on their way to Srinna Vossa where he was to be ordained a Ranger Apprentice. He worried about what would happen now. They were some of the oldest and most experienced, and it was a chance of a lifetime to be trained by even one of them, let alone all of them. They had so much wisdom and knowledge. Now, will anyone ever learn their secrets? How had it happened, how had the Velshari managed to capture them? And then worse, behead them all. They should have had the skills to evade the dark magic. It didn't make any sense.

1-That Should Draw Them This Way

About 301 rotations since The End of the Realms –E.O.R

Heavy gusts whipped through the barren wasteland. The radiating heat stung their lungs as they barreled over the uneven ground. Long strands of purple haze lined the night sky. Murky shadows played tricks on their senses as they dodged the tiny night insects. Turkill snagged a small stone as he turned a sharp corner. He placed it in the pocket of his sling and swung it over his head. He regained his footing and twisted at the waist. He let the momentum propel the stone. It sliced through the air like a razor and hit the Jaduuk square in the forehead. The creature fell backward in an instant. The pack of Jaduuk still behind leaped over their fallen packmate. They dug their hind legs into the ground and leaped over scattered boulders with ease.

Ladtwig ran onto a half-fallen tree and slammed his walking stick into the ground. His small frame launched into the air. He pulled his arms and legs in tight and rolled through the smelly, orc-like-wolf-hunter's arms. He somersaulted onto a jagged boulder on the other side and scurried over the edge.

"Send our scents into the breeze," Shaz said.

Serin twirled her hands, spinning the air before launching it toward the Jaduuk. The Jaduuk hunter snarled. Drool dripped from his long fangs at the sides of his mouth. Long ears at the top of his head twitched, and his snout-like nose puckered as he caught the scent. He skidded in the soft dirt and shot off toward them. Turkill leaped behind the boulder Ladtwig was behind and rolled to a stop.

"That should draw them this way," Shaz said.

"And then what?" Serin asked.

"We set a trap," Shaz said.

"How those things are twice our size, and we have no idea what they're capable of?"

"Then we find out," Shaz said.

"You know, I'm starting to doubt your logic here," Serin said.

"Here, help me with this rock."

Serin called the air and sent a puff under the immense boulder. Even with her air magic, the boulder was almost too heavy to move. She gripped the ground with her toes and stretched her arms out as far as she could. The boulder inched gradually. Shaz thrust his shoulder into the stone and heaved. It moved into place and Serin dropped her arms. They hurried behind the rock and crouched into its shadow.

Serin gripped the cold stone for support. Shaz could tell she was becoming weaker, and he did rely on her air magic more than he should. *Think, think, what would Grandfather tell me to do?* He thought.

"Do you think you could make a sandpit, while I keep them busy?" Shaz asked.

Serin studied him with a little surprise. She understood from his expression that he knew she was tiring. She sucked in a deep breath and nodded. Shaz touched her shoulder, and she became aware of his energy. It tickled her skin and gave her a little more confidence. Shaz gripped the hilt of his sword and rounded the boulder. At first, he couldn't see anything, but then, a funny image played out in his head. He sucked in a deep breath and the image became a little clearer.

"One, two, three, four, five," Shaz counted.

He found the Jaduuk scents and a blurry image of where they were settled into his consciousness. Three were larger than the other two, and he surmised they were the males. He pulled the sword from his side and allowed the energy to surge through his arm. He took several steps from Serin and then ran toward the smaller beasts.

Serin slipped off her boots and wriggled her toes into the soft sand. She hadn't understood why Shaz wanted the boulder moved, but now she could tell it was because the ground was softer here. She gathered the strength she needed and began filling the sand with air. A steady stream of wind burrowed into the sand, making the top bubble and bounce. Serin's arms ached. She closed her eyes and tried to focus on the wind, but she found it difficult. She breathed heavily, and her body sagged. The wind continued to burrow deep into the ground, making the circle widened. She had no idea how big to make it because she had no idea how big the beasts actually were, or if they could jump high, or at all.

Shaz clenched his fist. The pounding of the ground intensified as the pack quickened their paces. He was confident they had him locked into their senses and the only way out was to fight. A high-pitched snarl echoed over his shoulder. The enormous jaguar leaped over Shaz and sank her claws into a Jaduuk. The creature recoiled. A strong odor wafted through the air, and Shaz covered his nose. Jagwynn gripped the sand and slid on her haunches. The Jaduuk snarled and roared. Jag returned the roar and leaped at the Jaduuk. The Jaduuk dug its claws into Jag's flesh. Jagwynn yelped and her eyes widened. She opened her jaws wide and gripped the Jaduuk's face with her claws. She sunk her teeth into the thick leathery texture of the beast's neck. The Jaduuk reared back and tried to shove the huge cat off. Jagwynn swung her tail to keep her balance as her hind legs pushed herself onto the beast. They toppled to the ground and the more the Jaduuk wriggled, the tighter Jag clenched.

Shaz ran at one of the smaller Jaduuk. He flipped the sword and sliced the beast's chin. The beast roared and stumbled backward. Shaz spun and brought his blade over his head. The slight glow of the sword's markings made a mark in the night sky. He pulled it down with ease and listened to the whipping-sound it made against the howling of the wind. The blade sunk deep into the shoulder of the on-coming Jaduuk. A high-pitched howl pierced Shaz's head, and he flinched.

Shaz flew several lengths from another Jaduuk's fist, hitting him in the ribs. Shaz struggled to breathe as the pain raced to his brain. The cold, gritty earth found its way into his lungs as he gasped for air. Shaz coughed and gagged as a mixture of blood and sand escaped his lungs. The metallic taste the blood left sank into his consciousness. The heat of the Jaduuk's breath ripped down his spine. He couldn't make his body move. No matter how hard he tried and how much he yelled in his mind, it wouldn't respond.

"Stay here," Turkill said.

"What are you going to do?" Ladtwig asked.

"I don't know yet, but I have to help," Turkill said.

"We are way too small, they will eat us alive," Ladtwig said.

"Maybe that's the way we fight," Turkill said.

"How do you mean?" Ladtwig asked.

"Well, they can't fight something they can't see," Turkill said.

"But they see with their noses," Ladtwig said.

"Yep," Turkill said.

Turkill pulled all his leather armor and clothes off, clear down to his skivvies. Ladtwig's eyes popped out of his head. Turkill pulled his knife from his belt and sliced several desert plants off their stems. He rubbed them vigorously until his bronzed skin no longer showed. Ladtwig quickly followed and covered himself too.

"This plant stinks," Ladtwig said.

"Uh-huh."

Turkill removed his sling and gathered several rocks and shoved them into his pouch. He secured them around his waist and crept out from around the boulder. Ladtwig filled his pouch and grabbed his dart gun.

"I thought you were out of darts?" Turkill asked.

"I am, but you never know."

The steady wind had long dried all the water from their bodies. It was hard to move around without feeling the sting of their skin cracking. The heavy clouds thinned, letting a soft hint of the moon's light shine over the wasteland. Turkill caught a glimpse of the pack running toward Shaz and Serin.

"Over there," Turkill said.

Ladtwig nodded and hurried around the other side of a broad-faced rock. They froze in place when they heard Jagwynn snag her prey. Seconds later, Turkill waved to Ladtwig, and they maneuvered closer.

The largest Jaduuk waited at the back of the pack. He twisted his ears back and forth and sniffed the air. Turkill crept up to a desert plant and cringed as a twig snapped under his foot. The Jaduuk cocked his head and flicked his long pointy ear backward. Turkill froze and held his breath. The beast turned and studied the landscape. He sniffed again and sank his massive claws into the ground. A deep orange glow radiated from the creature's eyes. Turkill's heart sank, and he pushed the bile back into his stomach. Ladtwig tossed a stone across his path onto the other side, and the beast turned. The Jaduuk meticulously searched the night.

Turkill laid a stone into his sling and sucked in a deep breath. His arm shot above his head and his wrist flicked the sling so hard that the motion didn't even take half a second. The rock soared through the air like lightning and sank into the back of the beast's skull. The Jaduuk stopped mid-step and hesitated. He touched the back of his head and felt the stone. He turned around in slow motion and tried to make sense of what happened.

Turkill held his breath as he tried to understand why the rock didn't take him down. The beast shook his head and the orange glow returned. Turkill gulped and sunk low to the ground. Ladtwig flicked his sling, sending another stone into the Jaduuk's temple. The beast stumbled but didn't fall. Turkill scoured around in his pouch for the sharpest stone and loaded it into his sling. He stood, raised his arm and flicked his wrist. The stone shot out of the sling and ripped across the sky.

The fierce rotation of the rock became like a razor as it sliced its enormous bicep. Ladtwig slipped as he stepped over a rock and fell. He rolled over and rubbed his hiney. He hurried to his feet and positioned himself behind a rock. He reached for another stone, but his pouch wasn't there.

"Blast," he said.

The Jaduuk turned and moved toward him. Ladtwig hurried to the bush to search for his pouch. Turkill moved behind a dead tree trunk and loaded his sling. He peeked over the trunk but couldn't see the beast. He moved to the end of where it had been, but it wasn't there either. He hurried to the other end and peeked under the haggard roots. He could barely make out the Jaduuk and crept to a closer rock.

Shaz gripped his ribs and closed his eyes. A strong sensation coursed through his torso, calming the pain to a tolerable degree. He caught a glimpse of Serin stepping back behind the boulder. His heart swelled with undeniable gratitude for her. He shook his head and flung the Honor Blade behind him, letting the motion carry him back to his feet. The Jaduuk jumped back, but not far enough. The tip of the blade raced over its belly.

Shaz parried and sidestepped. The Jaduuk pulled a battle-ax off his back. Shaz studied the images in his mind and readied himself. Shaz threw up his sword and caught the ax at its head. He spun the blade and yanked. The Jaduuk gripped the long-hardened wood shaft tightly in his paw. Shaz let the blade slip away and parried back. The Jaduuk pounded its chest and howled. The grounds vibrations rippled into Shaz's body and the pit in his stomach clenched tighter. Shaz identified the remainder of the pack and learned they had mobilized toward them. Still keeping the beast in his sight, he checked to see if Serin was ready.

Serin leaned against the boulder and wiped the sweat from her brows. Her lightweight cotton tunic stuck to her slender frame. She tried to steady her breathing but found it difficult. She rubbed her aching arms and shivered from the wind as it blew against her wet skin. She examined her sinkhole and was confident it would at least take a few of the beasts. Serin brushed off her feet and slipped them back into her boots. She boosted herself from the boulder and curled her tongue between her teeth. A high-pitched whistle whipped over the air. The long-draping fur at the top of the Jaduuk's ears curved over to shield its inner ear from the noise. Shaz closed the gap and brought the sword up to a side strike. The blade made contact at the base of the creature's neck. The ridiculous stench wreaked havoc on Shaz's senses and he struggled to keep his nerves. The Jaduuk staggered, swaying back and forth until it lost consciousness and fell with a thud. Shaz searched his night vision and determined the rest of the pack wasn't far behind.

Jagwynn released the lifeless body and searched for her next target. She narrowed her eyes and slunk close to the ground. The coolness of the red dirt felt good on her warmed fur. At the back of the pack, she found the smallest Jaduuk and made her way. Jagwynn lay in the taller straggly grass and waited until the Jaduuk came close enough. She lunged with her forceful hind legs and released her claws. Jagwynn sunk her claws into the Jaduuk's shoulder and flung it to the ground. She flipped around and lunged again.

The Jaduuk went sprawling to the ground. Its look of shock and instant fear fed Jagwynn's excitement, and she sank her teeth into its neck. The Jaduuk squealed and flailed around, but Jagwynn gripped tighter.

Ladtwig found his pouch and tried to tie it back onto his breeches. The hot breath of the Jaduuk caressed his bare skin. The hairs on the back of his neck stood out and his body shivered. He gulped and turned around. His head lifted upward as far as it could go. The orange glow was now dark red. Its long snout flared, and drool dripped from its giant fangs that crested its eyebrows. Ladtwig searched his pouch, but his heart sunk when there were no stones. He slid his foot backward.

Ladtwig didn't see the rock behind him and toppled over it. He scooched backward, scrambling to figure out what to do. As he grappled the ground, he brushed up against a prickly plant. He broke off a long stem and jammed it into his dart gun. The Jaduuk opened his mouth wide and roared. Ladtwig sucked in and blew the stick hard and fast through the dart gun. The stick shot out and lodged into the back of the beast's throat.

Stunned, the Jaduuk dropped its ax and grabbed at its throat. Ladtwig scurried out from under its extensive claws as it staggered around. Turkill shot across the dirt and loaded his sling. The rock ripped across the sky with a whistle and embedded into the Jaduuk's throat, crushing its airway. Ladtwig jumped to his feet and darted back to the boulder they had left their clothes behind.

"One, more second," Shaz said under his breath. Serin whistled again and peeked out. Shaz dug his boot into the ground and lunged toward her. He crossed the distance at full speed and slid to a stop as he rounded the boulder. "Are you ready?" he asked, breathing heavily.

"Yes, but I have no idea how many it will hold?" she said.

Shaz nodded and peered around the rock.

"In about ten seconds, run that way as fast as you can and don't look back," Shaz said. Serin scowled and searched his face. He wasn't playing, and a hint of fear crept into her chest. "Go!" he said.

Serin propelled herself from the rock and dug her boots into the sturdy ground. She was glad the clouds had thinned, letting her see enough of the landscape, so she didn't have to stumble around. The pounding of the beast's heavy claws drowned out the blood beating in her ears. The sudden boost of adrenaline surged throughout her body, giving her a satisfying renewal. She leaped over a fallen tree trunk and caught herself as the loose ground moved under her feet.

From the corner of her eye, she found Ladtwig and Turkill huddled under the lowest ledge of a substantial rock. She picked up a rock and chucked it at them. They jumped, grabbed their things and darted toward her. She slowed her pace so they could catch up.

"Don't stop running," she said as they met up with her.

"Where's Shaz?" Turkill asked.

"He's coming," she said.

2-That's Not How You Catch A Fish

Turkill peered over his shoulder and caught a glimpse of Shaz shooting out from behind the rock. The first orc-ish creature slammed his foot into the ground to round the rock tightly, but his weight was too much for the air-filled sandpit. He slid across the others and bowled them into the pit. A deep growl echoed over their heads. Shaz leaped over the fallen tree trunk, closing the distance. Three more Jaduuk crashed into the sandpit and onto the others. Jagwynn padded up behind Ladtwig and nestled her nose between his legs. She lifted him over her head and onto her back. Turkill grabbed her fur and slammed his feet into the ground and propelled himself onto her back.

"We need to make it into those trees," Shaz said.

"What trees?" Serin asked.

Shaz pointed, but Serin couldn't see any trees. She understood he could see farther than she could, so she shifted her weight and dug into the ground. Her body ached, and her chest stung from the exertion and hot air. The night crept away with the faint hint of day. As the sun illuminated the backdrop, tiny white peaks formed against the soft pink and orange sunrise.

"What about the Jaduuk?" Turkill asked.

"We lost most of them for now." Shaz said.

"That's just perfect," Turkill grumbled.

Ladtwig attempted to say something but grabbed Turkill's waist so he wouldn't fall off. Jagwynn's long strides caressed the earth, but Ladtwig bounced. Turkill was a natural and hovered over her sleek frame as though he wasn't even sitting on her back. A Jaduuk howled from the distance.

"We may have outsmarted them for now, but they won't stop," Shaz said.

"That's just swell," Turkill said.

"I'm not sure how much more I can go," Serin said.

"Let's get into those trees first," Shaz said.

Shaz noticed Serin was falling a few steps behind. He grabbed her hand to keep her moving. The tree line came into view and they pushed even harder. The sun crested the horizon, casting a soft honey-glow on the desert behind them. They stopped several lengths into the trees. Serin struggled to keep standing. The heat had taken so much of her strength, even before digging the sandpit. Turkill and Ladtwig studied her, trying to decide if they needed to help her. Shaz pulled her into his arms and held her tight. Serin buried her face in his shoulder and sagged into his embrace. Shaz knew he had asked a considerable amount of her, and he felt completely helpless. His warmth soothed her scattered energy, and she soaked it in.

"Those are the Bairr Mountains," Shaz said, pointing to the small peaks in the distance.

"Hurmph," Turkill said.

"Is there any chance we can stop for breakfast soon?" Ladtwig said.

"Are you serious?" Turkill asked.

"What? It's almost time for breakfast and with all that running, I'm starving."

"What are we going to eat, Ladtwig?" Turkill asked.

Ladtwig searched for his satchel and then slouched.

"Blast. It's gone," he said.

"We need to put more distance between us, then we can stop for food. Any chance you could do your air buff?" Shaz asked.

She looked up at him and his heart sank.

"Are you trying to kill her?" Turkill barked.

"I'll carry you for a while," Shaz said.

His voice was soft and his blue eyes sincere.

"I'll try, but I can't guarantee how strong it will be," she said.

"It's ok, we just need to put a little more distance between us and find a shelter to rest in," Shaz said.

Turkill glowered at Shaz. Serin nodded. Shaz squeezed her one more time, and she cast her air buff spell on Shaz and Jagwynn. She figured she didn't need to buff the Minca since they were riding Jag and Shaz would carry her. Shaz knelt and Serin climbed onto his back. He winced as her thigh gripped around his torso.

"Oh, no, your ribs," Serin said.

"It's just a bruise," he said.

He gripped her legs and pulled her onto his back. She was certain he was lying, but she could hardly stay awake enough to argue. The small gap between them and the earth allowed them to move briskly and with ease. Shaz and Jag maneuvered the forest at a decent pace. The deeper they went, the thicker it became, until the air buff faded and Shaz's feet touch solid ground. Serin stirred and Shaz set her down.

"How are you feeling?" he asked.

"Better," she said.

"Good," Shaz said.

The sun reached the top of the sky. A whipping sound emerged from the treetops as a hefty black-bird shot from the sky. Shaz darted out of the way, falling into a roll and drawing his sword as he stood. Serin leaped behind a log, and the Minca and Jag raced to a bush. The sqwall pulled up and twirled to lessen its ascent and bent in half and plummeted back toward them. The deep black eyes glistened in the speckled sun rays. Shaz shoved his foot into the side of a tree and propelled himself into the air. He pulled the blade through the debris as it twirled around in the air from the forest floor.

The enormous crow-like bird screeched and Shaz narrowed his eyes. The blade contacted the side of the creature's neck. Deep rusty-red blood spurted. It recoiled and staggered from the sky. Shaz flipped head-over-heels and landed softly on his feet. He didn't understand at the time why Grandfather was always trying to coerce him to practice leaping onto trees and flipping and rolling. Now it was so natural and the more he did it, the higher he could leap and the farther he could propel himself.

"Find cover," Shaz yelled.

Serin searched the forest.

"There," she said.

They maneuvered the uneven terrain and veered left into a thick layer of underbrush. A loud bang pounded the air as the bird transfigured into a human-like form. The dirt and debris sizzled when the sqwalls blood hit it. Shaz scrunched his nose and parried around it. It gasped for air and tried to squeal, but the blood gurgled in its throat before it sagged lifelessly. Shaz returned the sword and studied it for a moment. The body twitched and Shaz kicked it. A small trinket fell out of a pocket. Shaz cocked his head with curiosity. He bent over the beast and found that the feathers weren't all attached to its body but were more like clothes. He padded the pockets and found several odd pieces of debris, beads, twine and other things a bird might find interesting.

He figured it must be the scavenger nature of the blackbird. In the last pocket, he found the small sapphire bead from his ceremonial neck collar. Serin and Jag hurried toward the bushes but were unable to stop in time as they noticed they were thorn bushes. Sharp thorns ripped into their skin as they shot into the cover. Jagwynn hissed and Ladtwig yelped and rolled off her back as an amply sized thorn embedded itself into his thigh. Shaz slipped the bead and the trinket into his pocket and hurried after Serin and Jag.

"We have to stop," Serin said. She hurried over to Ladtwig. "Let me see it."

"It hurts," Ladtwig said, trying to keep his lip from trembling.

Serin put her hand on his leg and warmed his skin with the tingle of magic. The pain eased, and she gripped the thorn with her teeth and yanked it out. Bright red oozed from the puncture wound. Turkill yelped when the red drips sank into his awareness.

"Don't tell me you can't stand the sight of blood?" Shaz asked.

"No, just his blood," Turkill said.

Serin drew in a breath and wriggled her fingers over the hole in his skin, and the deep azure-blue magic danced around the wound. The skin started to pull shut, but a heavy pounding echoed toward them.

"We need to keep going," Shaz said.

"We need rest," Serin said.

"We need shelter and a hiding place," Turkill said.

"We need food and lots of it," Ladtwig said.

It was hard not to grin at Ladtwig's insatiable appetite. Shaz searched for a place they could make a shelter out of. Vast trees emerged from tall grasses but narrowed at the top. The short, spindly branches wouldn't offer support. Several lengths away, mist rose from the ground.

"Over there," Shaz said

"What is it?" Turkill asked.

"No idea, but we may find some shelter behind that mist," Shaz said.

Shaz winced as he picked up Ladtwig and made his way between the thorn bushes.

"Look. Over here." Serin said.

A small waterfall poured from a high ledge. Shaz and Serin sunk several small lengths as they moved through the water-soaked ground. Turkill didn't sink as much because he was so much smaller and weighed less. Behind the falls an alcove was covered with tall reeds. The waterfall's energy ravaged the pond, causing it to dance and sway. Serin stepped on small uneven rocks protruding from the muddy edge. Shaz balanced on the first few. He handed Ladtwig to Serin after she made it to the landing. Turkill jumped across, but on the last rock he slipped and landed on his behind in the cold water. He jumped out of the water, cursing the whole way.

Serin sat Ladtwig on the cold stone and examined the wound. The puncture was now deep purple against his bronze skin. She pulled a stream of water from the fall and washed the wound. Ladtwig hissed as the cold hit his skin. Jagwynn plopped her plentiful hide next to him and licked his face.

"Looks like you two have this under control. Turkill let's scout the area and see if we can find some food," Shaz said.

Turkill reached for his sling, but it wasn't there.

"Well, that's just great. Just great! I lost my sling now too. What else could go wrong on this blasted adventure?" Turkill slammed his arms across his chest and huffed with a larger than usual scowl. The howl of the Jaduuk echoed off the walls of the falls. "No, no, no, I am not doing this."

"Come on, grumpy," Shaz said.

"This is not happening, this is not happening, this is not happening," Turkill mumbled as he scaled the rock that sent him into the pond.

Serin finished dressing Ladtwig's leg and rested against the wall. Jag laid next to her to share her heat.

"What do you think is going to happen?" Ladtwig asked.

"I haven't a clue. We must figure out a way to draw the Jaduuk off our trail. They are definitely good hunters," Serin said.

"What are the Jaduuk exactly?" Ladtwig asked.

"Creatures from the underworld who were brought here by the evil Necromancer as his foot soldiers," Serin said.

"I understand that, but what are they. Are they wolves, or humans, or what?" Ladtwig asked.

"I'm not sure, Shaz says they have hooves like horses and run on hind legs but can run on all four. They can see in the dark and hunt in packs," Serin said.

"Those didn't look like hooves. They were more like claws." Ladtwig said.

"Well, this is the first time we have actually seen one," Serin said.

"Packs? How many are there then?" Ladtwig asked.

"There were at least a dozen just now," Serin said.

"I'm starving," Ladtwig whined.

"Me too, but we'll have to wait until Shaz and Turkill return," Serin said.

"Uhhhgggg," Ladtwig moaned.

Ladtwig grabbed his stomach and rolled to the ground. A silvery movement under the water's surface flashed against the ceiling. Serin crawled to the edge and searched the soft blue pond. Several fish swam around a stalk of water weed. She reached in to grab one, but they swam away.

"That's not how you catch fish," Ladtwig said.

"Oh, well then you do it," Serin said.

Serin scowled at Ladtwig.

"First you have to climb in the water and walk very slowly. Then when you reach the right spot, you must stand still until the fish start to swim around you. You must be perfectly still, or they will swim away. Then when a fish is close enough, you have to throw your spear into their flesh before they sense your movement," Ladtwig said.

"Oh, is that all?" Serin asked.

Serin held out her hand and yanked it back toward her. A wave of water splashed on the ledge, leaving three fish flopping around. Ladtwig's eyes popped out of his head and his jaw dropped. The water splashed onto her skin and sank deep. She sighed with the little bit of rejuvenation it gave her.

"Now if only we had a fire," she said.

"I can help you with that," Shaz said, hopping onto the ledge.

"Did you find anything?" Serin asked.

"No, it would seem we have escaped them for now," Shaz said.

Turkill balanced on the rock before his nemeses and calculated the distance. He swung his arms and leaped across the water. His foot hit the center, and he leaped again onto the ledge.

"Glad to see you made it this time," Serin said.

Turkill blushed under a scowl. Shaz gathered the dry wood and twigs he had brought into the center of the alcove.

"We can't let it burn for long, so we better hurry," Shaz said.

He took out his flint and struck it against a stone.

"Aren't you supposed to be able to make fire come out of your hand or something?" Turkill asked.

Shaz gazed into his dark eyes and glared. He was right, but Shaz had never done it. The closest he came was when he made his palm burn with heat at Lucien's. Guilt sank a little deeper as he struggled with the insecurity he already had.

"Any idea where we are?" Serin asked.

"Yeah, in perdition," Turkill said.

"He gets like this when he is hungry," Ladtwig said. He pointed at the fish. "What are you guys going to eat?"

Serin glared at him and made another wave of water splash with more fish.

"I know his pain," Shaz said.

"You mentioned the peaks. About how long do you think it will take?" Serin asked.

Shaz appreciated Serin's effort to change the subject.

"I'm thinking the mountain range starts not far from here. It will probably take us several days to make it to the peaks though," Shaz said.

Shaz opened his hand and held out his palm. He thought back and tried to remember the feelings of when he was at Luciens but the memories of when watched the fire consume his childhood home came to the surface. All he could feel was anger, and a deep heat swelled at his center. His palm warmed, and the red swirl emerged. Turkill gasped and hurried behind Serin. Serin watched with wide eyes and studied his magic, noting his heartfire to make sure she knew how it acted when he called the fire magic. Shaz's brows furrowed as he concentrated. Little flickers of sparks danced from his skin and he smiled. He lowered his hand to the twigs and blew on the sparks. A flame popped into existence and danced from his hand.

"Look, I did it!" he said excitedly.

He hovered a dry twig over the flame until it caught fire and then sat it on the others. He folded his fingers over the flame, and it sizzled and faded. He shook his hand and blew on the little fire.

"That was fantastic, Shaz," Serin said.

"Yeah," Ladtwig said.

"Humph," Turkill said.

Shaz fileted the fish and impaled them onto a dried reed.

"Do you think we have time for a bath and to gather supplies before they find us?" Serin asked.

Turkill's skin reddened under his cheeks and Ladtwig snickered.

"If we hurry," Shaz said, trying not to blush himself.

"What about me? I can't walk," Ladtwig said.

"You can ride on Jag," Shaz said, rubbing Jag's ears.

The smoke from the fire hovered at the top of the cave and thickened. Serin checked the fish and handed them out. Shaz snuffed out the fire. Ladtwig scarfed the first fish in a matter of seconds. Serin rolled her eyes and Turkill turned away, shielding his from Ladtwig who was about to ask if he was done. Shaz finished his meal quickly and reached for another fish. He moaned and grabbed his side.

"Oh my, how could I have forgotten?" Serin said.

She set her meal down and scooted to Shaz. She rested her cold hands on his ribs and closed her eyes. Shaz didn't want to ask. It seemed that she was always healing him from something he did that was less than intelligent. He needed her so much and was sad that all he ever did was use her magic. Serin concentrated on his broken rib and imagined it growing back together. The heat the blue magic made surged into Shaz's core. A slight glow of sweat crested his hairline and the throbbing ache subsided. Then shame crested his core, and he pushed back the tears that tried to escape. Serin opened her eyes and gazed into his. She smiled gently and gave him a small nod as if to say, 'I know, and I don't mind.' It did make him feel a little better, but not much. Instead of dwelling on what he couldn't change, Shaz distracted himself with making his hand burst into flames.

He popped open his palm and at first, all he had was sparks. He went from one hand to the other and then both until it was instant fire every time. Serin watched his energy radiate around his core and gaged how much energy it took each time he engaged the fire. Each time he put his fingers over the small flames to extinguish them. It amazed him that fire sat on his skin and didn't burn him. He was concerned if other parts of his skin would burn if it touched the fire. He lit his hand on fire and hovered the back of his other hand over the flame and was pleased there was no pain.

"What are you doing?" Ladtwig asked.

"I'm finding out what part of me is subject to fire," Shaz said.

"Please be careful," Serin said.

He nodded and smiled, then moved it along his arm with no pain. He ran his fire all over his body, and the only places he could sense the heat or sting of the fire were on his chest. He pondered why the rest of his skin was exempt from it, but not his chest.

Serin sat on the edge and hung her feet in the water. The healing power the water gave her left her refreshed, but it was the rush of the falls that was so soothing she found it hard to stay awake.

"Let's make another sweep," Shaz said.

Turkill nodded and followed Shaz. Ladtwig whittled sharp points on several tiny darts he made out of the dried reeds. He explained to Serin how his dart blower worked and that it took time to fine-tune the points. He was very meticulous, which at first bothered her.

Serin waited until Ladtwig had fallen asleep and stepped into the water and made her way to the other side of the pool. Tall reeds swayed in the breeze the falls made. She swept the reeds aside and peeked into the other side. Another smaller pool glistened in the fading sun. She crossed the reeds into the smaller pool and pulled her dirt-stained tunic over her head. It amused her that at one time it had been a soft pink color. She removed her leggings and hung them on the reeds and pulled out the band that held her hair up.

Her long brown hair rested against her skin. She laid back into the water, letting it energize every bit of her. She swayed back and forth a few times and sat up and washed her face. She washed her clothes and laid them over the reeds to dry. She rubbed her skin under the water and viewed the dirt melt off her skin. She finished her bath and peeked through the reeds. She slipped out of the water and onto the warm stone. She pulled her cloak out of her backpack and covered herself and lay on her bag. Late in the afternoon, Serin woke to Shaz's and Turkill's hushed voices.

"You're awake," Shaz said.

"What's going on?" Serin asked.

"We can stay the night but there are heavy clouds sitting at the peaks and I'm afraid we will get caught in bad weather if we stay any longer. Do you think Ladtwig can travel?" Shaz said.

"I'm sure he can, but we might have to convince him of that," Serin said.

She sat up and her cloak fell from her neck. She caught it before it showed too much, but Shaz and Turkill turned away.

"It's going to be nightfall soon and I'm not convinced we have lost the Jaduuk," Shaz said.

"What makes you say that?" Serin asked, reaching for her clothes.

"I found some tracks, but it's hard to tell how old they are," Shaz said.

"Why?" Serin asked.

"They are underwater," Shaz said.

Serin nodded and rubbed her chin.

"I wonder if I could tell."

She pulled her tunic over her head.

"You can't tell through water," Turkill argued.

"I might elicit a feeling from the water. Maybe it will tell me," Serin said as she pulled her leggings on.

"It's too far away to make it back before nightfall. We'll just head out first thing and stay alert," Shaz said.

They returned to Ladtwig, who stirred and shifted.

"How do you feel?" Serin asked.

Ladtwig wriggled his foot and smiled. Serin helped him stand, and he tested it.

"It's better," Ladtwig said.

"Good, then we'll leave in the morning," Shaz said.

"Do we have any supplies?" Serin asked.

"Do we have food?" Ladtwig asked.

"Well, if you wouldn't eat so much and save some, maybe you wouldn't be so hungry all the time," Turkill said.

"If you wouldn't make me have to leave my entire stash behind because you couldn't keep your mouth shut," Ladtwig said.

"Really?" Serin said, her tone sharp.

The little men opened their mouth, then closed them. Shaz smirked.

"We found a beehive and some roots," Shaz said.

"I'll go with you," Serin said.

Shaz nodded, and they left, leaving the little men to continue their argument.

3-There's An Intruder On The Island

Riddick slipped around a large waslick tree and gripped the rope, lifted the clank precisely, and stepped onto the weighted wood platform. The double pulley system effortlessly lifted Riddick into the dark canopy of the lush green waslick tree. Riddick felt the cool night air become warmer the higher he went. The platform reached the outer wooden walkway around the tree hut. Riddick stopped and listened. Clanks and crashes sounded from inside. He slipped the loop over the peg and tip-toed toward the back door. He gripped the hilt of his battle-ax and delicately lifted the latch.

The room was dark, and Riddick knew no one should be home. Grandfather had left shortly after Shaz did and hadn't been back in over two moons. Merrick was also gone on another trip through the

Turbulent Reef. He slipped through the entry, closing the door behind him. The clashing stopped, and Riddick made his way over the broken and disheveled furniture. When he reached the other side of the room, he leaned against the wall and put his ear toward the hallway, which connected the general meeting room with the kitchen. He peeked around the corner and held his breath. He hurriedly made his way to the end of the hall and stopped short of the exit. He listened again and gradually let out his breath. A faint scratching came from the next room.

It sounded like a bird's claws were scratching at the wood planks. He peeked around the corner and examined his next route. The chairs and tables were strewn about, along with dishes and miscellaneous kitchen items. He rounded the corner and crept over the debris. He moved deliberately. His long legs maneuvered with ease. His bright red hair caught a glimpse of the three moons' light as he moved past the window.

His heart raced. He wiped the small bead of sweat off his forehead, then shot into the room that Grandfather used to study his old books. He brought his battle-ax up in a cross-strike and stepped into the thrust. A deep ripping sound filled his ears as the blade sank deep into the creature's flesh. It recoiled with a sharp screech that took Riddick by total surprise.

His nose wrinkled as he made out the details of its beak-like nose and black eyes. It lifted its arms, that appeared to be like a mix between a cape and feathered wings. With a deafening crack, the creature turned into a giant crow. The burst of sudden air blasted Riddick across the room. He coughed and sputtered as the pain shot up his spine. He bent in half and struggled to gain his breath back. The creature flailed around the room, knocking books and trinkets to the floor.

Riddick grabbed his ax off the floor and flung it upward, trying to hit the bird as it flew over his head and out of the house. He rolled onto the floor and laid there until he could breathe again. His head pounded as he stood holding onto the wall. He put his ax back and started leaving the room. His boot kicked a small wooden box, and he picked it up. He moved to a nearby window and found it was the puzzle box that he and Shaz used to play with. He maneuvered the levers and slid the lid off. Inside sat a small round medallion with a silver dragon on one side and gold dragon on the other. He ran it through his fingers and tried to figure out what all this was about.

What was that thing, and why was it in Shaz's house? What was it looking for? he thought. A sharp zing rippled through his fingers, and he almost dropped the medallion. A flash of light crossed the sky, leaving a tingle on his skin. He stared out the window and witnessed a lightning cloud move across the sky. He slipped the medallion in his pocket and hurried from the house. He made his way to the elevated platform and released the latch. He gripped the loop, and held onto the rope, as the square platform hurried to the ground. Riddick leaped over the trail, leading toward his own house, and hurried through the thick underbrush toward the village.

His heart thumped against his ribs as he ran through the trees. Shaz lived on the outskirts of the island, in the tree huts where the forest is the thickest. It would take about half an hour to reach the village if he kept this pace. Riddick's mind raced through the last few moons on the island, since returning from Ebassia. He hadn't pieced together all the strange things that had been happening. Now, seeing the creature, it started to make more sense. Whatever it was, it was trying to find something, it believed, Shaz had in his possession. His long legs caressed the ground like a deer gliding with ease. It was one of the things that always gave him the advantage over Shaz.

He ducked and maneuvered the tree limbs and stumps without missing a beat. It didn't occur to him at first, but the farther he ran, the more a funny sensation coursed through his body. Tingly and invigorating. He wondered if it was the residue of the lightning, but the idea of his earth magic crested his mind and he smiled. The sky lit up as he broke through the tree line. Three purple moons shone a soft glow onto the dark world. Crickets chirped and the soft clatter of the aspen leaves in the breeze eased his mind of the constant worry, which now sat in his chest.

Little specks of light sprinkled the night, as he made his way toward the outer edges of the settlement, and near the tree buildings. He veered right toward the edge and passed around the backside. The massive trees came into view, and he found the main road into the village. It was quiet, and his boots slipped on the night dew. He breathed at a steady rate to slow his heart, as he hurried the last several lengths to the center tree structure.

"Halt, who goes there?" the guard asked, breaking the silence.

"It's me, Riddick. I need to speak to the Chairman."

"Yes sir," the guard barked.

The guard stepped aside and pulled the heavy, wooden door open.

Riddick ducked slightly as he entered. He brushed his long hair from his face and searched for the private quarters. He moved with ease and finesse, for his height and stature. He was a good foot length taller than Shaz and had an extra 20lbs on him. All of it muscle, of course. He remembered when he shot past Shaz's height because Shaz pouted about it for over a moon's cycle. The slight scruff of his chin had filled in over the last rotation, as well as his broad shoulders. He stopped in the middle of the receiving room, which was decorated with delicate carvings and old paintings. One caught his eye. A tall red-haired man with deep green eyes appeared to be looking back at him. A shiver ran down his back and he shuddered. The door opened with a slight creak and a short pudgy man, dressed in a night robe, rubbed his eyes.

"What is this all about Riddick? Do you know it's the middle of the night?"

Riddick stared at the man,

"Oh, really? I hadn't realized, it was so dark outside I couldn't tell," Riddick said.

The chairman scowled.

"Did you come here to annoy me, or do you actually have something important?" the Chairman asked.

Riddick thought better of his next comment, which would normally fetch him getting in trouble.

"There's an intruder on the island," Riddick said.

"What do you mean, an intruder? The watchtowers would have spotted any ships and alerted me already."

"It's not that kind of intruder, sir."

"Then what kind is it?" Riddick opened his mouth and then shut it. He wasn't sure how to explain it or was it that the Chairman's lack of intelligence wouldn't understand. For a second his eyes shifted around his head, trying to find the right words. But nothing came. "Well, what do you have to say?"

"I'm sorry for disturbing you. I guess I need to find out more information before I can explain."

"Very well, but the next time you wake me in the middle of the night, I will have you on border patrol."

"As if," Riddick taunted.

The chairman glowered from under his bushy brown eyebrows and returned to his room and shut the door with a loud clunk. Riddick found himself full of confusing emotions. He started toward the door when the same picture jumped into his mind. The more he studied the face, the more it became familiar. He moved closer, enough to see the plaque under it, which read, *General Walter Kenon Brouderic.* The man's eyes gave Riddick the impression that he knew him from somewhere, but the memory was just out of his reach. He shrugged and left quietly. He found himself going toward the docks instead of home. He pressed his hand into his pocket for the medallion. He pulled it out and studied it with the small bits of light from the starlit sky. The lightning storm had changed course and wandered out to sea. He noticed a fastener on the back of the medallion that could connect to his belt. He removed the old hook and then secured the medallion to his belt.

He casually observed the calm harbor for a bit, listening to the soft ripples against the poles, before stretching through a long yawn. He made his way home and crashed onto his bed, which wasn't long enough for his tall frame. Morning came too soon, but Riddick dressed promptly and popped a plump piece of bread, slathered in butter, into his mouth, kissed his mother's cheek and raced to Shaz's place. He wanted to examine Shaz's house in the light and see if he could find any more of Grandfather's secrets.

He pulled the loop and latch and soared to the top. He secured the pulley and listened for any signs of movement. He couldn't hear anything, so he moved silently through the back door. It made him angry that anyone, or whatever it was, would do this. And for what, what were they looking for? Riddick picked up a small chair and set it back in its place. And then another. He rearranged the pillows on the sofa and straightened a picture on the wall. He stepped over a shattered glass vase, and into the room where the creature had been. Thick dark rust-red, almost black, puddles of blood had dried, and seep through the cracks of the wood floor. He wrinkled his nose as the odor of rotting flesh hit his brain.

"It looks like someone was looking for something," Grandfather said.

Riddick jumped out of his skin and spun around. He gripped the hilt of his ax so fast that Grandfather didn't even see him do it.

"Grandfather! Where did you come from?" Riddick stammered.

"Well, originally I came from Denasia, but *most* recently I was in Ebassia," Grandfather said.

"I mean, when did you return?"

"Only a moment ago," Grandfather said. One of Riddick's brows raised as he tried to figure out how he would have arrived moments ago. It takes over an hour to travel from the docks. He studied the old man for a moment. The tickle of his being a most powerful wizard etched at Riddick's mind, "What happened here?" Grandfather asked.

"It was some kind of creature. It was dark, but it looked as though it were part-human and part-crow," Riddick said.

"Ah, a sqwall then," Grandfather said.

"A what?"

"You remember the stories I told you as a child?"

Riddick searched his brain and then remembered.

"You can't be serious?"

"Well, you're the one who saw it, you tell me."

"Fine, it was a sqwall. What did it want?" Riddick said.

"I think it was looking for the medallion," Grandfather motioned to Riddick's new buckle, "Shaz wears his on his belt also."

"Shaz has one of these?" Grandfather nodded, "What is it any-way?" Riddick asked.

"It is the passkey to the portals," Grandfather said.

"Yeah, about that," Riddick said.

Grandfather chuckled, "You sound like Shaz too."

"I liked it much better when all this was just your stories."

"I guess the next question is, what are you going to do with it?" Grandfather asked.

Grandfather sat into the soft padding of the small sofa.

"What kind of question is that?"

"Remember the Rangers?" Riddick nodded and picked up a roomy chair, the only one in the house he fit in, and sat down, "The Rangers were an elite band of warriors. They started out as a group of Travelers, a low class of people with no inherent powers. But what they had, was stealth and loyalty. Queen Ambrosia was raised by the Travelers and taught in all their ways. When she became the Queen, she changed the way society treated her people. She created a secret group of highly skilled Travelers, to take ancient artifacts into the different realms, to keep them from Gavin Rhill and the Shadow. Over time, the Rangers grew, to not only be the Travelers but anyone with a pure enough heart and became the Dodjen."

"How did she know who had a pure heart? I mean, people lie all the time," Riddick said.

"You see, she had the power of 'Intuition' and could perceive a person's true intentions, without even hearing them speak. The secret to her rule, she never told anyone of her ability. That would have tainted the scales, making her a target," Grandfather said.

"So, what do these Ranger Dodjen's have to do with me?"

"You are a Ranger, it is in your blood. Your father came from a very long line of Rangers. The first, Yannick, was very close to the Queen and her family. You have inherited the gifts of the Rangers as well as being an elemental."

"Me?"

Grandfather nodded, his light blue, almost gray eyes became a bit glossy, and he stared at Riddick, almost through him. Riddick squirmed in his chair and rubbed his hand over his scruffy face.

"You have the birthmark of a Ranger, on your hip," Grandfather said. "Yannick gave his life protecting Shaz's father, Reinholt. You and Shaz have been connected before you were even born, and now you have as much responsibility and he does to protect the artifacts,"

"Artifacts?" Riddick almost didn't want to ask.

"There are four artifacts of particular importance to Gavin Rhill. You remember the Sev-Rin-Ac-Lavah. They have been hidden for centuries. Ever since their creation, in fact. It was after a supreme war wizard tried to use them to become a God. It didn't end well, and the Sun Goddess organized the Dodjen, a secret organization made up of the Rangers as well as elementals, to search out the evil and purge it from the land. In doing so, they defeated the wizard, but not without tremendous loss," Grandfather said.

A warm and fuzzy sensation sank into his chest with its truth, but he tried to make the logical connections and came up empty. He did have a birthmark on his hip, but lots of people have birthmarks.

"How do you have all this information? It seems like a lot of made-up stuff," Riddick asked.

"I was there," Grandfather said.

Riddick's eyes popped out of his head and he sat forward.

"You were there? That was hundreds of rotations ago," Riddick said.

Grandfather nodded and closed his eyes.

"It was, many long rotations ago, that's true, but time hasn't always been this way. In fact, here on the islands, the time turns at a different rate than do the other realms."

"How did it used to be?" Riddick asked.

"Srinna Vossa was once the most exquisite group of islands known. It was the central location of all the realms. Considerable trade came in and out of her ports. All the peoples and creatures lived with respect and care for one another. In each realm, a group of peoples existed with the creations of the God of Glory, that got along with one another, separating those who would fight with each other. But time had to revolve around the creatures, so within each place, the universe accommodated."

"What happened to Srinna Vossa? Does it still exist?" Riddick asked.

"No, remember Gavin Rhill destroyed it and Queen Ambrosia buried it."

"That's kinda harsh," Riddick said.

Grandfather smiled. It was almost all he could do. Riddick could see the rotations had indeed impacted the man. It seemed his age caught up with him faster than even a few moons ago.

"Maybe, but she had to secure the ancient scrolls from Gavin Rhill. He would stop at nothing to attain what he wanted."

The mid-morning air warmed the tree hut, giving a soothing tone to the room. Sprigs of light now peeked through the tops of the heavy tree canopy. A dusting of rays danced around the soft breeze.

"Is Gavin Rhill alive?"

"We do not know for sure, but it is speculated he is somewhere between life and death," Grandfather said.

"How comforting," Riddick said.

"When Queen Ambrosia sank the city, she used the power of the Sariandi Comet and the Incantation of Undin. A mighty spell that harnessed the magic of the Teorran Belt, the magic that once spewed from the earth like a fountain. It was the force that held the floating islands and united the realms. The islands plummeted to the earth and were swallowed up by the ground," Grandfather said.

"So, you're saying those stories *are* true and fighting it isn't going to change anything. Shaz is going to have to bring back the city and destroy Gavin Rhill," Riddick said.

Grandfather nodded.

"And he's going to need your help," Grandfather said.

"What can I do. I'm just a big awkward guy," Riddick said.

Riddick knew that wasn't true, but without having a full understanding of his own powers, he felt as helpless and the next guy.

"Oh no, you are a highly skilled combat fighter and the Earth Sage, and you must now learn how to control the element and become the force you were saved to become," Grandfather said.

Riddick scrunched his face and stared at Grandfather.

4-I Won't Let You Fall, I Promise

Shaz and Serin waded through the reeds, around the edges of the pond, toward a small outlet at the south end. Ladtwig and Turkill had to swim in some parts because the water came up to their chests, and Jagwynn sunk barely under the surface so that all you could see was her head as she paddled under the water. The sun had yet to crest the mountaintop and a cold breeze came in from the west. Once over the bank and onto dry ground, Jag shook, sending a spray of water all over the group, earning herself a stern scolding from everyone. Ladtwig and Turkill climbed onto her slick back and held on tight. Serin buffed the crew, and they hurried through the deep forest. The wind rushed past, giving their wet skin the chills. The shadows didn't make it any better, and Serin slipped her cloak on.

Shaz's newfound heat kept him warm and comfortable, and he hardly felt the discomfort the others did. They were headed toward the mountains and toward the direction the sun comes from, so it would be several hours before its heat would be of any benefit. The air buff made it so much easier to maneuver the terrain and make good time traveling across the world. Jag even got excited when it was time to re-buff. The Minca were adjusting to the magic, and they laughed and made jokes at every chance they found. Shaz's map indicated that they would have to do some climbing, so at the last settlement, they secured the needed climbing gear.

The higher they moved toward the tops the colder it became. Serin cinched up her cloak around her neck and pulled the hood tightly over her head. Ladtwig and Turkill layered more clothes onto their little frames, and Jag puffed out her fur. Shaz dutifully scanned the horizon and searched the terrain for the best possible routes. He reached into his pocket to pull out the compass, and instead he found the little sapphire bead. He pulled it out and twisted it between his fingers.

"What's that?" Serin asked.

"It's a sapphire bead I found on the sqwall."

"Explain found," Serin said.

"Its feathers were more like a garment with pockets," Shaz said.

"Pockets?" Serin asked.

"Yeah, and this too," Shaz said.

He pulled out the trinket and handed it to her.

"What do you suppose it is?" Serin asked.

"Not sure, but the bead is from my neck collar," he pointed to his neck, "and I have this exact thing at home," he said pointing to the trinket.

"How?" Serin asked.

Shaz shrugged. Serin stopped.

"What is it?" Shaz asked.

"How did it get it? Did it get it from your home or from some-one?"

"Serin, I don't know, it could be anything. I'm not entirely sure it is that."

"What is a neck collar for?" asked Turkill.

"It's a symbol of my rank, as a paladin fighter," Serin scrunched her brows, and Turkill and Ladtwig looked at each other and shrugged. "Well, let's just say it is the symbol of my position on my island," *Come to think of it, only a few people wear them.* He thought. It was a gift from Grandfather, not the Islanders.

"Which is what?" Turkill asked.

"It's the highest, and most skillful at hand to hand combat and weapons training. According to Grandfather anyway."

"Oh, that's Turkill too. He was the very best at all the tests in our village," Ladtwig said with a big smile.

Turkill blushed and turned away.

"So, how did the sqwall get then?" Serin asked.

"I've been trying to figure that out myself. Last time I saw this was at home on my island, if it's even mine."

He turned the miniature statue in his fingers.

"So, the sqwall has been to your island?" Ladtwig asked.

Jagwynn hissed. Shaz stopped. The thought of sqwalls attacking his island again made his stomach churn. His mind raced around the memories of his tree hut burning, and glowing black eyes in the forest as he came home from the cave, shot to the surface. Shaz's heartfire gripped his lungs, and he gasped. The rage gripped his being, and he wanted to explode.

"What is it?" Serin asked.

Shaz's eyes clouded over and sweat formed on his face and neck. The memory wreaked havoc on his nerves and Serin too found the memory play in her mind. His energy shift was strong and immediate, and she tightened her fists. A soft blue glow pulsed, and she put her hands on his chest. The cool healing magic seeped briskly into his heartfire. The fire subsided back to its normal size and Shaz sucked in the cool air.

"Thank you. I don't know what happened."

"I do," Serin said. She nodded, and he understood that she also witnessed what he had gone through. The passion for revenge had gripped his being. In a way, it terrified him, but in another, it invigorated him. "Come on, let's keep going," she said.

The forest thickened the closer they came to the mountains. The gentle floor disappeared under sharp and broken shards of stone that protruded from the now hardened dirt. Strong winds picked up as they toiled up a steep shoulder of the mountain, clinging, like lizards, to its rugged surface. Shaz dug his toes into a deep crack and gripped a small hold high above his head. The grip was covered with a dusty substance that made it hard to hold on to. He flexed his biceps and tightened his fingers and pushed himself intently until he found a second hold. He pulled an iron spike from his waist pouch and slipped it into a crack and lodged it deep. He gripped the flat end and sent heat into the metal. The spike went red and melded to the mountain and then cooled quickly with the cold of the fading sun. He slipped the rope through the notch at the end of the stake and tied a knot.

He passed the rope to Serin, who untied the last knot and secured it around her waist. The sun was now shining on them from the distant sunset. The higher they went, a crystal-blue mist formed, causing a thin layer of ice on their eyelashes. Serin struggled to stop her shaking hands in order to grip the ragged stone. She relied on the rope to help her navigate the face of the mountain. Shaz moved upward, scaling the hand and foot holds until he found another suitable crevice while the others united and re-tied the ropes to the new stakes and made their way up. They had loaded Jagwynn into a weaved net and was being heaved by a system of pulleys attached to the last rope. She was not happy about it either.

Shaz sank another stake into the mountain and repeated the process and again scaled the ridges. He came to an overhang that extended too far overhead to climb over, and the surface was too slick and there were no holds to grab onto. Shaz checked the rope that was tied around his waist and secured to the last stake and took in a deep breath. Serin watched as his tight muscles lurched his body out and away from the cliff. Her heart jumped into her throat and she nearly choked. She was mostly confident he would make it, but that little bit of doubt surged to the top of her brain and she shouted.

Shaz's momentum carried him far enough out and up that he was able to reach the ridge of the overhang. He gripped his fingers tightly into the cold stone and threw his leg toward the ridge. The middle of his body flopped onto the ridge and he wriggled the last few lengths over the overhang.

"I'm all right," Shaz called and peeked over the edge. Serin shot him a glare and Shaz chuckled. Shaz secured another spike and then tied the rope onto it. He wrapped a rope under his hiney and sat into the rope-like saddle. With one hand on the rope leading to the stake and the other holding onto the edge under his rear, he lowered himself down the mountain to where Serin was.

"You're going to have to climb the rope," Shaz said.

"I'm not sure if I can," Serin said through chattering teeth.

"Put your foot in my hand and I'll push you up," Shaz said.

Serin peeked between herself and the mountain face, down toward Shaz. She put her foot in his hand and he pushed her up. She gripped the rope tightly and wrapped her legs around it. The uneasiness of the swinging motion made her dizzy. Her stomach churned in all directions and her knees went weak.

"I can't do it," Serin said.

"Yes, you can. I won't let you fall. I promise," Shaz said.

Her heart understood that, but her brain screamed a different message. She inched up the rope until she could reach the ledge. She found a hold and gripped it as Shaz shoved her from beneath. She rolled over into the shelter of the crevice and let out a silent cry. She didn't want to let the others find out she was scared to death of heights. She wiped her eyes quickly and tied her rope to the next stake. She lay on her belly and reached over the edge and grabbed Turkill and Ladtwig's hand and helped them over as Shaz push each of them up. After helping the Minca, Shaz grabbed the pulley and reeled Jagwynn up. Serin had buffed her with her wind-walk, making her weigh much less so that the pulley would be able to lift her massive size. Jagwynn hissed at Shaz as he shoved her away from the mountain and left her dangling hundreds of lengths above the earth. Serin and the Minca pulled her over the edge and Shaz scaled the last little bit and pulled himself onto the ledge.

"This is about as stupid as ever," Turkill said, glowering at Shaz.

"You're the one who suggested we come this way. Besides, I'm the one doing all the work," Shaz snarled.

"Hurrmmppp," Turkill stomped.

"You're right, and we couldn't have done it without you," Serin said.

Shaz took in a deep breath and reached into his pouch.

"Let's hope we're almost there, I'm almost out of stakes," Shaz said.

"What do you mean, let's hope?" Turkill asked.

"I'll climb up a few lengths while you rest for a bit," Shaz said.

Shaz grabbed the wall and launched himself a few lengths upward. Serin sat against the wall and closed her eyes and tried to keep her emotions from flooding out. Several lengths passed, and Shaz lowered himself back to the ledge.

"We're so close, only one more stake, and then we're at the top," Shaz said.

"And just soon enough," Ladtwig said, pointing to the sun dropping below the horizon.

Shaz checked everyone's ropes and helped them up the last length. Serin climbed over the edge and rolled onto her back. Ladtwig popped up and over the edge and then Turkill. They all helped pull the pulley's and Jagwynn rolled over the edge. She clawed at the net and Serin untied the knot at the top. The net fell off her and she snarled and hissed at it. Serin smiled and reached for Shaz's hand as he reached the top. They pulled all the satchels and packs and untied the ropes. The Minca rolled up the ropes and Shaz and Serin studied the map and discussed the best way to go. They secured their packs and started over the frozen ground.

"Look, we're nearly to that clearing up ahead. Let's hope there will be some shelter," Serin said.

"I'll take a look," Turkill said.

"No, I will," Shaz said.

Shaz moved in front of Turkill before he could launch himself to the next patch of stringy grass. Serin rubbed her sore and blistered fingers and used her magic to calm the heat and heal the skin. Ladtwig flailed his hands at her and let her heal his too, then his big toe that stuck out of his worn-out boot. Serin chuckled and wondered how he always managed a hole in the same shoe by the same big toe.

"There's a cave on the other side of the clearing we can camp in," Shaz said.

"Another cave," Turkill grunted.

"Is there food?" Ladtwig asked.

Turkill reached down and pulled a wiry plant from the ground and nudged Ladtwig. Ladtwig scowled and then sniffed the plant.

"Smells sweet," Ladtwig said.

Turkill rolled his eyes and started toward the cave.

"It's like a little valley," Serin said.

"We still need to be careful, there are plenty of crevices for things to hide in," Shaz said.

"Like what?" Serin asked.

"I'm not sure, but there's a funny feeling in the air."

"Oh, sorry," Ladtwig said.

Ladtwig waved his hand behind his backside, trying to expel the odor. Serin scowled and Shaz blurted a quick snort, then coughed to gain control.

"I think it's something else, Ladtwig," Shaz said.

Ladtwig looked around and moved toward Serin, who frowned. Jagwynn hunkered down and as Turkill was halfway across the mossy green surface, a bright flash and loud boom erupted from the other side of the bowl-like valley. An enormous ball of crackling embers exploded a few lengths from Turkill, sending him flying backward. Shaz and Serin dove to the ground, and Ladtwig scurried behind a rock.

5-I Think There Might Be More Than One

Shaz rolled over to the edge of the rock face and searched for the culprit. A tiny movement flashed, and then another ball of explosive's shot across the sky. Shaz leaped and threw out his hand. The energy of the fire element came to life in his palm, and a blast of flames surged across the frigid air. Turkill regained his footing and darted back toward Serin and Ladtwig. The funnel of fire created so much heat that a wave of warmth engulfed the crew. Serin covered her head, and Turkill leaped over the rock as the heatwave blew through his hair.

A deafening crack thundered off the walls, as the fire consumed the ball of dancing sparks. High-pitched squeals burst from the ball as the powdery substance ignited. A burst of bright white caused Shaz to cover his eyes. He blinked several times and hurried to the other side. He peaked around a tall stone and searched again. Several lengths passed with no more explosions. Shaz waved to Serin and the Minca, who hurried to the boulder.

"What in the blazes was that?" asked Turkill.

"That was amazing fire shooting," Ladtwig said his little grin ear to ear.

Shaz felt guilty at how good it felt to harness the elements of fire. The destructive power, the power to take life. His heart pounded with both exhilaration and dread. It felt so, so, well, he couldn't explain even to himself how it felt.

"I have no idea, but the movement came from over there," Shaz said.

"Movement?" Serin asked.

"It looked like another one of you," Shaz said, looking at Turkill.

"Me? What are you saying?"

"I mean, it was another being that looked just like you," Shaz said.

"That's impossible!" Turkill said.

"Are you sure?" asked Ladtwig.

"Yes," Shaz said.

"There are old stories about our ancient relatives," Ladtwig said.

"Oh, no you don't. You are not going to go on about those stupid stories that father used to tell us," Turkill said.

"Why not? How can you be so certain that they're not true?" Ladtwig asked.

"Enough," Serin said sternly. "Ladtwig, tell us about the stories."

"Well, it's said, that when the tremendous destruction happened, our father's, fathers had been separated by the immense barriers."

Shaz rubbed his chin and mumbled under his breath.

"What is it, Shaz?" Serin asked.

"Grandfather tells a very similar story," Shaz said.

"Great, just great, so now everyone is going to sit at the fireside and sing too," Turkill grunted.

"What is your problem?" Ladtwig asked.

Turkill turned with his arms across his chest and harrumphed.

"Ignore him," Serin said.

"We must be getting close to the portal," Shaz said.

"To the Bairr Tiornecht Mountains?" Serin asked. Shaz nodded. "Where, I don't see anything?"

"I don't either, but I wonder if the portal is actually within the mountain," Shaz said.

"How do you suppose we get there, with that other Minca out there?" Serin asked.

"I think there might be more than one," Shaz said.

"You know I hate it when you say that. The last time it was the Jaduuk," Serin said.

Shaz chuckled. Shaz and Serin began moving toward the next rock, half-crouched.

"So, I guess we're not stopping for supper?" Ladtwig asked.

Turkill grunted and pushed passed Ladtwig, who puckered out his lower lip and sulked. Halfway around the bowl, another blast echoed toward them. Serin raised her arms and whipped them over her head. A powerful gust of wind gripped the crackling fireball and threw it to the side before it exploded. Three more shots barreled toward them. The loud boom it made each time, reverberated in their heads and they struggled to see straight. The blasts were so close that

Serin couldn't pull enough wind from the air, and they had to leap out of the way as it shot passed and slam into the wall behind them. The blast ripped through their bodies with a chill-like sensation, nearly taking their breath away.

A plume of smoke bulged from the explosion and entombed them. It was dark, bitter, and smelled of burned minerals. Serin managed to pull enough movement to dispel the vapors.

"That's it. The next time there's another blast, use your magic to form a shield of smoke around us so they can't see us," Shaz said.

"That's brilliant," Ladtwig said.

"Yeah, so we can head straight to our deaths," Turkill grumbled.

"Don't you want to find out if they're really are our ancestors out there?" Ladtwig asked.

"No," Turkill said.

"Well, be grumpy all you want, but we are going to find out," Serin said.

A loud burst sounded from the same spot and they made themselves ready for the explosion. Serin pulled clean wind around them, and at the same time kept the billowing debris from settling to the ground. They hurried toward the cave that was underneath where the blasts had been coming from. With a few lengths left, the smoke dissipated enough that the little militant could now see them and reloaded another shot and lit it up. Shaz's energy shifted, and he understood the portal to be close.

"Hurry!" Shaz called.

Ladtwig and Turkill, as fast as they were, were still not as fast as Shaz and Serin. Jag gripped Ladtwig in her teeth by his breeches. His dangling body under her clenches flailed about like a wild pig about to be devoured. Turkill never missed a chance to leap on to her back.

She made the last few strides with ease and disappeared into the darkness. Shaz and Serin leaped into the shadows as a blast crested their heads.

"Alright, so now what?" Serin asked through heavy breaths.

"I'm working on it," Shaz said.

"Well, maybe sometime before this moon's cycle is over, I would like to eat," Ladtwig said.

"Ladtwig!" the three scolded.

Ladtwig cowered behind Jagwynn, who gave a little hiss.

"The blasts are coming from above us. Maybe I can sneak up the edge and take a look. The portal is on the other side of that crevice," Shaz said.

Serin sent a blast of damp, musky air from the cave. Shaz hurried to the wall and climbed to the top. He peeked through the jagged surface. A little man with a long white beard huddled over a pile of the fireballs. He was the same size as the Minca with similar features, except his skin wasn't as dark and his eyes were blue. He was several rotations their senior but still had the muscle tone of a young man. Shaz noticed a long cannon, skinny at the top and a bit pudgy at the bottom. A long wick stuck out from a hole in the top.

The little man gripped a ball and hurled it into the chamber. They were obviously heavy for him, but he executed his movements with skill and precision. He pulled a long skinny stick that was glowing red hot and touched the wick. The blast shot the ball into the sky. Shaz didn't have time to ready himself and tried to cover his ears before the blast. He slipped and almost fell, but caught himself. The little man ran by to another mechanism and began the same routine. Shaz realized there was one person but several machines. He slipped back down the cliff-like wall and hurried into the cave.

"There's only one," Shaz said.

"Only one, then how can there be so many blasts," Ladtwig asked.

"He's using little cannons," Shaz said. He moved his hands around, trying to show the relation of size and shape. "Stay here, I will take him out and then you can climb up."

Shaz conscientiously scaled the rock face. He waited until the little man was at the end of the crude walkway. He rolled up over the edge and somersaulted to the other side, where a small edge was that he could half-hide behind. The Minca let off another blast. He ran with a slight limp back toward where Shaz was hiding. Shaz stepped out in front of him.

"Oiy," the Minca yelled.

He reached for his dagger at his belt, but Shaz snatched it out of his small grip.

"Now, I'm not going to hurt you," Shaz said.

"But I'm going to hurt you," the man growled.

He stomped on Shaz's toe and tried to round him. Shaz grimaced but grabbed the collar of the animal skin jacket he wore.

"Like I said, I'm not going to hurt you. My friends and I just need to pass through that crevice and into the portal."

"Oh, no you don't," the Minca said.

He squirmed and clawed at Shaz, who turned the little man around, so he couldn't reach any vital body parts.

"Oiy," Turkill yelled.

The little man froze. Turkill stomped over the uneven surface.

"I told you to wait for me," Shaz said.

"Well, I didn't," Turkill said.

"I see that," Shaz said.

"Who are you and why are you here?" Turkill asked. The little man's lighter skin went pale. His eyes widened. "What you've never seen another Minca." The man didn't answer. "Did you hear me?"

"I heard you, I just can't believe it?"

"Believe what?" Turkill asked.

"That you still exist."

Shaz chuckled at Turkill, who scowled even more as if that were possible. Turkill heard and shot him a glare.

"Alright, let's start at the beginning," Shaz said, letting go of the little man's collar.

The Minca shifted his clothes back in place and harrumphed. Shaz found it remarkable how much he resembled Turkill.

"I'm Shaz, this is Turkill, and we are looking for the Bairr Tiornecht Mountains."

"Why?" the man asked.

"Well, usually when someone tells you their name, you reply with your name," Shaz said.

"Huuummmph." the Minca grumbled.

Shaz burst into laughter.

"You're not helping," Turkill said.

"I'm not supposed to be," the man said.

Turkill looked between Shaz and the man and dismissed the misunderstanding.

"What did you mean by 'I still exist'?" Turkill asked.

The man thoroughly searched Turkill's face. His blue eyes narrowed and widened as he took in the details. Turkill gave him the, 'if you say anything, I will have you strung and beaten' look.

"Never mind, I thought you were someone else."

Shaz noticed the shift in tone and studied the little men. Ladtwig scurried over the edge and started running at the old Minca. Turkill put his arm over Ladtwig's chest to keep him back.

"How did you find this place?" the man asked, keeping the charade.

"Oh, we've be- "

Turkill nudged a pointy elbow into Ladtwig's side.

"It seems we aren't getting anywhere. Let's go," Shaz said.

Serin slipped over the edge and rolled to standing, and Jag leaped from a couple of small ledges and landed behind Serin.

"Oh, no you don't," the man said.

He started toward the machine but Serin threw a ball of air around him which picked him up off the ground. Panic hit him, and he flailed and hollered.

"Put me down."

Serin lowered her hand.

"No, leave him there until we're through the portal," Shaz said.

The man's eyes popped open, and he turned a tint of green. Shaz studied the rough edges of the rock for the key or pass phrase. He found the glyphs disguised as a handhold and muttered their meanings. The dark surface rippled from the center, showing Shaz how to part the opening. He put his hand into the misty wall and pulled as if it were a curtain. Serin and Jag stepped through and then the Minca. The man's eyes widened, and he wrung his hands together. The magic bubble popped, and the little man fell to the ground a second before the curtain closed.

A warm sunset greeted them from the northern sky, sending a rippling of colors over the landscape. Vast fields of mixed greens and browns draped over gently rolling hills. A cool breeze sauntered across the tall grasses to the east, letting a hint of Creeping Dewberry ease into Shaz's senses. Shaz scrutinized the scent as it was familiar from somewhere but couldn't quite place it.

"Where do you suppose we go from here?" Serin asked.

Shaz shrugged. He searched the horizon and found a tiny hut in the far distance. Shaz pulled out the map that Inelius gave him. The shimmering orbs lifted off the surface and hovered in the air. Turkill and Ladtwig moved closer. The sense of uneasiness that had been over Turkill surged. A bead of sweat crested his black hair and Ladtwig shifted in his clothes. Shaz ran his finger over the map, Turkill recognized his home village and swallowed hard.

"It says that the entrance to the Bairr Tiornecht mountains is going to be that direction," Shaz said.

Turkill gulped and Ladtwig searched his brother's eyes.

"How do you suppose we will find the entrance?" Turkill asked.

Shaz looked between them and was becoming annoyed.

"All right you two, tell me what is going on," Shaz said sternly.

"This is our homeland," Ladtwig blurted.

Turkill elbowed him and scoffed.

"I figured there was some relation," Serin said.

"So why the secrets?" Shaz asked.

"We must first speak to the chief before we can say anymore," Turkill said.

Shaz was about to begin a series of interrogating questions when Serin noticed the pleading look on Turkill's face.

"How far is it to the chief?" Serin asked.

"Over a day's journey, even with your air spell," Turkill said.

"It's gotten dark real fast, why don't we make camp and head out first thing in the morning," Serin said.

Shaz glowered at them and pulled his bedroll out of his backpack and placed it under a low-lying tree nearby. Serin snickered and pulled out her bedroll.

"But what about supper?" Ladtwig asked.

Turkill pulled out a half-eaten block of cheese and tossed it to him. Shaz grumbled and Serin laughed. Serin slipped a small piece of dried meat into her mouth and covered herself with her heavy wool blanket.

Jag curled up next to her and yawned. The buzzing of night insects echoed the chirping of the other creatures that came out at night. Serin found the soft ground a pleasant relief from the last several moons and sagged heavily and yawned. Partway through the night, Shaz heard a rustling in the tall grass and listened. He heard one of the Minca slip through the grass. He assumed it was Turkill and rolled to a crouch. He followed the rustling a few lengths, then hunkered close to the ground.

"Why did you come back? You know the Chief is not going to like this," the old Minca from the portal said.

"I had no choice. If I don't escort the big people, they will find out too much," Turkill said.

"How did you get wrapped up with them, anyway?"

"They are my friends, they have saved Ladtwig and me on count-less occasions, I owe them my life. The Chief will just have to get over himself," Turkill said.

"Good luck with that."

"Are you going to tell him about us?" Turkill asked.

"No, I'll leave that up to you, but you should tread lightly. There have been many strange things going on around here."

"Thanks, Tomos, I owe you," Turkill said.

"Yeah, but for much more than that," Tomos said.

"I know, I haven't forgotten," Turkill said.

Shaz witnessed the old man turn and disappear into the darkness. He crouched into the shadows as he hurried back to his bedroll. Turkill returned to their camp and listened to their heavy breathing before climbing into his own bedroll.

6-If You Want Him To Like You

The Minca village, at first, was spread out among the fields of tall grasses. The tops of the little huts barely reached over the soft cream colors of the wheat stalks. Straw-thatched roofs blended into the hues of the encompassing fields before they transformed into deep greens of the jungle foliage and trees. Shaz and Serin noticed little groups of people that had assembled around the little houses.

Turkill and Ladtwig walked with their backs straight and heads held high. Shaz followed suit but wondered why they would need to ignore their people. He wasn't familiar with all the customs, only a few that the brothers had tried to explain to him. Shaz understood now why Turkill had been so cranky. Turkill had recognized that they would be going to his homeland. Shaz wondered why he had kept it a secret. Every time he'd asked why they had left their homeland in the first place, the Minca shook it off by giving some random reason or petty occurrence with someone in the village that had happened rotations ago. Shaz and Serin had no real understanding of what their issues really were and what the night before with Tomos meant. Shaz understood the need for secrets. He only wished it didn't have to be that way.

Minca women would observe them warily until they saw Jagwynn, then they would rush their children into the hut or pull them behind them. Minca men held out their chests, showing they were not afraid of the big people and that they would gladly go to arms if needed to protect their homes. Serin wanted to find out what made them seem so threatened. Serin was fascinated by their little skin coverings and thought them to be very pretty people. Their skin tones were an array of rich chocolate browns to deep sand-colored hues. Their dark brown eyes had a glint of orange surrounding the black pupils, eyes that she had never seen before.

Shaz knew the type of warriors they were when Turkill and Ladtwig took out a Jaduuk with their poisonous darts and Ladtwig, with his clever thinking, always had extensive escape routes and plans. At one-point Shaz felt a small tinge of jealousy of Ladtwig's cleverness, although he would never admit it. It seemed there was another story to be told between the two, and Shaz was curious to find out. As they walked through the tall grass that came up to their shoulders, Shaz took in as many of the details, noting the surroundings, distances, hiding places, and counting the lookouts that were hiding among the shadows.

Ladtwig tried very hard not to fidget. Turkill was also a bit nervous, but mustered all his strength to give no notion of weakness. It had been several rotations since the two brothers had been home, and they were worried that they would no longer be welcome. It was foolish in the sight of the elders to gallivant all over the place. It was unwise, and the elders didn't allow the women to marry men who didn't stay home and take care of them.

Near the last hut that sat about twenty lengths from the trail stood a beautiful young woman. Her long black hair was twisted and braided into hundreds of tiny braided twists that were bunched and draped around her head. Small ivory tusk earrings hung from delicate ears. Her large glistening eyes stood out on her delicately carved features.

A small smile crept on her face before she remembered she was angry at one of them, and then it turned to a scowl. Serin studied the woman but didn't see that Turkill was glancing at her out of the corner of his eye, not wanting to show his disrespect, but wanting to take in all of her beauty. He then remembered, too, that he had left her for his silly exploration of the secret treasure in a faraway castle, instead of marrying her. His shoulders sagged ever so slightly, then stiffened, and he kept onward.

Soft bird calls echoed in the treetops as they neared the tree line. Ladtwig and Turkill knew this to be the alert system from the borders to the inner village. Turkill was dreading his meeting and introduction to the chief because he had made a fool of him when he chose his ridiculous dreams over stability and village life. Now, looking back, he did have some regret. He questioned why this woman was in a grass hut and not in the jungle. Did she marry that jerk Feungrid and was his one true love never to happen? Well, it didn't matter now. The world was now much bigger than his little village and without stopping Gavin Rhill it wouldn't matter what happened. They would all be dead, anyway.

The trail became narrow and uneven, Shaz and Serin both had to scrunch down to squeeze under the tree trunks that were growing in an arch over the path. The Minca were small enough that they didn't even seem to notice.

"What do you think father will say?" Ladtwig finally broke his silence.

"Dunno, don't want to think about it," Turkill said.

His voice harsh, his posture stiffened even more than before and the muscles on his neck pulsed. A small bead of sweat formed on his forehead. It was very humid in this part of the jungle, and being fully dressed made it much worse. A small clearing emerged behind a tall prickly bush and Turkill halted. Shaz and Serin stopped and waited for them to continue.

"Shaz, remember what I told you about how to approach the chief if you want him to like you, it is utterly necessary," Turkill said.

He turned back to him. His eyes showed no emotion, but Shaz detected the tenseness in his brows and neck and understood the tremendous favor he had asked of him. Shaz felt bad for getting on his case a few days earlier.

Shaz nodded to continue with a grateful half-smile. Turkill continued into the clearing. In the center, Turkill stopped and Shaz removed his boot from one foot and then the other. Placing them in front of him, he knelt and sat on his feet, then clasped his hands in his lap and stared straight forward.

The hut on the other end of the clearing, that almost didn't look like a hut, was covered in bulky vines concealing it from view. What seemed like several lengths passed, then an elderly man emerged from the small opening, bending in half just to exit. He rose to full height, which for a Minca he was a tall man. His skin sagged slightly on his bare chest and his trousers were strapped on with a belt made of old small braided and twisted vines. The legs were cut down the side and tied together at regular intervals, leaving gaps open where you could see his bare skin. He wore a band around his head with intricate carvings and details of stones, bones, teeth, and things similar to Shaz's neck collar. His black hair had been matted into tiny twists sticking straight up from his head, and the sides were shaved, leaving a soft gray and black fuzz.

The chief walked stately toward them. His hands down at his sides. His eyes moved from Shaz to Ladtwig and Turkill, Serin then back to Shaz. He stopped in front of Shaz and studied his boots, sitting half slumped without any foot to hold their shape. They were old and worn and, according to Serin, stinky.

"Why are you here?" he asked.

His voice was surprisingly soft and gentle. The way Turkill spoke of him Shaz had guessed him to be harsh and burley, for a Minca that is, anyway. Shaz sat up, kneeling now on his knees, as to be eye level with the leader.

"I come in search of an artifact from the Sev-Rin-Ac-Lavah."

The leader shot Turkill a nasty glare, and Shaz now understood why he feared this man. He then returned his gaze to Shaz.

"What makes you think that I know anything about this artifact you speak of and if I did, that I would tell you?"

"I respect your commitment sir, I am Shazmpt of the Tooatha De Danann, this is Serin, and Jagwynn, we desire to find the sheath of the Honor Blade," Shaz said.

Shaz turned to Serin as he introduced her and Jag, who was standing tall next to Serin, then returned his attention to the Chief. The chief witnessed the connection between them, he had seen it before. He waved his hand to Serin, inviting her to come to him. She had been instructed not to approach the chief until asked. Serin smiled gently in her humble way and began to kneel, and the chief motioned for her to stay standing. The Minca men revered their women highly, and it was respectful to leave the women on a higher plane than the men.

"You are Dodjen?" the chief asked.

Shaz nodded.

"How do you know?" Shaz asked.

"You're wearing the emblem of the Sun Goddess," the Chief said, tapping on his crown.

The chief's collar was swathed around his head as his crown, as it was too large to fit around his neck. Shaz now made the connection between the neck collars: Grandfather, his father, Yerild, Riddick, and he wore and understood that it was the symbol of the Dodjen. The chief motioned for them to follow him into his hut, then stopped and looked back, a confused look on his face, then he looked around. There was nowhere he could take them they would fit. He summoned some blankets and several little men scurried out of nowhere to bring blankets to sit on and food to eat and drink.

Shaz was invited to put his boots back on. He sat on a hand weaved blanket and slipped his feet back in his boots while Serin sat next to him and Jag with Ladtwig and Turkill on each side. After the men finished bringing food, they returned to the edges of the clearing and vanished. Serin had been intently watching as much as possible as did Shaz, both for different reasons. Turkill still had not let down his guard and was uneasy, Ladtwig had completely melted into the treatment. Shaz wondered what had happened between the two, but knew better than to ask.

"Tell me exactly what you are in search of?" the chief asked after taking a big swig from his mug.

"I am searching for the sheath for this," Shaz said.

He tapped on the hilt of the blade.

"The answers you seek are in the Crystal Catacombs, but in order to enter you must have the blood key," the chief said.

Shaz frowned.

"I am the blood key, the heir to the crystal city," Serin said.

Shaz turned and stared at her. His brows scrunched and his mouth partly opened.

"You have been traveling for some time. It is taxing to enter that realm," the Chief said.

"We are in quite a hurry," Shaz said.

The Chief studied Shaz's face and understood his urgency and nodded.

"Why have you not returned until now? Are you aware of how much worry and pain you have caused your mother?" the Chief asked Turkill.

Turkill hung his head.

"Father, I told you already, and I never meant to worry you or mother. I'm sorry," Turkill said.

Shaz choked on the food he was about to swallow.

"Father? He's your father?"

Shaz blurted before catching himself and threw another bite into his mouth. Serin too looked from the chief to Turkill, then to Ladtwig. The chief peered at Shaz and then back at Turkill.

"You did not tell them?"

"No, father I swore to you I would never tell anyone about our people and I never have, that I swear," Turkill said.

A gentle smile came over the chief's face and he nodded with approval at his son. It was the first time Turkill had ever seen his father show his approval publicly, and especially in front of strangers. It took him by surprise, but it turned into acknowledgment and pride.

"How did you find this place?" the Chief asked.

"The sword has been guiding me to the sheath."

"And my sons?" the Chief asked.

"We found Ladtwig and Turkill at my family castle and have been traveling together ever since," Shaz said.

"What were you doing at his family castle?" the chief asked.

"I, we... were..." Turkill began.

"Searching for the invisible door," Ladtwig blurted.

Turkill shot him a seething glare which Ladtwig chose to ignore, Serin now saw the family resemblance.

"Your sons have been a tremendous help to us," Serin said.

She wasn't sure if she was allowed or not, but at this point, she was impressed to interject. The chief studied her for a moment, then nodded approvingly. Shaz sat his plate down.

"Where would one go to... um... well..."

Shaz, not wanting to ask directly where he might take a pee, felt a bit awkward. Turkill understood right away and jumped up eagerly.

"Follow me," Turkill said.

Shaz and Turkill left the clearing and faded into the forest.

"Thank goodness you had to pee," Turkill said, "I was dying to escape that place."

"Father? You never said anything about him being your father."

"I couldn't, I had to keep the secret of our people or risk their destruction. We are the keepers of the catacombs which hold incredible secrets and many controlling spells and magic, as well as ancient artifacts and secrets."

"I thought you were afraid of magic?" Shaz asked.

"I am. Because we don't possess magic, we are not tempted to achieve gain from the artifacts or secrets. That is why we are their keepers."

"What about all the superstitions you have about magic?" Shaz asked.

"Oh, I am still superstitious. We have been taught to stay away from it out of fear for our lives. If someone that does were to trick us and got in, we would have failed our promise to the high council and would be punished. That is why our ancestors started the superstitions, to scare our people from ever getting too close."

"Then how come you allowed me and Serin to come?"

"You would have found it anyway, this way I can make sure it's for the right reasons," Turkill said.

Turkill stopped and pointed to a bunch of trees about fifteen lengths away and then turned so Shaz could take care of business. Shaz, seeing he had changed the subject and really needing to pee, hopped and skipped over the underbrush and made his way to the trees.

7-You Don't Seem To Be Yourself Lately

"Tell me, Serin, how long have you and Shaz been bonded?"

Serin choked on her water and tried to daintily wipe her mouth before answering.

"I have no idea what you mean. Shaz and I are just friends helping each other," she said sternly, wanting to dispel any rumors that she had feelings for him, which of course she did.

"Oh, I am sorry, I did not mean to offend, it's just that you have all the markers that you have bonded your magic's and are now united in cause. Plus, you would have to be the heir of Queen Ambrosia to be the blood key."

"Yes, I am her daughter, Lady Fortuna mentioned a bonding as well, but I don't know what it means, would you please explain?" Serin asked.

"Oh, I see," he paused, then continued, "I don't think I am the one to explain." He stood up from his blanket and turned to face the jungle. "I can say, however, your connection with him is strong for not being bonded and there is an extreme energy that surrounds you when you are together. But you must be careful of your growing strength."

Shaz came up behind Serin and sat back down in his place. He scooted close to Serin and leaned over to talk quietly to her. But before he said anything, the chief turned back around.

"Will you please explain that to me?" Serin asked.

"Good night." the chief said.

Serin scowled, her anger and frustrations were about to overcome the better of her. He bowed his head slightly, his hands straight down at his sides, and then excused himself and returned to his hut. Shaz leaned over to Serin.

"What did you talk about? I can tell you're angry. Is everything all right?" Shaz asked.

"Fine," she snapped.

"Alright, I was just asking, don't get all worked up," he replied and sat up.

"I'm sorry, I didn't mean to snap, I'm just tired and there is so much we haven't learned, it's like we're just running from one place to another with no reason or purpose. It's chaotic at best," Serin said.

She slumped over her knees and rested her elbows on her legs, placing her face in her hands. She didn't want to cry, but her emotions were teetering on overdrive and she didn't have any way of letting them out. Shaz wanted to quiz her about her being the blood key, what that even meant exactly, but he was certain she wouldn't talk to him in this state, so he left it for now.

"Hey, why don't we go play with water. I found a stream you can let out some steam by practicing your manipulations." Shaz pointed in the direction he came from with a small smile. "Maybe you could teach me something?" He said nudging her with his elbow.

"Sure, I guess, it's worth a try," Serin said.

She sat up, a small red mark covered her face where it had rested in her hands. Shaz smiled and then rose and handed his hand to Serin, which she took this time. He wasn't sure she would because she usually didn't. He could tell she was really having a hard time, and he started to worry. They walked through the heavy underbrush, pushing sizeable leaves out of their way and ducking under branches covered with heavy bark. Jagwynn padded alongside Shaz. The sound of the water rushing over the rocks and splashing into itself blocked out the birds and insects chirping and squawking overhead.

As they approached the river, they found a few Minca women at one edge where a small inlet allowed them to dip bulbous pitchers full of water and then carry them back toward their huts. The women were uneasy when they approached and hurried away.

Serin pointed down the river to a low section that allowed the water to pool calmly before it continued down the hill. They made their way over some rocks and through thick mud, then Shaz stopped and cased the area.

"Are we far enough away that our magic won't make waves?" he asked.

He caught his own joke he didn't realize he was making and laughed out loud. Serin too giggled and then nodded.

"I think so, and so what if it does?" She said half-serious-and-half-not.

"That's the Serin I know," Shaz said.

He winked and stepped into the water in his boots and all. Serin smiled, pulled off her gloves that went to her elbows and covered her tattoos, Shaz suggested she wear them to keep strangers from taking notice and running the risk of a secret Velshari finding their wear-a-bouts. The water was cold, and it sent shivers up their backs, leaving bumps all over their bodies. Serin reached down and put her hands in the water and waved them around a little, making a swooshing effect in the water. Shaz didn't know what to do, so he just stared. Jagwynn lapped up some water and curled into a ball and rested her head on her paws. Serin's hands glowed under the water, which he had never noticed before. She wriggled her fingers, and they glowed a brighter hue of green and blue than moments before.

"What are you doing?" he asked.

"Hum? What?"

"That thing with your hands, what is that?"

Serin looked at her hands and for the first time identified the colors that danced from her fingers.

"I don't know, I am just wriggling my fingers."

"Must be what color your magic is."

Serin looked up curiously.

"Maybe. Alright, now you do it, I want to see if it's the same," Serin said.

Shaz leaned over and waved his hands around, wriggling his fingers, but nothing happened.

"Nothing's happening," Shaz said.

"Hum," Serin's lips puckered in a contorted manner while she thought of why they didn't do anything. "What does the water say to your soul?"

"Say?" Shaz asked, "I dunno, nothing really," Shaz closed his eyes and thought about the cold water for a moment, "Nothing."

"What are you thinking about then?"

"Everything, the chief, the sheath, the last attack of the Jaduuk, the Minca, the catacombs," Shaz paused, "well you get the picture."

"Yeah, I do, but you have to push it out and only think of the water, try again," she said.

Shaz really tried, but he still couldn't get his mind to clear.

"Still nothing," Shaz said.

"There has to be something," she said, "think, or better yet, feel, simply close your eyes and feel."

She pulled some water into her palms and then dripped it back into the river. Shaz closed his eyes and brought a bright light into his focus. The light pushed out all the thoughts that had camped out in his mind. The water was cold and soft but had a strength about it; it didn't want to be moved, but moved freely at the same time. He couldn't hold it in his hands like dirt because it sifted out. It was always moving, never sitting, but was as still as glass. It gave everything life but also took away life.

Serin was amazed as bright colors, that spanned them all, shifted and swayed around his hands. Jag perked up and watched the floating colors begin to follow the tide downstream. She wanted to swat at them, but she was not about to go into the water to do it.

"Now open your eyes," Serin said.

Shaz opened his eyes and stared into the water, he wasn't surprised to see all the colors, he remembered that his magic ball at the earth portal looked the same, but he smiled he had made his magic surface.

"I guess you're right, it's the color of your magic," Serin said. Serin was feeling more energetic now. "Now tell the water what you want it to do."

"Just tell it, like telling a dog to sit or something?"

"Yeah, like that," she said.

"What do I want it to do?" he asked.

Serin stood up straight and put her hand's palm down, facing the water's surface.

"Touch my hands," Serin said.

The water splashed up and touched her hands and then splashed back down. Shaz mimicked the same thing, and the water obeyed. It reached up and touched his hands and splashed down.

"See, there you go. That's quite good. It took me a while to learn that." Then feeling silly she had just admitted that she followed up with, "but I was young then."

Shaz had hardly paid any attention, he was busy thinking of what next to tell the water to do.

"Stand back, I want to try something," Serin said.

Shaz took a few steps back with his hands still in the water. Serin closed her eyes, then opened them, her brows tight with concentration and her lips pursed together. The veins in her neck even flickered with determination. She took a step back and arranged her arms in a delicate half-arch-half-swoop around her head. The soft silvery purple vines etched barely under her skin illuminated. She had been wearing the gloves for some time, and Shaz hadn't seen them glow when she used her magic. She then swooped around her body and rose onto her front foot. She let the back foot raise slightly in the water. She balanced for a second and then stepped back again, releasing her arms to swing around in a figure-eight pattern, maneuvering around her body like a dancer in a play. The water responded and began following her movements, only it danced around a few lengths in front of her.

Shaz stared at the glistening droplets as they danced in and out of the last bit of sun rays shining through the treetops. The longer the water held its position in her dance, the deeper the colors matched her colors. Then in the center of the dancing fountain, a deep-blueish-purple dot formed and stretched from top-to-bottom fading into the casting colors at the edges.

Serin had been concentrating at first, but then relaxed and allowed the water to do its own thing. There was a sensation that the water was trying to make a replica picture of herself. A sense of fear crept through her chest and not wanting to be exposed, even with a made-up picture from water, she let the water collapse.

"Wow! That was amazing! How did you do that?" Shaz asked.

"I'm not sure, let me think about it and I will teach you later, I am tired. I am going back to see if there is a place to lie down."

Shaz figured she had secrets that ate at her too, which he hoped would explain her weird behavior as of late, and climbed out after her. They walked back to the clearing in silence.

"There you are, I have a place for you to retire to. Follow me," Turkill said abruptly.

Shaz passed off his shortness as being home with his father. Turkill led them across the clearing, on the other side of where the river was, to a shelter similar to the huts the Minca lived in. Except this one was a bit taller and enclosed on all sides. The walls were mostly circular but had five corners in the one room.

"You can sleep here, we have made beds for you and I'll see you in the morning."

"We? We are both in here?" Serin asked.

Her arms folded across her chest.

"Hey, it wasn't my idea, I'm just following orders. You can take it up with the chief in the morning if you want." Turkill grunted.

He huffed away, swaying his shoulders back and forth heavily with agitation. Shaz shrugged and climbed inside the small doorway with Jagwynn behind him. Serin stood outside for a moment, trying to figure out what she was going to do when Shaz popped his head out.

"You coming?"

"Uhhggg," she grumbled.

The hut was comfortable, and Shaz could barely stand up completely, which was better than bending half-way over. There were two beds made of soft leaves and dried underbrush covered by several blankets that were patched together to make one full-sized one. A small trunk-like basket sat at the bottom of each bed where they were to put their things while they slept, and a couple food baskets sat on top with a water bag on each. Jag turned around in circles a few times and lay down in the open spot at the side of the hut.

"They have gone through a lot to make us comfortable, considering we will be here for a little while," Shaz said, trying to remain neutral.

"Yeah, I guess," she mumbled.

She pulled her boots off and unlatched her knife and pouch belt and sat it next to the trunk. She slipped under the covers and was surprised to find the bed as soft as it was. She rolled onto her side and stared at the wall of the hut. Shaz finished his inspection and took off his boots, knife and pouch belt and then his sword. He placed all but the sword at the foot of the bed. The sword he tucked under the front edge. He reached over his head with one hand, grabbed the back of his collar and pulled his tunic off in one sweep. He tossed it at the foot of the bed and climbed in under his blanket. He laid there with his hands under his head, staring at the roof, wanting to ask Serin what was wrong, but not wanting to make things worse. He debated for a time.

"What's wrong, Serin? You don't seem yourself lately?"

Serin pretended to be asleep. She couldn't explain to him what she was feeling because she didn't understand herself, so what was the use in talking. She couldn't help feeling as though there was a chaotic power struggle between them. It was becoming worse and harder to control, and sometimes she felt like she might be going crazy. After what the Chief too had said about a bonding, she couldn't shake the idea that a power was drawing her closer to Shaz and yet pulling her away from him at the same time. None of this made sense, so she didn't want to bring it up and give Shaz more to have to worry about. Shaz waited a moment and then rolled over and fell asleep.

8-We Can Definitely Not Stay Here

A large sailing ship crept around the north end of the island. The sun beat down on the gritty sand, which radiated the heat back. The peer was one of the busiest places on the island. There were over thirty islands in the Turbulent Reef. Less than half had actual settlements, Turob being the biggest. Riddick stood with his hands clasped in front of him. His long red hair was pulled up and away from his face. His soft green silk tunic blew in the ocean breeze. Several men scurried about the docks, pulling in ropes and latching them to the bird dropping encrusted poles.

"Is that the new Mirabella?" A scrawny sailor asked.

"Aye," Riddick said.

"I didn't think she was due back until later in the month?"

"Aye," Riddick said.

"Did she return because of bad weather?"

"Aye,"

"Is that all you can say?"

"Aye,"

Riddick slapped the man on the shoulder, nearly knocking him over, and chuckled. He made his way to the end of the pier, passing several smaller sailing ships and two-man runners. The waves began slipping higher and higher as they bounced off the large hull and returned to the docks. The splashes of the cool water felt good on Riddick's sun beat skin.

The massive ship slowed to a near crawl and swayed on the waves, stopping only a few lengths from the dock. A large plank was lowered as several men scurried around securing the sails. Captain Yerild barked orders as he brusquely made his way down the gangway.

"Captain, you said you needed to speak to me immediately?" Riddick asked.

Riddick gripped Yerild by the forearm and slapped his shoulder.

"Aye, but not here," Yerild said.

He motioned down the peer. Yerild was a thick-skinned, weatherbeaten, excellent sailing captain with many rotations at sea. Even when they were sucked into the hurricane last season, Yerild didn't show this kind of urgency, and Riddick cringed at a sudden sink in his gut. He followed Yerild several lengths down the shore.

"There be strange things happening at sea," Yerild said.

"What kind of strange things?"

"Well, for starters, I've seen more of the sea serpents. None have attacked the ship and they keep their distance, but they are there. But that's not the worst thing."

"So, what is it then?"

Yerild looked around and then said softly, "New islands."

"New islands? Where? How many?"

"I'm not sure, maybe a handful. I don't think any of the other sailors even noticed, but I could see them in my looking glass."

"Why are you telling me this? Why not the chairman?"

Yerild spewed a throaty guffaw, "That swindly Chairman ain't a real chairman. I wouldn't trust him farther than I could throw him. Ever since Shaz's grandfather returned to Ebassia, there's no one to keep him in line. Besides, I think this is a new development, a magical development."

"I still don't know what I can do about it?" Riddick said.

"I'm sure you will figure it out."

His deep brown eyes narrowed in on Yerild, and the glint in his eye reflected his understanding of what Riddick was. A feeling of inadequacy ripped through his being and panic sat in his chest. Riddick ran his hands over his face and sighed heavily.

"I guess we go check them out. But we can't take the Mirabella, she's too large, and we want to do it as secretly as possible."

"Aye, I'll organize a small skiff and a few men. When do you want to leave?"

"We don't want anyone to find out, so we'll leave tonight after dark."

"Aye," Yerild said.

Yerild returned to the Mirabella and Riddick returned home. Riddick's mind raced around the stories from his youth and he tried to pull all the earth sage stories together as he gathered his things. He dressed in a lightweight leather tunic and leather belt that secured his hunting knives. He secured his battle-ax and loaded his satchel with traveling items and waited until dark before leaving. The small skiff sat in the shallow rim of the port, behind a ridge of several large rocks. Yerild slung his pack into the boat and checked the rigging. Riddick secured his pack before he padded through the silky sand with his soft leather boots.

"Who else is coming?" Riddick asked, setting his pack in the boat.

"Sebastian and Batovi," Yerild said.

"What about us?" Sebastian and Batovi asked in unison.

They looked at each other and chuckled.

"Good, we're all here," Yerild said.

"What's all this about?" Batovi asked.

"Remember when we went through the barrier and back," they nodded, "well, things have been changing. I saw new islands through my looking glass a few days ago and we are going to go check them out." Yerild said.

The two tried not to show how their stomachs lurched and they swallowed hard.

"We need to keep this an absolute secret. We can't go making trouble when we don't even know what is going on." Riddick said.

Sebastian and Batovi threw their packs into the skiff and slogged through the murky bottom. Riddick helped Yerild push the boat and then climbed in after him.

"How are we going to navigate our way with all this cloud cover?" Sebastian asked.

Yerild searched the darkness with his scope and shifted the rudder a small degree.

"We will follow the edges of the islands through the archipelago until we reach the open sea. By then, it should be about dawn, and then we will be able to navigate to the new islands." Yerild said.

Batovi unlatched the small sail. The wind jumped the small boat, and he pulled back to hold the sail before securing it to the end of the spinnaker pole. The little boat picked up speed over the choppy waves. As the crew moved around the south end of the main island, they swung wide to avoid getting sucked into the under-toe from a small inlet. The skiff maneuvered so much easier than the Mirabella, that several times Batovi over-corrected and nearly dumped them into the sea, earning him several curse words and some scowls.

As they maneuvered around cliffs and inlets, the clouds shifted enough from covering the stars for them to keep their bearings. It wasn't long before they reached the open sea and braced themselves for the bigger waves.

"If you could keep us from capsizing for the next hour, the winds will let up," Yerild said.

Batovi scowled. Yerild checked his looking glass and studied the sky every time he had a chance. Batovi, Sebastian, and Riddick passed the time telling tall-tales and making up new ones.

"There it is," Yerild said.

He handed the looking glass to Riddick, who peered through the long barrel.

"It looks like it might be quite sizable," Riddick said.

"Aye, it does."

"Maybe we should sail around it first," Batovi said.

Riddick nodded, then leaned to the center of the boat. The sail billowed and popped as they shifted directions toward the island. At first, all they found were sharp jagged peaks, but the closer they came, they were able to make out a lush green jungle and soft sandy shores. Not much different from their own. The sun was nearly an hour still from the horizon, as they banked left toward, what looked like, a small sea cave. The skiff had a hard time making progress toward the jagged rock-face and fought the waves on their way out. Batovi moved the sail back and forth, making the boat move in a zig-zag pattern. Thunder rippled across the sky and the crew looked behind them. Dark clouds seeped over the last bits of starlight and left them with a pit in their stomach.

"I think we will explore the island on land," Riddick said.

"Aye," the three agreed.

They managed to get around a large peak, strutting from the deep blue ocean, where the wind was calm. Riddick slung a hooped rope toward a smaller peak, snagging it over the edge, and dug his feet into the ridge of the skiff. He heaved and pulled them into the cave. Sebastian rolled the rope into a circle, as Riddick brought it in, to keep the extra length from getting sucked into an under-toe and pulling them in. The cave was dark and cold.

"How do you suppose we get onto the island; the water is too choppy to be able to swim to shore," Batovi said.

Riddick gripped the jagged rock of the peak and shoved the boat the last few lengths into the cave. The rocks gave him an unusual sensation as his skin touched it. He searched his mind for an explanation but found nothing. He shrugged it off and searched the uneven surface.

"There, that might lead us to the top," Riddick said.

"What is it?" Sebastian asked.

"Looks like stairs," Batovi said.

Riddick grabbed his pack and stepped out onto a small ridge, protruding from the rock-face above the water's surface. It was barely big enough to stand on, and he had to grip the ledge above him, to get the balance he needed. He reached out to Yerild, who gripped his wrist and helped him onto the ledge. Sebastian and Batovi climbed onto the ledge behind Yerild.

"It's slick, so be careful," Yerild said.

Riddick's long legs had no problem scaling the half-carved stairs. He peeked his head over the last bit of cliff, and searched the top, before hopping onto the soft green grass. He laid on his belly and reached down to Yerild, who struggled slightly with his rotund belly and shorter legs. Riddick helped him over the edge and rolled him onto the grass.

"There will never be any mention of this, ever happening, do you hear me?" Yerild said, rolling into a sitting position.

"I have no idea what you're talking about, as far as I know, you leaped over the edge with the grace of a gazelle," Riddick said with a grin.

Yerild smiled and rolled again to stand up.

"Remind me to lay off those biscuits Ole' Baggins makes," Yerild said.

"How is Ole' Baggins?" Riddick asked.

"Ornery as ever," Yerild said.

Sebastian and Batovi crawled over the edge and rolled to their feet.

"We don't have a lot of time before the sun rises, and we need to find shelter," Riddick said.

"What you do expect to find here?" Batovi asked.

"I'm not certain, but if it's only become visible since we opened the barrier, then I should imagine, other beings of some kind would be here too," Riddick said.

Batovi and Sebastian shared a slight grimace and then tightened their packs over their shoulders.

"I want to make it over this ridge before the sun rises, so we need to be quick," Riddick said.

"Lead the way," Yerild said.

Grass covered the uneven surface, leaving sharp edges of rock sticking out. The farther they went, from the crashing noise of the waves, they heard the night beetles singing their annoying crackling tune. Riddick had to keep a slower pace than his usual, and for some reason, an irritating pulse sat in the bottom of his stomach. It wasn't like him to be nervous with this kind of thing, he usually loved exploring new things. Like the cave, he and Shaz had explored as kids. He hadn't thought of that in forever. A sudden memory shot through his mind of the writings Shaz said he could see, but Riddick couldn't. At the time he was annoyed that Shaz kept making stuff up until he stopped talking about it. Now he knows it wasn't made up. *When I get back, I'll have to go search the cave again. Maybe things will be different now,* he thought.

Riddick made it to the top several paces before the others. He laid on the ground, which was nearly perpendicular. He peeked over the edge and found a lush jungle scene, several lengths below them. It was almost too real to be real, if that was even possible. His mind struggled to understand what his eyes were seeing. Tall, skinny trees covered the earth's surface and were shielded by shrubs and vines. Brightly colored flowers speckled the shaded terrain and were vastly different, but the same as the ones back home. They seemed to shine, like everything was covered in a bubble of water, and reflected in every direction.

He waved to the others, as they approached, to get down and they crawled the last few lengths.

"What do you see?" Riddick asked Yerild.

Yerild peeked over the edge.

"A jungle."

"Does it look different than usual?" Riddick asked.

"No, why?"

"Never mind. There's tree coverage over there. We can set up camp and then start to look around." Riddick said, pointing to a bunch of shrub-like trees.

They scuttled along the top of the slope until it dropped several lengths. They scaled the other side and ran into the jungle floor. A sudden flash of a heavy odor stung their noses. Batovi scrunched his face and Sebastian nearly gagged. Riddick held his arm over his face, and

Yerild plugged his nose. It wasn't the cool, refreshing ocean breeze they were used to. It was musky and moist soil which had a heavy twist of animal dung. The persistent wet, exotic plants oozed but weren't sweet smelling like on Turob. They were bitter and had a sharp sting of rancid oil.

"We can definitely, not stay here," Sebastian said.

"What size animal do you think leaves this kind of smell behind?" Yerild asked.

Riddick shot Yerild an 'oh-no' look and lowered himself closer to the ground.

"Let's keep moving," Riddick said.

The crew navigated through the rough terrain, climbing over and under plants, with leaves larger than their arms. Their boots sank into the soft earth a few lengths, and the farther they went, the harder it became to walk. They stopped several times to scrape the thick mud off the bottom of their feet, so they weren't so heavy. Batovi slipped under a large leaf with a pocket-like structure at the base. He didn't realize it was full of water, until it flipped back at him, drenching him top to bottom. Everyone laughed, except Batovi, who scowled and cursed.

The sun was now partially over the landscape, bringing with it a shimmer of light. It heated up the humid air, making it hard to breathe. More and more animals and birds started chirping and humming as the day went on. It had seemed rather quiet before, and Riddick wondered why. Riddick slowed his pace and calculated his bearings. Sebastian took out his parchment he had been using to draw the island. He scratched some more details onto the rough paper and then rolled it back up and slid it under his tunic. Riddick noticed a large stack of smooth rocks had been placed onto one another and steered toward them.

Riddick stopped under a large leafy bush and motioned for the others to get low. He studied the area, then crept a few lengths closer. He repeated the process several times until he was sure there was no one around and was close enough to clearly see the stones. He crept out from under his hiding place and moved toward the structure. It was only a few lengths taller than him, with several markings he recognized from his new belt buckle.

He couldn't read what it said, but it was clear to him it was part of a portal. He reached out and touched the markings with his finger. A surge of electric energy shot into his arm. He jerked his arm away and stepped back. He looked around but couldn't see any fuzzy sky shifts or dancing rain particles like the one on the ocean. There was no swaying of trees or rushing winds. He walked around the structure and then rested his hands on his hips.

"Well, what is it?" Batovi asked.

"I don't know?" Riddick said.

"It's an earth portal," Yerild said.

"Is that like the one on the ocean?" Sebastian asked.

"No, not quite, it's more like an opening of information. They teach you things, if you have magic to access them, that is. Otherwise, it's just a unique structure of some kind," Yerild said.

"How does one with magic access it?" Riddick asked.

"That, I don't know. I am only an informant for the Dodjen." Yerild said.

Riddick touched the symbols again. This time he embraced the energy it sent into his body. A burst of light shot from the center symbol. Riddick tried to cover his eyes, but his body didn't respond. He watched as images of large creatures galloped across the surface of the island. He saw hunters in red cloaks using magic to slaughter and capture them. He saw a long staff made from the horns of the animal, hidden against a tall tree and covered in thick underbrush.

What came next took his breath away. He struggled to inhale as a chilling, dark and sinister face emerged from the shadows. Riddick's heart thumped so hard, it felt like the inside of his ribs were bruised. The black eyes flickered and stared into Riddick's soul.

Riddick threw up a shield around his mind and heart, and the eyes flickered. They moved about as if they were trying to find what it had seen. Riddick used all his strength to pull his hand off the rock, and the visions vanished. He sunk to the soft ground and panted heavily.

"You alright, mate?" Batovi asked.

"What in the tarnation just happened?" Sebastian asked.

Yerild studied Riddick and gave him a slight nod when he finally had the strength to look up.

"Yerild, you're not telling us everything and I'm not going another step until I get some answers," Batovi said.

"I will explain as soon as I can, but not here," Yerild said.

Batovi threw his arms over his chest and scoffed.

"We need to find the Kar-ka-dannon," Riddick said.

"The what?" Batovi sneered.

"Look, I don't have all the answers yet, but I do know, there are things far greater than ourselves at play, and we are a crucial part of it. I won't hold it against you if you want to leave, Batovi." Riddick said.

Riddick struggled to his feet and held out his arm to Batovi with a softened brow. Batovi relaxed and gripped his forearm.

"Alright, but I don't like being left in the dark."

Riddick nodded.

"What kind of beasts are you talking about?" Sebastian asked his voice was a slightly higher pitch than usual.

"The Kar-ka-dannon, are large creatures that look like a mix between a horse and a wyvern-like lizard, with a long black horn in the center of their foreheads," Riddick said.

"That's comforting," Batovi said.

"Those are only a myth," Sebastian said.

Riddick smiled and started passed the rock structure. Sebastian cringed. It seemed like Riddick wasn't going to tell him anything, at least not yet. The men slipped in behind. After several hours slogging through the moist and stinky jungle, they found a large tree with several bulky branches, spiraled around the center trunk. Several thick vines hung in and around them, offering a kind of shelter.

9-The Legend Of The Kar-ka-dannon

"The legend begins, centuries ago, after the God of Glory cursed the world with hostile creatures to chasten his rebellious sons. One such beast was the Kar-ka-dannon. In the hot winds, that blew through the barren desert of Yune, the winds sucked up the harsh gritty sand and thrashed it around for moons. The Kar-ka-dannon hunched down and buried its head under its long mane. Its long black horn protruded from the center of its forehead, nestled under the cool surface. The magnificent creature stood several lengths taller than a man, and resembled a horse, but had a shorter snout which looked almost, lizard-like.

Its mane stands out around its face and drapes down its back and chest. One would hardly see the creature, even with its size, because of its golden-yellow and orange color that blended into the desert sun. The thick coat protected it from the harsh heat and dryness of the desert.

"The Kar-ka-dannon was a solitary creature who roamed through the wastelands searching for water. When it finally found water, it would cry tears of exhaustion and then drink. The Travelers would say, the tears would form into beads of healing. They would string them around their necks, to keep them from falling to illness, as they moved from realm to realm." Yerild said.

Sebastian sat wide-eyed, taking in every detail, but Batovi sat with his arms crossed and slunk against a tree. Riddick listened with his eyes closed and remembered the story from when Shaz's Grandfather told it. This time, however, he understood it was real, and the beasts were out there.

"It is also said, if the Kar-ka-dannon, washes its horn in the water, he gives some of its magic to the water, and the person who drinks from it would have everlasting life," Yerild continued.

"So how come no one has ever seen one of these Kar-ka-dannon?" Batovi asked.

"The Kar-ka-dannon only appears when a sage is born. Without the magic of the Teorran Belt, there have been no sages born in about 300 rotations. And before that, the Velshari searched out and captured the beasts to use their horns to make healing potions. Because of how effective its magic is to heal, it was always being hunted, so the creatures searched out the most barren and harshest of climates to hide in."

"You can't be serious, this is all ridiculous," Batovi said.

"But it makes for a good story," Sebastian said.

"I wish it were, but it is very true," Yerild said.

"And how would you know?" Batovi asked.

"I have seen one of the beasts, rotations and rotations ago when the last sage of the Bairr Tiornecht was born. A baby boy with bright red hair," Yerild said.

Sebastian and Batovi stared at Yerild, not knowing whether to believe him or not. It was so outrageous of a claim, it could either be true or not true. But the words hit Riddick dead center of this being. A sudden realization pounded in his chest and he swallowed hard.

He had been trying to piece all the weirdness of the last several moons together, and now it came full circle in his mind. Like the fact that he, like Shaz, hadn't been told who his parents were. He didn't look like anyone else and was taller than everyone. That Grandfather took him and Shaz on so many 'hunting' trips and told them so many different 'stories'. He wasn't quite sure he wanted to think about it anymore, because that meant his future was about to change in a very drastic way.

"Come on, let's set up camp," Riddick said.

Batovi grabbed his knapsack and pushed a large leaf out of his way.

"You have to admit, having everlasting life wouldn't be so bad," Sebastian said, dropping a pile of semi-dry wood onto the soft dirt.

"I suppose, but you would have to never get sick, or tired, or have to eat or experience pain, otherwise what's the point of living forever and dealing with it all?" Batovi said.

"That's what the Kar-ka-dannon would do," Sebastian said.

Batovi shrugged, gathered a few logs together, and pulled some dry kindling from his pouch. He nestled it under the wood and pulled out his flint and stone.

"We won't be making a fire tonight," Riddick said, stepping through the thick wall of underbrush.

"Why not?" Batovi asked.

"We're not alone," Riddick said. Batovi stood up and took a mental note of the place. Sebastian huddled near a trunk and sucked in his belly. "We will be safe here, but no fire."

"How do you know, we've been together this whole time, and I haven't seen any signs of anyone," Batovi said.

"I didn't say it was human," Riddick said.

Yerild twisted the chewed stick in his mouth and spit it out. He pulled out his cloak and wrapped himself in the heavy wool.

"What do you suppose it is?" Sebastian asked.

Riddick shrugged, "We'll find out tomorrow."

The group nestled into the warmest places in the jungle tree and tried to sleep. Riddick tossed and turned for what seemed like hours. The images from the earth portal swarmed his head. The pit in his stomach increased, and an unsettling energy radiated through his core. Halfway through the night, he climbed out of his spot and stepped over Batovi, who was quietly snoring into his sleeve.

Riddick pushed the long leaves away and ducked under a heavily covered mossy branch. Long vines draped all around him, and he maneuvered through them with a sense of order. The soft humming of the night insects echoed through the jungle in patterns as if they were talking back and forth. Riddick's nauseousness softened, but the tingle grew. Each time he took a step, he interpreted more and more of the power of the earth. His pulse quickened, and his blood surged through him.

Riddick's soft-soled boots allowed for him to feel the unevenness of the ragged jungle floor. Riddick stopped in the center of the hanging vines and turned in a circle. The night was dark, but the goodly sized fungi illuminated bright casts of greens, yellows and white light. He had never seen such a remarkable sight. He took in every detail and breathed deeply.

The moist night air filled his lungs, and he held onto the feeling of power it gave him. As he spun around, he realized he had seen this place before. When he was traveling back through the barrier from Ebassia, as he drifted to sleep on the ship. But in his dream, he wasn't wearing any shoes. He sat on a nearby rock and slipped off his boots and socks. He set his feet on the cold dirt, and a shiver coursed through his body. He gasped as the power of the earth shot into his frame.

The feeling was so intense his toes gripped the gritty surface. He put out his hands to steady himself and closed his eyes. In his minds-eye, the colors of the earth raced through his body. First his legs and into his core, then to his arms and back. Riddick reached down and sunk his fingers into the earth. The energy shifted from a tingling to a pulsing, and he heard the heartbeat of the earth.

Riddick struggled to make sense of everything. Even if he was the sage Yerild was talking about, he wasn't convinced he was anything special. Shaz was the one with the special powers, not him. He was the tall, lanky, awkward boy who was always in Shaz's shadow. He had complete loyalty to Shaz, but sometimes felt he was nothing, and would never be as good as Shaz. Even all the girls found Shaz more interesting.

Riddick listened again and heard a second heartbeat, but it wasn't of the earth. He searched the images the pulsing power gave his mind, and he sensed another human nearby. He rose, letting the dirt sift out of his fingers. He opened his eyes and searched as he turned in a circle, still letting the power of the earth ripple through his body.

Riddick stopped and focused through the vines. He saw two eyes peering over a rock. His heart skipped a beat, but then he realized it was Sebastian.

Sebastian had stirred with the sound from the swooshing leaves and searched for Riddick. When he didn't find him, he anxiously crawled out from under the wide fern he was under. He stayed several lengths back but followed Riddick. He stopped and huddled behind a rock and had been watching Riddick. Their eyes met, and Sebastian was certain Riddick had seen him.

Riddick sat down on the rock and pulled his socks and boots back on. The pulsing stopped as he covered his skin, and the tingle left his body. Sebastian slipped back to camp and pretended to be asleep before Riddick made his way back. Riddick climbed into his spot, but this time, with a new sense of security.

The thick morning mist consumed the landscape, hiding the bright greens of the jungle under a mucky gray. Riddick made an inventory of the contents of his pack. Yerild fancied a piece of bread with a few squished berries and shoved the whole piece into his mouth. Sebastian stretched, then pulled out a water bag. He gulped several long draws and wiped his mouth. Batovi returned after relieving himself and gathered his things.

"What direction are we headed?" Sebastian asked.

Riddick's gaze met Sebastian's dark brown eyes. He gave him the 'I-won't-say-anything-if-you-don't' look and gripped his shoulder as he passed. Sebastian nodded and threw his bag over his shoulder.

"I'm thinking we should head east," Riddick said.

Batovi looked around. "What direction is that you can't even see through this dreadful stuff."

Riddick was a few heads taller than Sebastian and Batovi, and even more than Yerild, who had been shrinking with age. Riddick pulled back the vines and pointed.

"This way."

"How do you know?" Batovi asked.

"Because we came from there, and we came from the northeast, so that makes this, east."

Batovi slipped out, passed Riddick and agreed. The crew started out, taking it slow. The heavy fog made it hard to see too far ahead, and the ground was covered in mossy roots. The jungle rains had washed much of the dirt away over the rotations, leaving the roots exposed. Some trees were so large, they could climb underneath their roots, and others they had to climb over. The deeper they went, the larger the trees became, and the harder it was to scale the vegetation. A low grumble rippled across the sky as a crack of thunder escaped the foggy surface.

"I don't think it will take long until we are all wet," Yerild said.

Riddick nodded, "Maybe we can take shelter under there." He motioned to an oversized wall of hanging vines. "That way we can take a rest for a bit."

They agreed and made their way over to the vines. Sebastian pulled back the vines and peeked inside. It was dark and cool, unlike the hot humid air they had been breathing for days. He warily stepped inside and held the vines for the others.

"Does this place smell normal?" Yerild asked.

"Compared to the rotting stench of animal dung, I'm not sure I know what you mean?" Riddick asked.

"I guess that singed my nose hairs off the first day," Yerild said.

Riddick laughed, and Sebastian cringed at the thought. Batovi felt around and found a rock protruding from the edge of the cave, and draped the vines over it to allow as much light in as possible. They each searched for a comfortable place to sit and pulled out some provisions. Riddick steadied himself on the wall and waited for the same tingle from the night before. He wondered why the rocks and dirt were different from the trees and vegetation. He guessed the life force would be different, because the plants are always growing, and the earth is steady and unmovable. He liked the feeling and tried to keep his skin on the rocks if possible, but without looking strange.

"So, I thought the legend said, the Kar-ka-dannon lived in the desert. This, is most certainly, not a desert." Sebastian said.

"Aye, that has been troubling me as well," Yerild said.

"Aye, there has to be a reason the earth portal pointed me this way," Riddick said.

"Well, I for one would rather be on the open sea, than in this forsaken place," Batovi grumbled.

"Why did you ask him to come along again? All he does is complain," Riddick said.

"He has his moments," Yerild said.

Batovi scowled and then realized he had been complaining an awful lot.

"It's just my magnetic personality," Batovi said.

Everyone rolled their eyes. Riddick rested his head. He agreed. The ocean was his first love. But sitting here, in this place, brought a deeper sense of self he had never known before. He pulled his wet curls from his face and secured them into a bun at the top of his head. His firm jaw tightened as he organized the recent events in his mind.

A cold drop of ooze fell from the ceiling and landed on Riddick's arm. He sat up, studied the droplet and then looked up. The ceiling glistened in the fading daylight.

"This can't be good," Sebastian said as he wiped a drop from his cheek.

Yerild looked up in time to get a glop right in the eye. He snarled and wiped the sticky substance, but it smeared across his face.

"I don't think it's safe in here anymore, I'm out of here," Batovi said.

10-More Like A Stupid Week

Everyone grabbed their packs and shoved whatever they had out back in and started toward the exit. The mist had lifted some, revealing the darkening of the eastern sky. They continued on for several lengths until they came across a swift river that ripped quickly over a bed of uneven stones and roots. Riddick balanced across a slender fallen tree, crossing over a deep pool in the center of the river. He focused on the life force the tree gave and walked with ease. A force created a suction on his body and kept him tight to the surface. Everyone else, however, struggled to scale the slick moss. Sebastian lost his balance and fell into the pool, landing on his back with a splat before being sucked into the undertow.

Riddick chucked his pack the remaining distance and dove in after him. He gripped the straps of Sebastian's knapsack and yanked. Sebastian popped out of the water, sputtering. Sebastian quickly got his bearings and paddled toward the other side.

"I'm really starting to hate this stupid day," Sebastian said.

"More like stupid week," Batovi said.

Riddick flicked his hair out of his face and grabbed his pack.

"Keep moving," Riddick said.

Everyone grumbled, even Riddick muttered under his breath. He crossed a steady spread of marshy sogg for several lengths until the ground started to harden. A small clearing opened, and he blustered through the fern-like bushes. A whistling echo rippled across the tops of the trees on the other side of the layer of mist that never went away as the others broke through the ferns.

"This doesn't look too bad. Maybe we should stop here for the night," Yerild said.

Riddick listened carefully but didn't move.

"What's wrong?" Sebastian asked.

Riddick turned to see a wave of tiny lizards leaping off the trees and swooping toward them.

"Watch out!" called Riddick.

The little reptiles were a deep green with dark spots. They soared through the air in a wavelike pattern. Riddick dove behind a boulder, while Sebastian and Yerild peeled off to the right and ducked under a large fern. Batovi fell to the ground and rolled out of the way. A loud boom of thunder shook the ground and the little reptiles swooped up and landed on a group of trees in front of them. Riddick rolled to his feet and darted across the small clearing. The insect-like creatures jumped from the trees and surged toward Riddick.

Riddick pulled his ax and gripped the handle tightly. He swung at the first wave in an upward arc and parried back, letting the ax's momentum carry it back toward the assailants in a downward thrust. The little creatures pulled in their scaly arms, collapsing their wings and nose-dived straight at Riddick. They were so fast that Riddick couldn't evade them all. The lizards sprung open their webbed limbs, and the tiny sharp horns on the edges of the wings sliced through Riddick's skin.

A screeching surge of heat pummeled his brain seconds before it registered as pain. Riddick ducked and leaped out of the way of the next wave. Small trickles of blood seeped from the tiny lashes. Riddick cursed as he inspected his arms and hands.

"Stay low and keep under the shrubs," Yerild said.

Batovi rolled under a fern and came to his haunches. Riddick motioned them to meet on the far side of the clearing, under the trees the lizards had originally launched from. Riddick yanked a fuzzy leaf from a nearby plant and covered his head as he darted, hunched over, toward cover. The lizards swooped up and landed back on the trees for a split second, before leaping off again. Riddick leaped into the underbrush in time to escape the next surge.

"I don't think they want us here," Batovi said.

"It would seem so," Riddick said.

Riddick searched the trees as he was lying on the ground with the leaf still over his head. A rustle of vines on an adjacent tree caught his attention. He studied the movement of a gigantic furry creature with sharp claws and a long snout, watching them with big red eyes. His stomach lurched, and he swallowed the bile hard. His heart pounded against his ribs and he felt as though he couldn't breathe.

The rodent-gorilla-like creature pulled back into the cover of the vines. Another crack of thunder filled the air. For a split second, Riddick saw a small glow behind its pointed ears. It was as if the vines covered another secret hollow. Riddick's brain shot into overdrive as he tried to run through all the images he had recently seen or stories he had heard. He was certain he had seen the orb that was creating the glow somewhere before.

"Let's not stay here for those lizards to come back for another round," Yerild said.

Riddick peeked out from under the leaf at the others huddled close to the ground. A gust of wind whipped from behind. There was a small opening in the trees behind them. He threw his long legs under his body and with two long strides was under the cover of the last bit of trees. They hurried through the opening. Heavy water droplets pelted them from all angles as the wind whipped around in a cacophony of confusion.

It was hard to see where they were going with the rain streaming down their faces. Even though it was freshwater, the stink of the jungle, which had eased into their hair over the last several days, now dripped into their eyes. The sting was uncomfortable at best. It made it worse, however, to try to wipe their eyes, so they forged on. Riddick found the sensations of the ground start to harden and was confused. It was usually the opposite; the water made the earth soggy and soft.

He stopped for a minute next to a tree with rough bark while waiting for the others and noticed the earth soften. His mind was struggling to make sense of everything it had been overwhelmed with. He was exhausted and wanted to eat a hot meal and go to sleep. He saw the weariness of his mates too, as they maneuvered the harsh terrain. A heavyweight of guilt overcame him for asking them to come along. He couldn't have guessed what to expect, but it certainly wasn't this. As they caught up, Riddick started to move but had to pull his feet out from the ground. They had started to sink into the firm, surface. A sucking sound echoed as he heaved his legs. His next step, however, was back on solid ground. His mind once again raced to find an explanation.

"When are we going to stop and rest?' Yerild asked through heavy breaths.

They were soaked clear to the bone. Yerild rubbed his aching back and Sebastian flipped his dripping hair from his eyes.

"Hopefully soon," Riddick said.

"Maybe that might work?" Batovi said. He pointed to a fallen tree propped onto another. "We could take some long branches and secure them over the top," he continued.

"Aye, sounds good," Riddick said.

They hastily moved toward the tree but had sunk a few small lengths into the ground.

"What in the world?" Sebastian asked.

"The ground is solid when just walking or running, but turns into a more liquid state the longer you stay in one place," Riddick said.

Sebastian endeavored to release his feet from the earth's suction, as did the others.

"This is the craziest thing I have ever seen," Batovi said.

It took a few tries, but they finally managed and speedily made their way to the lean-to. They gathered several long leaves, which were at least as tall as they were, and about an arm's length in width. Batovi strung several small vines together to make ropes, which they used to secure the leaves to the branches. After about an hour, they had made a sturdy ceiling that draped at an angle toward the ground. The rain hit the roof and ran off the back.

Yerild dug a trench around the back and away from their camp. The forest offered no dry wood, so instead, they pulled as many clothes off as they could to stay warm, then hung them on several branches to dry under the new shelter. Unless the rain stopped, it wouldn't do much good, but it made them think they were making progress.

"Does anyone have any idea where we are, or are we going to die alone out here?" Batovi asked.

Sebastian didn't want to say anything, but he felt the same way.

"Sadly, no, we didn't tell anyone where we were going," Yerild said.

"I knew it," Batovi said.

"No one is going to die out here. Although, you would make a nice corpse." Riddick said.

"And how can you be so confident? For all we know, you have gone insane and are leading us in circles around this creature infested prison," Batovi said with a scowl, then realized what Riddick had said and pouted even more.

"Oh, come on now, you're not having fun?" Riddick asked.

Batovi stared at him, his eyes dark and puffy. Riddick wasn't going to admit that he wasn't exactly having a good time either.

"No, I'm not having fun," Batovi said.

Sebastian snickered and Batovi shot him a glare. Yerild pulled out a stick of dried meat that wasn't so dry and started gnawing at the edge.

"How can you be so calm, your half the reason we're out here?" Batovi snarled.

Yerild shrugged, ripped off a piece and ate it.

"Well, I am not sleeping on this wet ground," Sebastian said.

He pulled his small curved blade from off his back and left the shelter. When he returned, he carried several long leaves, busheled under his arms. He spent the next hour weaving a hammock and secured it to the trees. They were impressed at how much weight the leaves held. It must be the many threads of sinewy like fibers that ran throughout them that made it so strong. Batovi and Yerild also made themselves a bed of some sort. Riddick's amazement showed all over his face as the rain hit the many sizes and shaped leaves and rolled off. He wondered how well it would work to use them as a covering for his supplies. He made himself busy making a sack-like arrangement and stuffed his pack inside.

It worked quite well, and the group did the same. As the last bit of daylight was sucked into the night, the crew had a nice dry dwelling. There would still be no fire, but at least they would be dry. The rain continued to fall heavily for over three days. Riddick noticed, the more it rained, the quicker and deeper the ground would soften as you would stand on it. They learned they had to keep moving or they would sink.

They tied everything to the branches and fixed their hammocks when needed. The plan was to wait until the rain stopped and then try to climb to the top of a tree and see where they were. But the rain didn't seem to be letting up anytime soon. Riddick decided he would try climbing the largest tree near the fort. It was slippery, and he had a hard time finding anywhere to grip onto.

He made several lengths of rope out of vines and heaved it into the highest branches. The rope fell to the other side, and then he tied the end to a large branch. He coiled it around his hand and hopped onto the rope. He wrapped his legs and tightened his feet around it. He stretched one arm up and gripped the rope as his legs pushed him upward.

He stopped at different branches on his way up to secure the rope around his hand, which was now aching heavily under the tightness of the vines. He hopped one more time on the rope, but the stress stretched the cord and it snapped. Riddick flung his arms out and caught himself before the rope rippled to the ground.

The moss-covered branch was hard to hold on to. Riddick tightened his core and griped hard with his fingers. He swung his body a few times and clasped one leg around another branch. He flexed his biceps and pulled himself onto the limb. He breathed heavily and wiped the rain from his eyes. He didn't have far to go and reached for the next branch. His fingers delicately searched for a solid grip, and when he found one, he pulled himself upward, using his feet against the trunk.

The dark sky lightened the higher he went, and soon he was at the top. He pulled the thin branches out of the way to see over the landscape. His heart sank, as all he found in every direction was more jungle. What was he going to tell the others? How was he going to take them home? Riddick let go of a branch, and a second before the leaves splattered water all over, he saw a flicker of light. He pulled the branch back and studied the horizon.

A tiny break in the clouds allowed the sun to shine off the wet surface. He narrowed his vision and pulled the fallen locks from his eyes. This time he found a flat stone wall reflecting the light. The shadows in the rock formed a face, just above a waterfall. It had to be something, and it would take less than a day to travel there. He scoured the horizon again for landmarks and structures he could use for directions and climbed down. It was as cumbersome to climb down as it was to climb up. He had to go slowly and keep a tight grip on the driest parts of the branches.

"Well, did you find anything?" Batovi asked.

"Aye, and it's only about half a day's travel," Riddick said hitting the ground softly, "but, I think we should leave our stuff here, and scout it out first."

"What is it?" Sebastian asked.

"A waterfall," Riddick said.

"Like we don't already have enough water," Sebastian said.

Riddick chuckled.

"There is an odd formation in the rocks above it. I'm hoping it will give us some clues as to where we are."

"Another earth portal?" Yerild asked.

"Not sure, but I hope so," Riddick said.

11-It's That Way

Birds chirped loudly as the morning sun heated the little hut. Shaz covered his head with the blanket. He was not a very pleasant morning person, so Serin was sure to leave him be as long as possible. Serin had been awake for a little while lying in bed thinking about all that had happened. She decided her stomach couldn't wait any longer, so she dressed swiftly and made her way into the village. Jagwynn yawned and crawled out after her. Serin liked all the different people she met and was always interested in learning about them. Serin had a pleasant demeanor, and most people liked her instantly. She moved around the little village, fascinated by how ingenious they were.

Pulley systems had been constructed all around the trees to carry water and small baskets of food to individual huts. Little people scurried and scrambled about with even smaller children going here and there. The woman wore thin fabric dresses covering one shoulder and cinched at the waist with a type of tie made of ropes or fibers. The men wore lightweight trousers. Some had belts, and some had straps from their trousers up over their shoulders that connected on the other side.

By mid-afternoon, many of the women chatted casually with her while the men tried not to be occupied by her beauty and height. For most of them, they had never seen other humans at all. One woman stopped her to ask where she had come from and what the world was like until her father came after her and whooshed her away. They definitely had superstitions, most of which were not true, but Serin didn't want to upset the world as they understood it. Which would be sure to happen soon enough. Shaz stirred again as a bird sat on top of the hut and squawked loudly.

"Shoo, get out of here," Shaz grumbled.

He rolled over and tried to hide his head under the small pillow. The bird squawked again, louder. Shaz sat up, feeling a mix of irritation and caution. He combed his disheveled hair out of his face and slipped out of bed. Throwing his tunic over his head and maneuvering his arms into the sleeves, while half bent over, wasn't that easy. Shaz grabbed his sword and fastened the belt as he climbed out of the little hut. The bright sun, nearly overhead now, blasted his eyes. He shielded his face and searched the surroundings. Shaz never went into anything without taking a quick inventory of his surroundings, often counting people, exits, and weapons belted or lying about. He turned toward the hut and saw a mighty hunting bird. Shaz relaxed the muscles in his neck and stood tall and inhaled a deep breath. Shaz straightened his tunic to hang slightly over his belt and adjusted his sword to his liking.

"Squawk," the bird said again.

This time softer and more like a casual conversation.

"Good afternoon to you too," Shaz said.

He stretched his arms high over his head and bent back, giving in to the morning tiredness from sleeping too long, and yawned. He didn't like that he slept so long, but it eased the headaches. The bird ruffled its feathers and stretched its neck out and then settled onto the hut.

"Gavin Rhill has summoned an army of Jaduuk from the Banished Realms," the bird said.

"When, how many?" Shaz asked.

"Too many to count. You must hurry and find the sheath and get to the Timeless Plains."

"I'm doing the best I can, I have no idea where it even is," Shaz said.

"You must hurry," the bird said and leaped off the hut and disappeared into the sun.

Shaz went back into the hut and finished getting dressed. Shaz was glad Drafang's tooth, that hung around his chest, allowed him to talk to animals, but sometimes it was too much, and he was still trying to figure out a way to shield all the noise he sometimes had in his mind. He pulled out his map and searched for the Timeless Plains. He found the Banished Realms and studied the landmarks and structures the map showed. The one thing he had learned is that as neat as the map was, it wasn't as accurate as it once had been.

He rolled it back up, grabbed a yellow melon from the food basket and went to find Serin. He walked down the little path that had led them to their hut from the river the night before. He could tell it was new because of the freshly broken branches, and the grass underfoot was barely bent and half flattened. The sun felt good on his skin and he soaked in the strength the light gave. A slight smile formed on his face as he felt its warmth.

Shaz made his way around small huts and into the clearing, where he glanced around to see if he could spot Serin. She was sitting next to some village women learning how to work a loom. Often, as they would be traveling, Shaz would gladly listen to her tell him stories about all the people she had met. He didn't mind because he loved the sound of her voice and it soothed his mind that she trusted him enough to share her thoughts. In all the chaos that was between the shadow magic and the elemental magic, it was a nice distraction. He made his way around several small children playing a game that involved a stick and a ball and tried not to be hit by either one. He nearly missed one ball only to get pummeled in the side of the head with another before he was able to make the break. He rubbed the side of his head and leaped over a tree trunk that had been dragged by the carpenters who had stripped the bark to make wares and goods.

"Oh, good your awake, I have made contact with the council and you may access the catacombs. I will send someone to take you there," the Chief said.

Shaz nodded before he crouched behind Serin.

"The Chief said we're good to go," he said quietly.

Serin nearly jumped out of her skin and spun around.

"What the-" Serin said.

"Oh, I'm sorry I didn't mean to startle you," Shaz said.

He held his hands up to avoid any backlash she might be ready to throw at him. Serin scowled and breathed in heavily.

"Shaz, you don't just sneak up on people like that," she said.

"I didn't," he exclaimed.

Shaz was getting irritated that she always made things out to be his fault. Her agitation was growing, and Shaz couldn't help feeling there was something very wrong.

"Where's Jag, we need to go," he said.

He turned and walked away. Serin jumped up and politely excused herself from the other women as they giggled softly. As Serin walked away to catch Shaz, she heard one of them say, 'Young love' and then they laughed again. Serin blushed, at first with embarrassment and then with anger.

"Shaz wait! I'm sorry, you startled me, and I didn't handle it well," Serin said.

She had an 'asking' tone in her words as she took several long strides to catch up to him. He didn't slow down. *Why is she the only one that can be irritated or upset or feel anything? Whenever I'm upset, I always have to 'calm down'.* He thought to himself, focusing on all the times they had disagreed or felt irritated and she got to express her feelings and he didn't, or so he felt. Serin grabbed his arm to swing him around to talk to him, but he jerked it out of her hand and kept walking. Serin slowed her pace. She realized she had angered him and thought she better let it go for now. Maybe after giving him some space, she could talk to him later. She kept a few paces behind him as she followed back through the clearing around the children playing and then through the fresh trail back to the hut. They both retrieved their satchels and traveling things, one at a time.

"Will we be gone long?" Serin asked.

"I wouldn't think so," Shaz said coldly.

"Shaz," Serin started. She paused to see if he was going to look at her. He finished sliding the strap of his satchel closed and then looked at her. He saw the hurt in her eyes and felt bad that he had let his temper get the best of him. The ache of shame settled in his stomach, which gave him a queasy feeling, like just before racing down a steep hill. "I'm sorry," Serin said.

Her eyes softly gazed into his. His blue eyes were stunning, and she loved looking into them whenever possible. Shaz relaxed and softened his scowl.

"Me too," Serin smiled and secured her satchel. "I think most of the day is all," Shaz said.

Serin nodded and threw her satchel over her shoulder.

"Where are you two going?" Turkill asked.

"Turkill, good you're here. We are going to need your help," Shaz said.

"Oh no, I am staying right here," Turkill barked.

"What's wrong with you I thought the chief sent you to go with us?" Shaz asked.

"Not me," Turkill grumbled. "I have... certain plans with-" his voice trailed off. He shifted uncomfortably and stared into the trees.

The beautiful young woman from the hut stood holding a basket. Her long, braided hair hung in front of her shoulders, covering the small bit of rust-colored cloth that barely covered her. Her eyes deepened the way they do before someone starts to cry.

"Ah, I see," Shaz said.

Shaz combed his hair with one hand while still holding his satchel in the other.

"Ladtwig can take you," Turkill said.

"All right, we'll take Ladtwig. Besides, it's just the day and we will be back before nightfall," Serin said.

"Yeah, that's right, where might we find the little bugger?" Shaz asked.

Turkill bowed to Shaz, which was a gesture of his commitment to him and their cause, and turned on his heels and walked into the trees and disappeared with the young woman.

"It sure would be nice to have some horses. Then you could give them your air spell and we could be back in no time," Shaz said.

"I don't think they have horses here," Serin said.

"Nope," Ladtwig said.

"I guess we're on foot," Shaz said.

"I'll buff us when we're out of the village," Serin said.

Ladtwig was about to make a joke about being buffed when Serin shook her head and gave him a sideways glare that said, 'you would be wise to not'. Ladtwig cleared his throat. Outside the village, Serin cast her air spell on them. It didn't take long to reach the edge of the jungle that now merged into marshy bogs. Jag let Ladtwig ride her, so they could move speedily. It became more and more that she allowed them to ride her. Shaz thought she secretly was developing feelings for them, but he wasn't going to bring it up.

"We're here, we can stop to eat, then you can continue while I wait outside," Ladtwig said.

"Oh, good, I'm starving," Serin exclaimed.

She pointed to a spacious flat rock a few lengths away.

"You should have said something," Shaz said. Serin was about to start in on him. "No, you're right, never mind."

The wind-walk faded and Shaz slogged over to the boulder while Serin settled herself on the warm slushy surface softly. Ladtwig had already stuffed a piece of bread into his mouth and tried to maneuver while trying not to drop the bread at the same time. Shaz chuckled for the first time all day when Ladtwig barely caught himself from falling. Serin smiled too and sat down next to Jag and opened her satchel, retrieving a loaf of bread and some dried meat. Shaz searched the forest. He observed the bark on the trees looked different from those near the village.

Several faint markings had once been engraved into the bark. Shaz recognized a few of the markings to be the same as ones from the cave back home and from the earth portal. *This must be near the portal,* he thought as he pulled out some bread and popped it into his mouth. The feeling of chewing the soft middle made his stomach lurch with excitement. He hadn't realized how hungry he was. The bite was too big for his mouth, but he didn't care.

Soft chirping echoed through the tops of the trees while the hums of the leaf people bounced around the branches. Ladtwig was being so noisy, crackling dried leaves and snapping dried twigs as he made his way to the big rock. Shaz stretched his legs and back a bit while stuffing more bread into his mouth. Then he studied the marks to see if he could make any sense of them. Serin noticed his gaze and searched the trees.

"What do you suppose they are?" she asked.

"Symbols of the ancient language," he said.

His thoughts were distant. A tingle of magic lifted the hairs on the back of his neck. His hand gripped the hilt of the sword and at the same time his neck muscles tightened. The tingle of magic tickle the hairs on Serin's arms and she grabbed for her bow that was attached to her satchel. Ladtwig was still messing with his bag and didn't notice anything, quietly humming to himself and smiling at a big block of white cheese.

"Be careful. I'm going to see if I can find the portal to the catacombs," Shaz said.

"It's that way," Ladtwig said.

Shaz spun around instantly and took two long strides over to where Ladtwig was fussing with his over-sized trousers.

"Where?" Shaz asked.

Ladtwig looked up surprised and stepped backward. He looked at Shaz and then at Serin and back at Shaz.

"I'm sorry Ladtwig, I'm not mad, it's just urgent that I, I mean, we find it," Shaz said.

Shaz softened his tone and relaxed his muscles. Ladtwig swallowed hard and then pointed into a tall group of trees off to one side.

"But you can't enter, there is no key, and the door has a keyhole. Not even magic can open it, so we have been told," Ladtwig said this time less timid.

"Who told you that, Ladtwig?" Serin asked.

"The elders, we are the keepers of the catacombs, we are not supposed to tell anyone about them though," Ladtwig said.

He stared blankly, and after a second, he realized he had told them where it was and stammered, trying to take it back and or make excuses.

"I thought the Chief told you to take us here?" Shaz asked.

"Oh, I understand, but I wasn't supposed to tell you about us being the keepers," Ladtwig said.

"Turkill already told me," Shaz said.

"You didn't tell me," Serin said.

"I guess it was for Ladtwig to tell you then," Shaz said.

Ladtwig's little narrow face blushed under his deep tan skin. He turned in the door's direction and started walking, standing a little taller and trying to imitate Turkill's swagger. Serin snickered and Shaz smiled as he stepped in behind him. They had traveled barely a few lengths into the trees when the shadow magic again pricked his senses.

12-Work Faster, I'm Tired Of This Stench

"What is that smell?" Serin asked.

Her nose crinkled, and she covered it with her hand, Shaz too puckered with the putrid stench. Ladtwig pulled a scarf from around his neck and tied it around his face to repel the stink. Shaz stepped intently over a fallen tree trunk. He steadied himself as he crossed the slick bark. The bark wasn't rough as he had expected, but slimy, he looked closer and found a pool of a slimy substance that covered the tree.

"What is this?" Shaz asked.

Ladtwig looked back to see what he was talking about and suddenly turned stone white. His eyes bulged, and he began to quiver.

"Th-th-th-the Shade Beetle."

"The what?" Serin asked.

Shaz drew his blade. The sound of the hardened steel hummed as it was pulled from its scabbard. Jag hissed and lowered herself to the ground. Shaz crouched gently as he moved around the tree stump. Using unified steps, keeping his weight on his toes, giving them the flexibility to lunge or tuck and roll, he motioned for Ladtwig to move behind him. Ladtwig was still frozen with fear, but managed to move a few lengths as Serin fell in next to Shaz. Serin was an excellent aim with a bow. She gripped the long delicate carved bow steady and pulled an arrow.

"Ladtwig, what kind of beetle are we talking about?" Shaz asked.

"I d-d-d-don't kn-kn-know exactly. W-w-we have n-n-never seen it. We have o-o-only heard about it," he answered.

The stench lifted slightly as a soft breeze came in from the north. A distant rumble echoed, and the sky dimmed with the cover of clouds above.

"Wonderful. Rain," mumbled Ladtwig.

That was the thing he liked least about being back home, all the rain. The trees thinned slightly the farther in they went, hearty round brownish-green balls scattered the ground making the stench even more grievous than before. Serin nearly gagged.

"What are these nasty things?" she asked.

"Beetle dung," Shaz said without even as much as a flicker in his face.

"How can you not be disgusted by the smell?" Serin asked.

"I can't be distracted; I have to stay focused," Shaz said.

"Yeah but-"

"Shhhhhh. I think I hear it, over there," Shaz said.

He pointed toward a stone wall that had been erected in the middle of nowhere. There were no walls connecting it to another, and it stood there all alone. There was a door in the middle with what resembled a keyhole in the center. Off to the side, there was a huge black mound. The dimming sunlight reflected off the shiny glass finish. The mound moved up and down slightly, Ladtwig stood silent for the first time since they had met him.

"Th-th-that's it," Ladtwig whispered

"I figured," Shaz lifted one foot over a rock. "We need to surround it," Shaz said.

"And then do what?" Serin asked.

"Kill it," Shaz said.

"That's what I was afraid of," Serin whispered.

A loud crack of thunder came barreling in at them, making Ladtwig jump. Shaz flinched and Serin covered her ears. The clouds swiftly darkened the sky and a soft mist moistened the air. Shaz was sure the window of opportunity would close fast with the rain, but he didn't know what the creature was or how to kill it. The thunder rattled the sleeping beetle, and the beast fluttered its wings slightly under the hard-protective shell. Ladtwig tried to find a hiding place and slipped on a rock.

The unusual noise woke the beetle, and it rose onto its skinny insect legs. It turned around to reveal broad, pincher-like fangs that had several layers of jagged teeth meant for ripping its prey to shreds. Black beady eyes flickered and popped open. It first saw Ladtwig laying on the ground trying to keep still.

"Oh man, I'm dead," Ladtwig cried.

"Quiet. It can't hear well and be still," Shaz said.

Jagwynn prowled around the outer edges of the area. Her yellow-orange eyes scanned the distance to find a vantage point to use.

"How can you tell?" Serin asked.

"That hard shell that covers its head, but it smells very well and can see in the dark. Serin, can you make it rain harder?" Shaz asked.

"Maybe, I can try," Serin said.

She secured her bow and arrow and rubbed her hands together. She focused on the water in the clouds and imagined it come crashing onto the earth. The energy from one hand to the other grew when she pushed them together to where they couldn't touch each other. She opened her hands wider, filling the space with more energy, and repeated the movement a few times. She dug into the ground and with a sweeping dance. She released her energy into the sky. A fluid-like motion left her hands and soared into the clouds. The clouds opened, and rain dumped down on them. They gasped as the sting of the unsuspected cold crashed through their senses. Jagwynn hissed and leaped onto a branch and shook heartily to remove the water, but it was useless, and she snarled with displeasure.

The beetle stomped and snorted. It moved toward Ladtwig, but the rain washed their scents away quickly and the beast was now confused about where to go.

"Ladtwig," Shaz called. Shaz pointed to the wall and yelled, "Run!"

Ladtwig rose quickly and ran right in front of the beast. The shade beetle was too fast, and it opened its fangs and with a loud clicking noise sprung into the air. It swung down swiftly, clasping its pincers together, grabbing onto Ladtwig's clothes. It swept him up and flung him around. The force threw him right out of his oversized coat. Shaz released the sword from its on-guard position and the blade flashed as it came slicing through the air. The beetle felt the sting of the blade hit his head. The creepy insect's protective armor was stronger than Shaz had thought, and his blade was repelled by its force, throwing Shaz backward. Jagwynn leaped down and caught Ladtwig on her back and scurried out of its reach. Shaz leaped back and steadied himself, his arm ached from the jarring.

A loud clicking came from its belly as the beetle turned to face Shaz. The hard-outer shell lifted, revealing wings that unfolded as they stretched out. The wings hummed as it spun around and hovered a few lengths off the ground. The legs spaced out around its body, which made it steady but had no turning radius.

"Blast!" cursed Shaz.

He noticed its underbelly was also covered with a protective shell. The rain faded to a slow shower. Shaz and Serin wiped the water from their faces and searched for a hiding spot. The enormous insect sat itself back on the ground. Its giant fang-like pincers opened, spreading apart, and revealed several layers of razor-sharp teeth. A thick gooey slime dripped off the end of the fangs splashing onto the wet ground leaving a rancid order in the air.

"This thing is just nasty!" Serin exclaimed.

"And scary!" Ladtwig said.

Ladtwig hunched behind a rock that sat next to the wall.

"Serin, you make some noise and attract its attention. I am going to circle around and look for a week spot," Shaz said.

Serin nodded and winced, having to remove her hand from her mouth. She grabbed her bow and knocked an arrow. She calmed her breath and aimed. The arrow left the string with a soft whistle but missed its mark by a half-length and hit into the armor instead. The beetle looked in her direction but didn't move.

"You're going to have to make it turn on you and keep it distracted," Shaz said.

"Yeah, right, let me go ahead and become beetle food," Serin said.

Shaz rolled his eyes and was about to return her snide comment with one of his own, when Jagwynn leaped onto the beast's back and released her razor-sharp claws. The outer edge of the beetle was too hardened, and she slipped off with a screech. Serin threw her arms out and sent a solid ray of water straight into the creature's face. The beetle spat and sputtered as it coughed out the water. Small insect legs that sat under the pincers cleared the water from its face. It lifted into the air and started toward Serin.

"Now what?" Serin asked.

Shaz's eyes widened with surprise and admiration. She blushed slightly, then turned away. *Stupid, stupid self, why do you let yourself feel this way.* She thought. A loud slap of the pincers barely a few lengths away from her smacked her back to reality. She leaped into a tuck and roll onto the soggy ground. Covered with mud, she pulled her small blade attached to her thigh. She darted toward the beetle and slipped under its head, sliding through the muddy ground to the other side. Hot blood dripped down her arm and the beast let out a loud bellow, almost like a distraught cow.

Shaz had made his way around the beetle and behind the free-standing wall and back to where Serin was.

"Well?" Serin asked.

She wiped her eyes, leaving a smudge of mud and insect blood in its place. Shaz smiled. She was even more attractive with mud and grime from battle covering her body. Realizing she had seen him staring at her and the fact that the beetle was getting ready to make another attack, he cleared his throat.

"I think the only weakness is between the shells, the best spot is in its neck," Shaz said.

"And how do you suppose we bi-pass the massive fangs?" Serin asked.

She mimicked the pincers with her fingers in front of her mouth and made a face.

"I'm working on that part," Shaz said, trying not to laugh.

"Well, work faster, I'm tired of this stench."

"Yeah, yeah," Shaz said. Shaz ran through several scenarios. Different attacks and outcomes, then decided the best option would be to take out the fangs. "If we take out the fangs first, then there will be nothing to protect its neck. Serin you distract it again and I will take out its fang from the side."

Serin nodded, not wanting to do any of this, but decided she better stop being grumpy and step up. She burst from their hiding spot and ran again, sliding underneath its head. With a raised arm, she slashed at its neck barely above the under-carriage armor. More blood trickled down her blade and onto her arm. The warmth felt good as the rain had brought a certain chill to her skin.

The beast realized its imminent danger and reared backward in pain. Shaz jumped from a tree branch and leaped high into the air. He swung with all his might, thrusting all his energy into the sword. The blade sliced through the fang with ease. Shaz was bewildered at why the difference between this and his first attack. It was the same armor plating that was on its head. Bright green blood spurted from the severed limb, splattering his tunic. The beast, instantly stunned with pain, flickered its eyes. The deep-black armor plating turned a fire-red and then singed into a blood-red color.

"It's mad now!" yelled Shaz.

He landed on the ground and back stepped toward the tree. Serin ran toward the tree, but the beast caught her arm with the other fang enough to slash her skin. She yelled out with pain and grabbed hold of the cut. The rain stung as it fell against her skin. Shaz blocked the next attack as Serin made it to the tree. Jag ran under the beetle and rammed into a hind leg. The leg bent backward and broke halfway. Jag gripped the ground and spun around to make her next move. The beetle steadied itself on the remaining seven legs, then lurched at Shaz with its remaining fang and small front arms. Shaz parried forward, lifted the blade in a blunt block, then stepping sideways, he swung the blade down and back around in an uppercut motion. The beetle blocked by tilting its head, landing the blade tip into the heavy armor. Shaz rotated his wrist to bring the blade back down and shielded his body by crossing the blade from his knee up to his shoulder. The sword fight with a one-fanged beetle lasted for several minutes. Shaz blocking then striking, and the beetle blocking then striking, Jagwynn snarled and lunged, and the beetle blocked.

Serin grabbed a handful of mud and infused it with a Waterbloom flower, which had excellent healing properties and grew on the bark of the trees and smeared it on her arm. The mud made a temporary bandage, keeping it from bleeding and the plant to aid, so it wouldn't become infected until she could heal herself properly. She didn't have any idea what effects the beetle's fangs might have on her if the thick ooze had a toxin or not. Shaz slipped on a wet flat stone and fell on his butt. The initial shock of falling was replaced with anger. The beetle's head came down at an angle, intending to impale Shaz. Serin saw him slip and as the fang came moving at high speed, she reached back and pulled out her bow, knocked an arrow and released before Shaz could secure his footing.

The arrow landed its mark this time and pierced into one of the glowing red eyes. The already in motion, fang slammed into the ground a second after Shaz leaped out of the way. The fang stuck in the muddy earth, and Shaz flipped his blade in his hand and ran full speed at the pincher. The beetle frantically tried to dislodge its last weapon. Shaz spun around, holding his blade outstretched, and slammed into the tentacle, piercing through the armor once more with ease. The beetle lurched back from its force of struggling to free itself and fell onto the ground. Several cracks sounded as the small insect legs buckled underneath the heavy body armor, leaving it writhing in pain.

Shaz sliding in the mud turned and ran toward the beetle. He leaped high into the air, doing a forward somersault. Stretching out his sword, he sliced off the creature's head. It rolled across the clearing and came to a stop right in front of Serin. The awful sight and stench were too much for her to handle. She lurched forward and vomited. Shaz landed onto the body and slid off the domed shaped armor. Sloshing and slipping, he moved promptly back to where Serin was, and in time to watch her puke. He had to admit it was quite disgusting.

A sizzling popping noise came from the beetle and they both turned. The now blood-red armored beetle flickered with shades of red, yellow and orange. The shell cracked into hundreds of pieces. Gently crackling with the sounds of fire, the shells burned and disintegrate, falling to ash. Black plumes of smoke disappeared into the sky. Even though it was still raining, the water didn't affect the burning creature. Shaz and Serin stood amazed, watching the insect disappear, leaving a singed black mark on the ground. They found Ladtwig hiding behind the rock and under several leaves.

"Ladtwig, where are you?" Serin asked.

He peeked out from under a leaf.

"Is it-" Ladtwig began.

Shaz and Serin nodded, and Shaz helped him out of his hiding place.

"That's a great hiding place," Shaz said.

Ladtwig smiled weakly in appreciation.

"But I didn't help kill it," he said almost at a whisper.

"Now we need to get in that door," Shaz said.

Shaz patted Ladtwig's shoulder and Serin nodded and walked over to the door, stepping over a small mound of beetle dung. She studied the door for a moment, and then it occurred to her that the shape of the keyhole was the same shape as the pendant the lady in the stone gave her. She pulled it out from under her tunic and rolled it in her fingers for a moment.

"What's that?" Shaz asked, coming up behind her.

"The pendant the lady in the stone gave me," she replied.

"You didn't tell me about that," Shaz said.

"No, I didn't, and you don't always tell me everything either," Serin said.

Serin stepped toward the door and slipped it into the keyhole. She noticed Shaz's surprise to her sudden tone of annoyance and a mixture of regret and justification confused her thoughts. The key fell right into place and the door clicked open. Serin returned the pendant around her neck and pushed the door a few lengths, paused, and then pushed it enough for them to slip inside.

13-At Least You Don't Have To Use Blood Each Time

Once inside, the door closed on its own, sending a churning feeling into Serin's stomach. *I hope it opens back up when we want to leave.* She thought. The hallway lit up gradually as though someone was stoking a fire, making it bigger and bigger, but there was no fire. The walls glowed with specks of light. Serin studied the wall with her fingers as she speculated what the tiny glowing specs might be. Jagwynn sniffed at a glowing stone and sneezed.

Shaz searched for clues, but for what, he had no idea. The dimly lit hall opened into a sizeable room. With every step they took, the room lit up a little more. Serin noticed Ladtwig was not with them and turned toward the door.

"Ladtwig, what's wrong?" Serin asked.

He was hunched into a tiny ball next to the door, rocking back and forth.

"I don't like magic," Ladtwig said.

"It's not magic," Shaz said.

"Then how does the room light up on its own," Ladtwig asked.

"He has a point," Serin said.

"Alright, well, it's not bad magic then," Shaz said. Shaz turned and took another step, but he couldn't move any farther. It was like there was an invisible shield keeping him from moving forward, "Serin, check this out," Shaz said. Serin moved to the invisible wall and reached toward the darkness. The force shimmered and flashed, then went black. "I command this door to let me pass," Shaz said. The force remained dark and Shaz threw his arms across his chest. Serin looked around and found a small platform resting at an angle that stuck out from the wall next to the door. She put her hand on the smooth surface, but nothing happened. "If you're the *blood* key, does that mean you have to use blood?" Shaz asked.

Serin cringed.

"Maybe."

She took her knife and sucked in a deep breath and poked the tip of her middle finger. She squeezed a few drops onto the platform, but nothing happened. Serin put her hand on top of the blood and pressed it into the stone. The slate sucked in the blood and then glowed in the shape of her handprint. The force field faded and a long corridor opened. Serin looked at Shaz with a 'please-don't-ask' look. He softly touched her arm to reassure her he was content with the way things were, and he would wait until she was ready. A loud puff of air echoed down the corridor. Ladtwig ran to catch up to Shaz and Serin. He stopped a few lengths from Shaz, slightly panting.

"Don't go without me," Ladtwig said.

Ladtwig nervously played with Jagwynn's fur, and she didn't hiss like she normally would. Several long tombs came into view and they now saw four graves stacked on top of each other on both sides of the slender hallway. Small statues, delicately carved of what they supposed was a replica of the deceased, sat at the head of many of the tombs. The tombs had a soft, efflorescent glow that made the stone almost see-through. Ladtwig peeked between his fingers as he held onto Jag. As they made their way past the last tombs, another room opened. Several small tables sat throughout the room, also made of the same crystal-like rock as the walls, ceiling, and floor. Tall shelves circled the room and were covered with scrolls and old books of every size and thickness. Shaz and Serin walked around the room, taking in how vast it was.

"This is bigger than the library at the castle," Serin said.

"Strange place to put a library," Shaz said.

Serin was certain she was in the crystal catacombs of the ancient city of Srinna Vossa, and that she needed to somehow complete the circle, whatever that meant. She remembered back to Lady Fortuna and wondered how she was going to one, find out about this circle thing and two, how she was going to explain it to Shaz. Jagwynn stalked the edges of the room with her eerie glare as though she were skeptical of something in the room. Shaz noted how often she stopped and eyed a book or scroll and wondered what she was up to.

"Maybe it's how they kept it hidden," Serin said.

"Who's they?" Shaz asked.

"The Crystal City, Srinna Vossa," Serin said.

Shaz's eyes met Serin's briefly, and he wondered what she knew about the ancient city. An old book caught his eye and Shaz picked up the old leather-bound book that had shiny metal clasps on the edges, and a locked strap across the pages and ran his fingers along the binding. The book spoke to him in a way he hadn't heard before, not with words, but with familiarity, as if it were an old friend. He turned the book over and studied the locked strap and tapped his finger on the lock.

"Open," Shaz said.

The metal latch released from its holding and flipped open. Shaz, being pleased with himself, opened the heavy cover. The ink on the pages was a spun gold, unlike any ink he had ever seen. The symbols in the book matched that of the ones in the cave he had learned as a child and those on the trees that lead them here.

"What does it say?" Serin asked.

She was glad he hadn't pressed as to her knowledge of the old city but felt a bit odd not knowing what to share or not to share. She tried to read the strange markings, but she had no clue what any of it said. To her the marks looked like funny squiggles and fogy pictures of what could be just about anything.

"It's talking about the Tooatha De Danann, the Bairr Tiornecht, Lavari, and the Fir Bolg. The four children of the God of Glory. It says here that they were the first people of this world and had supernatural powers," Shaz said.

"So, you can read them?" Serin asked.

Serin pointed to one of the marks on the page, and Shaz nodded.

"Aye, well, most of it, some of the marks I haven't learned yet, but if I study it, I bet I can figure them out," Shaz said.

"Where did you learn about them?" she asked.

Serin hadn't figured Shaz to be the studious type. In fact, she pictured him being the funny one in the corner, always cracking jokes to keep the attention on himself.

"You have your secrets, I have mine," Shaz said.

He figured he wouldn't ask her, but he also wouldn't share his. He knew it was childish, but he found he didn't care like he should and wondered why they seemed to be aggravated with one another. He stepped around her and took the book to one of the tables. Serin winced at his words and stood silent with a defeated heaviness in her chest. She debated whether she should tell him about the lady in the stone who told her she is the queen of Srinna Vossa, a city that doesn't exist anymore, and her being a high priestess, of what she still didn't know. Shaz slipped into one of the chairs and skimmed the text while his finger ran across the page, stopping on the symbols he didn't know to think. Serin was confused about what to do, but she was certain she could trust him, so why did she feel the need to be upset with him.

"Shaz-" Serin started.

"I know what happened to Srinna Vossa. It says here that the city of Srinna Vossa was an extravagant and magical empire of floating islands. They sat in the Teorran Belt, which was a tremendous magical force, like a fountain that came from the center of the world, which caused them to float and gave them their power. The royal family oversaw keeping records of the world that were kept in *this* vault and secured by the royal blood," Shaz said.

Shaz looked up and straight into Serin's eyes. Serin bit her lip as a tear crested the corner of her eye, ready to spill over. Shaz now understood her need to keep her secrets and felt horrible for being a jerk.

"I found out in the forest when I met the Lady in the Stone. She told me, as the daughter of Queen Ambrosia, I am the next queen of the most powerful city in Edenocht. I mean, I knew my mother as a small child and all, and my father told me she was the queen of Srinna Vossa, but it never registered that *I* would be the next queen until the lady said it out loud. I guess I don't have to worry about it though because the city doesn't even exist anyway," Serin said.

"When I was young, I found a secret cave that had these same symbols in it. When my grandfather caught me doodling one of them on my studies, he realized he couldn't keep me from fulfilling my role as a war wizard. I can talk to animals. I can sense other's feelings and sometimes their thoughts. I can see, hear, taste and feel more than others, and someday I will have to sacrifice my life to save the world. How's that for secrets?" Shaz said with a smile.

Serin nodded and smiled and bumped him with her shoulder in that 'it's-all-good' kind of way, but swallowed as his words of his sacrifice sank into her deep thoughts. She didn't want to imagine what that would be like knowing that one day you would have to die by choice. Shaz smiled and picked up the book and kept reading. Serin searched for Ladtwig but couldn't see him anywhere. She found him curled up on the floor with Jag near where the wall had been, fast asleep. She pointed to him and put her finger over her mouth to tell Shaz he was sleeping, then sat down and opened a scroll.

The scroll was written in their language and she read it easily. It described different spells that would be useful in a kitchen. She returned it and brought several more back to the table. Sifting through each scroll, she learned things from household duties to healing spells. She found some particularly interesting and after she had found some blank paper. She copied a few to keep with her. Shaz had been studying the same book for some time, and Ladtwig finally stirred.

"I'm hungry, are we ever going to leave here, or do I just plan on dying here where I lay. Why are we even here? It smells funny in here?" Ladtwig mumbled.

They both looked up from their respective reading, Shaz stood to stretch his legs. Serin leaned back over her chair, letting her long hair, now dried back into their curls, flow over the back of her chair and stretched.

"We left our packs outside. I'll go get them," Shaz said.

A moment before he opened the door he called, "If I'm not back in five minutes, come looking for me."

Ladtwig sat up and cringed, and Serin chuckled. Ladtwig gave her a glare, which made her laugh. A few minutes later Shaz returned carrying the packs. He tossed Ladtwig's down to him and sat Serin's on the table next to her. Ladtwig had already pulled out an immense piece of cheese concealed in cloth and had taken a bite before Shaz sat back down.

"How much food did you bring?" Shaz asked, astonished that he had yet another plump piece of cheese.

"Apparently not enough," Ladtwig grumbled.

"We better stay here till morning, it's dark out and I don't want to go back in the dark." Shaz said.

"Sounds good to me," Serin said.

Ladtwig grunted.

"Would you rather leave in the dark and risk running into another beetle?" Shaz asked.

Shaz popped a piece of dried meat into his mouth. Ladtwig shook his head frantically and spun himself around, hoarding his food, and sat looking at the wall.

"This book has the whole history of the world. There is even a section that talks about Gavin Rhill and the Velshari, but so far nothing on the sword," Shaz said.

"I still don't understand what the Velshari is exactly," Serin said.

"Me either, other than the stories grandfather told me. The organization's no secret, but the members are. No one knows for sure if someone is secretly in alliance with them or not," Shaz said.

A thought crossed his mind, *that's why Mrs. Bailey told me not to trust anyone.* He rubbed his chin. Serin pushed the scroll she was finished with and reached up and grabbed another. This one had a gold ribbon tied around the center. She pulled on the string, but the ribbon would not budge.

"Blast, this one won't open," she said.

She sat back in her chair and folded her arms across her chest. Shaz looked up, reached over and touched the knot.

"Open," Shaz said.

The little knot slipped out and fell off the scroll.

"That's not fair," Serin grumbled as she leaned forward to open the scroll.

The large library was silent for what seemed like hours as the two read their respective findings. Shaz was more than halfway through the book when something made him angry and he slammed it shut, sending a loud slap echoing through the room. Both Ladtwig and Serin jumped in surprise.

"What's wrong?" Serin asked.

She set her scroll down and stared at him.

"Nothing," Shaz said.

"Well, it can't be nothing to have you that upset," Serin said.

"I don't want to talk about it," Shaz said.

"Fine," she fired back, flipping her chair around, so she wasn't facing him.

Shaz was well aware he was being immature, but he didn't care. He had just read the part where Gavin Rhill killed his father and he now understood that he and his mother were smuggled onto the islands of Turob by Grandfather, and why he was never allowed to use his magic. Shaz paced, trying to make sense of the memories and his new understanding of his past. He struggled to figure out the missing pieces of his memories, and his anger got the better of him. Serin closed her eyes and tried to search his energy. She found all the chaos in his mind and soul, and her frustration softened.

"Keep reading, it might get better," Serin said.

Shaz paced the room one more time and opened the book again. Serin stopped and pondered what she just read. Her mind circled around the new information like a whirlwind, and she couldn't help the power of its truth overcome her frame. She now understood what Lady Fortuna meant by 'complete the circle'. Shaz felt the energy shift and put his book down. Serin re-read the passage and looked up and found Shaz was looking into her eyes. Serin gazed into his eyes and tried for an explanation, but nothing came.

"Listen to this, Synergy-bound Magic- is the interaction or cooperation of two or more elemental traits which produce a combined effect more superior than the sum of their separate effects. The synergy of two or more elements and or powers allows for a sharing of the traits between the parties bonded. Synergy-bonding is an elevated status for elemental mages and can secure a more powerful duo during combat. The union allows for full access of powers to be shared or enhanced by the other parties for the duration of the bonding," Serin read.

"That's interesting," Shaz said.

Shaz's heart pounded, and he understood the moment he shared with Grandfather in his prayer hut the night he received the sword, was an addition to the original Synbond. A burst of heat flared in his heartfire, and all the bits and pieces he'd been seeing and feeling over the last several moons fell into place. He needed to create a new Synergybond with Serin. The spike in his heartfire always set her on alert, and Serin opened her mind to his energy.

"Synergy magic was used to keep the shadow magic from overpowering the war wizard. Without the bond, the chaos between the shadow magic and the light magic of the elements will overpower and kill the war wizard before the person reaches adulthood." Shaz sat up. "So why have you survived this long?" Serin asked.

"Well, that's a nice question?" Shaz said.

Serin blushed.

"No, that's not what I mean. It says that no war wizard lives to adulthood without it."

Serin pointed to the text on the page.

"Grandfather had a bond with me," Shaz said.

"That makes sense," Serin said.

Shaz now understood Grandfather used the Synmagic to keep him from using his magic as part of his shield he told him about.

"Only by bonding, or completing the circle, their magic with an elemental of healing, will it secure the war wizard's ultimate survival. Some symptoms of un-synergized magic, or a synergy with a non-healer, are headaches, irritability, frenzy, and manic episodes, both for the elemental and the Tooatha De Danann. Once the magic is bonded, it is permanent and cannot be removed or transferred, until the death of one of the unified. When needed two or more bonds can be made but it is discouraged as one will be dominant over the other. One must take extreme caution to whom one bonds to as this will be a lifetime connection. This bond is not limited to male and female relationships but prohibits the persons from having a romantic relationship. The bonding does not require the two persons to remain with one another, but distance can cause discomfort and an unpleasant demeanor," Serin said.

Shaz was now certain his first task was to meet and bond with Serin. The increasing need to bond with Serin filled his being, and he felt a new kind of devotion to her. He already loved her, but this new connection intensified his love to a whole new level. Serin found herself being drawn into his eyes. The power of unity coursed through her and she understood her need to bond with him. A realization overcame her as she allowed herself to be in love with him. This power wasn't asking for their permission, but rather commanding it to be done.

"Does it say how to use Synmagic?" Shaz asked.

Serin shook her head but couldn't pull her eyes from his.

"I bet we have to find another scroll or book," Serin said.

Shaz peeled his gaze from hers and sat his book on the table and started combing the shelf.

"It says here, that the Velshari tried to breed war wizards to harness their shadow magic, but the children were to unstable and they either killed others or died themselves," Serin said.

Serin cringed with disgust at the atrocity this evil man did. She looked at Shaz and understood *he* was a forbidden child. If they had known about him, he would have been put to death.

"How in the blazes are we supposed to find it?" Shaz asked. Serin sat the scroll on the table and went to help. "Show yourself you blasted scroll," Shaz said.

A dusting of rusty gold sparkles emerged and lengthened into a long shape that resembled a pointed finger. It hovered tightly to the books and scrolls as it searched the writings. The finger-ish tip swiftly made its way around the room and then stopped and pointed to a scroll on the other side. Shaz brushed passed her and hurried over to it and snatched it out of the pile.

"Sha-" Serin started.

Serin sensed his urgency and realized it had been a concern for him for quite some time, and now she understood he was feeling more desperate. Perhaps he was feeling the same intense need to bond as she was, but for different reasons. He unwrapped the scroll and started reading. Shaz looked up excitedly but found a concerned look on Serin's face.

"So, if Grandfather used Synmagic with you, then you shouldn't be bonded to anyone else-"

Shaz took her hand and gave her a gentle smile.

"The bond with Grandfather won't end, our bond will simply take first place," Shaz said.

Serin couldn't hide her worry that they might mess things up.

"I suppose," Serin said.

"This will help you too. It's been hard on both of us, the chaos of our magic's competing with each other, maybe your moodiness is a side effect from hanging out with me all the time, but it might be from the need to do this too," Shaz said with a smile.

"Well, I don't think it's *just* the magic aspect," Serin said.

"It's true, I'm not always easy to get along with," Shaz said.

He smiled and his blue eyes lit up with a sparkle Serin loved. Shaz tried not to show it, but he always knew when she was watching him and he liked it. Maybe too much.

He was so beautiful, amazing, strong, powerful, and incredibly charming, *you would be an idiot not to be his healer forever, even if you never get to marry him and bear his children,* Serin skimmed the spell trying not to show her growing eagerness to be with him and reasoned, *this would stop his headaches and my mood swings, and I would always get to be with him.* Shaz studied her face as he listened to her thoughts. He knew he would never love anyone else but Serin and his heart swelled with the fully formed devotion for her.

Serin suddenly remembered that he said he could sense people's feelings and hear their thoughts and blushed, realizing he had probably heard her whole thought. Shaz lifted her chin and leaned toward her. She closed her eyes as his warm lips touched hers. She had never known such a feeling. Something she couldn't describe. He pressed his lips into hers and she pressed back. Shaz wrapped his arm around her waist and pulled her tightly to his warm body. Serin sank into his strong grip and she placed her hands on his muscled arms. Serin didn't want to stop kissing him, but she pulled back and watched Shaz open his eyes.

"I love you Serin Svirtari," Shaz said. Serin's heart leaped in her chest. "I have loved you since the moment I saw you. I want you to be with me forever. I need you," Shaz said.

"I love you," Serin said.

"I want to marry you and live happily ever after, after I sacrifice myself, that is," Shaz said.

"That would be quite the feat, living happily ever after, after you're dead," Serin said.

"I could manage, if you were there to help me," Shaz said.

A strange comfort sank into their minds, and Serin scrunched her face in thought. Her mind whirled around the idea of being with him forever, then a sadness hit. *We'll never be able to have children,* she thought. *But Shaz is a forbidden child, so why couldn't we?* Shaz pulled her chin to his and kissed her again. The sensations rippled their energies like nothing they had ever felt before, and Serin didn't want to let go. She made an image in her mind of how this moment felt so she would never forget and then pulled away.

"Let's let that work itself out," Shaz said.

Serin blushed.

"I'm not sure I'm going to like this you hearing my thoughts thing," Serin said.

"Alright, I won't if you don't want me to," Shaz said.

"You can do that?" Serin asked.

Shaz nodded and Serin relaxed. *I guess it wouldn't be too bad as long as you don't laugh at me or get mad,* Serin thought.

"It's a deal," Shaz said.

"Are you sure about this?" Serin asked.

"Completely," Shaz said between kisses.

"Ready then?" Serin asked.

"In a minute," Shaz said.

He pulled her body close to his. Serin allowed his essence to surround her, and she crept onto her tiptoes and put her hands on his face and kissed him back with an eagerness she relished.

"Eeeeewwwww, what are you two doing?" Ladtwig asked.

Serin blushed and pushed Shaz away.

"It's called kissing," Shaz said.

Shaz snuck another kiss in before he let her go.

"Why would you do that?" Ladtwig asked.

Shaz chuckled, and Serin reached for the scroll. Shaz gripped Serin's hand tightly. Serin lifted the scroll and looked at Shaz. They repeated the words together. The soft blue energy of Serin's magic emerged from her skin and surrounded her body. Shaz's multiple shades emerged, and the magic forces grew until they connected. Strands of Serin's soft blue magic intertwined with his multi-colored strands as they encircled them. They finished the last words and the brilliant mixed shades wriggled and danced for a moment and diminished back into their bodies. Serin choked back the knot in her throat, but somehow had a reassurance that everything would work out. Shaz wanted to kiss her again, but refrained with the understanding that

that part of their relationship was now over. A knot formed in his throat and he tried to clear it without being obvious.

"What was that?" Ladtwig asked.

Ladtwig was peeking out from under a chair at the edge of the room.

"A magic spell that will help us defeat Gavin Rhill," Shaz said.

He figured Ladtwig didn't need to be bothered with the real details.

"Well, if we're done here using magic and stuff, I want to go home," Ladtwig said.

"You're right, but I still don't have any information about the sword," Shaz said.

"Make that magic finger thing find it for you," Serin said.

"Oh, yeah. Show me the writings on the Honor Blade," Shaz said firmly.

The sparkles popped into existence and rummaged through the materials. After several minutes, the magic stopped and pointed to a small leather notebook. Shaz pulled it from the pile and dusted off the cover. He untied the leather ties and opened the delicate binding. Serin scooted in next to him and tried to make sense of the scribbles on the page.

"Is that the ancient language?" Serin asked.

"Aye, but it looks like it might be a more complex system of the ancient runes, like a secret code or something. It's going to take me some time to decode it. I'll take this with and study it later. We need to head back," Shaz said.

They gathered their things, and the lights dimmed one by one until each one went out as they left the library. Shaz stopped at the entrance where the invisible shield was and tried walking through, but it didn't let him.

"Well, I guess I don't get to share that part of your magic," Shaz said.

"Do we even know what we do share now, exactly?" Serin asked.

Serin found the platform on this side of the shield and put her hand on it, and the doorway opened.

"At least you don't have to use blood each time," Shaz said.

"Good thing," Serin said.

14-You Will Bow To Me

A dark shadow crept across the stone floor. The fading light of the fire in the center left the room dim with a sense of loneliness. A stiff stench wafted around the barren and roughly carved walls. Water seeped from the rough corners, leaching the minerals, leaving a rusty stain on the now slick surface. The swoosh of the blood-red robe broke through the creaking of the mountain overhead. Soft clicks echoed through the corridor as the polished boots maneuvered toward the fire.

A tall, slender figure ran his long fingers over an invisible door and snapped. The force released a soft pop and the rock wall disappeared. He pulled a long iron rod from next to the wooden desk and stoked a small fire. A breath of fresh fire bit into the unburned wood and it grew with eagerness. The man lifted an old tattered book from the desk and sat into a tall chair. He thumbed through the worn pages until he found his marker. He read the heading and skimmed through the symbols.

His finger stopped halfway down the page. He sat up and brought the manuscript closer to his face. He studied the symbol with intense scrutiny. Semias Trevelis sat the book on the desk and removed a scroll from the desk drawer and let the long parchment fall to the floor. He scanned the symbols until he came to the missing one and dipped a ragged feathered quill into a jar of ink. He fully transcribed the symbol from the book onto the parchment. He blew on the ink and rested the quill back in its cradle.

He pulled a long staff from his cloak. A small red ball rested at the top and was protected by several rings of hardened metal. He brought the staff and the scroll to the fire. With a raspy voice, he read from the scroll. He gripped the staff tightly as the power of the scroll and staff surged from his chest and into his arm. A tingle turned to red hot searing pain. His toes curled in his tight boots as the pain radiated into his core and raced to his head. Sweat gripped his long brown hair and crept down it until it reached his shoulders. Semias breathed in heavily. He gritted tightly, and his chest heaved as he uttered the last few words of the ancient spell.

A surge of pulsing energy ripped through his body, causing it to crumple to the floor. The earth groaned and shuddered. Semias struggled to find air to fill his lungs as his life essence seeped back into his body from the staff. The drain on his body was more than he had ever imagined. Tears streamed down his now long hollow cheeks. The ground beneath him grumbled and groaned.

****

Darkness encompassed the landscape as Amirra crept from the cave opening. Amirra much preferred being outside. It was the one way she could stay away from Semias as much as possible. She pulled her hood over her cinnamon-colored hair and wrapped the sides around her tightly. The cave opening was tucked around a ridged rock formation, keeping it from direct view.

She hated living in this place. She hated being Semias's errand girl, but there was nothing she could do about it. She belonged to him. She was a slave, at least that's what he always told her. He had given her a long list of tasks, but at least it gave her a chance to be away from him and on her own as long as she didn't take too long doing them.

She unfolded the crinkled paper and read the crappy handwriting, then put it into her cloak pocket. The path from the cave entrance was steep and narrow. It winded up and around several peaks before descending to the valley floor. Amirra couldn't tell exactly where she was going, and the directions were vague, so it was going to take her some time to figure it out. She kept tightly to the side of the mountain for most of the climb up and then back down until the path widened. She had made this trek so many times before that she had made herself a small shelter off the path near a little stream. It was quiet and peaceful, and she had gathered bits and pieces of broken dishes she found to make herself a place to stay while away. The darkness shifted to a simmering gray, and she figured she could take a few hours to sleep before the sun rose. She pulled open the flap-like covering and slipped inside. She looked around to make sure her things were as she left them and then slid under a pieced-together bedroll and fell asleep.

A strong wind blasted her gently freckled face. She squinted and turned her face from the stifling power. The roar of wind pounded her ears and whipped her red hair around her head. Tears ran down her pale cheeks and she gripped the reins tightly. She struggled to breathe but managed to suck in a steady stream of air through tightly pursed lips. The beast she was on was warm under her thin leggings. Its massive wings slipped in and out of the air current without hardly a sound. The deep-red and black wyvern twitched its head ever so slightly.

"You have to stop fighting me, Ada."

"But I can't breathe."

"You will as soon as you trust me."

"I do trust you."

"You mostly trust me. But you have yet to let me into the deepest, darkest part of your soul."

"I can't do that, you will see who I am really am."

"And why do you think that I care about that? I am a creature of higher understanding, I don't peddle emotions, therefore I care nothing for your inadequacies."

"Well, that's part of the problem. If you don't care about who I really am, then why should I let you see it. What makes me feel that you will protect me and my deepest innermost parts."

"You make a very good point, Ada, for that I am sorry I have not conveyed my dedication to you. I suppose your 'feeling' would equate to my 'magic', therefore allowing my understanding of humans to increase."

"Yes, it's like the innermost parts of why I do or don't do something, and how I understand and learn my world," Ada said.

The wyvern dipped back toward the surface and slowed her pace.

"You have my word, that I will protect your feelings as you protect my magic. Is that a fair trade?"

"I suppose I can do that."

"Then close your eyes and do as I taught you."

Ada closed her eyes and tried to imagine herself standing in the center of her being. The whiplash of wind in her face eased as the wyvern descended, and she took in a couple breaths. She gripped the reins so tightly that her hands were now aching and the pain was fighting for her attention. She loosened her grip and found herself standing in the center of the darkness. She pictured what her inner aura looked like and let it encompass her whole frame. A warm bath of breath emerged and the fears and aches she had disappeared. A strong heartbeat appeared next to hers and she felt the magic of the wyvern. A dense wall of rippled colors surrounded their two hearts.

"Now open your eyes," the wyverns said.

Ada hesitantly opened her eyes and found the sting of the wind was no longer on her skin and eyes. She lifted her head and gazed around the soft puffy clouds that danced on the soft blue atmosphere. She breathed in as normal as she would on land. She eased on the reins and with a suction that kept her on the beast; she relaxed. The wyvern twitched its head, and for the first time, Ada now perceived exactly what the wyvern was going to do. She braced herself and sat deep into the saddle. The wyvern lifted her head and flapped her wings fiercely, shooting straight up into the sky. She then rolled several times. Each time she shifted her moves Ada understood and followed or gripped, whichever was needed. The excitement and accomplishment raced through her and Ada became one with her wyvern.

"Now, to give you a name," Ada said.

"Names are not necessary," the wyvern said.

"That may be so, but saying 'hey you' doesn't seem very bonding."

"Very well, what shall you call me?"

A twig pegged Amirra in the head and she jumped awake. She shielded her eyes from the mid-day sun and cursed that she had let herself sleep so long. She kicked at the grungy gray ribbard that was attempting to take her laces off her boots. The half-rat-half-bird flew through the air with a screech. Amirra brushed off the twigs and debris and examined her surroundings. She reconnected the dots as she shook her mind clear of the real-as-day dream and tried to forget it.

What is a wyvern anyway? Who is Ada, and why do I need to know about her? She thought. She pulled out a small chunk of dried meat and popped it in her mouth.

She made her way through a heavily wooded section carefully as not to be impaled by the sharp barbs on some of the bushes. She pulled the red robe off and stuffed it in her satchel. The heat of the day was making her hair glisten with sweat. She couldn't shake the dream. It was as if she were in the dream, as though she was Ada, not simply watching. She actually felt the heartbeat of the beast sitting next to her own heart. She felt its breath, its 'emotions'. She felt Ada's. Every time a thought of the dream came to her mind, she pushed it out by repeating the Velshari chants, but even they couldn't keep it completely at bay.

Several hours later, she stopped next to a small stream and refilled her water bag. She found herself daydreaming about riding this creature, not knowing what it really was. She imagined all the places she would go, and what she would do with the beast. She decided she liked the idea of being free. Of being able to fly on the back of the flying creature. To have such a magnificent being at her command. If they did exist, if they were real, if there was a way to find one, then maybe she could break the forces that bind her to the Velshari, and to the creepy Semias.

****

A soft rumble crept closer until his ears nearly burst. The pressure the earth released encased him in total fear. His body froze, even though he was screaming in his mind to make his limbs obey. Rock fragments released from the ceiling and crashed to the floor. A jagged rock sliced through his side and impaled itself into the floor. His mind exploded with pain and everything went black.

Semias blinked, the ragged stench of putrid grime slithered into his senses. He wrinkled his face as he lurched forward and expelled the stomach acid. His senses cleared, and he realized he was under a pile of rocks. The room was dark, there was no sign of the old fire. He grappled through the debris and pulled the debris from his battered body. A rock, too heavy for him to move, secured his cloak to the earth. He slipped his body from its hold and crawled out of his almost tomb.

He searched around noting the sharp edges and tried to avoid them. Several times he knelt onto a small shard and winced with pain. He finally made his way to the wall, and feeling above himself, stood up. His entire body ached. He barely mustered short stifled breaths but was glad to be alive. He couldn't understand what had happened. In all his research, the spell was to summon the most notorious rune caster. He feared his research hadn't been complete and that he had been too hasty.

He shuffled along the edge of the wall, deliberately moving his feet over the rocks and crumbled walls. A quick burst of pitch from a spent fire touched his senses, and he reached down to find its remains. He closed his hands together and pulled the fire element from the air. A small flame burst from his palms and leaped onto the half-burned wood.

Semias scoured the debris for any sign of his staff. A pit in his stomach lurched into his throat and he grabbed a slick rock. He heaved the stone enough to roll it off the top of the pile. Then he pulled more rocks away from where he had been before he was encompassed with earth. His heart pounded heavily and dread sat in his bowels. A glimmer of red sparkled from the firelight, and Semias gripped the staff. He brushed the dust and dirt off and held it tightly to his chest.

Semias took an inventory of his long-time home. It had taken him longer than he could remember to find all the pieces to the spell that would make him strong enough to summon the ancient being. There was nothing left but a few sticks from the desk that protruded from the rubble. He caught a small glimpse of his red cloak. The coldness of the earth sank into his bones and he shivered. He found a few more pieces of wood and organized them into a triangle so they would burn more efficiently. The flame settled to a soft heat. Semias rubbed his hands over the warmth and rubbed his arms.

A gentle glow of green seeped around the corner of the doorway. Semias gripped his staff and crouched against the cold wall. He discreetly made his way over the rubble and listened at the edge. The green hues danced around a darkened shadow. He peeked around the corner as he sucked in his breath.

A short but stocky man stood bewildered at where he was. Semias could see that he was a Minca, but his skin had faint markings etched under the surface of his light skin. Semias came around the corner and bowed.

"Who has brought me here?" the Minca asked.

"Luthrous?" Semias asked.

"That depends on who you are?"

"I am Semias Trevelis."

"Which means what to me?"

"We have searched you out."

"Who is we?"

"The Velshari," Semias said.

The Minca studied the tall figure.

"For what purpose do you bring me from my slumber?" Luthrous asked.

"Gavin Rhill desires to recreate the Sev-Rin-Ac-Lavah. We need your rune casting to enchant new elements."

"I don't think you understand how this works. I can't make the Sev-Rin-Ac-Lavah. Nor any piece of it. Do you understand what you have done?"

Semias searched Luthrous's face. The Minca elder stared motionless.

"*I* don't understand? Can you even fathom the kind of power I have had to harness to bring you hear?" Semias snarled.

"That's my point, you have ripped the fabrics of time, you have severed the elements and unleashed a power you understand nothing about. You have cursed this world. Even if I do your bidding, it will avail you nothing."

Semias slammed his staff on the ground. A loud bang clapped and ricocheted around the small cavern. Luthrous flinched.

"Do not suppose to tell me what I have done. I am the only one, except Gavin Rhill himself, effective enough to evoke this spell."

"That may be, but you are certainly more foolish than that of a small child," Luthrous said.

Semias gritted his teeth and held out the staff. The red ball glowed hot and Luthrous was encompassed by the red mists of Semias's magic.

"You will bow to me and do as I tell you," Semias growled.

Luthrous's body suddenly bent in half and he fell to his knees. Luthrous coughed as the sudden force expelled the air from his lungs. The ancient magic possessed his reincarnated form, and he realized he was now subject to the shadow.

"You may be in charge of my body, but you can't control my mind," Luthrous said.

"Oh, you seem to not understand what *I* did," Semias said. Luthrous winced as pain shot into his head. He gripped it tightly and fell to the floor. Semias twisted his staff over Luthrous for over a minute, letting the pain work its way through his whole body. The crook of Semias's lips crept up his face and a glint in his eye flickered with pride. "Now let's get to work," Semias said.

****

Amirra capped her water bag and slung the thin strap over her shoulder. She stood and started fiddling with her knife belt when the earth under her rattled. She threw out her arms to steady herself. The rattling shifted from a soft motion to a jagged ripping. Amirra leaped to a tree trunk and threw her arms around it. The tree branches whipped back and forth, tousling her off the tree. Darkness clouded the sun as an enormous plume of black smoke and debris shot into the sky. A cold tingle echoed through her body and she scrambled to another tree.

Water from the stream swished back and forth, overflowing the small trench it had so diligently been making. The rugged bark bit at her arms as she locked her hands on the other side of the tree trunk. For several lengths the earth rocked and swayed with jarring movements. Her head was hurting, and her stomach lurched several times. She couldn't make out what was happening. The sky continued to darken as ash and soot fell to the ground. The rancid smell of minerals stifled her breathing, and she tried to hide her face. Repeating her Vel-shari prayer over and over in her mind, she pleaded to be spared from whatever was happening. The shaking eased to a slow rumble, and she examined the new landscape. She pulled out her cloak and covered her mouth. She found a plume of dust and smoke coming from the edge of the only mountain range there was in this realm. As she regained her bearings, she realized it was coming from Semias's lair.

She wouldn't mind if he was dead when she arrived, but the pit in her stomach said otherwise. That it was probably him, and he had found the last rune glyph for the spell. She started over the embattled grounds. The closer she came to the entrance, the deeper the soot became. It had become so dark that she could barely make out where she needed to go. She stopped several times to reassess her directions. Many of the trees had fallen and new rocks that now ripped up through the ground changed the landmarks she once used.

The small path she was trying to maintain ended with a wall of jagged rocks. She stuck her boot into a crevice and propelled her body upward. She found a handhold and then another foot grip. Several lengths up, she looked down behind her to see if she could make sense of where she was. Nothing was the same. Especially now, being under so much soot. Her nerves creaked as the magnitude of the earthquake sank in. She searched above her and found the trail still intact. At least at this part of the trail. She moved her hand over the edges and found a small grip. The cold, ragged rock bit at her fingernails and she winced. She kicked against the surface and managed to pull herself onto the rails. Once on the trail, she examined her fingers and cursed. She breathed minimally, trying to keep the heavy soot from suffocating her.

She moved hastily up the trail. She wasn't sure she was going to find the entrance. What if it had collapsed? Then what? Would she have to contact the Velshari and organize a search party, or could she slip into non-existence? She hoped the latter, but as she rounded the corner, she found the entrance to be intact. Her heart sank and the silent anger she held encompassed her being.

15-You Sure Have Made A Mess Of Things

The crinkled body of the Minca unfolded from the frigid floor and followed Semias. Several times they stopped to remove rocks and debris from the corridor. Semias made Luthrous remove as many as he was able, and then with irritation, moved the ones that were simply too heavy for the small man. They came to the entrance of a cavern, and Semias flicked his finger toward a torch resting on the sidewall. Several small torches lit around the room, creating an eerie glow of orange over deep-charcoal stones.

A sturdy worktable sat at the back of the cavern, and several old objects that Luthrous couldn't quite make out. He assumed them to be artifacts of things such as jewelry, pouches, tinderboxes and mundane objects. An all-encompassing circle etched into the floor covered the entire surface of the room. A long crack at the top of the circle was several small lengths deep as Semias crossed over it. Semias commanded Luthrous to remove all the rocks and debris from the rune-casting circle.

Luthrous had to obey. He pulled and heaved as many rocks as he was able to the edges of the room. With each one, his heart sank deeper into the pit of his stomach. A symbol emerged at the center of the circle.

The Hagalaz, the symbol for destruction, was embedded into the stone. A circle surrounded it with smaller symbols and a bunch of ancient rune letters. Luthrous understood this to be the infusion sign for 'ultimate rule'. He swallowed the bile that was now surging through his esophagus. He moved to the top of the circle and found the sign that stood for 'suffering', at the top.

"The final outcome- suffering," Luthrous whispered. He was certain he was standing in a Rune Casting Circle of Eltheeda the Deceiver. Luthrous didn't want to see what was in the other two circles. But his body moved without his consent and continued to clean the surface. "Pain is in the future," he said as he uncovered the east circle. Sweat dripped off his body, as the heat from the magic that forced him into bondage, bolstered around him like a heavy wool blanket. He finished with uncovering the west symbol which translated to, "The past is full of unfulfilled desire," Luthrous muttered.

He leaned against the wall and breathed in heavily. He wiped the sweat from his brow and closed his eyes. Semias returned to the room and blew on the flames in the torches with a cast of fire breath. The little flames grew and lit the room brighter. The oft cast from the flames that would normally be orange and soothing was tainted with green and was cold to the soul.

"Ah, you have cleared the rune-circle," Semias said. Semias set the oversized book on the workstation and walked around the circle, admiring the deep cuts and engravings. He moved to the center and set his staff in the middle. A bright light popped into the red ball and a beam focused on the center rune. "Ultimate rule is present, the outcome will be suffering, pain is in the future, and the past is unfulfilled desire," Semias said.

Luthrous observed the red light hit the center rune and illuminate smaller runes on the outer edges of the circle. Luthrous couldn't remove one of the rocks that hid the rune of 'Exception'. The symbol of Aesir, the Sun Goddess, flickered barely under the outer edge of the rock. Luthrous smiled to himself, being that his body wouldn't let his lips do it. The 'Aesir' sign stood for divinity and choice. Luthrous comprehended this to be the most paramount rune there is. He has only seen this rune twice before from any casting. He let the small flicker of his soul sit deep in his chest and was filled with a sense of calmness.

Semias spun around and lifted his arms. Shades of black crept into shades of green and danced around the room. The cover of the book opened, and several pages flipped until it rested on the recipe of the Honor Blade.

"Honor Blade, quite a hypocritical name, don't you think? I mean, who of any of the past that has ever held that sword was actually honorable," Semias said.

Luthrous squinted as he peered toward the book. He caught a glance of one of the symbols at the corner of the page and grasped that it was his very own book of notes. His eyes widened with desire. Images raced through his mind as old memories surfaced. He silently rehearsed his mantra of runes in the ancient language. He wanted to make sure that he would remember them all so that he wouldn't make any mistakes. He secretly wanted the chance to remake the Honor Blade. He would do a few things differently.

"The Honor Blade was not named for the beholder. It was named after the source in which it was created. The Honor Stone, the last magical Rune Stone. I am assuming you have enough rune-stone dust from the Honor Stone?"

Semias winced. He stepped over a rock and crossed the rune-circle with a gliding motion. He intently moved bottles and leather pouches that sat on the workbench. Luthrous dusted some remnants of stone from the edge of the casting surface and eased his way to the workbench.

"Don't touch anything," Semias said.

"Well, at some point you are going to have to permit me to examine the contents of your materials and search through that book," Luthrous said.

"I supposed your right. It would seem I do not have the needed runestone material," Semias ran his finger over the text and studied the recipe. "I do not see that ingredient listed here."

"That is because you do not read the ancient runes." Luthrous raised onto his tiptoes and pointed to a glyph near the top of the page. "This is the glyph for 'being of honor'," he pointed to another lower down, "but this is the one for 'Honor Runestone'."

Semias studied the two glyphs and found the smallest tic at the upper corner was facing opposite directions.

"How could I have missed that?" Semias said.

"It's easy to do. It was wise after all for you to have summoned me, so as to not make a horrible mistake," Luthrous said.

"Where do I find this runestone?" Semias asked.

"Oh, I am not sure you can. It was nearly impossible to find during my time. Now, who even knows? The person known to have had the stone was Nitida. But I can tell you it requires the essence of the spiny violet nightshade plant and a crow's foot to even verify its purity," Luthrous said.

"The Runecaster in the Mountain Temple?" Semias asked.

"Yes, my successor, and she became even more powerful than I," Luthrous said.

Semias flipped to the back of the book and scanned the lines for those elements. A dull echo rippled through the corridor. The candles flickered as a gasp of fresh air hit them. Strong boots intently clapped against the floor. Slender legs kicked the billowing red robe as a female figure emerged from the darkness. Semias turned and admired the young woman's hips sway as she crossed the distance. His desire for her was no secret, but he was prohibited to take her until his work was finished. Now being in the last hour of his work, his urges rippled through his body. The young woman watched his eyes look her up and down, taking in all of her curves. She tried to gag down the bile without being noticed. She stopped several lengths from him.

"Come closer," Semias said.

Semias's eyes gleamed as they stopped at the collar of her black leather tunic.

"No, thanks. You sure have made a mess of things." she said.

She gazed around the dim and half-destroyed cavern and found the Minca in the shadows. He returned the gaze with sad eyes. A feeling of understanding etched at her emotions. Semias studied her soft hazel eyes. Her long eyelashes cast a gentle shadow over them, and her high cheeks glinted a hint of pink on her warm skin. He couldn't help but find her stunning beauty intoxicating. She stared at him, her thin brows creased gently at the center of her oval face.

"Have it your way, but not for long Amirra. You will be mine."

"Who is this?" she asked.

"This my dear is the Minca Runecaster, Luthrous."

"So, it has begun then," She said. Semias nodded with a proud smile. Amirra tried to take a read on Semias, but he was too trained to let his true emotions show. All except his lust. That she had been fighting for rotations. Now that the Runecaster was here, her time would be short. She needed to figure out her next move. "Do you have a task for me or not?"

"Yes, while I await the sqwalls return, I need you to fetch these," Semias said.

He pulled a small piece of parchment from his robe and crossed the distance between them. *Great, another piece of crappy handwriting.* she thought. He leaned into her and sniffed in her scent. Amirra ripped the paper from his grip and whipped around. Her hood slipped off her head as she hurried out of the cavern, letting her long hair dance gently in the wake. If there was a door, she would have slammed it, so she kicked several small rocks instead.

16-A Very Large And Angry Gorilla, Thing

Riddick and the others took a few provisions and headed toward the waterfall. This time, with leaf hats made of the large, round, fan-like leaves secured to their heads. The rain softened to a steady drizzle, which also made it easier to navigate the rugged terrain. It had amazed them that there were so many trees and vegetation growing in one place.

They had lived on their islands their entire lives, but they had never seen such a jungle or seen such rain. They made good time knowing they couldn't stop, or they would start to sink, and before the day was half over, they found the waterfall. The torrential deluge of water fell with ferocity for several lengths into a well-like structure.

"What is this place?" Batovi asked.

"That is one big waterfall," Sebastian said.

"Where does all the water go? This pond is barely big enough to catch the water in the first place," Batovi asked.

"There must be an underground waterway that it follows," Riddick said.

"Best be finding a place to stand on," Yerild said, searching for one for himself.

Riddick hung his pack on a branch and scaled the side of the waterfall.

"What are you doing?" Yerild asked.

"I need to get up there and see if I can find anything. You search around here," Riddick said.

"What are we looking for?" Sebastian asked.

Riddick shrugged. Sebastian rolled his eyes and found a place to hang his things.

The ground here was a bit dryer, which made it a little easier. However, he still had to be careful. Riddick moved in a zig-zag pattern, using any ledge he could as he scaled the side of the face-like formation of the rock. When he was above the fall, he stepped out onto a small ledge. The rock face was straight up, and there were few handholds to grip onto. The familiar tingle of the earth's magic rang through his fingers and he stepped back onto the ledge. He pulled his boots off and felt the cold ground with his bare feet.

A chill ran through his body and then the energy of the earth. It was calming and invigorating. His mind opened and allowed the sensations to envelop his senses. He stretched across to the ledge and gripped a small divot. His biceps pulsed as he pulled his body close to the rock-face. His toes dug into the smooth surface. He focused on every movement. He looked below and realized how high he was.

He reached high above his head for the next hold and scooted along the narrow lip. He gaged his distance, and noting he was in the center, he looked for clues. His fingers and toes were sagging under his weight, and he hadn't yet found anything. He gave in to the pressure and started back to the side of the fall. When he returned to the ledge, he replaced his boots and climbed back down.

"Did you find anything?" Yerild asked.

Riddick shook his head, "There was nothing up there."

"So, now what?" Yerild asked.

"No idea," Riddick plopped himself on the edge of the pond and slumped.

"Hey, it's stopped raining," Batovi said.

"Aye," Yerild agreed.

"If we ever leave this blasted island, we can say, at least there are no other humans to have to worry about," Sebastian said.

"It won't be long until the other settlements find this place. Captain Bricker was spout'en off his mouth a bit ago, about taking the summer to search the seas," Yerild said.

"What does he expect to find?" Riddick asked.

"No idea, he's young and full of pompous pride," Yerild said.

"Thinks he's a regular explorer," Sebastian said.

"Just because he inherited his ship from his father, doesn't make him a ship's captain," Yerild said.

"I heard him making plans with the Chairman, something about, expanding the territory," Riddick said.

"That's not good, you know the Reef Councils will never give up their islands," Batovi said.

"Aye, but that's what makes him dangerous," Riddick said.

Yerild nodded.

"We better find a way out of this jungle and get back home," Batovi said.

"Then what? Hide the island? It's going to be found sooner or later," Sebastian said.

Riddick rubbed his scruffy chin. He had no idea what he was going to do, but he had to do something, especially if the Kar-ka-dannon was here, somewhere.

"Let's head back and see if we can make a map and retrace our steps. Maybe we can return to the skiff in a few days. We've learned much more about this place now, and I think it won't be too hard," Riddick said.

"But what about your Kar-ka-dannon?" Sebastian asked.

"It will have to wait," Riddick said.

Riddick picked up his stuff and started back through the underbrush. The sun was shifting the day to night when they heard the screeches of small monkeys. They picked up their pace and hurried back to camp. Riddick rounded a tree and pulled several vines out of the way. Several small, fluffy monkeys were ripping through their camp. Riddick pulled his ax and started attacking the little creatures. He didn't intend on hitting any, just scare them away. Sebastian picked up several rocks and chucked them into the canopy. Monkeys scattered, shouting loudly.

"Those little buggers, look, all of our stuff, gone," Batovi said.

"Guys, what's that?" Yerild asked.

A substantial tree flung back and forth from the ricochet of a very large force. Loud cracks in the trees sent shivers through their skin.

"I don't know if I want to find out," Batovi said.

"Me either," Sebastian said.

"Run, back to the falls," Riddick shouted.

Riddick waited until the other three passed him, and then he spun on his toes and launched into a fast sprint. It didn't take him long to outrun the others. He slowed his pace and peeked over his shoulder. An enormous gorilla gripped the top branch of a distant tree and threw itself toward them. It flew through the air and caught another branch. Its palm seemed like it was the size of Riddick's chest and its fingers, the size of his arms.

A lump formed in Riddick's throat, and he dodged a bunch of vines. Batovi grabbed a vine and swung over a tree root. Yerild and Sebastian rounded the root and dipped under another. Riddick gripped his ax, and with the other hand gripped a vine. He thrust his legs against a trunk and leaped onto a branch. He scuffled along the slick surface and nestled up against it. The enormous primate's deep black eyes had a red ring around the outside, and its fangs were long and sharp.

There was something unusual about this beast. Gorillas were aggressive, but they didn't act like this. There was a feeling of frenzy, perhaps, an element of being possessed. But by what? Riddick hugged the trunk. The whipping of the tree branches made his stomachache. The magnificent animal gripped a vine, and released the other hand, as it continued to fly toward the setting sun.

Riddick swung his ax and sliced the vine. The gorilla bellowed as it careened toward the thick underbrush. Loud cracks and pops echoed as the jungle floor encompassed it. Riddick gripped a vine and swung to another branch. He landed softly and huddled toward the trunk. He searched for the others and identified Sebastian nestled under a root, while Yerild and Batovi were peeking through a huge fern.

The gorilla pounded his fists against the ground, which shook the whole earth. The pit in Riddick's stomach grew and nearly choked him. He sucked in a deep breath and tried to steady his breathing. The gorilla searched the canopy. Drool dripped off his long fangs, and his breath steamed in the coolness of the evening. Riddick listened, but all he heard was his blood echo in his head. He grabbed the vine and leaped from his perch. He twirled his ax in his grip, so it was ready for a downward strike.

The ax's blade sliced through the creature's shoulder as Riddick landed behind it. It roared and spun on Riddick. Riddick leaped into a somersault and brought his ax up. The blade caught the gorilla in the chin. Riddick ducked as the beast threw a round strike, with its fist clenched tightly. It slammed its fists against the ground again and then circled Riddick.

Riddick sidestepped the roots, and ran straight at the beast, with his ax aimed at its neck. The gorilla swatted the blade with one arm, and with the other, hit Riddick square, sending him flying into the trunk of a tree. The pain seared Riddick's brain, and his lungs struggle to keep the air in them. Riddick gasped heavily as his body crinkled to the ground. The jungle floor merged with the surroundings and he couldn't tell if he was upside down or not.

The gorilla roared and pounded his chest. The red rings, around its pupils, radiated with its breath. It reared onto its hind legs and beat its chest while letting out another screeching roar. It gripped its fists into the ground and hurled itself toward Riddick.

Riddick opened his eyes and spotted the gorilla coming toward him. He shouted in his mind, for his body to move out of the way, but it didn't even as much as twitch. The gorilla barreled in on him, and Riddick was convinced he was going to die. The thudding of its hands and feet against the earth echoed in Riddick's ear as he lay motionless.

If only the earth would protect me, he thought. Instantly, the mucky dirt threw itself into a covering surrounding his entire frame. The beast slammed right into the wall of earth and fell backward. Riddick sank into the dirt. A soft sensation tickled his bare skin. It pulsed in and out and soon was running through his whole body. Riddick couldn't see, but he heard the beast beating on the earth around him. He hoped the others would be safe too.

The sensations returned to his body, and he lifted himself to his knees. He searched around but couldn't find his ax. A vine dangled in front of him, which gave him an idea. He imagined opening the earth on the opposite side of the beast and rolled out of the shell as the earth complied. He tipped-toed behind several trees, and when he was behind the gorilla, he hollered a war cry. Instant power surged through his soul. A power he had never had before. His body still ached from the blow, but his mind was invigorated.

The beast spun around, his chest heaving. Riddick gathered several vines and pulled them taut. The gorilla rushed toward him. Riddick took a deep breath and threw a vine around the beast's arm as it reached to take a swing. The vine tightened against its deep gray fur and yanked it off balance. A flicker of surprise ripped through its expression. It flexed its biceps and tore the vine from its secured place.

Riddick dug his toes into the ground and launched himself onto another vine. He soared into the air. He threw another vine around the gorilla's other arm. As he whizzed past the beast's head, he twisted his core, sending the vine around the beast. He gripped the vine tightly with one hand and leaned out. With three sturdy vines, he wrapped them around the gorilla's neck. Riddick ducked as the first arm came flying at him. He spun around, gripping the vine tightly, and let go. He fell to the ground, still holding the three vines that were coiled around the gorilla's trunk-like neck.

The ricochet slammed its enormous body against the earth. It roared and squirmed as the vines tightened around its neck. Riddick rolled into a dead run and secured the vines to a tree. He spun around, and with another few vines, leaped over the gorilla and secured them, tying the beast to the ground. The gorilla struggled and squirmed, but the more it moved, the tighter the vines cinched around its neck.

Riddick searched for his ax and found it wedged tightly between several roots. He darted to his weapon and gripped the handle tightly. He thrust his foot against the moss-covered tree and tried to dislodge it. His foot slipped on the bright green lichen, and he fell onto his rump.

He rapidly stood, and with a sharp rock, scraped the moss off the log and tried again. This time, after a few tugs, he pulled the ax free. A deafening crack of thunder stung the air and rippled over their bodies. Riddick rolled the ax in his hand and started toward the gorilla. Its helpless body pulsed as it breathed heavily. Riddick stood over it and studied its eyes. The red rings gave the impression that something had bitten off a part of the beast's soul and Riddick internalized a degree of sorrow.

He struggled with whether to kill it or not. He slipped his ax over his shoulder and hurried to the others. Yerild and Sebastian peeked out from the bushes, and Batovi crawled out from the nook in the roots.

"Come on, it won't take long for it to get loose," Riddick said.

"Alright, so this is going to sound dumb, but what in the tarnation was that?" Sebastian asked.

"A very large and angry gorilla, thing," Riddick said.

Sebastian scowled. Yerild snickered.

"I gathered that much, but why?" Sebastian asked.

"I think it has been possessed by something. Its eyes had a red ring around them. There was something definitely wrong," Riddick said.

Yerild rubbed his chin and whacked a leaf from in front of him. Riddick was confident he was thinking and would corner him later. They made it almost halfway to the falls when they heard one of the trees the beast was secured to snap and pop.

"Run!" Riddick yelled.

"This can't be happening," Batovi grumbled as he dashed through the shrubs.

Their exposed skin was being battered by the sharp edges of the leaves as they ran. Sebastian cursed as a blade of tall grass whipped him in the eye, slicing his flesh. A drop of blood flowed toward his hairline as the wind rushed by.

Another loud crack of thunder pulsed the darkening sky. Yerild stretched to reach over a root, but his foot slipped, and he hit it with his forehead before landing on the ground. Riddick stopped and helped him back up. Riddick turned to look behind him and saw a full-sized tree whip back and forth.

"Blast, it's coming after us. Hurry, to the waterfall," Riddick called.

Riddick didn't know what kind of protection the waterfall was going to offer, but a feeling in his gut told him that was where they needed to go. Yerild steadied himself and hurried as rapidly as his larger frame would let him. Riddick stayed behind him and made ready to pull his ax. This time he wouldn't have compassion for the beast. Sebastian skidded to a stop, nearly toppling over into the deep pool. Batovi took a hard right and round to a stop next to Sebastian. Yerild checked over his shoulder to make sure Riddick was still behind him.

"Yerild, stop!" Sebastian and Batovi yelled.

Yerild turned back in time to slam right into the two, knocking them over the edge, and toppling into the ravaging water below. Their bodies flailed about, grasping for anything, but there was only a sheer rock face all around them. Riddick witnessed Yerild's feet disappear over the edge and secured his ax into its fastener. Sebastian pointed his hands in front of him and straightened his body. Batovi followed, but Yerild struggled to reset his body from its panic mode. They sucked in a deep breath and dove into the icy cold fluid. Riddick launched off the ground and over the edge in a perfect arch. He hoped they would be already out of his way by the time he hit the water.

The sting of the instant cold stifled his brain, and he wanted to gasp. He allowed the water to swallow him up and lose momentum and then kicked his feet and pulled his arms through the water. He could barely see through the white foam and wasn't sure which way to go. He caught a glimpse of something moving and maneuvered his body toward it.

He found the other three huddled in a small corner of a cave-like cavern and popped his head up. The pocket of air was sucked into his lungs and the panic released his brain.

"Well, that wasn't my exit strategy, but I guess it worked," Riddick said.

"Worked? It got us away from that thing, but it most certainly didn't work," Batovi said.

"Whose idea was it, anyway?" Riddick asked.

Sebastian and Batovi pointed at Yerild, who sheepishly grinned.

"Any idea how we are going to get out of here?" Batovi asked.

"Well, the water has to be going somewhere, we need to take turns and find out where it goes, then follow it," Sebastian said.

"I like it, I'll go first," Riddick said.

He sucked in a deep breath and slipped under the surface. He rolled his body and pushed off with his feet. He felt the rocks around him and tried to determine which part of the water was moving. The temperature became colder and colder the deeper he went. He was about to return for air when a gurgle of air bubbles came into view. He made a mental note of what the surrounding rocks were like and returned to the surface.

"There are bubbles coming from a section that way," Riddick said, and pointed to where he had seen them.

"I'll go next," Sebastian said.

He took in a deep breath and dove under the water. He kicked the water and swam around the corner toward the bubbles. He continued to dive until he found them. It was hard to see anything, because of it being dark underwater, and it was after dusk. He scooted along the sharp edges, being careful not to cut himself. He found a hole big enough to swim through, then returned. He popped up and gasped for new air.

"There's an opening large enough to swim through, but it seems like there is something blocking the way," Sebastian said.

"It's a portal then," Yerild said.

"What makes you say that?" Riddick asked.

"That's the way most of them are," Yerild said.

"Then we swim down there," Riddick said.

"No, way, I'm not going into some different realm without knowing where I'm going," Batovi said.

"Then stay here," Riddick said.

Riddick dove under the water, followed by Yerild. Sebastian hesitated and then shrugged. He dipped down under the surface and disappeared into the darkness. Batovi grumbled, and then he too swam after Sebastian. Riddick felt a sudden shift of energy and he understood it to be the magic of the portal accessing his magic. He wondered if the others were going to be able to pass, and he made a mental command to the portal to allow them all through. Riddick looked back to see Yerild right behind him. He wasn't fast on land, but he was an expert swimmer. He noticed what looked like Sebastian and then kicked off the edges of the tunnel-like portal to propel him faster through it. A suction grabbed him and threw him to the other side. He straightened his body and soared through like an arrow. Yerild too felt the pull and allowed the magic to take him to the next realm.

Riddick popped through the surface on the other side and flung his hair out of his face. Hot air filled his empty lungs. He covered his eyes with his arm and squinted from the bright sun that was hitting the surface and reflecting into his eyes. He waited for a moment, and then Yerild emerged from the darkness. They started swimming out of the way in time for Sebastian, and then Batovi, to come to the other side.

17-Did You Find The Answers You Seek?

Serin buffed the three of them, and they hurried through the woods back toward the village.

"That's odd," Serin said.

"What?" Shaz asked.

"The treetops are swaying, but there is no wind," Serin said.

"What would cause that?" Shaz asked.

Serin shrugged. Shaz dug his toes into a boulder and thrust himself over the top. Serin rounded the boulder, and Ladtwig and Jag scurried over the top behind Shaz. Serin's air spell was getting stronger and lasted longer, but there was little warning when it wore off and Shaz leaped over a fallen tree trunk and hit the ground hard.

"I guess the magic has worn off," Shaz said.

"Let's take a breather for a few minutes," Serin said, coming to a quick stop.

"Yes, lets," Ladtwig said.

Ladtwig pulled some dried meat from one of his pockets and chewed diligently. Shaz rested against a tree trunk and Serin sat on a stump. The ground rippled and shook, sending some old branches that were barely hanging on, crashing to the ground. Shaz jumped up and gripped the hilt of the blade.

"What was that?" Serin asked.

"I don't know, but I don't like it," Shaz said. Shaz steadied himself as the ground rolled under his feet. "I don't think it's anything magic," Shaz said.

"Jaduuk?" Serin asked.

Ladtwig jumped and ran behind Shaz.

"No, I don't think so, I don't smell or hear them. It's something else," Shaz said.

"It feels like the ground is shaking," Serin said.

"Why?" Ladtwig asked.

"I have no idea," Serin said.

A loud cracking sound echoed from the distance and grew louder as it came closer. The surface bounced them, and they reached for whatever was near to steady themselves. They covered their ears and ducked as the vibrations shot over them. Shaz gripped Serin and pulled her tightly to him and lowered themselves to the ground. Ladtwig struggled toward them, and Shaz pulled him in tightly. The earth shook violently, lasting several lengths, and then went silent. It was totally silent. Even the birds and insects no longer made any sounds. An eerie sting sat in their stomachs.

"This cannot be good," Serin said.

"Come on. Let's go," Shaz said.

Serin buffed again, and they raced toward the village. The chief was coming out of his little hut when they approached. Shaz and Serin began to unlace their boots in the formal greeting, but the chief waved them to stop.

"We have no time for that, follow me," the Chief said.

The Chief motioned for his wife to take Serin and then beckoned Shaz to follow him into the woods. Serin started to object.

"The healers need your help Serin, please come with me," the Chieftess said.

Serin studied the little woman's eyes and found pain and sorrow in them. She nodded and hurried after her. The seven tribal elders walked briskly through the tall grass. The elders were speaking in a language Shaz had never heard before and found Turkill following behind him.

"Where are we going?" Shaz mouthed.

"Pay attention," Turkill mouthed back.

Turkill pointed up ahead. Shaz identified a hut, twice the size of the small ones they lived in, and several large mammoths milling about the long grass. Some had long beige fur all over, covering their large hoof-like feet, and others were smooth and leathery. The little men matched their animals. A couple had long fur coats with fur caps and boots and others had fewer clothes but slightly more than Turkill's clan. Shaz deducted they must be from the southern territories or high in the mountain regions.

The elders stopped and talked amongst themselves for a moment after reaching the prayer hut. The eldest Minca, that was in the middle, stepped through the others and entered the hut first. He lit a small lantern with a flint and hung it on a hook near the center. A soft aroma of sage, dockweed, and mulberry emanated from the lantern. Each of the chief leaders entered in a particular order that Shaz assumed was based on their ranking system.

"Now you," said the Chief and held open the blanket door so Shaz could enter.

Shaz still had to bend over, but once inside, the hut opened to where he could stand upright and even had a little room above his head. There were ten small blankets on the floor placed in a circle. A fire pit was in the center and small lanterns hung throughout the room. Some were meant for fire and others the same herbs. The first seven elders sat with their legs crossed, the ones with coats took them off and hung them on small hooks at the back. The Chief directed Shaz to a blanket in the circle. Shaz sat down, folding in his long legs like the others. Turkill rushed to the fire pit and struck a flint against the top stone, sending sparks onto the dried brush that was nestled under small twigs. A small flame popped to life and then caught hold of the twigs. Turkill added a few small logs as the fire grew, and then a few larger ones. After feeling confident the fire would last awhile, he moved to his seat next to Shaz and sat folding his legs. The Eldest folded his hands in his lap.

"Calamity has befallen our realm and we need the ancient's help. We must concentrate deeply in order to bring the spirits here," he said.

"I do not like this. He has brought these calamities upon us. *He* has doomed us all by his Shadow magic," one elder, sitting two men away from Shaz, said. Shaz perked up when he heard him call it shadow magic. "See, he knows what it is. Do you possess shadow magic boy?" the Minca asked.

Shaz wasn't sure if he should answer the question or not and sat staring back at the men. Shaz ran different scenarios through his head. All the men were staring at him, waiting to see what he was going to say.

"It is not our place to judge," the Eldest said.

"No, it's alright. To answer your question," Shaz said looking at the man, "Aye, I do have Shadow magic, I can't guarantee that I will not cause more harm than good, but I will die trying to protect others. It's a burden I didn't ask for, and I only hope that I will not fail."

An awkward silence filled the hut as the man digested the admission.

"Then we begin," said the Eldest.

All the men put their hands flat on the floor. Their palms touched the cool ground and all but Shaz began swaying in a circle together. They hummed in harmonizing tones for several lengths then, started chanting in the language they were speaking earlier. Shaz didn't start swaying but sat with his hands on the ground watching the men. A feeling of inadequacy overcame him. He was angry that everyone else appeared to understand more than him and no one was offering information.

How was he supposed to do all this? A game that Grandfather used to play came to his mind, and he understood that even if people told him what to do, he would still have to do it and learn for himself. Shaz sucked in a deep breath and closed his eyes. He tried to concentrate on the gentle chanting and take in the aroma of the herbs. His mind slipped in and out of old memories and recent events, and he couldn't force his mind to focus on any one thing until an image of Serin fell into place. His nerves settled, and he realized she was his calming voice. The chanting grew louder, which brought Shaz back to the prayer hut. He opened his eyes and stared into the fire that was now burning strong.

A woman came from the center of the fire and stood before the Eldest Chief. Her soft flowing dress was long and danced as though it were the flames. Her soft gaze eased the tension in the room.

"Ah, the Minca, what can I do for you?" she asked.

"Cornelia, it's good to see you again," the Eldest said.

"You too Laudus," she said.

"I'll get right to the point. What is happening to our land? We have been having earth-shakes which have ripped through the land," he said.

"Earth-shakes? Hummm, that can mean there has been a tear in a realm barrier."

"Will that affect only this realm or others too?" Shaz asked.

Cornelia spun around and shot Shaz a glare. Shaz suddenly realized he was not supposed to speak to her.

"Who are you? You are not Minca," she questioned sternly.

"No, I am Shazmpt," Shaz said.

Cornelia's brows raised, "Shazmpt, son of Reinholt, heir to the Tooatha De Danann?" she asked.

"Yes," Shaz said sheepishly.

"Oh my, this changes things," she said.

"How?" Laudus asked.

"I fear this means a tear in the *time* barrier."

A lump formed in Shaz's stomach.

"But why tear the fabric of time?" the Chief asked.

"There are many reasons, the Runecaster deep in the Bairr Tiornecht mountains will have the information you seek. I wish you well," Cornelia said and faded away.

The fire didn't fade, and Shaz saw another figure emerge through the flames. He noticed tiny glowing strings that were stretched from the Minca's hands were secured to the being in the middle, like chains to keep him confined as if he were a prisoner.

"Who seeks me?" the figure asked in a gruff and raspy voice. Shaz found that all the Minca had their eyes closed. "Who seeks me?" the man demanded.

Shaz questioned which of the Minca had requested this being. The hairs on the back of his neck started to tingle, and he wondered if it might have been himself that had brought this man here. He turned to the man and studied his half-faded form dance with the flames for a moment.

"I do, I am Shaz, son of Reinholt."

"Son of Reinholt, huh? Very well, what do you want?"

"Who are you?" Shaz asked.

"I am Sarud," Sarud said.

It didn't actually answer his question, but Shaz got the impression that he was somehow related to the Velshari. Shaz didn't know what to ask exactly, he hadn't even realized that he had wanted anything. Then the shadow crept into his mind. The uncomfortable feeling it brought made Shaz squirm. Shaz sensed this being had a level of shadow magic, so he guessed it to be about that.

"I come seeking instruction on shadow magic."

"Shadow magic? I have no knowledge of that."

"Yes, you do, I can sense it in you," Shaz declared.

The red-flickering image of a man stood surprised in the middle of the fire.

"Hum," Sarud said, rubbing his chin. Sarud studied Shaz for a few minutes. "You have a tremendous amount of shadow magic. Much more than I have ever seen. You must be careful as not to let it overtake you. The Shadow dwells in the hearts of all men and desires to control all men. Its only desire is power. *IF* you give into its enticing, the evil will take hold and tear you apart. It is fueled by anger, greed, selfishness, and fear. But the Shadow dwells *deep* within your soul. You must take extra caution," Sarud said.

"How do I control it?" Shaz asked.

"Control the Shadow? No one controls the Shadow, however, anyone trying to use the magic it offers will have incredible advantages, but it comes at a tremendous cost." Shaz knew that the shadow magic took some of his health when he used it, but for some reason Sarud's words implied something else, something more. "The Shadow needs a host to survive, and in return, it offers its services. Anytime it is asked to do something, it will require something from its host. But if it doesn't like the way you are using it, it will require even more from you. Do its bidding and it will help you and aid you. Only those who have a natural ability and aptitude to do evil can wield it without the constant drain on them," Shaz's stomach hit the bottom and came back up, leaving him the intense desire to puke. Sarud found a bit of delight in his discomfort. "Those desiring its power will suffer if they do not have shadow magic. When using shadow magic, people nearby may feel the backlash it sends when in use."

"What kinds of things can shadow magic do?" Shaz asked through pale lips.

"It can do anything you desire, although remember, it has a mind of its own and will make you pay to use it against its will." Shaz rubbed his hands together, feeling a very real dread about his powers. "You can evoke the power of the shadows and use your shadow to kill, steal, lie, cheat, it can even possess others, and shadow magic can force other's shadows to control them." He paused and peered more deeply into Shaz's eyes, "I see that you have the ability to create shadow warriors and anger the hearts of man, to cause contention and force loyalty and bondage."

Shaz took in a deep breath and thought, *Maybe I don't want to learn anymore*, the feelings weighing even heavier than before. His thoughts turned to Serin and the Minca. At least he has the bond with Serin now.

"I see you have been bonded to an elemental, whom you care very deeply for. She will be a considerable strength and a tremendous risk to you. She evokes the power of water, air, and light. A power that thwarts the shadows," Sarud said.

"Light? I was only told she controlled the water and air." Shaz said without thinking, then asked, "How can you tell?"

"I see her in you. The shadow magic knows what can destroy it, it too knows, and it seeks to rid her from you."

Shaz shielded Serin from Sarud, blocking any more information from him.

"Will it destroy me?" Shaz asked.

Shaz's hands wrung together tightly. That was the real question he wanted answered.

"Yes," Sarud said. A sly grin on his old wrinkled face told Shaz he secretly desired to harness the powers Shaz had, but the chains he was bound with forbade him. "But only if you give in to it with your selfishness."

Sarud looked longingly, Shaz sensed that that was what happened to him. Shaz watched Sarud's answers as if he had two faces, an evil one and a good one, as if he couldn't decide which one to choose.

"Can Serin destroy me?" Shaz asked quietly.

Sarud nodded, but then his heavy brows softened, and he leaned forward. His pure fatherly concern showed through momentarily.

"Or make you whole. With the correct balance of light and shadow, you can be very intense together, but if one overpowers the other, destruction will occur," Sarud said.

A deep ripple of truth coursed through his body and Shaz now understood that he could be both good and evil, as long as he kept them in balance and used them for the right reasons. Sarud studied him, searching to read his thoughts, but Shaz had closed off his thoughts and feelings. Shaz noticed Sarud's gaze move to the Honor Blade, and an uneasy sensation crept into his guts. Shaz put his hand on it to secure it. Shaz felt the deep desire Sarud has for the sword, but knew the figure in the fire was a spirit and couldn't actually take it from him.

"What about Gavin Rhill?" Shaz asked.

Sarud stood up straight. His brows hovered over his tortured, maddening eyes.

"I have said too much," Sarud said.

The image disappeared into the fire. The flames sank to a gentle burn. The small men released their leashes on the figure and sank onto the floor. Feeling the drain it took on them, they sat for a few moments to regain their strength.

"Did you find the answers you seek?" Shaz nodded. "Good, then we must get you to the Runecaster at Bairr as quickly as we can," Laudus said.

18-What Did The Earth Portal Tell You?

A light blue sky met the red and orange sand at the horizon, which seemed to never end. A few tall jungle trees stood around the smooth pond. A small lizard sunbathed on a smooth, wind-worn rock. A wave of heat rolled across the desert floor, making the distant hills look like they were swaying in a breeze. Riddick swam toward the edge until his feet met the ground. He stood and walked through the last bit of water.

The heat felt good. It had been a long week on the water-soaked island. But as he sat and rested under one of the trees, his heart sank. They had no provisions, no direction, and no idea what even lived in this realm.

"So, I guess we are no longer on the island," Sebastian said.

"Aye, just on the other side of a barrier," Yerild said.

"Which realm are we in?" Riddick asked.

"That, I have no idea," Yerild said.

"I guess we go after your Kar-ka-dannon after all," Batovi said.

Riddick remembered the images from the earth portal and stood to look around.

"It all looks the same," Riddick said, rubbing his face.

"Look around for anything we can carry water in," Yerild said.

They started to search the small oasis and found several round shells they filled with water. Batovi found that the outer shell was like a type of woven material, and he began pulling it off and weaving a rope to secure it to his belt.

"Maybe we can move some of those rocks and make a shelter," Sebastian said.

Riddick wandered a bit while the others heaved and pulled the largest rocks they could maneuver to make a small cave. He searched the distance for any clues at all. Anything he could use to determine which direction they should even go. He walked around the pool several times as if the next time around something would magically appear.

He picked up a rock and chucked it into the heat ripples. It landed several lengths away, and a lizard scurried away from the small dust plume it left. The sun was now heading toward the horizon, and the heat in the air diminished to a more tolerable temperature.

"It's going to be night soon," Yerild said, stopping next to him.

"Aye."

"I believe we are in the Realm of Yune," Yerild said.

"Have you been to all of the realms?" Riddick asked.

"No, not all, but many. Back when I was young and starting out as an informant to the Dodjen."

"Those are real too, I guess," Riddick said.

"Aye, everything Grandfather told you, is real. That was his job. He sacrificed his position as the Grand Cleric to take you, boys, into hiding."

"From Gavin Rhill and the Shadow?" Riddick asked.

"Aye, because of your being the descendants of the ancients that fashioned the original Sev-Rin-Ac-Lavah. Because you are the descendant of the Bairr Tiornecht and the sage of the staff of the Kar-ka-dannon. You have the right to the staff as your inheritance, but if Gavin Rhill destroys you, then there is no one to stake their claim and he can have them," Yerild said.

"The ancient artifacts Gavin Rhill is searching for?"

"Aye, it's no accident I asked you to go on this mission," Yerild said.

"Aren't there more than just us?" Riddick asked.

"No, Gavin Rhill hunted your ancestors, your family, and killed them all. Mathieu was the only one powerful enough to keep you hidden from the Shadow's power. Our island was the only one that had enough places to use as hiding places."

"The archipelago," Riddick said.

"Aye. That's why he brought you to Turob. I have no powers, but with this," he pulled an identical medallion from his shirt, "I can travel through the portals into any realm, and quietly. Gavin Rhill cast a spell on each portal to identify who was moving through them. It searched the magic imprint of each person, but I have none, so I was never detected. That's when Queen Ambrosia started the Teorran Travelers. Peoples of the Travelers have no magic, but have the fortitude for hiding. I was raised a Traveler of old, and we had many underground and hidden passageways. We used to keep from the magic folk. For many rotations, I roamed many realms, observing the doings of the shadow and watching the artifacts. I reported to Queen Ambrosia and Mathieu. Turob was my suggestion."

"Gavin Rhill murdered my family?"

"Aye, and Shaz's and the girl he travels with."

"Shaz travels with a girl?" Riddick asked, his eyes wide. "I wonder how well that's going?" Yerild chuckled. "So, what is this 'mission'?" Riddick asked.

"What did the earth portal tell you?"

Riddick searched his mind and tried to organize the images in a sensible order. He had a hard time making sense of it. An image of the Kar-ka-dannon, tied to a pillar, settled at the front of his brain.

"I need to find the Kar-ka-dannon," Riddick said.

"Then, that's what we'll do," Yerild said.

"I have no idea where to even start," Riddick admitted, his head hanging low.

"I have heard, if you just ask, the Kar-ka-dannon are eager to please," Yerild said.

Riddick scowled, and Yerild slapped him on the shoulder and returned to the others. Riddick walked around a few more times and then returned to the others and helped finish the shelter. The dropping sun brought a comfortable coolness, and the crew searched for food. Sebastian and Batovi, finagled a poorly rigged trap, to try and capture a lizard who was mocking their attempts.

Riddick stretched out on the warm sand and stared into the sky. Small patches of stars twinkled into existence. He scoured the dots and made patterns in his head, so he was sure to remember how to return to the portal. A group of stars, sitting in the high north section of the night sky, was familiar. Riddick stood and turned around. The belt of stars suddenly stood out.

"It's the constellation, Ophard," Riddick pronounced.

"Aye, the heavens are the one thing constant in the world of Edenocht," Yerild said.

"Then, I know how to find where we need to go. The earth portal showed me the Irias constellation. That's the direction we need to go," Riddick said, pointing.

He made note of all the constellations, mumbling as he made a map in his head. The night went by too fast and before too long, the heat of the next day was bearing down on them. Riddick found it particularly hard to keep the penetrating rays of the sun off his fair skin. It didn't seem to bother the others, but they had a protective layer of hardened, ocean-tanned skin. It would take several days to travel to the constellation Irias from where they were. Halfway through the day, a gusty wind picked up sand and blew it around them. The sting of the gritty dust ate at their senses.

They struggled to cover their faces and pushed forward. Riddick's lip cracked open, and when he licked it, he could taste the metallic hint of blood. He wasn't sure if they were going to make the several days' journey. The wind continued to gust from every direction, making it even harder to stay on course. Their legs became heavy, and they struggled to stay standing.

"Over there," Riddick said.

He motioned toward a fairly good-sized flat rock protruding from the sand. They veered toward the rock and huddled closely together. The wind rushed around it, giving them a bit of relief.

"We'll stay here for a while and hope the night will bring a calm," Yerild said.

They all agreed and hunkered down to wait out the storm. Small drifts of sand crept up onto their bodies, covering them from underneath. Sebastian and Riddick tried to brush the sand away, so it wouldn't swallow them up. Their skin was oozing from the gnawing of the sand. It was becoming more than they could bear, and Riddick slammed his fist into the earth. A wall of sand formed around them, shielding them from the onslaught. Sebastian and Batovi's mouth dropped, as they witnessed the sand crawl on top of itself and become solid.

"I didn't know you could do that," Sebastian said.

"It happened in the jungle too," Riddick said.

"I'm not arguing," Batovi said.

Riddick sagged into the sand and closed his eyes. Yerild and the others also found a comfortable place to settle into. It was warm and quiet. The sand wall was so thick, it was hard to hear the roaring winds whipping around outside. It was now dark and soon they were all yawning. The exhaustion overcame them, and they slipped into sleep. Riddick stirred and tried to re-adjust, but Batovi was nearly laying on top of him. He waved his hand and let a small hole open in the top of their sand bubble. Riddick could see a few stars and there was no wind. He shoved Batovi off him and stretched.

19-I Am Crolos The Desert Plains Warden

Riddick had no idea how long they had slept, but he was rested and starving. He pulled the bulbous root filled with water and took a swig. It had sat in there long enough to take on the sweet flavor of the root. It was refreshing and somehow satisfied the hunger. At least for now. Yerild stirred and Sebastian's arm smacked Batovi in the face. Batovi sat up straight and was about to belt Sebastian when he noticed Riddick studying the stars.

"How far are we?" Batovi asked.

"Well, we're not as close as I had hoped, but we're not lost either. I think we should try to gain some ground while it's cool and there's no weather," Riddick said.

"I'm starving," Batovi said.

"Drink from your root, it's sweet and satisfying, but not too much. We won't know when we'll find food next," Riddick said.

The others woke, and Riddick let down the sand walls. The cool night air filled their lungs, sending a shiver of invigoration to their brains. They traveled through the night making good time. They stopped every few hours to re-assess the stars, just as they would at sea. It was natural to them and brought a sense of comfort. Sebastian and Batovi even sang the familiar sailor tunes of the deep.

"Hey, look, a rash-fieldcress plant," Yerild said.

"What kind of plant is that?" Riddick asked.

"It's a plant that tastes delicious. We can stew it, boil it, eat it raw, and dry it," Yerild said.

Yerild broke off several twig-like pieces, twirled it around with his tongue and then consumed it. The others stood with perplexed looks and then gave in to their hunger and gathered their own.

"Wow, this does taste good," Batovi said.

Batovi gnawed at the outer casing until the soft inner core oozed into his mouth. He smiled as the taste of meat ran through his taste buds. Riddick searched around and found a few more plants, and tied a stack of twigs into a bundle, and secured them to his belt next to the bulbous root.

"Come on, let's keep going, we won't have long until sunrise," Riddick said.

The others secured themselves their own stock and continued to the north. They walked until the sun became overbearing, and Riddick made another sand covering. They rested and ate and told stories for over three more days.

"We're running out of water," Yerild said, rolling the last bit around the bottom of his root.

"Aye, and there is still nothing but sand as far as the eye can see," Sebastian said.

"Are you sure we are almost there?" Batovi asked.

"Aye, but who knows what we will find, or if we will find anything when we arrive there," Riddick said.

"But you said-" Batovi started.

"He said, that is where we needed to go, not that we would know what there would be when we got there," Yerild interrupted.

Batovi shoved a twig in his mouth and scowled. The dryness of the heat, even though they were traveling at night, made their skin continue to crack and ooze. Every time they moved, the scabs that had now formed, pulled and cracked. Riddick gingerly pulled a twig from his side belt and broke it in half. He opened his mouth slowly, so he wouldn't split open the skin again. He managed to place the piece in his mouth and then held his fingers to keep them from cracking. A loud billow came from the distance and shattered the quiet desert night.

"The Kar-ka-dannon," Yerild said.

"Are you sure?" Riddick asked.

"The legend says, it makes a loud and obnoxious billow. That sounded pretty obnoxious to me," Yerild said.

The sound came again, but this time, it was more like a cry for help. Riddick felt an instant sense of pain and anguish, as if it were his own. His brows furled as he scoured the night horizon.

"It came from that direction," Riddick said.

"How can you tell?" Batovi asked.

"I can feel it, it must be close," Riddick said.

"Look, over there," Yerild said.

Riddick turned to where Yerild was pointing and identified a human figure walking toward them. Riddick gripped his ax, and Sebastian and Batovi pulled their small curved knives and took attack stances. The figure came into view. He was wearing a dark robe with the hood drawn over his head.

"Steady," Riddick said.

Sebastian and Batovi looked back and forth between each other and Riddick and Yerild. Yerild had lost his blade, so he had picked up a rock.

"Stop, who are you?" Riddick called.

The figure stopped and stood momentarily and then lifted his arms to pull the hood off his head.

"We're armed and ready to fight," Sebastian said.

The figure took a few steps closer.

"There won't be any need for that, I am here to help," the old man said.

"Who are you?" Riddick asked.

"I am Crolos the Desert Plains Warden."

Yerild almost dropped the rock and coughed. Riddick turned back to him and witnessed his face fade in color.

"What is it?" Riddick whispered.

"He's from the old days," Yerild whispered back.

"What does that mean?" Riddick asked.

"I can't tell what side he is really on?" Yerild said.

Riddick started to pull his ax from his back.

"Now, now, there is no need for that. I am an old man and couldn't best you. But I can offer medicine for your skin, and shelter," Crolos said and held out his hand.

It shook gently from age and the early dawn crept over the man's face and they recognized deep wrinkles in his tanned skin. An uneasy curiosity surged through Riddick's core, but he secured his weapon. The man finished the last few lengths and held out his hand for them to greet. Riddick remembered what Mathieu had taught him. He closed his mind from any form of magic from seeing into his thoughts, then took his hand. The old man's eyes twinkled a weird glint, and Riddick was sure there was something about him.

"Come, you are a long way from home and are probably starving. I also have fresh water," Crolos said.

Yerild dropped his rock, and the others returned their blades. They followed the old man over a hill. As they came over the crest of the sand dune, a small dwelling came into view. Flickering lights from the windows cast a gentle glow on the red sand. A well, with a bucket to draw from it sat at the edge. It was hard not to want to run toward the well, but Riddick controlled his impulses. His mouth gripped tightly from the lack of moisture in his body. The old man lifted the latch and lowered the bucket. After a moment, he retrieved it and poured the cool liquid into a saucer.

Batovi grabbed the saucer from the edge of the roughly carved stones and followed the man into the house. It was warm and comfortable, but Riddick sensed an odd sensation as he stepped over the thresh hold.

"It's not much to look at, but it's home," Crolos said.

"How long have you lived here?" Riddick asked.

"Too long. I have been stranded here for quite some time. I hope maybe you can shed some light on the fate of this realm," Crolos said.

"I don't think I have much to offer," Riddick said.

"But, you might," Crolos said, peering at Yerild.

Yerild sucked in a deep breath and nodded. A shift in the energy in the room made Riddick question what was going on. Sebastian and Batovi busied themselves with dividing the water into cups and handed them around. Riddick sipped the liquid. The cold stung his cracked lips. The desire to guzzle it down surprised him. He understood, however, he needed to drink it slowly, to give his body time to take in the needed nourishment.

"What is the last thing you remember?" Yerild asked.

The man slipped off his traveling robe and hung it on a peg on the wall.

"Where are my manors, please, take your cloaks off and make yourself comfortable. Let me make you some supper. It has already been many seasons; I can wait a little longer."

"I'll help," Sebastian said.

Crolos nodded, and they disappeared into another room.

"What is going on?" Riddick asked.

"I'm not sure, I need to find out who he is and what he knows," Yerild said.

"What could happen?" Riddick asked.

"A lot!" Yerild said.

Yerild's face turned a bit of ash and he gulped hard. Riddick handed him a cup and Yerild sipped the liquid.

"You don't exactly exude confidence here," Riddick said.

"I know," Yerild said.

Yerild took another sip and turned as the others returned. Sebastian carried a platter of pieces of bread and cheese and some dried meat. Yerild stared at the platter with a perplexed gazed. Yerild gripped Riddick's forearm. Yerild gave Riddick a 'be-on-the-look-out' look. The pit in Riddick's stomach hit the bottom of his guts and shot back up, getting stuck in his throat. He swallowed a gulp and pushed it back down.

"Please, sit and eat, I am sure you are famished," Crolos said.

They were starving, and it was hard for Riddick not to want to stuff his face. They gratefully gathered pieces of the cheese and meats and ate eagerly. Even Yerild gave in to his hunger. Crolos helped himself, after they had all served themselves, and sat in his wooden chair in the corner. Crolos rested his head against the hardwood of the back of his chair. Riddick was sad for the man. He was sure he had waited for an excessive amount of time for any communication with anyone.

"Where are you from?" Riddick asked.

Crolos lifted his head and watched Riddick for a split second.

"From a time and place very far from here."

"Are you a traveler?" Riddick asked.

"You've heard about the Travelers?" Crolos asked, his brows raised.

"Only stories," Riddick said.

Crolos nodded and turned to Yerild.

"Please, tell me, how long has it been?" Crolos asked.

The crack in his voice was sincere, and Riddick sensed the dread in the question.

"Three hundred rotations," Yerild said. Crolos closed his eyes. A small tear escaped the corner of one. "What of the artifact?" Yerild asked.

"Not here, I gave up a long time ago," Crolos said.

"This isn't about that, Kar-ka-dannon thing, is it?" Batovi asked.

Crolos perked up and stared at Batovi, who slunk into his seat.

"Kar-ka-dannon? How do you know about the Kar-ka-dannon?" Crolos asked, his tone sharp.

"Riddick beheld them in a vision, on the other side of the oasis," Sebastian said.

Yerild shot them a penetrating glare that sent shivers down their spines, and they shut their mouths tightly. Crolos studied Riddick. Riddick felt his energy being attacked. He closed his mind even tighter and tried to find balance against the wall.

"I suppose you have a right to the information. The war wizard has emerged from the shadows, to take his place in the realms. The

Solstice of Yune will return shortly, and the realms will begin to align," Yerild said.

Riddick stared at Yerild as though he had spoken an unfamiliar language. He was about to open his mouth, but Crolos beat him to it.

"And the Queen?"

"No one knows yet," Yerild said.

"How long?" Crolos asked.

"Mathieu is gathering the council," Yerild said.

Riddick noted the two men's expressions as they talked back and forth, and Crolos wrung his hands.

"Gavin Rhill?" Crolos asked.

"Mathieu says he has been felt in the universe, but so far, hasn't made a presence yet," Yerild said.

Riddick noticed a conflicting flicker in Crolos' eye. He paid attention to the energy around the room and organized the scents, sounds, and feelings around him. There was one he had noticed when they first came to the camp. It was the same as the crazed gorilla's eyes, but he couldn't figure out why. A small stone statue, sitting on a shelf above the waning fire, snagged his attention. It was exactly like one on Shaz's mantle.

He studied it from across the room, trying to find a reason as to what it meant. It had to mean something if they both had one. Crolos realized Riddick was intently looking at the statue, rose from his chair, and picked it up. Riddick rubbed the back of his neck. His long wavy red hair was now slightly fallen from the tie he used to pull it out of his face.

"This is a Realm Tribute of Peace," Crolos said.

"How many are there?" Riddick asked.

"Only twelve," Yerild said.

"Yes, they were given to the council by Queen Ambrosia, as a token of the unified efforts of the realms," Crolos said.

"Only those who she found worthy received them as a reminder of their loyalty," Yerild said.

Crolos sat it back on the shelf and ignored the implication.

"The one relic I kept," Crolos said.

"There are many we need to gather if the Realms are to be reunited," Yerild said.

"Have all the heirs been found?" Crolos asked.

"All but one," Yerild said.

"Which ones?" Crolos asked.

"Tooatha De Danann, Bairr Tiornecht, and Lavari," Yerild said.

"Lavari? Really? I thought they had been completely eliminated," Crolos said, his brows high and his dark eyes wide.

Riddick pieced their semi-secret code together, and he was certain they were talking about he and Shaz. He didn't know the third, but he did know it wouldn't be long until he met up with them and he shivered from its truth rippling through his core.

"What is it?" Crolos asked.

"Oh, nothing, it just got warm and then cold all of a sudden," Riddick said.

"There is much to do, but we are exhausted. By chance, could we finish this conversation in the morning?" Yerild asked.

"Yes, of course. Here, I have medicine for your skin."

Crolos left the room and returned with three small jars and a bottle. He handed them to Sebastian and Batovi, who smeared the oily goop onto their faces and hands. Riddick smelled the ointment and immediately recognized its components. *I guess it's part of being an Earth sage.* He thought. He smeared the contents on his skin and breathed in the herbs and minerals. It was comforting to his soul, much more than he had ever understood before.

"I have blankets, but you'll have to share the floor. I'm sorry I don't have more to offer," Crolos said.

"You have been more than gracious," Riddick said, taking a blanket.

He propped himself against a basket, near the far side of the room, and spread the heavy wool blanket over him. It wasn't long enough to cover his entire body, and his feet stuck out a few lengths. He was used to it though and felt right at home. It didn't take long before he slipped into a deep sleep. He didn't even stir with Yerild's snoring, or the wheezing sound Batovi made in his sleep.

A pounding in his head stabbed at the back of Riddick's skull and he jerked to alert. He kept his eyes closed and listened. When he heard nothing, he peeked out from under his eyelids. The room was dark, with a gentle glow from the last bit of fire in the lantern across the room. He lifted his head and heard faint voices coming from outside. He searched the room and found everyone still asleep. He wanted to find out who it was, so he pulled in his long legs and rolled out from under the blanket and came to a half-crouch under the window.

Outside, near the well, he could see three hooded figures. The one he recognized as Crolos, the other two he had never seen before. They were both short, with their heads coming to Crolos's waist. His heart pulsed as he ran through every story Mathieu had ever told him. The taller of the two shifted from one foot to the other, letting the moon's rays hit the side of his bronze skin. Then he remembered the story of the Minca. Small men, half the size of regular men, but thin and agile. Warriors, hunters, and keepers of precious things. They had pure hearts and didn't seek after riches or power. They were used as guardians of artifacts, precious gems, and even secrets.

Riddick needed to move closer, to hear what they were saying. He lowered onto all fours and crawled toward the door. His bare hands steadied himself on the cold wood floor. He felt the energy of the earth tingle against his skin and he soaked up the power. A thought came to mind, and he put his ear to the ground. The earth responded to his need and carried the sound vibrations into his mind.

"The heirs have been found, the solstice will come soon, we must find the Kar-ka-dannon," Crolos said.

"We have been searching for so long, what makes you think it will show up now?" the taller Minca asked.

"Because the Bairr Tiornecht earth sage has come, and it will find *him*. Besides, I heard it in the distance just before coming across the sage," Crolos said.

"Are you sure?" the other asked.

Their voices were deep for little men, but not as deep as regular men. The vision the earth portal gave him resurfaced, and Riddick was confident the Kar-ka-dannon would be in trouble. He needed to find it, and fast.

"I will take the sage to the pillars, which will send for the Kar-ka-dannon, then we can-" Crolos started.

"Shhhh, I think someone is coming," the first Minca said.

"How can you tell?" asked the other.

"No, no, it's the sage, he is listening, we will meet again tomorrow, and follow the plan," Crolos said.

Riddick cursed under his breath and crawled back to his spot. He pulled the covers over him and pretended to be asleep when Crolos crept back into the house. Crolos stepped over Batovi, who had made himself comfortable in the walkway, and hurried to the back room.

Riddick wrestled with his thoughts the remainder of the night, falling in and out of sleep. Yerild snorted loudly, which startled him awake. He rubbed his nose and rolled over. Sebastian and Batovi stirred and then sat up. Riddick yawned, then opened his eyes. The early dawn crept through the window, casting a long shadow on the old furnishings.

Riddick hadn't noticed how old everything was the night before, and he chided himself. He took great pride in taking in every single detail there was. It relieved the uneasiness in his chest to know where everything was, even to compulsion. He pushed Yerild's large leg off his leg and rose. He stretched and then left the house to relieve himself. He studied the ground as he walked out past the edge of the makeshift grounds.

He didn't see any footprints. He fully expected to find three sets and wanted to see which way they went, but there were none. He searched the horizon. Small desert bushes speckled the landscape, and he now saw a jagged, red mountain range in the distance. His stomach growled, and he returned to the house.

20-We Need You Here

The sun had long slipped past the horizon, leaving a cool prick in the air. Shaz waited for the visiting Chiefs to leave the hut and then followed Turkill and his father. The soft clicking of night insects was calming, even though he was so far from his home. The comfort his new synergy with Serin gave helped soothe the heat that was constantly increasing in his chest. He understood it to be his fire magic, but he couldn't tell how much longer he could keep it under control. They quietly made their way to their huts and shelters. Shaz pulled the flap open enough to slip through. He unlatched his sword and set it at the edge of his bed. He slipped his tunic off and then his boots, setting them down quietly.

"How did it go?" Serin asked.

"Sorry to wake you, I had no idea it would take so long," Shaz said.

Shaz climbed under his covers and fluffed his headrest.

"I barely made it back myself. There were so many people that are injured," Serin said.

"You must be exhausted. Did you drink plenty of water?" Shaz asked.

"I tried, but the water supply is so low, and it was barely enough to make enough healing compresses that we needed. I also heard that some of the water supplies are poisoned with some kind of mixture of toxic fumes," Serin said.

"Could you separate the good water from the fumes?" Shaz asked.

"I don't think I can do anything, I'm so drained."

"Well, get some sleep and we'll come up with something in the morning."

"Uh-huh," Serin muttered.

Shaz listened to Serin's breaths slow and deepen. He closed his eyes, but he found no sleep. His mind circled around the prayer hut and the Synmagic. His bewilderment on how he could help Serin settled on his face. She used her magic so often and she was getting quite good and he had yet to even try his. That's what he was going to do, he was going to start helping. After all, he supposedly had water and air magic too. Maybe he could use his own water magic to keep his heartfire soothed. He tried to picture in his mind what his other magics looked like. He had a pretty good idea about the fire but had pushed out the others. He let himself relax and his body sank into the fluff. A calm overcame him as waves of blue crashed against his consciousness. The soft sound the waves made when they crashed into the shores back home filled his mind and a soothing calm came all over his body and he drifted to sleep.

Shaz woke with a start. He lifted his head and blinked. He half expected his head to hurt like it usually did when he didn't get enough sleep, but it didn't. The soft morning light lifted enough shadows that he could make out Serin still sleeping across the hut. He rested his head and watched her softly breathing. A soft thud sounded at the edge of the doorway.

"Shaz, you awake?" Turkill asked.

"Yeah," Shaz whispered.

"Let's go, we need to get a head start, we have a long way to go," Turkill said.

Serin stirred.

"I'll be right out," Shaz said. Shaz reached for his tunic and slipped it over his head and grabbed his sword, boots, and satchel and lifted the flap. "Stay here with Serin Jag." Jag looked up sleepily and yawned. He pulled his boots on as they walked. "Who all is coming?" Shaz asked.

"Me, Ladtwig, and a handful of others."

"Where is the closest poisoned watering hole?" Shaz asked.

"Why?" Turkill asked.

"I want to try something before we leave," Shaz said.

"It's on the way out," Turkill said.

Turkill moved through a growing crowd of people and bumped into a bulkyeir than usual man. The man turned around with a scowl, and Turkill started to apologize when he realized who it was and scowled. The man smiled a sly grin and squared his shoulders.

"Turkill," the man said.

"Feungrid," Turkill said.

Shaz smirked as the two men puffed out their chests. He wasn't surprised to see the exchange, but was now very curious as to their history. The woman Turkill spent the day with stood behind an older man, and Shaz guessed him to be her father. She smiled and waved a tiny half-wave at Turkill, and her eyes sparkled. Turkill held his head high and smiled back at her and then gave Feungrid a glare as if to say, 'back-off'. Turkill slammed his shoulder into Feungrid's as he moved passed him and let a big grin encompass his face.

They met up with the others at the edge of the village. Shaz slung his knapsack over his shoulder and listened to the Minca bark orders. They may be small in stature, but they certainly were not timid. He liked their tenacity and fire. They were all nearly as grumpy as Turkill was, which made Shaz smile. He followed them through the tall grasses at a very slow pace. Even Ladtwig and Turkill could move faster than this. He wished Serin had buffed them first, but he was positive they wouldn't go for it. Halfway through the morning, they reached the small retention pond. The surface of the water was covered in a thin layer of film. Several dead birds and rodents lie around the edges. The putrid smell of rotting flesh stung his nose and Shaz coughed. Shaz took off his pack and stepped over the corpses. He peered into the water and hesitated. He really wasn't sure if he could do anything and didn't want to make a fool of himself. He lowered his hand to the surface and hovered it a tiny bit away.

"Don't touch it, it will burn your skin," Turkill said.

Shaz found the other Minca men staring at him. He sucked in and held his breath. He focused on pushing the substance away from his hand the closer he went. The still water wriggled, and the film moved away from his skin. He put his finger into the water and pushed the substance even more. It obeyed and moved farther from his hand. He set his other hand in the water and concentrated on making the substance move farther away. The Minca stood in horror as they had never seen magic before. Turkill and Ladtwig chuckled, remembering how scared they were the first time they witnessed it too. Now it was almost an everyday activity. The substance moved to the other side of the pond and he pulled his hands out of the water.

He examined them to see if they were burned, but there was no sign of anything wrong. He gathered some into his cupped hands and took a sip. It tasted fine.

"I think this water is fine now," Shaz said.

The Minca wearily moved away as Turkill ran up to see the water.

"Um, I think it's moving back," Ladtwig said.

The film was moving back, and Shaz cursed. With a flash of anger, he shot a burst of flames from his open palm. The fluid burst into green flames and shot into the sky with a loud bang before resting to a simmer. The Minca ducked and scrambled away from the blast.

"Well, that might do it," Turkill said.

"If not, then maybe Serin can when she is feeling stronger," Shaz said.

He huffed off, feeling dejected. Turkill sent one of the Minca back to report their findings to the chief and was instructed to catch up with them. Turkill hurried to catch up with Shaz and the other Minca mumbled to each other while keeping their distance. Shaz's frustration was gently simmering under the surface. One because he hadn't even learned the basics of each of the elements and because the Minca moved so slowly. He was also used to the buff, and it seemed like he was crawling across the planet. Several times he found himself several lengths ahead and had to stop and wait for the others to catch up. He wanted to chide them, but it wouldn't do any good. He didn't stop for lunch, even with Ladtwig's incessant whining, and made them keep moving until the sun began to set.

"Shaz, we need to stop the others are falling behind," Turkill said.

"Fine, we'll make camp over there."

Shaz pointed to a thicket of bushes. Turkill made his way to the others and directed them to the location. They unloaded their things and gathered firewood, but much of what they found was covered in moist moss. It would take days for it to dry out.

"This is going to be one miserable trek," Shaz mumbled.

****

Serin rubbed her eyes and sat up. The heat of the mid-morning sun made the hut warm, almost too warm. She found Shaz's bed empty and quickly dressed. She combed through her hair with a little device one of the Minca women gave her. She couldn't believe how smooth her hair was. She twisted her locks in her fingers to bring out her curls and pulled the top behind her head, so it wouldn't get in the way of her healing. She grabbed a few of the smaller, deep red fruits and hurried from the hut. She jogged through the tall grass toward the healing huts that had been set up to take care of those who had been injured in the earth-shake.

"Oh good, you're here," the Chieftess said.

"How is everyone?" Serin asked.

"Remarkably well, I must admit I am a bit jealous of your magic," the Chieftess said.

Serin touched her arm gently and smiled.

"It's not always what it's cracked up to be," Serin said.

The Chieftess wasn't sure what that meant, and she followed Serin toward the isles of beds. Serin stopped at several and felt for signs of struggle. Her heart sank when she caught a glimpse of several small bodies that had been moved out of the huts and onto a wagon. Three Minca lifted the cart and heaved a leather belt around their chests. They heaved the bar that went across the front and began moving the wagon. It broke Serin's heart that they were being taken to their final resting place.

"Did Babbesh and Fionte return with those herbs I sent for?" Serin asked.

"Not yet, I expect they will return close to the end of the day," the Chieftess said.

Serin pulled the notes she had taken in the Catacombs and scanned through the lists of poultices and rubs. One, in particular, was of interest to her. It had a spell she could use to enchant the substances in Mrs. Bailey's pain relief ointment to make them stronger, and then she could show the Minca women how to make it. Serin pulled some bandages from a young girl's arm and examined the cuts. They were very deep, and she needed to mend it together. The other healers of the village had used some thin string and a needle to bring the skin together, but it needed more.

"Hey there, how are you doing?" Serin asked.

The little girl burst into tears.

"It really hurts," she said.

"Let's see what we can do about that," Serin said. Serin pulled her gloves off and put her cool skin on the girl's arm. The little girl peeked through teary eyes, Serin's tattoos gently glowed under her pale skin. A soft hue of sky blue wrapped around the girl's arm and sank into her skin. The little girl looked at Serin with wide eyes and she smiled. "Is that better?" Serin asked.

"It doesn't hurt at all," she exclaimed.

"But it is still hurt, I need to do a little more on it so that it will heal really fast too. Is that all right with you?" Serin asked.

The little girl nodded. Serin rubbed her hands together and formed the blue magic into a string. She delicately moved her fingers, wrapping the sparkling string around them as though she were tying a knot in real string. Serin held the girl's arm out so that she could examine the wound and started to 'sew' the magic into her wound. Starting at the deepest part, she fused the flesh back together, then moved onto the next layer. Several women gazed with horror and amazement, not knowing how to feel about the magic. They had been so ingrained to be frightened by it, but it was also such a divine miracle to be used for good. The little girl giggled as the tickling sensation moved up and down her arm. Serin grinned as the last layer pulled together. A soft reddish-brown line ran the length of the wound. Serin removed the old string and then kissed the girl's arm.

"There, good as new. And now you have something even the boys will be jealous of," Serin said.

"I can't believe it," one of the women said.

"Me either. I thought magic was evil. Evil can't heal," she exclaimed almost with a question.

"Magic is simply a force, it is either used for good, or evil, but it in itself is neither," Serin said.

She smiled, realizing she sounded like the Willow.

"I guess we can't argue that," the Chieftess said.

The other women agreed and chatted quietly amongst themselves.

"You must come quick!" a young woman called.

Serin hurried from the hut and into the bright sun. She shielded her eyes as they adjusted to the brightness. Several more injured were rounding the little road on a wagon.

"What happened?" the Chieftess asked as they pulled the wagon the last few lengths to the huts.

"The ground opened up and shot burning hot earth into the sky. It oozed everywhere; several homes were destroyed. We couldn't contain it, it just kept coming. We lost a lot of people," the man at the head of the wagon said.

"Melted earth?" the Chieftess said.

He nodded.

"I'll take it from here, you must tell the Chief right away," the Chieftess said.

The man agreed and slipped out of the harness and ran toward the Chief's hut. Serin and the others started pulling people off the wagon and getting them organized into cots. Those who were strong enough to be moved were moved into the homes of the local villagers to be nursed from there. Serin started examining each one, trying to find the most injured. Their skin was burned badly, deep red pockets sat under crusted skin. Some oozed, and some had already soaked through the bandages they had used.

"We need more water, go fill these washbasins," Serin said.

"With what? Our water is poisoned," the Chieftess asked.

Serin stared at her, not wanting to believe what she had heard. Serin clapped her hands and called the water element. The basins filled with water almost instantly. Serin didn't want to use too much of her magic because it took so much energy, but she had to do something. The vines on her forearms deepened and crawled up her arms. She didn't care anymore, it was no use hiding them from people. She sucked in heavily and filled her chest with her water essence. The deep blue-green flames within her surged and encompassed her whole frame. A dark cloud formed over the huts and a steady drizzle of rain fell from a miniature rainstorm.

"There, keep the basins full and soak every bit of cloth you can find. We need to keep these wounds cold and wet," Serin said.

The women were stunned but quickly started hustling about gathering the cloth.

"Keep the village-folk away as best you can, we don't have time to explain what's going on," the Chieftess said to her crew of personal warriors.

They nodded and moved several lengths and spread out into a circle. The Chief hurried through the barrier and skidded to a stop.

"Oh, my worlds!" the Chief said. He covered his mouth as the horrible scene became real. "How many?"

"Too many," the Chieftess said.

The Chief took a second look at the mini-rainstorm spinning around in circles off to the side of the huts.

"Where is Shaz?" Serin asked.

"He has gone to the Bairr Mountains," the Chief said.

"Without me?" Serin asked.

"We need you here," the Chieftess said.

The Chieftess's eyes were wide with pleading, and Serin nodded.

"What are we going to do about the melted earth?" the Chieftess asked.

"I'm sending out another group to evacuate the villages and bring as many as they can back here. I have dispatched several crews to organize more room for them and find as many supplies as possible. The Chiefs have gone to check on their people and will send word back as rapidly as they can. I don't think there is anything we can do about the melted earth, except keep out of its way. I am going to head out there to inspect it and get a better idea of the severity," the Chief said.

Serin feared she wasn't going to have enough energy to use for healing, so she decided to focus on pain relief first and then determine how much magic to expend. Serin swirled her hands in the water of each basin, sending her magic into the water. Then submerged the cloths in and out of the magic-infused liquid and handed them to the women, who started wrapping each wound. The moans and groans softened as the cool bandages soaked into their burned skin.

"Can I help?" the little girl asked.

Serin looked down at her and figured she was too young to be seeing all of this, but changed her mind when she detected the desire in her face. Serin nodded and gave her a wet length of cloth. The girl hurried to another small girl and wrapped her arm. She then kissed the bandage as Serin had and gave her a smile. The small girl stopped crying as the pain eased from the magic soaked wrap. Serin smiled and wiped the tiny tear from her eye. Then a spike of anger shot to the surface and she blamed Gavin Rhill and the shadow for causing all this chaos.

A man jumped out of the way and hollered as a tiny bolt of lightning shot from the cloud as he was trying to fill a basin. Serin took a deep breath and calmed herself, and the storm returned to its even drizzling. Late into the day, Babbesh and Fionte returned with the herbs. They were horrified to see how many people had been brought. Serin began teaching the women how to make Mrs. Bailey's pain relief ointment and showed them how to apply it. The young women took over their mothers' chores and gathered food and cooked all day long. Three groups of homeless Minca drifted in toward the late afternoon. The men began making more shelters. Some of the men, who tried to ignore the magical cloud, fashioned a receptacle to catch most of the water so that it wouldn't flood them out.

The little cloud operated perfectly by making the correct amount that it never overfilled the basin. What did seep out was made into a fun place for the children to make mud cakes and structures. Even Jag tried to help but found all she was good for was giving rides to the kids. She, however, as tough as she is, found her soft spot and let herself become attached to them.

Several times Serin needed to use her magic to repair a deep wound. One of the older gentlemen had lost an eye to the spitting earth, and she was unable to make it whole. A few men brought lanterns and hung them as close together to give off as much light as possible. The sun dropped below the horizon and the night chill soaked the landscape. Serin pulled on her cloak and tied it around her waist. It was much warmer closer to her body, so she asked if one of the women could sew her a new cloak. She quietly talked about her design as she washed her hands. Most of the patients had now been moved into family huts to recover. Only the ones with the more severe wounds stayed. Every hut was bursting at the seams with people, but Serin heard the children playing and laughing and the adults humming soft tunes of comfort. She would normally be exhausted, but she hardly felt any discomfort at all. She wondered if it was part of the synergy she now shared with Shaz. She wondered what kind of Shaz's magic she would have access to and didn't hear the chief at the door.

"Serin, the scouts have returned, you might want to get some sleep, there is a large group that needs you, but they are too sick to travel."

"I'm not tired, Jag, and I can go right now," Serin said.

"Are you sure?" he asked.

Serin nodded and grabbed her satchel of medications and tinctures they had made.

"Let me get Babbesh and Olfa to replace me here," Serin said.

The chief nodded and gave orders for a few of his guards to organize the traveling party.

21-Why Isn't The Door Opening?

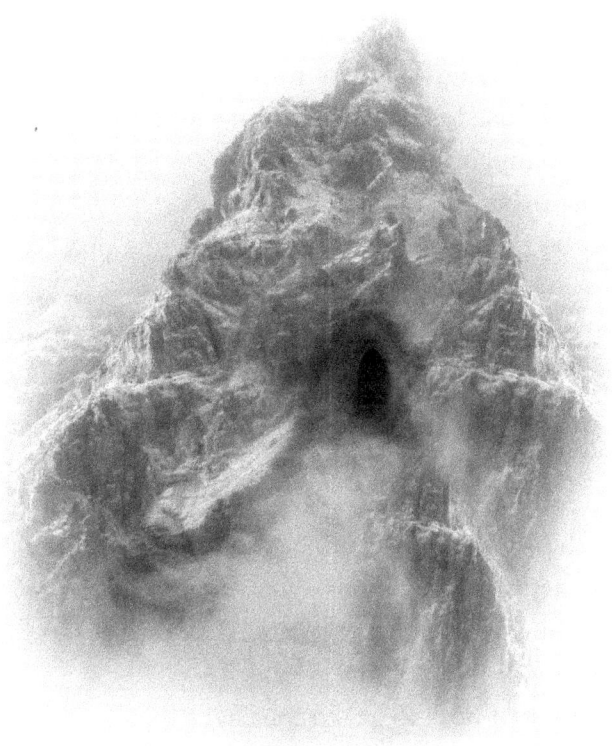

Miserable was an understatement. This trip couldn't have gotten any worse. Shaz thought that Ladtwig and Turkill argued. The little men found it pleasurable to debate every single aspect possible. From the types of insects in the world to the amount of sunshine in a day. Shaz would rather have been fighting shade beetles the entire time than listening to them. Shaz found that if he stayed enough lengths ahead, without being too far away, he could think his own thoughts. By this time, they had made it to the part of the jungle that was so damp they would never find dry wood to make a fire with.

They ate the rations they brought, which were now moist with the dampness and hard to chew. Shaz grumbled under his breath and felt like Turkill acted. Things didn't get better; they had slept on the wet ground and comfort was nowhere to be had. He woke with sore muscles and grumbled through another meal of dried meat and soggy bread. He wanted to use his fire to dry things out a bit, but he didn't think it would help much.

"How much farther?" Shaz asked.

"We would be there by now if it were just you and us," Turkill grumbled.

Shaz snickered. He hadn't wanted to say anything in fear of insulting Turkill's clan-mates.

"And if we had Serin's air buff," Shaz said.

"I never thought I would say this, but I miss the magic," Ladtwig said.

Turkill nodded, and Shaz studied the little men. They had matured since they met all those moons ago.

"So, what is the plan once we get there?" Turkill asked.

"I was hoping you knew," Shaz said.

"I'm only aware of how to get to the caves that serve as the portal," Turkill said.

Shaz scratched his chin. He pulled out his map, and they watched the little spheres jump off the surface. Ladtwig always enjoyed the colors and tried to make them move by putting his finger under or over the ball.

"It doesn't show anything, other than where the major cities or townships used to be, and I have no idea how old this map is," Shaz said.

"Maybe it will show more once we are on the other side," Turkill said.

"Maybe. It doesn't look like we have much farther from here. Maybe another day or so?" Shaz said.

"Possibly, if we can keep moving," Ladtwig said.

"Another few minutes and then we're heading out," Turkill barked at the other men.

Shaz rested against a tree and closed his eyes. He reached his mind out and tried to sense what Serin was doing. A faint image surfaced, but he couldn't quite make out what was happening.

"Move out," Turkill called.

Shaz waited for the little men to make a single file line through the thick brush. He played with the bead still in his pocket and pondered why the sqwall would want it. He searched for a missing spot on his collar and removed the latches at the back. He pulled off the collar and studied it. He found the broken strings that had held the bead. A memory flashed from when the sqwall had cornered he and Serin in the town square and wondered if that was when he lost it. He wasn't sure if the one in his pocket was the same one, but the hairs on the back of his neck shivered his spine.

"Are you coming?" Turkill called.

"I'll catch up," Shaz said.

Shaz was sure they wouldn't get too far ahead, so he started inspecting his collar. He wanted to figure out why the creature would have wanted it in the first place. There was nothing that particularly stood out. Each stone, bead, gem or piece of bone had a marking on it. He had never paid much attention before because he wore them against his skin. As he went to put it back on, the necklace slipped and landed on the ground. Shaz bent down to pick it up and noticed that the way it landed allowed the runes to line up. This time, he understood what it said.

He moved the pieces around in different patterns and learned that it was part of a recipe. He pulled out the little leather book and opened the first page. The symbols lined up the same. He had been wearing the recipe for the construction of the Honor Blade. He skimmed through the book, picking out as much as he understood. He compared the two together and learned that he had part of the recipe and the bead didn't have a mark on it. He wondered if the bead meant anything in particular but realizing the Minca were far off, quickly slipped the notebook into his tunic and secured his collar, placing the bead back in his pocket. Shaz ran to catch up and found the crew making as much noise as ever. He stopped in front of the line next to Turkill.

"We need to hurry. What do we do to make these guys shut up and move faster?" Shaz asked.

"Why?" Turkill asked.

"I know what Gavin Rhill is trying to do, I just don't know how," Shaz said.

"What is that?" Ladtwig asked.

"He's trying to recreate the blade," Shaz said.

The brothers looked at each other and cringed. Turkill stopped and waited for the others to catch up.

"From here on out, there will not be another word spoken unless you are spoken to by me," Turkill said. The power in his voice silenced the men. A look of shock crested their tanned features. "No more doddering either, our mission has just been upgraded to critical. Move out, now!" Turkill said.

Shaz was impressed that the little men did exactly that. Not a single word was uttered. They slunk close to the earth and doubled their speed. Shaz wished they had done this sooner, but took what he could. Turkill maneuvered the crew through the jungle floor and over the jagged rocks. The trail they needed to use was over the top of a small ravine. Shaz could have jumped it, but the Minca needed a way across. One of the men pulled out a rolled-up rope bridge. Shaz took one edge and with a running start leaped across. He hammered the flap ties into the ground with a rock while the Minca did the same on the other end. Turkill sent Ladtwig first, and then the others. He waited until everyone was on the other side and then started across. Halfway across, the bridge started to sway and Turkill lost his footing.

Shaz threw his hand out to catch him, but he was several lengths away. Turkill tried to snag the bridge, but his hand barely caught the edge and the rope popped off the wooden plank. Turkill grappled for another plank, but the swaying flipped him off the bridge. He fell backward into the darkness.

"NOOOOOOO!" Ladtwig cried.

Shaz threw both his hands into the air and gripped the air element. He commanded it to fetch Turkill and bring him to the surface. The wind obeyed and whipped past him, blowing his hair all around. Turkill emerged from the darkness flailing about like the first time Serin cast her air spell on him. It set him down next to Ladtwig, who leaped onto him in a hug. Turkill pushed him away but smiled.

"Are you all right?" Shaz asked.

He nodded. The other men were confused about what to think. They were starting to see that magic wasn't all bad, but still reserved judgment.

"Let's keep moving, we're almost there," Turkill said.

Turkill pointed to the path, and the men made their way over the last couple ledges. The sun was close to setting and they wouldn't have much light to scale the last part of the mountain path. They scooted against the mountain in several places. Shaz found the path had been made for Minca, not people his size, and several times had to grip a handhold and swing across the narrower places. The three moons crept into the dusk-stricken sky, giving a hazy glow to the mountainside. They turned a corner and found an opening big enough for Shaz to walk through without bending over.

"How are we going to see anything in there?" one of the warriors asked.

Shaz found a long wooden stick with an oil-soaked cloth at the end laying on the ground. He waved his hand over the tip and a flame burst into life. The Warriors jumped back, nearly knocking the last warrior off the edge. He cursed a string of profanities and powered his way into the center of the men. Turkill found another torch half-on-half-off a small ledge to the side and handed it to Shaz, who lit it. Shaz handed it to Turkill and started into the cavern.

"Are you coming?" Turkill asked the warriors.

"We'll stay here and keep watch," one said.

"Suit yourself," Shaz said.

The darkness nearly suffocated the torches. Shaz went one way and Turkill the other. They circled the edges of the cavern and each time they found a torch in the wall they lit it. The darkness lifted, and they now saw a tall stone-arched doorway. The peak came to a point at the center and protruded about four small lengths. Above the door were two grandly sculpted serpents that intertwined and circled each other, with a glyph engraved deep into the rock surface. The chiseled edges were ground smooth, and it came to a hard crevice in the center.

"That looks like your belt buckle," Ladtwig said.

"Aye, but that one has the symbol for Chantry of Runecasting in the center," Shaz said.

"Well, we are in the right place then," Turkill said.

"Look, there's the keyhole," Ladtwig said.

Turkill pulled out the artifact that the Chief had given him and stepped up to the door. He was barely tall enough to insert the long handle into the hole and spin the dial. A small round plate near Shaz slid open.

"What is this for?" Shaz asked.

"I don't know, all the Chief said was to put the key in the hole and spin the dial," Turkill said.

Shaz stepped back and studied the surface. The door itself was smooth, other than the keyhole. The door frame was also smooth but had small grooves from where it was molded into its shape. He held the torch closely and noticed several glyphs in the stone. They weren't engraved or raised, and he speculated how they might have been put there. He put his hand on one and it lit up with a deep-green glow.

"What does it say?" Ladtwig asked.

"It's only a letter," Shaz said.

Shaz touched each of the glyphs he found and read out the letters.

"This makes no sense," Shaz said.

"It doesn't tell you anything?" Turkill asked.

"Well wait, maybe it needs to read from the top down," Shaz changed the order of the glyphs and it read,

What is greater than the Sun Goddess?,

What is worse than the Shadow?,

The poor have it,

The rich need it,

And if you eat it, you'll die,

"What in the hay does that mean?" Turkill asked.

He threw his arms across his chest and harrumphed.

"It's a riddle," Ladtwig said.

"So, what does it mean?" Turkill asked.

"I have no idea," Ladtwig said.

"What is better than the Sun Goddess?" Shaz asked.

The Minca warriors outside huddled around the doorway. One of the warriors from the back pushed to the front.

"Cheese!" Ladtwig said.

"Moon mushroom cheese, or Baguto?" a warrior asked.

"Does it matter, cheese is cheese," another said.

"You certainly do not understand your cheeses then," the first said.

"Unless you put the cheese on sautéed grumbits, then cheese is nasty," a third said.

"This is blaspheming, you can't compare the Sun Goddess to cheese. Nothing is greater than the Sun Goddess," a fourth said gruffly.

Shaz snickered, "All right, what is worse than the shadow?" he asked.

"Drager's stinky feet," a Minca said.

"Hey, mine isn't near as bad as Frebin's," Drager said.

"That's if yours are clean," another said.

"Nothing is worse than the shadow," Shaz said.

Turkill and Ladtwig shared a sad glance.

"Moving on, the poor have it," Turkill said, silencing the laughter.

"The poor don't have anything, that's what makes them poor," Frebin said.

"If they don't have anything, then they have nothing, otherwise they would have something," one of the Minca said.

"It's NOTHING," Ladtwig said.

"Right, because otherwise, they would have something," the Minca man said.

"But you can't eat it," Drager said.

"Unless your Drager, then you could eat anything," Frebin said.

The men laughed.

"It's NOTHING," Ladtwig said.

"It has to be something, otherwise they wouldn't have asked us to figure it out,"

"No, it's just NOTHING," Ladtwig said.

"You're not making sense, Ladtwig," Turkill said.

"Wait a minute,

Nothing is greater than the Sun Goddess,

Nothing is worse than the Shadow,

The poor have nothing,

The rich don't need nothing,

And if you eat nothing you'll die,

The answer is NOTHING, Shaz said.

"I told you it was NOTHING," Ladtwig said with a big grin.

Shaz ruffled his hair and smiled.

"Now what?" Turkill asked.

Shaz took the torch and ran it along the smooth surface. When he came to the hole he tried to look inside, but he couldn't see anything. He handed the torch to Ladtwig and started to reach inside.

"What if there is something in there that will eat your arm?" Ladtwig asked. Shaz pulled his hand out and shot him a glare. "Well, it's possible," Ladtwig said.

Shaz called the fire to his palm. A hot glow emanated without a flame and he hovered it over the opening.

"It's a lever," Shaz said.

He reached in and gripped the lever. He jerked it forward and the latch behind the wall groaned as it shifted several spaces.

"How does it work?" Ladtwig asked.

"I haven't a clue," Shaz said.

Shaz pushed the T-shaped handle as far back as it went. He counted each time the pulley gripped the next gear.

"There are the same number of groves as there are letters," Shaz said.

"So, if the answer is NOTHING, start with the space for the N," Ladtwig said.

"Good idea," Shaz said.

He returned to the beginning and counted out the spaces.

"Now go to the space for O," Ladtwig said.

Shaz did, and then the T until he finished spelling the word. A loud rumbling echoed, and the solid rock slab fell into the ground with a thud. A plume of dust shot out of the crevice and everyone coughed and sputtered. Shaz grabbed the torch and waved the dust out of his way.

"Are you kidding me, another door?" Turkill asked.

A solid rock door, like the last, but with a complicated system of gears in the center and three different sized wheels remained. A half-circle of runes had been carved into the stone, several small lengths from the largest wheel. Shaz gripped the hearty handles and tried to twist. He commanded the gears to turn, but not even his magic was going to open it.

"It's not going to budge. We'll have to figure out how to activate the runes," Shaz said.

Turkill turned around to find the remainder of the Minca now standing behind them. He noticed a circle chiseled into the floor.

"Hey, check this out," Turkill scuffed the floor with his shoe and a small billow of dust rippled away. Small individual circles were evenly spaced around the larger one. "Help me dust this off," Turkill said.

Everyone went to a different part of the circle and started to brush it off. One of the warriors stepped into the center of the smaller circle and it sank slightly, and he jumped off.

"Did you see that?" Ladtwig asked.

"What?" Shaz asked.

"One of those runes lit up when he stood on the disc," Ladtwig said.

"Do it again," Shaz said.

The Minca hesitated but stepped onto the circle. One of the center symbols lit up and stayed lit until the Minca stepped off again.

"All right, everyone pick a circle. One at a time, step into the center," Shaz said.

"What about those three?" a warrior asked.

"After I see which symbol goes to the one you're on, go to one of the others," Shaz said.

The warrior nodded. Each one took their turn and the corresponding glyph lit up until they were at the last one.

"It didn't move," Frebin said.

"Maybe you're not heavy enough," Shaz said.

"Hey, what are you saying, that we're not fat?" Drager said.

"NO," Shaz said.

"Oh, so you're saying that we're small," Frebin said.

"NO, it's just-" Shaz said.

The Minca burst into laughter and Shaz turned red. Frebin stepped on the plate with Drager, but it still didn't move. The smallest of the group, Harmus, climbed onto the shoulders of the other two.

"Ouch," Drager said.

"Will you," Frebin said.

"Uuhhgg," Harmus said.

"Are you about done?" Frebin asked.

They finally stopped wobbling around and the plate sank. They cheered and Shaz read the glyph. Shaz watched and tried to make sense of them, but they were out of order to say anything.

"Is it another riddle?" one of the Minca asked.

Shaz shook his head.

"No, it's more like directions. Go here, then do that, then do this and so on," Shaz said.

Ladtwig sat on the floor in front of the door and peered up.

"What are you doing?" Turkill asked.

"I'm looking at the wheels from the perspective of the floor," Ladtwig said.

"Why?" Turkill grunted.

"No, that might just be it. The symbols are similar to the directions one would use to steer a ship or navigate with a compass. I'll say the direction and you tell me what it looks like to you," Shaz said.

Ladtwig nodded, and Shaz signaled for the men to step onto the circles again.

"Levante, or East," Shaz said with the first one.

Ladtwig studied the gears and handles on the wheels.

"All right, spin the center handles so that the one on the right is facing East," Ladtwig said.

Shaz spun the handle to that position and a latch sounded behind the door.

"Now step off the circle," Shaz said. The circle stayed in place. "Now you," Shaz pointed at the next man. He stepped onto his plate and another glyph lit up. "Libeccio, Southwest," Shaz said.

"Try the biggest wheel and turn it half-mark to the South by Southwest," Ladtwig said.

Shaz pulled on the arm and tried to twist it, but it didn't move. He moved the smallest wheel, and it fell into place. He pointed to the next

Minca, who stepped onto the plate, and then the next. None of the plates worked.

"Remember, the three of you need to stand on the last one," Shaz said.

The three Minca maneuvered themselves back onto the plate and tried to hold still. Shaz pulled the long lever again and the latch behind the door fell into place with a rumbling. The Minca hopped down and did a victory dance.

"Two down," Shaz said.

Shaz organized the men to stand on all the plates again, and they continued running through each possibility. Yet, the smallest wheel wouldn't budge.

"There are more than eight directions on a compass. We need to stand on two or three at a time and see if new glyphs light up," Shaz said.

Turkill directed the men to stand on each different combination of the remaining plates, and Shaz read the new glyphs.

"Maestro-Tramontana, North by Northwest," Shaz said.

Shaz gripped the small wheel and gave it a heavy heave. The dial slipped into place and the latch ground to a thunk. Everyone held their breath.

"Why isn't the door opening?" one of the men asked.

"That's a good question," Shaz said.

"Oh, you didn't push the button," Ladtwig said.

"What button?" Shaz asked.

"This one," Ladtwig said.

Ladtwig pointed to the center bolt. Shaz pushed it in, and it sank into the gears with a clunk. The door popped open a few small lengths. Shaz gripped the thick rock slab and pulled it open.

22-I have Been Waiting For You

Amirra pulled out the paper and read the scratches, Semias called language, and tried to pick out the parts that she was able to read. She had been schooled by the   as a child and then given to Semias as his personal bondservant. She excelled at most of the requirements, except she showed no signs of magic abilities. It was her punishment for not being able to at least harness her tongue, which she used quite regularly.

Amirra calculated the descriptions with the few reaming land formations and decided on an easterly direction. The wind came in strong and whipped her hood off, leaving her skin exposed to the cold sting. Her eyes watered as she squinted. She tried to pull her hood back over her head, but the wind caught hold of the pocket and ripped it from her hands. Amirra stopped and turned around, searching the forest. A wind funnel left eddies of debris flailing around.

Most of the forest noise was stifled by the heavy soot and the whooshing the wind made. A strong sensation gripped her stomach, and she froze. Her heart pounded in her chest and she wobbled. A tiny white light reflected off what seemed to be a wall. Amirra moved slowly around a tree as she considered that what she was seeing was real. The glimmer rippled up and down, allowing the reflection of the forest to sway back and forth. Her mind yelled to leave and quickly, but she found her legs weren't listening and she stared into the reflection.

What she couldn't understand was that her reflection wasn't there. Her curiosity was greater than her fear, and she reached up and touched the energy. A shot of ice-cold wreaked havoc on her senses and she recoiled. The wall stopped swaying and became still. A faint image of a small woman came into view behind the wall. Her long silver hair hung above her waist. The closer the figure came, Amirra could make out the details of her age but wasn't sure she understood all the markings on her skin. Amirra pulled away from the barrier and began to turn away.

"Amirra, I have been waiting for you," the woman said.

Amirra froze again. The voice was remarkably familiar, and she had a sudden rush of love race to her heart. She couldn't place why the voice was so soothing, or why she even recognized it, but she did. She turned around and found the woman standing on her side of the barrier.

"Why do I recognize you, but have never met you?" Amirra asked.

"It's the calling of the Runes," Nitida said.

"Runes?" Amirra asked.

"The power of words both spoken and written," Nitida said.

"I don't understand," Amirra said.

Nitida unlaced her velvet bag and pulled the cord. The top fell open, and she reached in and pulled out a few of the runestones. The smoothly polished white and bronze stones clinked against one another. Dark symbols engraved on one side sat deep in the surface. Nitida held them out and motioned for Amirra to take them. Amirra hesitated, and Nitida motioned again. Her soft smile and gentle brows reassured Amirra, and she held out her hand. Nitida set them in the palm of her hand. A jagged pain ripped at the back of her neck and she cried out. She dropped the stones and gripped the back of her neck. Raised skin puffed out under her hand and was hot to the touch.

"What did you do to me?" Amirra yelled.

"Nothing, the Runes have called you, they have chosen you to be the next Runecaster. To take my place when I am done here," Nitida said.

"I can't, I belong to the Velshari. The shadow won't let me leave," Amirra said.

"Is your desire to leave the Velshari?" Nitida asked.

"Very much so," Amirra said.

"Then the Shadow has no control over you," Nitida said.

"I wish I could believe that. I have tried so many times to leave and the pain the Shadow inflicts on me is unbearable," Amirra said.

"Here put this on, just for a time," Nitida said.

Nitida handed her a gold and silver pendant tied to a silver chain. The small amulet dangled gently in the fading sun. It was delicately carved with fine details and was very pretty.

"What is it for?" Amirra asked.

"It will shield you from the Velshari for a time so that you can come with me. I have much I want to share with you," Nitida said.

Amirra rubbed the back of her neck and felt the heat of the new marking soften. She deliberated for several minutes with every scenario she knew of, and the one that kept coming back was that she might be able to have freedom, even if it were for only a little while. She took the necklace and braced for the pain, but when it didn't happen, she unhooked the small latch and secured it on her neck. The cool metal was soft on her skin and it gave her a sense of comfort.

"Shall we go?" Nitida asked.

Amirra nodded, and Nitida put her hand into the curtain of mist. The energy parted, and she guided Amirra through the portal. The forest was now a towering wall of bright stone. The hues of whites and grays danced between lines of silver. Glyphs decorated the walls in all kinds of patterns, from delicate and swirly to organized and linear. Amirra had never seen such majesty. Her brain couldn't process enough of the details that her eyes soaked in.

She ran her finger along one of the linear lines and was surprised when a tingle tickled her skin, and she explored the possibilities that were now coming to her mind. She followed Nitida slowly through the long corridor that was brightly lit but by what she couldn't tell.

"What is this place?" Amirra asked.

"This is the Chantry of the Bairr Tiornecht Mountains. The Hall of Runecasters. This is your new home if you accept the calling," Nitida said.

"Calling?" Amirra asked.

"The Runes have chosen you, but you must accept of your own free will and choice. They will not force you to do anything you are unwilling to do. The path may be difficult, but it will always be your choice," Nitida said.

Amirra liked the sound of that, but was certain it would never happen. She knew firsthand what kind of torment the Shadow was capable of.

"How long have you been here?" Amirra asked.

The stone corridor faded away and merged into a soft blue sky. A beautiful waterfall cascaded down the last bit of the stone wall and splashed into a deep blue pool. A delicate fauna of vines, grasses, blooming plants, and insects decorated the immense new world. Amirra gazed into the sky and found a mixture of clouds and rock formations. The smells of the blooming plants mixed with the wet earth to send a comforting aroma around the new world.

"Is the outside, inside a mountain?" Amirra asked.

"A very long time and yes, you're quite observant. The Chantry is but a part of the ancient civilization of the Bairr Tiornecht people. One of the son's of the God of Glory and younger brother to the Tooatha De Dannon used his unique supernatural powers and gift of the earth's energies to create a world within a world in order to protect his people from the Shadow and its organization the Velshari. It served many purposes throughout history, including the formation part of the Sev-Rin-Ac-Lavah," Nitida said.

"Oh yes, I know about that. It's all Semias has talked about for most of my life," Amirra said.

"I am sure you are hungry, perhaps we should eat and then we can begin your training," Nitida said.

"Training? For what?"

"To be the next Runecaster, I thought I explained that," Nitida said.

"How long will it take?" Amirra asked.

"It is a lifetime pursuit, no one really ever finishes," Nitida said.

"Oh my, I can't be longer than a few days. Semias won't permit anything longer than that," Amirra said.

"Well, I suppose that's if you choose to stay with him," Nitida said.

"I told you, I have no choice."

Nitida understood Amirra was not at a point to understand the power of choice and that she would need some time to find a new path. Nitida waved her hand in the air and a door on the far side of the waterfall opened. A soft amber light cast a glow on the vegetation. Nitida motioned for Amirra to follow her and started across the intricately carved bridge that attached the pathway to the stone walkway around the gardens. Amirra rubbed the back of her neck and found it hard to keep her mind from racing.

The delicately carved glyphs mixed with the ridged ones created a mixture of emotions she had never had. She ran her finger over the glyph encrusted handrail and was amazed when they glowed under her touch. She found a few symbols she recognized and some that she now understood. It was a feeling of power, control, happiness, pleasure, and most of all, freedom.

Nitida showed her a pleasant housing unit that was decorated with soft colors and fabrics. She ran her hands over the soft fur blanket that covered the end of a modest-sized bed. The sensations tickled her mind, and she smiled. The fragrant flowers and herbs rested on her senses with a security of peace. It was so amazing, too amazing to be real. The Velshari chants came rushing to her mind, and she pulled her hand off the blanket. She wrapped her blood-red cloak around her body and muttered the chants.

"What are you saying, dear?" Nitida asked.

Amirra looked up, her eyes barely looking at the old woman.

"The Velshari chants," Amirra said.

"Those won't work here. Here is a different chant you can use if you would like." Nitida handed her a small scroll. Amirra stared at the scroll. She wanted to rip it open and learn as much as possible, but she was so afraid of the Shadow that she didn't dare. Nitida held it for a moment and then set it on a small table next to the bed. "Well, when you are ready, it will be right here. I'll have some food for you shortly."

Nitida left the room and pulled the door partially closed. Amirra gazed around the room. It was wonderful, everything she had ever imagined her own space to look like. More even, she couldn't even fathom such wonderful things existed. She spent the rest of the day, or night, she couldn't tell which, examining the trinkets, tins, jewels, clothing, fabrics and the soft bed. At first, she sat down and then lay onto the padding at the top. Her head sank softly, and she closed her eyes. She wanted too much for this to be true, to be real, to be happening to her. She wanted so much to make her own choices, not that she would be able to, but she wanted to try.

Images of the Shadow hung at the fringes of her mind and she tried to ignore them. She found herself drifting off to sleep and stirred to keep herself from falling asleep completely, but eventually, her body gave in and she fell asleep.

23-You Are The Heir To The Fir Bolg

She tossed and turned between pleasant dreams and nightmares, but ultimately woke with a start after feeling the Shadow grip at her mind. It was trying to find her, but she was barely out of its reach. Amirra sat up and felt the pendant that Nitida had given her fall onto her skin. She pulled it up to examine it better and noticed the front could open.

She popped the lever and opened the lid. The image of the woman from her dreams sat in the center. It was too much. She needed to find out what was going on. She closed it back up and hurried from the room. She found her way down a few corridors and into an unfamiliar room. It was as spacious as the last one, but instead of vegetation and waterfalls, there were books and scrolls. Soft draping fabrics framed tall windows that allowed light from the outer world inside. She still tried to make sense of it, but searched until she found Nitida at the far side. She rounded several tables and chairs and navigated the rows of shelves.

"Oh good, you're awake. Did you sleep well?" Nitida asked.

"Not really, I guess better than usual," Amirra admitted.

"What can I do for you?" Nitida asked.

"Tell me what is going on, I mean what is really going on," Amirra said. Amirra opened the locket, "I have seen this woman, but, how have you?"

"I see, I am sure you have many questions. Please come," Nitida said.

Amirra followed Nitida through the shelves to a sitting area and motioned for her to sit. Amirra sat on a soft cushioned chair and Nitida brought over a sizable leather book. She sat it in her lap and pulled open the cover. Nitida read from the book the story of the God of Glory and explain the history of Edenocht. Some of what she said she already knew, but she was taught from the perspective of the Velshari, so she struggled to organize the new information. The Velshari taught her they are only trying to get back what was stolen from them, their powers. That they are forced to use the shadow as a way to be as powerful as the Tooatha De Dannon and the Biar Tiornecht.

Nitida continued to explain the legend of the war wizard and the relationships between the missing heirs. Amirra caught herself both absorbing every detail and confused as they conflicted with so much that she had been taught. Amirra pictured the details and hanging on every word. Nitida finished the story and looked into Amirra's eyes. Amirra shifted in her seat as a heat emerged in the center of her being.

"What does all this have to do with me?" Amirra asked.

"You are the heir of the Fir Bolg," Nitida said.

"How do you have this image of this woman?" Amirra asked.

"She is your mother, and you are destined to unite with the heirs of the others," Nitida said.

Amirra stared at Nitida. She wasn't sure if she had heard her correctly. She picked up the locket and opened it. She stared into the eyes of the image. Even without saying anything, they spoke to her. She blinked and rubbed her eyes. She wanted so badly to believe it all, to find out where she came from, to learn who she was, but now that it's all here, she wanted to forget it. Pretend she didn't hear it and that she will never know.

"How can I help? I have no powers. I have no magic," Amirra said.

"You do, the power of words have their own intensity of force, unlike any other universal truth there is," Nitida said.

"I really wish I could believe that. I wish I could believe all this," Amirra said.

"You will in time," Nitida said.

Amirra's stomach grumbled, and she blushed.

"You were asleep by the time I returned, I have food for you, come follow me," Nitida said.

Amirra followed Nitida through the library and into a comfortable kitchen. The smell of freshly baked bread wafted around the room and brought with it a hint of rosemary. Nitida put her hand on the counter in the center of the room and a glyph lit up. A series of levers opened several doors, revealing cups, plates, and serving utensils. The wonder let a smile cross Amirra's soft pink lips. It had been so long that she had been happy that she wasn't sure what it felt like.

Amirra gripped the sleeves of her cloak and pulled it off and rested it over the back of a chair. She took the plate Nitida offered her and slid in under the table. A crinkled piece of paper caught her attention and she reached down and picked up Semias's scribbled note. She unfolded it and read the hatch marks. A pit in her stomach formed and sunk deep into her gut. The wonderful food that was now in front of her somehow no longer looked or smelled good.

She shoved the parchment back into her robe pocket and forced herself to eat. After a few minutes, her nerves relaxed some, and she was able to feel content about the food. She noted Nitida rummage around the kitchen as though she had something important to do, but Amirra could tell she was making herself busy while waiting for her. She finished the last bit of fruit juice and dabbed a napkin over her lips. The more she wanted to believe all this could be true, the more she was convinced that it wasn't. She needed to find the items on the list quickly and get back to Semias.

"Thank you, you have been most kind," Amirra said.

"Are you ready?" Nitida asked.

Nitida rested a cooking pan in a holder and moved toward the entrance. Amirra nodded and followed her. Once again, they navigated a series of pathways and corridors until they returned to the library. Nitida gave her several books and scrolls to begin reading and instructed her to practice the chants at the end of one of the books. Amirra found a comfy chair and set the books on a nearby table. She opened one and pretended to read. She waited until Nitida was gone, and then she started to look around.

The instruction hadn't made sense at first, but now that she was in the library, she realized she was looking for a set of numbers. She scanned the edges of the books and compared the marks etched into the stone or wood shelves. Halfway through the library, she found the marks that indicated that the items she was after were close. On the very top shelf were baskets and pouches. She looked around and found a stool and climbed onto the narrow platform. She quickly made note of the marks and climbed down and scooted the stool over a few lengths. She climbed again and reached into a basket. The contents were too low to reach, so she pulled it off the shelf. She caught herself as she became unsteady on the small surface. She pulled a few pouches to the side and there was the pouch she was looking for.

She didn't want to alarm Nitida, so she pulled out her own pouch and poured out half the dark blue powder into her own bag. It had a funny smell to it, but she couldn't quite put her finger on it. She tied the string tightly and stuck it in her pocket. She returned the pouch and basket and climbed off the stool and returned it to its place.

She repeated the process until she had completed the list. Amirra removed the note and checked off all of the items. Now she needed to find a way to get back to Semias without Nitida finding out. She took the smallest book and slipped it under her arm and headed back to her room. As she rounded the corner of the hallway, she thought she needed to take. She saw several impressive arched windows on one side. A soft purple haze danced on the stone floor and she stepped in front of the first arch. She felt a bit guilty for disturbing the drifting particles that danced in the night light.

The Chantry cave ceiling was a replica of the night sky. She wondered how the magic that was used, made the inside reflect the real outdoors. It was amazing, and she longed to remain the rest of her days, which wouldn't be long if she didn't get back to Semias. She breathed in the night air and it was remarkably similar to the real outside. She swallowed hard and hurried down the corridor. She found her way back to the room and slipped a few of the gems into her pocket. She wrapped her cloak around her and drew the hood.

After turning around twice, she established the correct path back to the waterfall and into the passage that took her out of the Chantry and through the portal. She stopped and amazed at the shimmering curtain before stepping through it.

A heavy heart rested in her chest and she wiped the tears that now poured down her cheeks. The hours passed by slowly until she reached her makeshift dwelling. She climbed inside and plopped onto the semi-soft bed. The book she put in her pocket jabbed her side and she rolled off of it. She pulled it out and thumbed the pages. The night had shifted to early dawn and she could now make out the symbols. A few pages in, she came to a chant she had never read before.

I believe in Choice,

I believe in my power to make a Choice to change my life.

Choice can change the world,

I can make magic by intentionally choosing my actions.

Her heart swelled and her chest heaved as the tears flowed down her cheeks once again. She was such a mess; how could she have let this nonsense even enter her mind, let alone stay there and make her cry like a child. She put the book down and repeated the Velshari chants. Her mind settled, and she drifted off to sleep. She didn't sleep for long with the usual ache in her guts and hurried back to the lair.

She had no idea how long it had been and feared Semias would be angry. Loud pops and sizzles rippled along the corridor as she blinked to adjust to the darkness. She rounded the corner to find Semias swaying back and forth with the chants Luthrous was using. Amirra somehow understood what he was doing, and she felt sick. She touched the back of her neck and saw the symbols on the stone floor begin to glow brightly, then dissipated and back again. She recognized some of them from the Chantry and understood them to be runes.

Luthrous stopped his chanting and turned to her. His dark eyes flashed and Amirra stepped back. He studied her like he was reading her thoughts, as though he knew where she had come from, and what she had seen. She then understood who had written the instructions on how to find the powder.

"Do you have the powder?" Semias asked.

Amirra pulled out the pouch and tossed it to Luthrous. Luthrous picked it up and opened the string and poured out a small amount into a dish. He pulled the herbs needed to check its purity and then nodded to Semias.

"If that's all you need, then I am leaving for a while," Amirra said.

"No!" Semias shouted.

"You're in a bad mood, what's your problem?" Amirra sneered.

"It would appear that the war wizard has killed my precious sqwalls, and I don't have the sapphire I need," Semias growled.

"That's not my fault," Amirra huffed.

Semias turned and walked quickly to Amirra. He grabbed the back of her hair and yanked her face upward. She winced in pain but kept her expression tight.

"No, but you are going to get it for me and bring me the war wizard too," Semias said.

"Why would I do that?" Amirra asked through gritted teeth.

"Because I said so," Semias said.

He released her hair, and she nearly fell forward.

"What if I don't want to?" Amirra asked.

"You don't have a choice. The shadow will make you," Semias said.

A scowl quickly formed on her face and a sharp pain hit the back of her head so intensely she blacked out.

24-How Exactly Does This Cave Protect Us?

The smell of cooking meat rippled through Riddick's nose as he entered the house. He looked around and found Yerild organizing his pack.

"Where are Sebastian and Batovi?" Riddick asked.

"Helping Crolos," Yerild said.

"So, what side do you think he's on?" Riddick asked.

"I'm still not sure. He seems to be genuine, but most of them are, just before they try to take your soul."

Riddick raised an eyebrow and folded his blanket and set it on the chair.

"What artifact is he supposed to be finding?" Riddick asked.

"The Staff of the Sev-Rin-Ac-Lavah," Yerild said.

"Why?"

"It was the next to be relocated, but it was never found before the realms were closed."

"Why was it the next one?"

"Because the Fire Festival of Litha was near, and the staff's beacon would become active when the sacrifice was complete."

Riddick studied Yerild's face. He searched the database of stories and remembered the one he was talking about.

"Then Gavin Rhill could find the staff," Riddick said.

"That's correct," Crolos said.

Riddick and Yerild turned to see the old man standing in the doorway.

"Queen Ambrosia needed to move it out of its current realm so that it wasn't seen when the Fire of Litha was lit," Yerild said.

"And that was your job?" Riddick asked Crolos.

He nodded with a heavy head.

"I have never given up, not even to this day. That is why I am about to ask you a very important question," Crolos said.

He walked around a chair and stopped directly in front of Riddick. Riddick put up his guard and searched the old man's face.

"What can I do?" Riddick asked.

"Help me find the Kar-ka-dannon. It is the only way now to find the staff," Crolos said.

"What would I have to do?" Riddick asked.

"Go with me, to the altars of Litha, and summon it."

"Why me?" Riddick asked.

He already had the answer but wanted to play as dumb as possible. There was something about the old man that Riddick didn't feel right about.

"I think you know. You are the Earth Sage. You alone can summon the Kar-ka-dannon," Crolos said.

Riddick studied the man and then Yerild, who gave a nod, then nodded.

"Alright, when do we go?" Riddick asked.

"After we gather supplies, it's a few days' journey from here," Crolos said.

"I'll gather my things," Yerild said.

"No, we must travel alone," Crolos said.

"No, we must certainly not," Riddick said.

Riddick burrowed deep into the man's eyes and sent a pulse of the earths' magic into him. Crolos shuddered and stepped back in surprise. Riddick was several lengths taller than the others, and Crolos quivered.

"Very well," Crolos said.

They all gathered what supplies secured their packs and traveling equipment. The sun had already penetrated the barren world, leaving an almost unbearable heat. Crolos made sure they took as much medicines as he had. They fashioned brimmed hats from some old wicker baskets to keep the sun off their faces. But the heat radiated off the ground and back at them. They took in slow, steady breaths so that their lungs wouldn't choke and heave the air back out. They traveled most of the day without much conversation. Riddick picked up a stone every time he came across one, hoping to perceive a new sense of the earth's magic.

At one point, he detected small feet moving over a ridge of sand and understood them to be the little men from Crolos's house. The farther they went, the closer they came to the mountain range he had seen from the house. The wave of heat made it hard to see much, so he focused on trying to think of every detail he could remember about the stories of the mysterious beasts and the Earth Sage Grandfather would tell him as a child.

A sense of power and courage being the Earth Sage overcame him, but he also understood the hefty amount of pressure that went along with it too. He allowed his mind to wander and before too long, the sun was setting behind the peaks of the red rock.

"We can find shelter in a cave just up ahead," Crolos said.

"It's about time. I was made for water, not sand," Batovi said.

"Water?" Crolos asked.

"Aye, sailors of the deep," Batovi said.

"You're quite a ways from any water, my friend," Crolos said.

"You're telling me," Batovi said.

"What made you come on this trek in the first place?" Crolos asked.

"We were scouting out a new island near our own, and we found our way here," Sebastian said.

"New island?" Crolos asked.

"Aye, the war wizard opened the portals when he penetrated the barrier," Yerild interrupted.

"I see," Crolos said.

"War wizard? Another one of your silly stories?" asked Batovi.

"Aye, another silly story," Yerild said.

Crolos acknowledged their lack of understanding of the whole matter and stepped behind a boulder.

"In here, we will be safe for the night here," Crolos said.

"Safe from what?" Batovi asked.

Batovi checked over his shoulder as he followed Crolos into the cave.

"Sand mites," Crolos said.

What are sand mites?" Sebastian asked.

"Little insects that live in the sand and suck your blood while you sleep," Crolos said.

Sebastian and Batovi hurried into the cave. Crolos hobbled over a rock and pulled a striking stone from his robe. He smacked it against the stone wall and a spark shot into life. It fell onto a torch and flames consumed the oil-soaked cloth. A faint glow illuminated the cave and Crolos lit another, then another. The cave had a couple of half-rounded trenches that were used as beds and a fire pit in the center.

Crolos pointed to a stack of wood, and Sebastian gathered several sticks and a few logs. He placed them into the fire pit and used the torch to lite a fire. Crolos pulled a ragged make-shift door, made of sticks tied together, across the opening. Small ice-blue flowered pods with long spindly vines surrounded the twigs.

"So, how exactly does this cave protect us from the sand mites?" Riddick asked.

"It doesn't, those pods do. Frozen Hops is poisonous to them," Crolos said.

He adjusted the rope around the top and bottom of the door and made his way to one of the trough-like beds.

"Frozen Hops, how can anything be frozen in this place?" Sebastian asked.

Crolos chuckled.

"They aren't actually frozen Sebastian, they just look like they are, and they only grow on the peaks of the Yune Mountains," Yerild said.

Sebastian's eyes lit up and then he adjusted the logs on the fire.

"They can heal a variety of ailments, actually," Riddick said.

Yerild and Crolos gazed across the flames at Riddick.

"I'm aware of a few uses for them, maybe someday you can teach me all of them," Crolos said.

"Aye," Yerild said.

Riddick dusted an empty spot in the cave and made himself a bed. The sand was softer a few inches down and his body sank into the coolness as he lowered into the bed. He laid quietly thinking, while processing all the new sights, sounds, and feelings he had had throughout the day. The earth opened his thoughts and helped organize them into cohesive groupings of information. He didn't know how long it took, but when he stirred, everyone had fallen asleep and the fire had died down to a simmer. He noticed Crolos wasn't in his bed. He quietly made his way to the door and peeked through the spaces in the lashings.

He brushed the soft peddles of the Frozen Hops out of the way and searched the dark night. He couldn't see anything, so he pulled the door open and slipped out. The night air was hot, and his lungs stammered with its surprise. Riddick didn't want Crolos to hear him or sense his presence this time, so he thought about what it would take to make the earth shield his presence. Several ideas circled his mind, but one circled more often. He made the mental image in his mind and became aware of a strand of energy leave his body. The warm surface of the cliff rested in his being, and he searched for Crolos's energy. He found it around a bend and at the top of a small peak.

Riddick crossed the sandy path to the other side in no time flat and started to climb the ragged rocks. He kept himself close to the surface to feel the surrounding energies. He stopped at a lower ledge and listened. He heard the same small men and Crolos talking. He crept around the edge and lifted himself with his arms to where his feet reached the next foothold. His muscles bulged, but he kept a secure grip and lifted himself over the ledge. Riddick placed his ear against the hard, cold stone and closed his eyes. The vibrations of the earth gave him a funny picture in his mind. He was uncertain how he was going to ever figure this out. He started examining the images and understood the higher frequencies to be of the plants, and the lowest ones were from the rocks beneath. He tried to focus on the mid-tones and remembered what Crolos's voice sounded like. A picture emerged, and he opened his mind.

"What if he can't help us find the staff?" a Minca said.

"Then we have him call the Kara-ka-dannon, kill it, and take the horn to Semias to make another one."

"You wouldn't?" one of the Minca asked.

Crolos shifted his weight and rubbed his chin. He stared at the ground; his eyes heavy.

"Now that there is no Queen, no Council, no Dodjen, I am not staying here another day longer than I have to. I am done living in this blasted place. I will make them show me the portal and then we can get out of here," Crolos said.

"Have you gone mad?" a Minca asked.

"I can't help how angry I feel toward the Queen and her selfishness. If she hadn't destroyed the realms, we would have left rotations ago," Crolos said.

Riddick swallowed hard. He had had a hunch that there was something wrong with Crolos. Now he was certain his loyalties were in question. He wondered if Yerild knew too.

"I am tired of this too, but there has to be a better way to solve this. Maybe we should just ask the earth mage to help us find the staff and then secure it like we were supposed to before," One of the Minca said.

"Where, we have no idea if there are any realms left in the first place," Crolos asked.

"Well, they came from somewhere, didn't they? What if we forget the staff and assume it is well hidden and have them show us where the portal is that they came from?" the other Minca asked.

"What about Semias?" Crolos asked.

"What about him? He doesn't have to find out. Besides, if what Yerild said is true, then can Gavin Rhill's enchantment even tell who is going through the portals anymore? Even if he knows where we are, he won't know if we have the staff or not," the other Minca said.

"As far as I'm concerned, you're the one that made the deal with Semias, that's on you now," a Minca said.

Crolos' eyelids flinched, and the heat of regret forged in his heart.

"Very well, we will take them to the rune circle of Yune and then get them to take us to the portal," Crolos said.

The Minca agreed and shuffled off toward the far side of the sandhills. Riddick slipped back down the mountainside and hurried back to the cave. Even with his height, he was still one of the best sneakers there was. Riddick closed the flower-covered door and laid down. He sucked in a deep breath and let it out as though it were a snore as Crolos entered the cave. He listened through the earth's vibrations and witnessed Crolos cross the opening, stepping over Sebastian and Batovi. He tried not to grin, but his new understandings made him feel a sense of power and knowledge.

25-I Am The Runecaster Nitida

A strong odor met Shaz as he crossed the threshold into the Bairr Tiornecht Mountain Temple. He couldn't quite figure out what the mix was, but he could tell there were several herbs mixed with some kind of mineral.

"Let me check it out first, stay here," Shaz said.

The Minca warriors stayed back, but Turkill and Ladtwig crept behind Shaz. Massive hand-carved stone pillars lined a black river. The walls vaulted hundreds of lengths above them, showing intricately carved windows that stretched most of the length. The magnificence of the structures was breathtaking. Three boats sat at the edge of the smooth tiled floor a few lengths from the entrance. Daylight cast sparkling rays over the black river.

"What is this place?" Turkill asked.

"It's ginormous," Ladtwig said.

"How can there be daylight inside the mountain?" Turkill asked.

"I have no idea," Shaz said.

"So now what do we do?" Ladtwig asked.

"Go get the others," Shaz said.

Ladtwig turned to the door and kicked a torch. He handed it to Shaz and fetched the others. Shaz looked for a place to set the torch and found several sconces on a nearby wall. He set the torch into the cradle and noticed several runes engraved into the stone. He put his finger on the first one and started to read. The runes glowed green as he touched them.

"What does it say?" Turkill asked.

"It's instructions. We need to take the boats to the end of the river and no matter what we do, do not touch the water with anything."

"Why?" Turkill asked.

"It doesn't say."

"That's lovely," Turkill said.

"Oh, come on grumpy," Shaz said.

Shaz chuckled at the astonished faces of the Minca as they gawked at the enormous cavern.

"Grab a few torches and climb in those boats, and whatever you do, do *not* touch the river," Shaz said.

The Minca tiptoed to the torches. Most of the Minca flinched as Shaz lit them from the fire in his palm. Shaz held the edge of the boat as four of the Minca climbed in one and the other four in the next.

"How do we steer this thing?" asked one of the Minca.

Shaz climbed into his boat and searched for the sail. All he found was a funnel-like tube at the back. Black dust covered the lip of the opening and Shaz rubbed his finger over the soot. It smelled like the explosives that Tomos used in his cannon's. He searched the platform and found a pouch of a black and gritty substance.

"Yep, this is it," Shaz said as he crinkled his face from the rancid smell.

He scooped the powder with the metal scoop hanging on the wall and carried it to each boat. He poured it into the funnel of the first boat and a dull putter sound echoed from under the hull as if there was a mechanism that was ignited by the powder. The boat moved away from the ledge and Shaz filled the next boat. He had to retrieve more from the bag to fill his boat. He didn't have time to return the scoop, so he heaved it onto the platform as far away from the edge before the boat pulled away. The Minca discussed the idea of the self-propelled boat and the huge pillars. Shaz sat quietly, studying the fine details. There were lines that ran from each glyph that was etched in each pillar. The lines ran up and down and around the glyphs and other pictures of creatures and symbols that connected them together. He was so deep in thought as to their significance that he didn't notice an argument between two of the Minca break out. A splash broke the stillness of the water, and Shaz leaped to his feet.

"Hurry, grab him!" Turkill shouted.

The other men gripped his arms and yanked, but the water wouldn't release the little man.

"Come on, pull," called a warrior.

They yanked again. The boat was starting to pass the Minca, and the others scooted to the back edge of the boat to keep a solid grip. They shoved their feet against the edge and heaved forcefully. The three men lost their grip and tumbled back into the boat. Shaz leaped into the black water and instantly learned that it wasn't water at all. The black substance was thick and gooey. He stretched his arms and tried to propel himself forward the way he would underwater, but his body didn't move. He couldn't open his mouth to let air out because he couldn't reach the surface to take more in.

Panic raced to his brain, signaling his body to flail about, but he barely mustered a few tiny lengths. Shaz focused on relaxing his body. He tried to think of how to do Serin's air bubble, but nothing came to mind. He focused on his heartfire and allowed his body to radiate heat. The substance began to loosen and thin out. He raised his head and swam slowly back to the surface. The now thin black ooze dripped off his face, and he expelled his breath and sucked in a new one. Shaz wiped it from his eyes, but it stung as he opened them to find out where the Minca was.

"Are you all right?" Ladtwig called.

"Sort of," Shaz said.

"I'm not!" the Minca called.

The ooze was slowly sucking his small but bulky figure downward. Shaz found him a few short lengths away, and he stretched his arm and kicked his feet. He snagged the back of the man's collar in time to keep him from sinking completely.

"Hold on," Shaz said.

Shaz radiated his heat around the Minca and started toward the boats. The boat had continued moving forward and Shaz had to move rapidly to catch up. The sludge melted as he swam through, but the Minca's extra weight, which wasn't really that much, made it so he couldn't move quite fast enough. Shaz searched for the ending, but there were several more lengths still to go. His muscles started to fatigue, and he wished Serin was there to buff him with her air spell or something. She always found the solutions. He focused on the heat his body was making and turned it up. The sludge thinned even more and lessened the resistance. He kicked harder and closed the gap to the boat by several lengths. He gripped the Minca's tunic and pulled him close enough to shove him onto his boat. With one more kick, he snagged the back of the boat and tugged the man toward it.

"Grab hold of the boat and I'll shove you up," Shaz said.

The Minca stretched and gripped the edge as Shaz steadied the other side. The black ooze stuck to the Minca, which made it very hard for him to move. He heaved himself with all his strength and Shaz pushed him upward. The Minca rolled over the edge and plopped to the bottom. He breathed heavily as Shaz pulled himself into the boat.

"What is the tarnation is that stuff?" the Minca asked.

"Are you all right?" Turkill called.

"I have no idea what this stuff is," Shaz said.

Shaz waved to Turkill. Everyone scooted into the center of their boats and didn't say another word until they reached the end. The boats bumped the edge of the next platform and the putter from underneath stopped. Shaz steadied the boat against the edge as the Minca climbed out and then hopped onto the smooth stone platform. He bent down and steadied each boat as the Minca climbed out.

"Now where do we go?" Ladtwig asked.

Shaz studied the glyphs and pictures.

"There should be a door around here somewhere," Shaz said.

"Another door!" a Minca said.

"Here," Shaz said.

He located the lever and twisted, pulled, and pushed the latch until it unlocked and allowed him to open it. Shaz peered through the opening, but it was dark.

"Wait here, I'll see if we can find something to light," Shaz said.

Shaz popped a flame from his hand and hovered it around the opening until he found a lever on the other side of the hallway. He gripped it and thrust it upward. Several lights in the ceiling ignited and glowed brightly, illuminating the walkway.

"This way," Shaz said.

The Minca followed Turkill down the hall, except for the man who fell. Shaz returned to him and put his hands on his shoulders. He brought his heat to his hands and ran them near the man's body wherever there was the black goo. It melted off his body, allowing him to move freely again.

"Thank you," the man said.

Shaz nodded and patted his shoulder. They caught up with the others about halfway down the walkway.

"You know, this is getting a bit irritating, all these tunnels and walkways and puzzles and stuff," a man said.

"That's for sure," Turkill said.

"Let's hope we're almost there," Shaz said.

The walkway widened as they neared the end and small bright green plants crept out of the cracks that were now growing wider apart. Shaz watched the lights high above slip into a daylight lit ceiling. It was hard to tell if it was a ceiling or the sky itself. The walls blended seamlessly into intricately carved clear windows. The small green plants grew together in tight bundles and spread throughout the vast cavern, following their vines. Statues in the walls between the windows depicted women in flowing gowns and crowns on their heads. A waterfall at the top of the cavern dropped a steady stream of crystal blue water into a pool that drained into a river and circled an elaborate gazebo in the center.

"I'm guessing this is the temple?" Turkill asked.

"Possibly," Shaz said.

Shaz stepped onto an intricately carved bridge and rested his hand on the railing. A gentle tingle touched his senses, and he crossed to the center. Shaz was interested in the stories that had been engraved in just about every surface of the cavern. From the handrails of the bridge to the walls and even the structural supports of the gazebo.

"Do NOT touch anything," Turkill said to the others.

Ladtwig quickly put his hand behind his back and pretended not to have touched the soft yellow flower that was as tall as he was. Shaz found a small stone altar in the center of the gazebo. Sudden memories of Serin on the altar with the witch made his skin crawl and a pit form in the bottom of his stomach. He shook his head and walked around the altar.

"What is this place?" Ladtwig asked from across the stream.

Shaz waved to the Minca and most of them crossed the bridge. A few of the warriors stayed behind and pretended to be standing guard.

"It says here, that this is the altar of the Runecaster," Shaz said.

"What's a Runecaster?" Turkill asked.

"Someone who casts runes?" Ladtwig said.

"Well, that is obvious, but what does that mean, I mean cast runes to do what?" Turkill said.

"A Runecaster is a unique individual that has the fortitude to see into the runes and understand them," an old woman said. The company jumped and gripped their weapons. "Runes are the written language spoken with the intent to utilize the magic forces of this world to make an effect on someone or something."

"Who are you?" Shaz asked.

"I am the Runecaster Nitida," Nitida said.

"You're a Minca!" Turkill said.

"Yes," Nitida said.

"But Minca don't have magic," Turkill said.

"That is correct. The study of runes is an art, not a magic. BUT the powers the runes evoke are a strong magic," Nitida said. "Now, why are *you* here?"

"We need to find out how to repair the torn time barrier and find the Honor Blade's sheath," Shaz said.

Nitida studied Shaz intently and rubbed her fingers together at the tips. Shaz read the glyphs under her skin as they illuminated. He understood her to be performing a truth casting.

"You must be the war wizard if you have the sword," Shaz nodded. "I am sorry to say, that I have not seen it for quite some time. I am, however, glad that he does not have the blade, but that begs the question, what are you to do next?" Nitida said.

"I'm sorry, but I don't follow," Shaz said, as a pit ripped through his guts.

The old Minca woman's eyes glistened, and her long white hair swayed as she walked to the small pillar at the back of the gazebo. She pulled a blue velvet sack off the platform and loosened the ties. She returned to the altar and put her hand in the center. A rune casting circle lit up and glowed, the outer circle glowed orange and the inner circle a deep red. The compass danced between blue and purple, and the small circles at each point were a bright yellow.

"Now pay attention," Nitida said.

Ladtwig scooted in close and watched intently. Several Minca men tried to watch at a distance. Nitida reached into the bag and pulled out the runes. She wriggled them in her hand for a second and released them onto the altar. The small polished blue stones scattered around the circle. Some landed upside down so the marking couldn't be seen, some halfway and the rest face up. The wrinkled old woman set the bag down and hovered over the circle. Her trembling finger moved from each symbol as she muttered to herself.

"This is one of the most complex castings I have ever seen," Nitida said.

"What does that mean?" Shaz asked.

"Have you ever had a casting before?" Nitida asked.

Shaz shook his head.

"Is it like fortune-telling?" Shaz asked.

"Far from it. When the very first people began writing their words, they learned that the written language was more powerful when spoken," Nitida said.

"So, the power comes from the reality of the words?" Shaz asked.

"Words create reality, not the other way around. That is why the power and magic of the ancient language are so overpowering. If one truly understood the power of words, they wouldn't say what they say," Nitida said.

"How so?" Shaz asked.

"The skin will heal the cut of a blade, but the wound that is inflicted by the words of disapproval or anger will cut deeper than any blade could, and there is no skin to heal it," Nitida said.

Shaz understood this to be a truth he couldn't argue with.

"So, what about this, is so complex?" Shaz asked.

"You have cast the Thuraz rune, but it is inverted. When Thuraz is inverted, it suggests that you have been surrounded by difficulties and problems for quite a while. Things will become worse before they are better."

"That's most certainly true," Shaz said.

"You have the inner strength and resolve to overcome whatever has been put in your path if you will believe it to be true. You must act so that things do not drift any further out of your control." The hint of insecurity stung Shaz's mind. "However, do not act in haste as that may not be the best course for you to take. Try to ensure that you have all the facts in hand before proceeding," Nitida said.

"That's just the thing, I understand that, but I haven't figured out how to apply it. I can't even find the sheath to the sword, let alone figure out how to destroy it. Or if I even want to destroy it." Shaz said.

"Why destroy it?" Nitida asked.

"That's what Ceros told me I was supposed to do," Shaz said.

The warriors had found pleasure in quietly discussing the unique vegetation and structures and had wandered around the cavern.

"Ceros. Now, I haven't heard that name in a very long time," Nitida said.

"You know him?" Shaz asked.

Nitida nodded. She examined the stones.

"You are trying too hard, try taking a step back from the events and see the full picture. This will allow you time to analyze and reflect on the situations that have been surrounding you. Progress may be slow, but you will be moving forward all the same. A positive outcome is possible, but you have to believe that you can succeed," Nitida said.

She moved to the next stone.

"The Kenaz, the present, is also inverted. This indicates you are feeling as though you are lacking new ideas and creativity. Don't fret, for this is temporary. Look deep within yourself, see if you can identify what you may need to change. In order to get your life back on the right path. If you look closely, you probably already know in your head, what you need to do. Remember, the smallest change can have the largest impact. There are things you need to learn to progress. These will appear to you when you are receptive to their messages and are at a stage, on your path, when you will be ready to accept the lessons they have to teach."

"You understand all that from one symbol? It sounds like you are making this up as you go," Shaz said.

Nitida scowled. She touched the center of his chest and closed her eyes. She took in a few deep breaths and then gazed at him.

"I understand why you are hesitant and have feelings of animosity for this task. But you must understand, it may feel like the future is all gloom and doom, but if you believe, all things are possible, you can make a difference. Which leads me to the last glyph." Nitida pointed to the Raidho stone. "This one is the future stone and is in its correct orientation and suggests that there is an important journey in your future. Not only physical, but spiritual as well. Take heed to understand, that the journeys will be a direct result of the decisions you make. You must trust your instincts, for they will guide you well. This is the time for action and decisions to be made. You have the knowledge to judge which is right, and they have far-reaching effects. Most of all, enjoy your journey. Find fun and peace with your friends, in your companions, in your lessons. You are the only one that can choose your path. Don't let those around you, those who think they have superior knowledge, make your choices for you. The pathways you take are chosen by you, so ensure you choose the routes you want to travel."

Nitida rested her shaky frame on the altar. The magic she used to make the cast took its toll.

"Tell us what to do about the earth splitting open," Turkill said.

"You must mend the tear in the weaves of time. That will be no easy task. You will need the four descendants to repair it, for they are who made it," Nitida said.

"How do I find them?" Shaz asked.

"You travel with one already and the other will meet you soon. The last I fear may not be so easy to find. She hasn't figured out how to free herself from the bonds of the Shadow."

"Can I free her?" Shaz asked.

"You can, however, the Shadow will take its toll and may be more than you can bear. She has the power within herself, but she must believe and make her own choice," Nitida said.

"Where do I find her?" Shaz asked.

"Your paths will cross and be made known to you shortly. This I can tell you; your path will cross the old with the new. You will find what you seek and will possess the power," Nitida gathered her stones and secured them back in their pouch.

26-This Is Getting Out Of Control

Shaz thrust the heavy door several times before it budged a few lengths. A plume of soot fell from the top of the doorway and plopped on their heads. The Minca warriors coughed and sputtered as the extremely fine debris lined their lungs. The men tied whatever spare pieces of cloth they had over their nose and mouths. The door plowed through a pile of fresh soot and they made their way out into the outer cave. The cave opened to an inky sky and they could hardly see any farther than their feet.

"What in the world is going on? What is this?" Frebin asked.

"Soot," Shaz said.

"Soot? What would cause this much soot?" he asked.

"Either a volcano or an earthquake," Shaz said.

"What makes you say that?" Turkill asked.

"We had a volcano erupt on my island when I was young," Shaz said.

"Oh no! We must get back to the village as fast as possible," Turkill said.

"Why?" Shaz asked.

"I'll explain when we get there," Turkill said.

Turkill slipped passed Shaz and started to climb the soot. He couldn't even make his way to the top of it because it was like powder and he fell through it.

"I wish I had Serin's air-walk spell," Shaz said.

"Well, could you use fire to do something?" Ladtwig asked.

Shaz thought about it, but it made no sense. The soot was already burned particles, so it wouldn't do much to burn it out of the way. He could try to use the wind to blow it away...*that's it, I'll explode it out of our way.* He thought. Shaz focused on his heartfire and remembered when he made a loud clap in the village with the beaten woman. He slapped his hands together and shoved the combustion forces from his body. The weightless soot shot out of the cavern and disappeared into the murky sky. The Minca jumped and Ladtwig scurried behind Turkill.

"Let's go," Shaz said.

They began a fast pace back toward the village, with Shaz shoving the soot piles out of their way as they made it back down the narrow and rigid path. Shaz held the rope bridge steady as they crossed. The soot was deep in some places and in others it still swirled around, making it very difficult to see where they needed to go. Shaz began to understand more about the force of the fire element, realizing that it wasn't just making fire, but using air and heat to create a combustion of particles. The more force the combustion has, the hotter the fire.

"Shhh, did you hear that?" Shaz asked.

"No, what?" Turkill whispered.

"I'm not sure, it's coming from over there," Shaz said.

Shaz motioned toward the noise and put his finger on his lips. The warriors lowered to the ground and gripped their weapons. Shaz motioned for Turkill to take the left side and half the warriors to follow, and the other half went with him to the right. They searched the surroundings, moving intently.

A faint scuffle echoed around the trees. Shaz rounded a tree and found a girl yanking on a chain that was bound to her wrists. The chain was around the trunk of a tree and secured at the back with a bulky lock. The girl's cinnamon hair was covered in soot and her cheeks were bright red. Shaz stepped on a branch and snapped it in half. The girl froze. Turkill stationed the men with him around in a circle and made his way to Shaz.

"What is that?" Turkill asked.

"A woman in a trap," Shaz said.

"I know, but why? And where did she come from?" Turkill asked.

"I have no idea, this is your realm," Shaz said.

"We don't have any other humans here," Ladtwig said.

"Then what is she doing here?" Shaz asked.

"You're the smarty pants, you tell me," Turkill said.

Shaz scowled.

"We have to help her," Shaz said.

"No, we have no idea what she is doing here. We can't take strangers into the village. Besides, someone tied her up for a reason," Turkill said.

The look of pleading made Shaz's heart confused. He understood that no one, not even him, was supposed to know about the Mica and the secrets they keep, but this woman was obviously in need of help.

"What if we let her go, and then wait until she is gone before we return to the village," Shaz asked.

Turkill thought for a moment and nodded. Shaz stood up and walked toward the girl.

"Get away from me," Amirra yelled.

"I'm not going to hurt you," Shaz said.

"If you come any closer, I'll hurt you," Amirra said.

"I can see that you mean that, but I don't think you will. Let me just take the chains off and you can be on your way," Shaz said.

Amirra hesitated and searched his eyes. She softened her soot-stained face and held out her wrists. Shaz stepped close enough to touch the chains, and a tingling on the back of his neck pricked his awareness. He studied the metal rings latched together and searched the surroundings with his magic.

"What's wrong?" Amirra asked.

"Nothing, I'm checking for traps," Shaz said.

Amirra's heart rate jumped, and her blood quickened in her ears. Shaz felt the shift and scanned her energy. He could tell there was a conflict within her, but didn't sense that she had any elemental powers. He walked around the tree and hovered his hand above the chain. He focused on the energy the chain gave off and recognized it as the same force as the altar Serin had been bound to moons ago. *The Velshari* he thought. He called the same force from his core and commanded the chains to release. The iron cuffs clacked and fell with a loud clank.

"How did you do that?" Amirra asked.

"It doesn't matter. You're free to go now," Shaz said.

Amirra rubbed her raw skin and gazed into Shaz's deep blue eyes. Her heart skipped a beat, and she blushed.

"Thank you," Amirra said.

"How did you get here, and who did this?" Shaz asked.

"All I remember is riding my horse through the countryside and then getting hit with something and waking up here," Amirra said.

Amirra rubbed the back of her head and found blood on her fingers.

"Your hurt," Shaz said. He was certain she was lying, and that there was a much deeper story involved.

"It's nothing, I'll be all right," Amirra said.

"What is taking so long?" Turkill said.

Turkill came out from under a bush. Amirra screamed and jumped close to Shaz.

"It's all right, this is Turkill, he's with me," Shaz said.

"You mean, you're with me," Turkill grunted.

"Here let me take a look at that," Shaz checked Amirra's head and Amirra glared at Turkill. Turkill peered at the human girl with a scowl. There was definitely something up with her, but Shaz couldn't place it yet. "Serin should take a look at this, it looks deep," Shaz said.

"No, she can't come with us," Turkill said.

"He's right, I'll be all right. Besides, I need to continue on to where I was going," Amirra stepped away from Shaz. "If I even knew where I was in the first place," Amirra said, looking around.

Shaz wondered if this was the girl Nitida told him about. He needed to find out, but how, *perhaps the Chief will know,* he thought.

"We'll take her to see Serin, then help her find where she needs to go. I'll send you ahead and you can bring Serin and meet us," Shaz said.

"Fine, but I don't like this," Turkill said.

"Noted," Shaz said.

Shaz maneuvered around the tattered ground behind Turkill, who caught up to the others. Amirra tried to keep her balance, but she kept stumbling. Shaz put her arm around his shoulder and his around her waist and helped her maneuver the terrain. A knot in the bottom of his stomach settled in and didn't leave, causing Shaz to wonder what was up with her. He was positive he needed to figure her out, that she somehow had information he needed, but he also needed to stay cautious.

"I can hardly see where I'm going," Shaz said.

"I thought you could see far distances?" Turkill asked.

"Well, yes, when there's not a wall of soot three lengths in front of me," Shaz said.

"What do you suggest we do?" Turkill asked.

"I need to get a bird's-eye view of where we are," Shaz said.

Shaz helped Amirra sit on a rock and gripped a low-lying branch and pulled himself onto the limb. He reached for the next branch and stuck his toes into the trunk and leaped toward a higher branch.

"It's even worse up here," Shaz said. "Wait, I think I see something?"

Shaz studied the distance. Even though he was above the trees, the sun was nowhere to be found. He spotted the tops of the grass huts in which several were buried under soot. A sudden wave of worry hit his brain, and he was committed to making sure everyone was alright, but he was certain he couldn't trust Amirra yet. He climbed out of the tree and motioned for Turkill to come close.

"I see the tops of the huts, but they are buried in soot. We need to make sure your people are safe, but what do we do with her," Shaz whispered.

Turkill studied Amirra and was convinced she couldn't be trusted, but he needed Shaz's help to save his people, which would mean that she would have to find out where the village was.

"I guess we bring her along, but any indication of trouble and I lock her up myself," Turkill said.

Shaz nodded.

"I'm sorry, I never even asked your name," Shaz said.

"Amirra," she said.

"Can you walk?" Shaz asked.

Amirra stood and steadied herself.

"I think so," Amirra said.

"Good, because we're going to need your help," Shaz said.

Hopelessness sank into the men's bones the closer they moved to the village, that was now covered with several lengths of soot.

"We need to check for survivors," a warrior said.

"Split up, we'll cover more ground that way," another said.

They each hurried to a hut and shoveled the soot away from the doors.

"No one is here," Drager said.

"Me either," Ladtwig said.

"Not here," Shaz said.

Amirra shook her head.

"Keep checking," Turkill said.

They checked several more huts, but each time found no one there.

"We're almost back to the village, let's find the Chief," Frebin said.

Little people emerged the closer they got to the center of the village. They were covered in soot and carrying sacks and bushels of food and supplies.

"Looks like they escaped before the soot cloud got there," Shaz said.

"Let's hope so," Turkill said.

Amirra took in all the little people and how many of them were hurt. A pang of anger surged and for the first time she didn't only want out of the Velshari for herself, but because she now saw what it was doing to others. The soot was much less here, barely a sprinkle. They maneuvered through the throng of people until they came to the central square. Amirra grew angrier as she took in the carnage of death and injury. She was well acquainted with Semias's evil doings, and this time she was a part of it.

"Father, father!" Turkill said.

The chief stood up from tending to an old woman. He turned and Turkill and Ladtwig embraced him.

"What happened?" Shaz asked.

"The mountain, it just broke open. The earth shook for days,"

"Days? What do you mean *days*?" Turkill asked.

"It's been weeks," the Chieftess said.

"How can that be, we weren't gone that long," Turkill said.

"Who is this?" the Chief asked.

"This is Amirra, we found her trapped on our way back from Bairr, she is hurt, and we needed to check on the grass huts," Turkill said.

"This is getting out of control," the Chief said.

A darkness hit Shaz's chest as he tried to search for Serin's energy but couldn't sense it.

"Where is Serin?" Shaz asked.

The Chief pointed to their hut. "Resting, I hope, she has been non-stop since you left."

The pit in Shaz's stomach leaped to his throat, and he hurried through the people. He pulled open the flap to their shared hut and found her laying on her bed. He knelt next to her and reached out to her with his magic as he checked for breathing. She stirred.

"Serin, you awake?" Shaz asked softly.

Serin rolled over and blinked. Her eyes were deep red with the lack of sleep. Shaz realized how drained she was, and his heart sank.

"Shaz?" Serin whispered.

"It's me."

She tried to sit up. Shaz lifted her up, and she hugged him and buried her face into his neck. Shaz held her tightly, his heart sinking even deeper.

"I'm sorry it took so long. What happened?" Shaz asked.

"The earthquakes have opened holes all over, some with spitting earth, some with poisoned water, and lots of soot. I have been healing people for days," she said with her face still in his neck.

"You have nearly killed yourself," Shaz said.

"I'm fine, I just need a little nap."

"No, I can feel it, you're not fine," Shaz said. Serin could hardly keep her eyes open and her body hung on his. Shaz reached into his inner strength and pulled it to the surface. The magnitude of colors danced and rippled from his body, surrounded them both, and then sank into her body. "There, any better?" Shaz asked.

"Yes, thank you," Serin said.

She gazed into his eyes and smiled.

"You scared me," Shaz said.

"I'm sorry," Serin said.

Shaz watched as the green of her eyes returned and then he kissed her. His warm lips covered hers and she sank into his embrace. He was surprised that his feelings for her were now even stronger than before, and they were steadily growing more and more. Serin pulled away.

"We're not supposed to be doing this," Serin said.

"Says who, I can't stop the way I feel about you," Shaz said.

"You're a war wizard, and I'm elemental, this is forbidden," Serin said.

"Shhh, I don't believe that. Besides, if *I* am the war wizard, then I will find a way to make this work. I won't lose you for anything," Shaz said.

Serin studied the deep concern in his eyes.

"Shaz, what's wrong?"

"There's more to this puzzle, I can feel it, I just can't decide what it is yet," Shaz said.

"Like what?" Serin asked.

"Never mind, you get some sleep and we'll talk later," Shaz said.

He tucked her in and put a hand on her forehead and sent another boost of his magic. She closed her eyes, and he kissed her forehead. He sat with her for several minutes to make sure she would be all right and then returned to the square.

27-He Wiped The Sweat From His Brow

Luthrous didn't want to, but his body obeyed its master and moved toward the center of the rune circle. A partially forged steel blade sat in the center. Luthrous picked it up and felt it's cold against his hand. The energy the steel gave was of very high quality and his heart skipped a beat. Even though he didn't want to be doing this, he couldn't deny the love he had for the art of rune magic. Luthrous turned it over a few times, watching the green lights reflect off its surface. His mind opened and the runes, from so long ago, came rushing to the forefront. A sturdy energy surged through his body as the runes danced around. He slowly sucked in a deep breath and then exhaled.

His body moved and swayed with the rhythm of the ancient text. He let out a low hollow song-like string of words.

True power comes from pure intent, evil or good,

Sword, Unbreakable, Forever Sharp, Eternal Smiting, Discernment,

Incisive wit, truth-verifier, truth spell caster, winds to control and command, fire to propel ignite, earth to trust and unite, water heal the mighty of might,

Keen intelligence, eagle eye, wisdom untold, mineral found deep in the earth of Bairr Tiornecht, used for its density for the building of indestructible weapons.

Poison, Accurate, Piercing, Bashing, Reach, Trip, Finesses, Light, Defensive, Resist elements, Resist Shadow, Grace under pressure,

Luthrous chanted with intensity and devotion, bringing the majesty and strength of the words into existence. The more he chanted, the stronger the spell became. Only a skilled Runecaster would be able to discern when there was no more cosmic energy to strengthen a casting. Some spells would take days to complete. The blade was still rough, and Luthrous recognized it as the stage between the fully hardened stage and the spring steel stage.

Luthrous wasn't the sword-smith, but he was fully aware of the process of forging a blade. A good sword-smith takes the raw nugget and forges it into a block by subjecting it to a massive amount of heat, then taken out and hammered into a thinner block. The hammering creates an interlocking connection of mineral components. The block is then scored and folded transversely and longitudinally several times to bond the components even deeper.

A normal sword made from regular steel compounds would only be folded about twenty times, but the Honor Blade being made of the Bairr Mineral, Severa, would need to be folded over a hundred times to create the same hardness or softness for strength and sharpening.

This process would take many moons to perform. Luthrous studied the intricate mineral patterns that evolved through the process and wondered what poor sap was forced to make this blade.

Luthrous kept his chanting steady and imagined the words infusing to the patterns in the new steel. Luthrous created a fierce swordfight in his head and focused on each part of the blade as he chanted. The strongest parts would be down the center and at the neck where the pummel would be attached and the slightly softer reserved for the edge where the sharpness would be finely honed.

Slight green hues of color began to ripple up and down the dull blade. Luthrous closed his eyes and gripped the first rune symbol in his mind and focused on securing it into the top of the blade under the section saved for the stone of ownership. The sharp-edged symbol Teiwaz appeared. At first very faint but grew to a deep mucky green before settling on mist color. The Teiwaz symbol was the infusion of masculine energy, bringing, as a result, anxiety to conquer.

Teiwaz is the Rune of courage, dedication, and absolute trust in one's own resources.

In situations on interpersonal relations or devotion to a cause, Teiwaz advises perseverance, at the same time reminding one that patience can sometimes be a kind of perseverance. The strength to analyze the foundation of one's life will allow the user to harness their deepest and most powerful resources.

As with the original process of molding the minerals, and when Luthrous was confident the symbol was fully infused, he quenched the blade in cold water, allowing the metal to cool and harden in its new form.

Luthrous viewed the bubbles and steam spew from the water until they simmered and then disappeared. He pulled the blade out and wiped it down with a soft cloth. His stomach grumbled, and he rested the sword on a holding stone. He admired his work and was now confident he would be able to finish the rest of the runes.

Luthrous chanted through his beginning chants again several more times as he focused on the next rune to be made. After several minutes, the swooshing pattern of the Sowelu rune settled at the front of his mind.

This Rune means Wellness, a rune of great power that indicates a moment of profound regeneration, a search for totality. It signals the need to become aware of your essence to express it in a creative manner, thus increasing your vital force. It also points to the need of admitting something that you have long denied, something that has remained under the shadows: now it is time to bring it out into the light. It might be prudent to stay away from a pressing situation, remembering that withdrawing at the right time is a sign of force and not of weakness.

Luthrous steadied his crippling hand over the newly formed glyph. His mind was alive and vigorous, but the new body he was in couldn't keep up these long hours. Luthrous muttered the ancient language as he searched deep within his soul's magic. Semias had given him a list of enchantments to make, but this wasn't an amulet that would allow the wearer to withstand stuff. It was a mighty weapon that could change the course of the entire planet. Luthrous understood the desires Semias had required and did his best to find the needed elements. However, rune casting doesn't work that way. If he simply followed the list, the sword would be a hot mess of magic and very unpredictable.

The sword conformed again to the next glyph engraved into its surface, and Luthrous repeated the process. The physical components of the metal were already exceptional, but Luthrous added the runes of *Unbreakable* and *Sharpness*. He infused the control of the elements and higher divination. Seven more times he searched for the proper castings. His limbs were sagging heavily on his frame and his head started to sway.

He wiped the sweat from his brow with a dirty cloth he managed to tear from Semias's shredded red robes. Luthrous held his breath and tightened his closed eyes. Images swirled around his mind and he grabbed each one and pushed it aside until he discerned the one he wanted. Dark green, nearly black, lines shadowed the edges of the symbols that made up the words. Swirling hues of green and gray wafted around his mind as he brought the symbol from the back.

A sharp pain hit the back of his head and crashed through to his eyes. He gripped his head and sucked in as much breath as his lungs had room for before his body gave way and he hit the cold stone. Tears seeped from his now black eyes. He tried to move, but there was no response from his new limbs. The pain moved around his head for what seemed like hours before it eased to a heavy pounding. Luthrous tried to make sense of what was happening, but no solution presented itself.

"Luthrous, Luthrous, are you, all right?" Semias asked.

Semias lifted Luthrous's head and felt for a pulse. It was weak, but still there. Semias slid his long arms under the little man's frame and took him to where he could lie down. He covered him with a warm blanket and fetched some water from a nearby depository. He puckered Luthrous's dry lips open and dripped water into his mouth. The cool sensation eased through his core and the throbbing settled a bit.

Luthrous sank into the soft cushion and allowed his mind to relax. Soft specks of mist eased the pounding, and the pain subsided. He wriggled his fingers and toes. The fact that they moved meant he was still 'back' alive, but that also meant he was still trapped. He wasn't sure if he wanted to sigh with relief or a sigh of dread. He settled on a mix of both and opened his eyes.

Semias was hunched over the old book, running his fingers along the symbols. Luthrous understood them to be the 'Old language' but not the 'Ancient language'. Semias shut the book and set it at the side of the table.

"What happened?" Luthrous asked.

"I was hoping you could tell me. I found you writhing on the floor," Semias said.

"Writhing? Well, it certainly felt that way," Luthrous said.

Luthrous rubbed his face and tried to remember what he was doing. The dark lines of the symbol danced in his memory, barely behind the forefront of his waking mind, as if it were taunting him. Then he understood. He had forgotten to access the 'key' rune of his own memory. He had placed it there for this exact purpose. What he didn't expect was for the pain to be that intense. He allowed himself to believe it was the new body that couldn't handle the pain.

"Are you fit to continue?" Semias asked.

Luthrous started to climb off the bed, then shook his head.

"It would seem there is a limitation to this new form," Luthrous said.

"What's that?" Semias asked.

"It seems to require food, drink, and sleep," Luthrous said.

"You haven't even eaten?" Semias asked, surprised.

Luthrous shook his head.

"It's been days since you started the sword," Semias said.

Luthrous rubbed his face and closed his eyes. It certainly seemed like it had been days the way his body ached. Semias left the dim, but warm, cavern. He returned with a plate of food and a pitcher of water.

"I will make you a dwelling, and then when you have recovered, we can continue."

"Have you the sapphire?" Luthrous asked.

"As soon as Amirra returns," Semias said.

"And Nitida?" Luthrous asked.

"I am not worried about her," Semias said.

"You should," Luthrous said.

"She has her hands too full to be bothered with some missing dust," Semias said.

"You mean the girl?" Luthrous asked.

"Amirra? Amirra would never betray me," Semias said.

Luthrous studied the delusional expression on Semias's face and understood that he truly believed that Amirra loved him. He smiled inside with the understanding that Amirra would be the next Rune-caster and hoped she would be the cause of his demise.

28-I Guess I've Always Known

The air was so hot that it was nearly impossible to fill their lungs. Crolos woke the crew up during the middle of the night and they traveled while the sun wasn't beating down on them, but it was still more than a day's journey. Riddick tried several times to bend the rocks overhead, but he barely made small avalanches that earned him some strong words. Riddick easily picked up the sand and moved it about in waves like the sea, but he was more interested in making the rocks move. Late in the morning, they took shelter under an alcove. Crolos studied Riddick intently while trying not to seem obvious, but Yerild could tell he was thinking about something.

"I need you to take reconnaissance on Crolos," Yerild said.

"Why?" Batovi asked.

"He's up to something and I need to find out what, but he is on to me," Yerild said.

"Aye, aye, what am I looking for exactly?" Batovi asked.

"I wish I knew, he has been here for so long, I'm not sure if he is really all there, or where he actually is," Yerild said.

"That sounds lovely," Batovi said.

Yerild patted his shoulder and sunk into the rounded corners of the stone wall. Sebastian wasted no time finding as many stones as possible and hurled them at Riddick. Riddick held out his hands and pushed the projectiles out of their paths. They crashed into the sides of the canyon walls and shattered into small shards that plopped into the soft sand below.

"Now, throw as many as you can, as fast as you can," Riddick said.

Sebastian's eyes widened with glee and he began scavenging more rocks. Riddick waved his arms around and several rounded objects surfaced through the sand and made their way to Sebastian. Sebastian nearly slipped as he stepped backward onto a moving rock.

"That's pretty creepy," Sebastian said. Riddick smiled. "You ready?" Sebastian asked.

Riddick nodded. Sebastian began chucking rocks at Riddick as fast as his body allowed. Riddick threw the oncoming threats out of the way without even a sweat. Sebastian, on the other hand, was dripping. His gray tunic was half soaked, and his disheveled hair stuck to his face. Batovi joined the fun, and Riddick gleefully swatted the rocks like flies. Panting and out of breath, Sebastian and Batovi collapsed to the ground. Riddick pulled an umbrella-like structure of sand over them to protect them from the searing heat of the sun.

"That's pretty impressive," Crolos said.

"I guess," Riddick said.

"When did you find out about your being the earth sage?" Crolos asked.

Riddick was aware that he intended to do some digging, so he shrugged.

"I guess I have always known," Riddick said.

It wasn't a bold-faced lie, exactly. He did somehow always feel a certain connection for the earth, but until Grandfather stopped shielding him, he didn't have access to it. It kind of bothered him he had hidden it from them, but he understood why. Grandfather's magic was enough to keep them out of Gavin Rhill's magical reach, but not enough to battle him. At least this way, he had a chance to learn it now, now that he was strong enough on his own. Crolos watched Riddick's expressions as the thoughts ran across his mind.

"How much farther do we have?" Riddick asked.

"We should reach the alter by nightfall. If we leave soon," Crolos said.

Riddick let the sand canopy slip back into the surface, and Sebastian and Batovi gathered their things. Yerild gave Batovi the eyebrow-raise and Batovi settled into Crolos' left side. Batovi was the best interrogator anyone had ever seen. The interesting part was he never even asked direct questions. He rounded the bush so many times that it seemed like it would shrivel to anyone who was aware of what he was doing. He was congenial and made the best jokes that his victim never even caught onto what he was doing.

Riddick pulled out the salve that Crolos had given him and smeared it onto his lips. He rubbed them together and felt the tingling of the medicine soothe his skin. Riddick slipped the jar into his satchel and examined the sky. The sky was exactly the same as everything else, yellow-orange. Riddick missed the deep shades of green from his island and wondered what Shaz was up to. What fun adventures was he having without him? A tinge of anger mixed with jealousy etched at his heart. The day continued to wreak havoc on their sun beat skin and dry out their lungs. Their pace slackened, and their steps shortened. Yerild found another plant and pulled the stems off, handing one to each person. Batovi and Sebastian sucked theirs dry, but Riddick and Crolos delicately consumed the sweet water.

"It won't be long till we can rest," Crolos said.

Batovi made his way to Yerild and gave him the signal that he had information on Crolos. Yerild returned a slight gesture and re-situated. Yerild lagged behind Batovi. Crolos, Riddick and Sebastian moved on ahead.

"So, what did you find out?" Yerild asked.

"He was a tricky one. But it seems as though he has been working with another group of people, The Minca, I think he called them. They have been following us for some time now. I don't believe they are any threat, but Crolos definitely has his own agenda, one in which I don't think was the original plan from the time before the end of the Realms."

"How, so?" Yerild asked.

"Well, that's just it, I don't know, I mean, he rambled on about some ancient set of artifacts called the Sev-Rin-Ac-Lavah, but I don't think he even knows what he is saying," Batovi said.

"What did he say about it, EXACTLY," Yerild asked.

"He said, 'the story is that Gavin Rhill already has the first part of the Sword and the original recipe of the Runes that made it, even before the sinking of Srinna Vossa,'" Batovi said.

Yerild chuckled at Batovi's nearly exact mimicking of Crolos, but it turned to a quick scowl.

"So, it is true," Yerild said. Batovi nodded. "Common, let's catch up."

A heavy gust of wind picked up and pushed against the travelers. Riddick shielded them but still found it hard to push through. Several minutes passed, and the wind stopped. The sudden calm took everyone by surprise as they nearly stumbled forward of their own force.

"Are we there?" Batovi asked.

"Yes, the Alter of Yune," Crolos said.

The lifeless desert was now a delicate ecosystem of small flowers mixed with thin vines. Nothing like the jungle, but Riddick had the sense that they were nothing to be trifled with. Sprigs of fine grass decorated small crevices in the hardened ground. Several stones protruded from the flat surface. The compacted earth emerged from the soft sand. Riddick started toward the center of the circular stone, but Crolos grabbed his arm.

"We must wait until the cycle of the moon is in alignment over the center stone," Crolos said.

"When will that be?" Sebastian asked.

"Sometime tomorrow in the mid-morning," Crolos said.

"How can we tell when they are aligned?" Riddick asked.

"The alter will illuminate the path the mage is to take to reach to the center," Crolos said.

"Till then, let's get some sleep," Yerild said.

Crolos led them to a patch of ground on the other side of the circle and they pulled out their bedrolls. The sun was less intense here, as if a type of shield covered the landform. It was quite a bit cooler, and the crew found it very easy to find sleep as the light faded into night. Except for Riddick. His senses were overwhelmed with the earth's new surroundings. His mind raced around the shifting energies and the new sensations of the earth. He laid there with his eyes closed, but he stretched out his essences and found he could 'walk' around the surroundings. He inspected and analyzed the type of dirt and vegetation and the materials the stones were made of. He found he could understand it all. Except for one part, the very center. There was nothing he could sense with his magic.

He circled it several times and searched for any signs of energy, but it was a complete void. Riddick wandered away from the center until he came to the shield of energy that protected the alter. He followed it around until he returned to the same spot. He sucked in a deep breath and reached into his core and closed his eyes even tighter. The darkness under the flat hardened earth was a few lengths away, and he wanted to understand what was underneath. A cold shiver ran through him and he decided he better not push any further. He returned to his body and was reassured with a calmness as the soft dirt encompassed his feelings once more. He was confident he had a good understanding of the alter and relaxed enough to fall asleep.

Riddick stirred and sat up. The others were still sleeping, and he went to lay back down but a feeling of panic filled his chest. He got up and witnessed from a dream-like state, Shaz covered in soot and little people dead all around him. He blinked several times and this time a mountain split in half with bright red liquid earth was seen rising from the center of the world. Plumes of steam plagued the torn earth and there was soot covering the entire earth's surface.

Pockets of poisonous gas from the earth's core killed everything in its path. Riddick looked to see if he could find Shaz, but all he saw was destruction. The smell of iron sank into his nostrils and rested on his tongue, giving him a sour taste in his mouth. Darkness crept over the horizon, and Riddick felt the breath being squeezed from his chest. He turned around to find his way back to the patch of ground, but there was nothing there. Darkness surrounded him, and he sank to the ground. His red hair flopped over his face as he buried it in his hands.

"Riddick," a voice came.

Riddick lifted his face and squinted. A bright light appeared at the center of the circle where the altar was.

"Riddick, come here," a strong female's voice beckoned.

Riddick rose and walked toward the light with his hand shielding his face. A tall, thin woman appeared. Her long brown hair cascaded down her slender frame like waves of the desert. Dark brown eyes rested on high cheeks and her skin was a soft, smooth walnut color.

"Who are you?" Riddick asked.

"I am the essence of this world, Edenocht,"

"The essence, the energy I sense from the world, that's you?" Riddick asked.

"Yes, you are the Earth sage, my human protector."

"Protector? What do I protect you from, you're the world, the largest force there is?" Riddick said.

"Not the largest, evil is greater than I, that is why I have come to you. I am in need of your help. The evil Necromancer Semias has ripped the fabrics of time and has reincarnated the Runecaster Luthrous and in doing so has ripped open my core."

"Can't you fix yourself?" Riddick asked.

Riddick's cheeks reddened as he regretted his words before he was even done speaking them.

"I could, but my energy is a very slow-moving energy. That is why humans cannot see the trees or grass growing. It would take so much time that all humans would cease to exist before I could heal the gap."

"What can I do?" Riddick asked.

"Your magic is growing but you are not strong enough on your own, you must get the war wizard and the healer to help you, but you must fuse the earth shut before all the spitting earth escapes."

"I don't know where Shaz is, or the split in the earth, how can I get there?" Riddick asked.

"I will take you," Mother Edenocht said.

"Through the realms?" Riddick asked.

"Through the earth." She spoke quietly. "You must never tell anyone, except your friends how you traveled, and you must go now."

"But what of Yerild and the others, the Kar-ka-dannon, and the staff?" Riddick asked.

"You can find the staff as soon as you close the earth's crust, and as for your friends, I will return them to your island. The Kar-ka-dannon will be safe and will meet you wherever you are when it is time."

"How?"

"That is not your concern right now, you must go."

"Will I be able to travel like this all the time?" Riddick asked.

"No, there are only very rare extremes where this level of travel is acceptable. Are you ready?" She asked.

"I suppose," Riddick said and swallowed hard.

The image of the woman merged into a long oval opening.

"Step through and you will be moved to where your friends are, please hurry," Mother Edenocht said.

Riddick looked back at his friends and found Yerild standing at the edge of the platform. He nodded at Riddick, who then stepped into the earth. Riddick gasped as the floor fell out from under him and he fell through the bottom of the inside of a tree. A tubular casing formed around him, and he saw small branch-like structures shooting off in all directions. Riddick guessed he was on the inside of the world's largest root system. The force that propelled him both pulled and pushed his body. His chest was heavy as he sped through the passageways, and the pressure nearly overwhelmed his frame. He closed his eyes and focused on the inner strength the planet's magic gave him, and soon the movements became smooth and effortless.

The tubular expressway dipped and turned. In some places he bent in half and others a little more than half. Normally, this would have made him sick. He was always the first to get seasick, however, this time it was as smooth and comforting as he had ever been. His ride seemed to take quite a long time, and he wondered how many time zones he would pass through. He speculated what the different realms looked like, what lived there and all the secrets that might be hidden. After a time, the force against his body eased, and he slowed down. The dimly lit corridor intensified a moment before he was shot to the surface.

29-We Minca Are The Keepers Of Many Things

The pounding of the heavy mallets against the tight rawhide of the warning drums broke the silence of night. Shaz jumped out of bed and grabbed his sword in one fluid motion and hurried out of the tent. He raced into the square and found Turkill and the Chief discussing loudly. Several torches secured in the ground around the formal square had been lit and gave a soft glow to the dark night.

"What's going on?" Shaz asked.

"There is poisonous gas pouring out of a crevice not far from here and it's heading our way," Turkill said.

"Will it dissipate before it gets here?" Shaz asked.

Amirra emerged through the darkness and stopped a few lengths from the Minca. Shaz noticed her watching him and realized he hadn't grabbed his tunic. Amirra blushed and rubbed her nose. A sense of sadness overcame her when she saw all the scars on his body, and she wondered how much pain he had suffered.

"It has been for days now, but the wind is changing, and it has already started to kill the remaining livestock we have left," the Chief said.

"We need to see if we can make the wind blow it back the other way. Where is Serin?" Turkill asked.

"She's not strong enough yet, I'll go," Shaz said.

Amirra smiled softly and moved toward Shaz. Shaz kept his focus on the Minca but kept his energy on hers. He still didn't know what she was about, and things had been so crazy that he didn't have the time to question her.

"I can do it," Serin said.

Shaz turned to see Serin standing behind him.

"I don't think you're strong enough," Shaz said.

He took her hand and squeezed gently. Serin peered around him at Amirra. Amirra folded her arms across her chest and glared at Serin.

"Who is that?" Serin whispered.

A wave of energy rushed through Shaz's body as though he were stuck between two darts of jealousy.

"I'm Amirra," Amirra said.

Amirra stepped next to Shaz with determination, as though she were telling Serin that he belonged to her now. Serin glared at her with a slanted eyebrow and then looked at Shaz. He had a slight grin on his face and a look that said, 'She has no idea who she's messing with'. Serin smirked. Amirra felt the blood under her cheeks and turned away. Shaz wrapped his arm around Serin's waist and walked her several lengths away.

"I know you are as determined as I am to make things right, but you are still too weak and I'm not going to lose you to anything, remember," Shaz said.

"So, what are you going to do then, Mr. Smarty pants," Serin said.

"That's my girl," Shaz smiled and kissed her.

"I mean it Shaz, what are you going to do?" Serin said.

"Teach me how to move the wind and I will do it," Shaz said. Serin nodded, and they walked back to the Minca. "Serin is going to teach me how to move the air," Shaz said.

"I'll go with, you'll need someone to watch your back," Amirra said.

"That means *I* will go," Turkill said.

"Me too," Ladtwig said, trying to imitate Turkill's swagger.

Turkill pushed passed Amirra and Shaz, and Serin smirked. Serin saw the frustration on Amirra's face and tried to figure out what her intentions were. She had mixed emotions, which made it harder for Serin to sift through. The Chief found a sense of pride in the devotion his sons had for them and understood their connection was built on total trust and friendship.

"Where is Jagwynn?" Shaz asked.

"She's not in your hut?" Turkill asked.

Shaz shook his head.

"I'll go find her," Turkill said and hurried into the darkness.

"You two will need to hurry," the Chief said.

Shaz and Serin nodded and returned to their hut.

"So, are you going to tell me about Amirra?" Serin asked.

"I don't actually know anything about her. We found her in a trap on the way back from the Runecaster. We weren't going to bring her here, but we needed to check on the huts and she was with us, so she ended up coming too. Turkill and the chief weren't too happy about it either," Shaz said.

Shaz slipped on his soft blue tunic, then his gray leather jerkin, and then realized the tone in Serin's voice and rolled his eyes. Serin chuckled.

"She's hiding something for sure, and she definitely thinks highly of you," Serin said.

"Oh, I hadn't noticed," Serin slugged his shoulder, and he chuckled. "Are you going to be alright with her here?" Shaz asked.

"Yes, why wouldn't I? Is that why you wanted Jagwynn? You don't think I can protect myself from a powerless girl," Serin asked.

"No, that's not it. And just because she doesn't have magic doesn't make her harmless. Maybe you could set the village woman on her case and find out more about her. They love a good gossip," Shaz said.

"Are you saying that women are nosey?" Serin asked.

"Yes, well, no, that's not what I mean." Shaz was about to get frustrated but relaxed when he found Serin smiling at him. "Just teach me what to do," Shaz said.

It was good to see Serin bantering again. He had hoped she would improve quickly, but it had been longer than he had expected, and he was getting nervous. Shaz had tried to help the women with the heal but he kept getting in the way and they shooed him out. He was quite amazed by Serin's little rain cloud that somehow made the perfect amount of water and never overflowed the basin that had been made for it. They left the hut and found a clearing big enough for them to stretch, and Serin began showing him the movements she used to summon the air. Shaz felt a bit silly moving his arms around his head and raising onto his toes. It didn't take long for Serin to realize this approach was not going to work for him.

"Alright, let's try something else," Serin said.

"What, you don't like my moves?" Shaz asked.

She chuckled. She did realize it wasn't his style, but he was quite cute.

"All right, think of the wind being a flame and call it to you," Serin said.

"Like calling a pet?" Shaz asked.

"Shaz, be serious," Serin said.

"I am, I mean like 'here wind, wind, wind'."

"No, like 'wind, come now!'" Serin said.

"Alright. Wind come now!" Shaz demanded.

Shaz ducked as an instant gust of wind whipped over his head. The wind whipped around, forming a funnel next to him.

"Well, that worked. Now tell it what you want it to do," Serin said.

"Wind, blow the toxic fumes away from the village," Shaz said.

The wind fizzled to the ground and disappeared.

"That didn't work," Serin said.

"Don't worry. I'll work on it. Come on," Shaz said.

"I hope so," Serin said.

They returned to the square and started gathering supplies.

"Is Turkill back? We need to leave," Shaz said.

Jagwynn's dark-yellow eyes peered through the darkness and faded into the light. Turkill had a grin from ear to ear as he leaped off her back. He stood tall and strutted passed the warriors next to the chief. Serin hurried to her, and Jag nuzzled her gingerly. Amirra gasped and threw her hand over her mouth. Shaz studied Amirra and watched her eyes gleam when she noticed Jag's collar. A small rock formed in the pit of his stomach. She had no magic, he knew nothing about her, and until now she gave him no indication that there was anything amiss about her. Except that she kept trying to win his affections.

"You better get going," the chief said.

"You watch after Serin," Shaz whispered to Jag.

Jagwynn rubbed up against him as she walked past him.

"We'll be fine, come on Jag, you can come with me, I guess I need a babysitter," Serin said and returned to her hut.

Shaz grabbed the satchel from the Chieftess and slung it over his shoulder. Turkill and a party of warriors each grabbed packs, and they started into the night. The sun soon lightened the sky and Serin woke with a severe grumble in her stomach. It was the first time in days she was hungry. The chilly morning air stung her skin, and she shivered. Her teeth chattered as she hurriedly threw on several layers of clothes, her boots, and a cloak. She hadn't realized so much time had passed that the seasons were now changing to the cold moons. In fact, she had no idea if the weather even turned cold in this realm. She crept passed Jag, who was curled up in a tight ball. The early morning light barely made it through the soot-filled sky. Serin pulled her cloak tight around her neck as the tiny particles of soot she stirred flew into the air and dance around the breeze.

Serin found a few of the women tending to the sick and started helping. She was pleased to see her little rain cloud still diligently making freshwater. Serin pulled up her sleeves and rested her hands on the surface. She pushed a surge of healing energy into the pool and soaked up the energy the water gave her in return.

"You're feeling better?" Britta asked.

"Yes, much. It's good to be back to work," Serin said.

"Don't overdo it. Shaz will have my hide if you do," the Chief said.

Serin studied the chief and found a gentle glint in his eyes. When they first arrived, he was certainly the one in charge, but now it seemed that Shaz had earned his strongest allegiance. Serin smiled and soaked a handful of cloth and began wrapping the head of a young boy. The Minca were shivering and their lips were purple.

"We need to find warm clothes for everyone," Serin said.

"We don't have any," Britta said.

"We don't have the cold here," another woman said.

"Then why is it so cold?" Serin asked. They shrugged. "I sure hope Shaz hurries, then we can figure out a way to change this weather," Serin said.

"How are you going to do that?" Amirra asked.

Serin peered over her shoulder at the red-haired girl. She wasn't a child but had a certain youthfulness about her. Not playful, more inexperienced, which made her seem even younger. Serin contemplated telling her, but decided she wasn't ready.

"Would you mind helping here for a bit while I talk to the Chief?" Serin asked. Amirra's eyes widened, and she took a step back. "The ladies here can show you what to do."

Britta took Amirra's hand and gently lead her to the water and showed her how to soak the linens. Serin followed the Chief out from under the tent and walked to the other side of the clearing.

"What do you think about Amirra?" the Chief asked.

"She's hiding something," Serin said.

"That is what I think too, but what?"

"That I can't say, do you think she is dangerous?" Serin asked.

"Does she have magic?" the Chief asked.

"I didn't sense any of her," Serin said.

"Shaz didn't either, he said there is magic about her but not in her, he thinks she is carrying an amulet or something that has been enchanted," the Chief said.

"That would make sense. Have you searched her hut?" Serin asked.

"Yes, but we found nothing," the Chief said.

"We need to keep a tight watch on her," Serin said.

"You need to watch your back too," the Chief said.

"Me, why?" Serin asked.

"Every time she looks at you, she has anger in her eyes," the Chief said.

"That's because she thinks she can have Shaz for herself," Serin said.

The chief blurted out a hearty guffaw.

"That will never happen," he said.

"Why do you say that?" Serin asked, not that she didn't agree.

"Synmagic doesn't work that way," the chief said.

"How does it work then?" Serin asked.

"Well, with Synmagic, the two bonded can *only* love the one whom they are bonded to," the chief said.

"That's not what the scroll said, it said we *couldn't* be together because of the forbidden child," Serin said.

The Chief waved his hands in objection.

"Synmagic is not only between two people, it extends to their offspring, for the purpose of harnessing untrained powers. The parents of elemental children absorb the extra energy until the child is old enough to handle it on their own. It is the way the universe accommodated for the nature of love," the chief said.

"I guess I don't understand exactly what you're saying," Serin said.

"A very long time ago, the Velshari tried to use Synmagic to try and manufacture War Wizards and caused great havoc among the world, so the Council had it written that all unions of Synmagic were forbidden to engage in a romantic relationship so that they would not result in children. That is also why Shaz is the only war wizard left in the realms. But the truth of it is, that there are many kinds of Synmagic. The kind of synergy *you* share isn't just a magical one, but one of love, trust and devotion. Love is a whole different kind of magic, a whole different kind of synergy. Synergy was designed *for* the creation of elemental beings. Shaz's mother and father were united first by love, and then by Synmagic. That is the missing piece Gavin Rhill never had, nor is he capable of love. When Gavin Rhill started hunting Shaz's parents, they extended it to Mathieu, or Grandfather, which is how he was able to keep Shaz from the destruction of the shadow magic. Synmagic is simply a synergy or cohesive balance of powers between two or more entities, but *love* is the ultimate force," the Chief said.

It all made sense, that is how Shaz was able to be bonded with Grandfather and her, but that it was the kind of bond that made the difference.

"How do you know all this?" Serin asked.

"We Minca are the keepers of many things, including secrets," the chief said with a smile.

Serin's heart nearly burst. She no longer had to keep her feelings locked down in fear they would cause chaos and pain. She didn't have to keep him at arm's length, she didn't have to pretend she didn't love him, she didn't have to make up reasons as to why she couldn't show her affection for him. Serin couldn't wait until she could tell Shaz all of this and *really* kiss him.

The Chief smiled at the joy that was now written all over her face. He left her with her new excitement and walked away, giving orders to several men to gather as many skins as possible to make coats for everyone.

30-There's A Whole Lot More To This Mess

The night turned into day, but it hardly made a difference for the crew. A distant glow hovered on the other side of the heavy soot-filled clouds, giving enough light to make out half the details as they struggled through the overshadowing drifts of heavy soot. The particles from the melted earth were so fine that when they tried to step onto the mounds, they would fall right through them, sinking to the bottom. Shaz had a much easier time because of his size, but Turkill and the other warriors cursed every few minutes.

"How much farther?" Shaz asked.

"That ridge is as far as we can go," a warrior said.

A misty green hue floated and billowed from behind a low-lying ridge. The cloud was pushing the soot back toward the ground and making its way toward the village. The misty green made the sky seem like it was going to crash down on them at any minute. A rancid metal taste formed in their mouths and they covered their faces with cloth.

"Let's stop here," Shaz said.

He had moved as close as he dared to use the wind tunnel to funnel the gas into the sky. He closed his eyes and searched for his magic.

"Wind, come here!" Shaz called loudly.

The wind element shot toward him from all angles and instead of ducking, this time he grabbed it with his hands and swirled it around. The wind fell into place and formed a whipping funnel, opening wide at the top and sitting in the palm of his hand at the bottom. His hair whipped around his face and he moved around to keep the funnel in balance. He tried to move the air toward the mist and struggled to make it bend enough to suck the gas into the funnel.

Little by little the gas moved toward the hand-held tornado, and Shaz focused on making it larger and larger. The surrounding air cleared, and he stepped closer to the gap in the ground where the poison was coming from. He bent down and set the tornado on the ground near the hole and crawled out from under the wind. The Minca watched the green mist pull backward into the funnel. The clear wind-tube became the same green as the gas and spiraled it into the sky, keeping it from escaping into the atmosphere.

"You did it!" Ladtwig said.

"So, it seems," Shaz said.

The Minca slapped each other on their backs and started back toward the village. After several lengths, a crashing noise came from behind them.

"What was that?" Turkill asked.

Shaz turned to find the funnel had become imbalanced and was thrashing around wildly. The green mist was being flung everywhere.

"Get out of here," Shaz said.

Shaz covered the Minca as a large branch flew through the air missing them by a tiny length.

"Well, that didn't work," a warrior said.

"What happened?" Turkill asked.

"The force must have been too much for the funnel," Shaz said.

"Now what do we do?" Turkill asked.

Shaz shrugged and then thought, *What would happen if I tried to burn the gaseous cloud*? He stood up and called the wind to stop. The funnel dropped, and a plume of gas billowed toward them.

"Watch out," Shaz said.

Shaz ignited the flames in his palms and shot the flames toward the mist. The flames hit the gas and a shocking blast ignited the sky. Flames shot out in all directions, throwing the men head over heels several lengths. The gasses gave off a sizzle a regular campfire could never imagine. The heat was so intense it melted full-size tree trunks. A cacophony of wind, flames, and soot shot around Shaz. The Minca covered themselves as the heat roasted their hiny's. Dark black ash shot into the sky, pushing whatever soot was left from the earth-shakes back toward the ground. The flames were sucked back toward the crevasse as the force of the fire and heat created a vacuum. Shaz pulled himself from the soot and ash and rubbed his eyes. The sting raced to his brain, and he moaned and blinked several times.

"Look, the flames are consuming the gas," a warrior said.

The orange and yellow flames were now tinted with a green hue at the base, but by the time the flames died out into the sky the gas had been burned. There was not even a dark cloud of soot or ash.

"Now we can get rid of the gas," another warrior said.

"But how long will it burn?" Shaz asked. Everyone shrugged, and their pleased expressions turned sour. "Are there any more?" Shaz asked.

"There are a few more this way," Turkill said.

Shaz used his new air magic and tunneled through the soot and kept it away from their faces. Shaz repeated the process with each gas plume, but each time he stood as far away as possible. Each time the flames shot from his palms farther and farther, however, he still found himself being thrown several lengths from the blasts.

"There, this ought to do it," Shaz said.

He brushed off the soot from his face and pulled his hair out of his eyes as he stood back up from the last blast.

"Let's hope so," Ladtwig said.

The sun was shining a bit brighter as the gasses were now eliminated from the sky.

"Let's get back to the village," a warrior said.

Shaz once again managed his wind spell and blew the soot out of their way.

"They're back," a small Minca boy shouted.

Serin came out of the hut and snickered at all the men with the best windblown hair and black smudges all over their bodies that she had ever seen. She wanted to rush to Shaz and tell him what the Chief had told her, but she would wait until they were alone, and the time was right.

"I take it things went a different way," Serin questioned.

"They sure did," Turkill grumbled.

Turkill kicked a basket out of his way as he pushed passed her.

"He's not exactly thrilled with the way I handled things," Shaz said.

"I can see that. So how did you handle things?" Serin asked.

"Are you hurt?" Amirra asked.

Amirra stepped between Shaz and Serin and gazed at him with wide eyes. Serin scowled. *And now she thinks she's going to tend to his wounds.* Serin thought.

"I'm fine," Shaz said.

"Did you know your bleeding?" Amirra asked.

Amirra put a cloth on his forehead and took his arm to lead him to the tent. Serin felt the blood under her skin begin to boil. *I can't believe the nerve of this girl.* Shaz pulled away gently and moved her hand from his arm.

"I'm fine, plus Serin is the one that heals me," Shaz said. Shaz smiled with a polite head-nod and moved passed her and took Serin's elbow and walked her back to their hut. "Don't let her under your skin, Serin," Shaz said.

He pulled off his leather jerkin and winced as the pain in his shoulder hit his brain.

"What happened?" Serin asked.

"Well, the wind tunnel worked for a minute, but then the energy became unstable and it thrashed around. So, like my normal stupid self, I lit it on fire. It exploded and shot us across the forest," Shaz said.

"We heard the blasts and feared something horrible had happened. At least the earth didn't tremble again, so we knew it wasn't an earth-shake," Serin said.

"My head is trembling, does that count?" Shaz said.

"Do you have a headache? I thought those were gone now?" Serin said.

"Aye, but not one of those headaches, more like the 'just got your-can-kicked' kind." Serin stared at him, "Never mind," he said. Serin helped him pull his tunic off and examined the cuts and bruises. She put her hands on his skin and Shaz sighed as the pain eased from his body. A warm and cool tingle enveloped him, and he eased into her magic as it pulled the skin that was separated back together. "You have gotten really good at this," Shaz said.

"Yes, lots better from the first time in the forest. I'm still trying to figure out how to heal without leaving scars though," Serin said.

"I'm sorry you have to do this," Shaz said.

"Why are you sorry?" Serin asked.

"If it weren't for me, you would still be at Mrs. Bailey's learning about herbs and stuff. Safe and sound," Shaz said.

Serin stepped in front of him and pulled his face toward hers. His bright blue eyes were dimmed and pained.

"If it *weren't* for you, that's *exactly* where I would be, but why do you think that is where I *want* to be?"

Shaz shrugged.

"I feel so bad that I have put you through so much, your too good to me and you don't deserve this," Shaz said.

"I deserve to be with you, wherever that is, or however that is. That is what *I* choose." Serin pulled his chin toward her and leaned in and kissed him softly. His lips parted and he let her embrace him, slowly at first, but then her new freedom to love him escaped. He kissed her back and wrapped his arms around her waist and pulled her tight. The moment seemed to last forever until Shaz pulled away.

"Have things changed between us?" Shaz asked.

"Things aren't going to be better anytime soon. We still have to defeat Gavin Rhill wherever or whenever that is. But we are together. Isn't that what you say?" Shaz nodded, "all right then, no more pity party," Serin said.

"All right, but there seems to be something else about you," Shaz said.

Serin hesitated, she debated telling him about her new information and then remembered that he was probably already listening to her thoughts anyway, so she rehearsed her conversation with the Chief. She watched his thoughts move from several places, but since she couldn't read his thoughts, her fears began to get the best of her and she started to worry, so when he said nothing her heart sank.

She pulled away and started to gather his things to take them to the wash, but he took her hand. Shaz pulled her tight and held her. She wrapped her arms around him and listened to his beating heart. It was the most comfortable place she had ever been, and he wanted her there. Words didn't have to tell her that. His grip tight around her was enough to calm every fear she had had. He kissed her forehead and let the moments pass quietly.

"Shaz, Serin, are you all right?" the Chieftess asked.

"We're fine. Why? What's going on?" Shaz asked.

"Nothing, it's just that you hadn't come back, and we got worried," the Chieftess said.

"Thank you, we'll be out in a bit," Serin said.

Serin heard the Chieftess's soft shoes through the tall grass leaving the hut and nudged Shaz.

"Are you hungry?" Serin asked.

"Very," Shaz said.

"Then let's go," Serin said.

"That would mean I have to let you go," Shaz said.

"Are you alright?" Serin asked.

"Aye, why?" Shaz asked.

"Because you are acting different," Serin said.

"Because I am in love with you, and now we're free to be in love forever?" Shaz asked.

"Well, yeah, and because you've never just held me like this before," Serin said.

"Because I haven't been allowed to, Serin, the only time I don't feel the internal conflict of my shadow magic is when I am holding you or kissing you or as near to as I can possibly be. For whatever reason, I can push the constant pull the shadow makes me feel when you are close. It is the only time I don't feel the pit in my stomach, the anger in my chest, and the chaos in my mind," Shaz said.

Serin squeezed him.

"I didn't know that. I'm sorry you have to feel that. I do wish that wasn't your burden," Serin said.

"I can't do it without your help," Shaz said.

"And now you don't have to," Serin said.

He kissed her again and then let her go. It was still very cold, and Serin shivered as she helped him with a clean tunic and his leather jerkin.

"How is Amirra doing?" Shaz asked.

"I think she is doing better. She just needs some guidance and some friends. I don't know where she comes from or her past, but I think she hides behind a wall of toughness not because she means any harm but because she has been hurt and is trying to protect herself. She has really been a big help with all the chores and the other women seem to like her," Serin said.

"You're always giving people the benefit of the doubt, that's one thing I adore about you, Serin," Shaz said with a smile.

"I think if we play our cards right, she can become a good friend and ally," Serin said.

"Alright, then we give her more leeway and I'll follow your lead," Shaz said.

"She has a lot to learn, maybe Jagwynn can help keep an eye on her," Serin said.

"Where is Jag?" Shaz asked.

"I haven't seen her. She was around earlier. I bet she's out patrolling with Turkill or one of the other warriors," Serin said.

They made their way to the campfire and dished themselves the meager soup. It was quite a difference from when they first arrived. Much of the livestock had been killed and the vegetables and roots were no longer trusted. Amirra was sitting near the back of the fire with a scowl on her face. Shaz had agreed to give her a chance, but he knew there was still a level of confusion within her. As though she wanted something she couldn't have. Amirra noticed them return and tried not to look longingly. Serin waved to her and motioned for her to join them. Amirra hesitated but agreed and moved her way through the little groups of people and sat next to Serin. Serin wrapped her arm around her shoulder and gave her a squeeze, and Amirra smiled. She didn't quite know what to do. It was the first time she felt like she might have a friend.

"Thank you, Amirra, for all your hard work over the last several days. I know how hard it can be, especially for someone who doesn't even know us. That really takes someone with integrity," Serin said.

Amirra peered into Serin's eyes with a questioned look.

"I'm not sure what to say," Amirra said.

"Has no one ever given you a compliment before?" Serin asked.

Amirra shook her head.

"I don't even know what that means," Amirra said.

"Well, from now on, you're going to hear a lot more of them," Serin said and squeezed Amirra's hand and smiled.

Shaz found himself staring into the fire and thinking of all the things that had gone on. He tried to make sense of the events, but things weren't lining up the way he thought they should. There were gaps in time, there were gaps in places, and with people, with Jag.

Shaz jarred from his thoughts as the ground rumbled. The Minca scurried toward their huts and Serin gripped Shaz's forearm. A loud pop and a thud echoed through the village. A hole opened in the ground and a bright light shot across the clearing. A very tall tree root emerged from the hole and then opened in the center. A bright red-haired man stood in the center of the root. Riddick's pale face and freckles stood out from the brightness, and Shaz rubbed his eyes.

Riddick stepped out of the root and blinked several times. Shaz leaped over a Minca and raced toward his best mate. Riddick's eyes adjusted barely in time to see Shaz throw his arms around him.

"Is that really you, Riddick?" Shaz asked.

"Aye, it's me alright," Riddick said.

He gripped his friend tightly, and the light faded as the root returned underground.

"How is this possible? Where did you come from? What are you doing here?" Shaz let him go and stood back. "Did you grow even taller?" Shaz asked.

Riddick laughed his hearty bellow and slapped Shaz on the shoulder.

"Mate, I have so much to tell you." Serin walked up next to Shaz. Her soft green eyes smiled as she watched Shaz reunite with Riddick.

"Who's this?" Riddick asked. His eyes bright and hopeful.

"This is Serin," Shaz said.

"I thought so."

Riddick took her hand in his and kissed the back of it. Amirra made her way toward them, and Riddick noticed her from the shadows. Shaz motioned for her to come closer.

"This is Amirra, and these are the Minca," Shaz said.

The Chief and Chieftess made their way as well as Ladtwig and Turkill, who had his arms over his chest with his usual hurmpf look.

Riddick nodded to them all and then turned to Shaz. His expression deepened.

"We need to talk and quickly," Riddick said.

"Let's go to the prayer hut," the Chief said.

"Just Shaz and I," Riddick said.

"It's all right, the Chief, Turkill, Ladtwig, and Serin need to hear this too," Shaz said.

Riddick nodded, and they made their way through the crowded people. Once inside, Riddick rehearsed what had happened with the new island, the portal, and Crolos. Shaz filled Riddick in on all the things that had happened with the Minca.

"So, you're the Earth Sage?" the Chief asked. Riddick nodded. "That means we have three of the four original descendants of the Sev-Rin-Ac-Lavah," the Chief said.

"So, who is the fourth?" Serin asked.

"Well, Shaz, you are from the Tooatha De Danann, Serin you are of the Lavari, and Riddick you are from the Bairr Tiornecht. That leaves Akraven, the city of the Fir Bolg. I have a feeling it is Amirra," the Chief said.

"What makes you think that?" Riddick asked.

"I heard her telling one of the others she was told she was from Akraven as a child."

"Nitida alluded to that as well. I wondered if it was her. We need to go ask her," Shaz said.

"We need to get to that huge crevasse and get it closed before the liquid earth spills out and kills everything," Riddick said.

"How do we do that?" Serin asked.

"I don't know, I was hoping you would," Riddick said, turning to Shaz.

"Nitida told me the only way to fix it was to mend the weaves of time," Shaz said.

"That would make sense since it was torn when Semias brought Luthrous here," the Chief said.

"How are you going to do that?" Turkill asked.

"The catacombs, there might be something there," Serin said.

"What are the catacombs?" Riddick asked, a hint of worry in his tone.

"It's a library," Shaz said.

"With dead people? That's interesting. I guess it makes sense. Books usually boarded me to death too," Riddick said.

"You sound like Shaz too," Serin said.

Riddick chuckled.

"Hey, where is Jagwynn?" Riddick asked.

"I haven't seen her," Serin said.

"Us either," Turkill said.

"She hasn't been with you?" Shaz asked the Minca.

They shook their heads. Shaz gripped his blade and moved toward the door.

"What is it?" Serin asked.

"Nothing good, that's for sure. Let's go," Shaz said.

Shaz ducked through the small opening, and Serin followed. Riddick had to bend nearly in half, and the Minca laughed at his height. He was like a giant compared to them. The Minca had to run to keep up with Riddick's long strides, and Shaz and Serin even found it uncomfortable. They searched for Amirra and Jagwynn but couldn't find either of them. One of the warriors detailed seeing Jagwynn going with Amirra into the jungle, however, only Amirra came back. Shaz closed his eyes and searched the surrounding energy. He recognized faint traces of their energies, but nothing more. Riddick put his hands on the cold ground and used the earth's energy to make a mental picture of where they had gone. The earth showed him their tracks that lead all the way to the mountain, but then was lost halfway up.

"They went to the mountain. But Amirra came back and Jag didn't," Riddick said.

"How did you do that?" Shaz asked.

"Pretty cool, huh?" Riddick said.

"Why would she take Jag there and then come back?" Shaz asked.

"So, I could make sure you went after her," Amirra said.

They spun on their heels and were shocked to see Amirra wearing a blood-red cloak that covered her head. Dark shadows covered her eyes.

"So, that's what all this is about. You're a Velshari," Shaz said.

"I don't understand, I thought we were becoming your friends. What do you want with Jagwynn?" Serin asked.

Amirra winced, she blinked the tear from the corner of her eye.

"I don't need Jagwynn, I just need her collar," Amirra said.

"Her collar? Why?" Shaz asked.

"It's the recipe of the Runecaster that is needed to enchant the honor blade that Semias and Luthrous are recreating. Except after getting it from her, we found she had only one of the two sapphires needed to reverse the effectiveness of *your* honor blade. It would seem that *you* have the other one on *your* neck collar," Amirra said.

Shaz reached for his neck, but the collar wasn't there, and he remembered he had taken it off and left it in his satchel. Amirra pulled it from behind her back.

"Thanks for helping me earn my freedom," Amirra said, her tone nearly cracking.

"And how do you think you are going to get away from here? It seems you've forgotten where you are," Turkill said.

"Like this."

Amirra rubbed a small amulet and vanished, leaving a puff of soot twirling around.

Shaz reached into his pocket and pulled out the sapphire.

"So, that's why they were after it," Serin said.

"I wonder what will happen when she finds out it's not on the neck collar?" Shaz said.

"So, there's more to this collar than just looking awesome?" Riddick questioned.

He noticed the Chief touch his crown, which was very much like their collars.

"There's a whole lot more to this entire mess," Serin said.

"And all we are, are pawns in Gavin Rhill's sick game," Shaz said.

"Come on, let's go get Jagwynn," Serin said.

31-It's Not My Choice, It Never Has Been

Semias paced back and forth, stabbing the tip of his staff into the cold stone floor with each step. The persistent chanting was aggravating his nerves. The green-tinted fire cast shadows along the walls with a dreary wave. After hours of chanting, now came the part where the Runemagic would infuse the elements into the sword. Luthrous scanned the pages of his old notebook, remembering the ages gone by. Luthrous organized every ingredient that he had and marked the pages he would need.

His crooked finger slipped under the next page, and he turned it respectfully as not to ruin the delicate paper. The once black ink had faded to a deep brown. The page was now covered in smudges of a substance he didn't recognize, but it made the writing nearly impossible to read. Unless you were the one that wrote them. He read the warnings he had left and secured it in his mind.

When working with runes, there are many processes that could change the total outcome. It was a very delicate art. It took decades to reach even an average understanding. That's why the first rune skill the Runecaster learns is the extend-life casting. An intricate balance of health and fervor with a desire to continue living even when there is little to look forward to.

Luthrous was one of the oldest known Runecasters in his day. He had confided in Nitida his involvement with the Sev-Rin-Ac-Lavah and made her promise she would protect the Honor Runestone to her last day. He trusted she would be strong enough to withstand Semias, that is the reason he told him where it was. In a way, it was his own selfishness. He wanted the chance to recreate the sword, but more so, that maybe he could return and take his place as a Runecaster again. Heavy clunks echoed in the hallway, jarring Luthrous and Semias from their introspections.

"It's about time you returned," Semias said.

"Don't patronize me," Amirra said.

"Where is the cat? I should pleasure in extracting her magic when this is all done," Semias said.

"She's in the dungeon," Amirra said.

"I must ask, how did you make the last of the Sakura follow you? As the personal assistant to the Sun Goddess, they are not easily deceived," Semias asked.

His eyes settled on Amirra's with his eager greed. She found it even harder to look at him and wanted to spit in his face. The question pricked the back of her mind also. Her heart was torn in half. She had betrayed people that were starting to trust her. People *she* could call friends, people she *wanted* to call friends. A sharp stabbing pain hit the back of her head as the shadow magic that controlled her reminded her of her place. She winced but kept her knees tight. She wasn't going to obey for much longer, even if that meant her own death. She had finally found another reason to live, and now it was too late. Amirra tossed the collar on the floor. The beads slid across the smooth surface and came to a stop a few lengths from Luthrous.

"Why do you need this if you already have the recipe?" Amirra asked.

"It is a recipe, yes, but it's the stones I want," Semias said.

"Why?" Amirra asked.

"I told you so that the sword will extract the war wizard's magic with each hit and store its mighty forces until *I* unleash them on Gavin Rhill," Semias said.

Amirra cringed. She wanted Gavin Rhill destroyed, but not by Semias. The sudden realization that he was going to kill Shaz for his magic made it all too close now that she had met him and even fallen for him. She needed to get Serin out of the way and find a way to stop Semias.

"You don't have much time. They know it was me who took the collars and Jagwynn. One of them is an earth sage, and he has tracked me here," Amirra said.

A glint in her eye flashed and Semias was turned on even more. He loved her fierce spirit and was looking forward to taming the beast inside her. Amirra nearly gagged, but swallowed hard.

"I think we can buy enough time," Semias said.

"How, they are already on their way?" Amirra asked.

"I will send the Jaduuk, they will keep them busy," Semias said.

"It won't take long for them to take out your pathetic pack," Amirra said.

"I have been growing my pathetic pack while you have been making new friends and falling in love," Amirra tried to hide the surprise on her face, "Yes, I can tell you think you love him, but I assure you, he loves another, and he would only break your heart. I, on the other hand, will give you majesty that is why I will kill him," Semias said.

Semias slammed his staff into the ground and the wall behind Amirra opened. The stench of bad breath and dung hit her in the face. Her heart sank seeing the hoards and hoards of the beasts. Semias strode next to her and pulled a red lock away from her burning cheek. Amirra froze, her anger raging. She had already experienced the shadow magic consume her with the most terrifying pain and knew she had to stifle the anger and quickly or suffer the pain again. She turned her head from his hot breath breathing on her now exposed neck. Semias pointed his staff toward the entrance.

"Go and bring back the war wizard. I shall use his magic to defeat Gavin Rhill," Semias said.

The huge orc-like wolf at the front lifted his snout and howled. Drool dripped from his upright fangs and splashed onto the floor. He dug his hoofed claws into the floor and reared onto his hind legs. The packs howled in return and grunted and growled. Amirra's adrenaline raced through her body with both the sheer magnitude of the beasts as well as the terrifying fear she had for the Minca and her friends. The lead Jaduuk thundered across the cave and disappeared through the darkness.

"Aren't they magnificent?" Semias asked.

Amirra stepped away from him in time to avoid his lips touch her neck. She couldn't breathe, her chest was about to cave in. The feelings of dread overcame her and then the sting of the shadow magic begin to numb her conscience. This was the very thing she had been fighting for so long.

"You can stay here and watch Luthrous as he completes the sword and then take your place beside me," Semias said.

Amirra crumpled to the floor as Semias strolled out of the corridor and returned to Luthrous. Amirra thought of Jag. *How did she get her to follow her?* At first, she thought it was her amulet that forced her to follow, but now that she thought about it, she hadn't even said anything to her, and her amulet wouldn't be strong enough to force the handmaid of the Sun Goddess. *What have I done?* Amirra struggled with the details of why the giant cat would come willingly.

"Unless," Amirra said.

She stood up and hurried into the long corridor. Fire lit the torches on the walls as she rounded several corners and descended deeper into the mountain. The stale stink of minerals intensified as she passed the last of the hallways.

She gripped the heavy latch and slid the cold steel pin from the lock. It hit the back of the lock with a deep ping and Amirra yanked on the iron bolted door. She pulled a torch from the wall and stepped into the cell. She searched the small room for the cat but couldn't see anything. Looking for a black as night cat in a black as night room proved irritating at first. Jag opened one eye and watched Amirra circle the room. Jag blinked and stretched with a large yawn. The light caught a glimpse of her teeth and Amirra froze.

"Why did you come with me? You knew this was going to happen? You betrayed your friends?" Amirra asked.

"I did not betray my friends. I have come to help one of them," Jagwynn said.

Jagwynn's voice was soft and smooth. A soft purr echoed at the end of her words.

"What do you mean?" Amirra asked.

"You Amirra, daughter of Ada Yonsforth, are the last descendant of the Fir Bolg and heir to Akraven. The Sun Goddess needs your help to defeat Gavin Rhill," Jag said.

"You know who I am? I don't even know who I am. Semias has been my keeper most of my life," Amirra said.

"The Sun Goddess knows that, we have been watching you," Jagwynn said.

"I can't break the bonds of the shadow magic. I have tried so many times. It's not possible," Amirra said.

"It is possible, but you have to believe in yourself. The shadow can only control you if you allow it to. Your new friends can help you. And then you must return to Nitida and accept your calling as Runecaster," Jag said.

"If they will even look at me ever again with the way I tried to get between Shaz and Serin and betrayed them," Amirra said.

"Their bond is unbreakable, they have synergized their magic, and they have chosen each other. No one can stand in the way of agency. But they can help you."

"But will they?" Amirra asked.

"I guess that is up to you. What will you do to show them that they should?" Jagwynn asked.

Amirra thought of several things to help, but each time the sting of the shadow ate at her mind.

"It's no use the shadow isn't going to let me anyway," Amirra said.

"Then that is your choice," Jagwynn said.

"It's not my choice, it never has been. Ever since I was a child, I have been forced to do things against my will!" Amirra shouted.

Red hot anger surged through her, and she shook with fury. She thrashed and kicked about, letting out the anger she had held in for so long. Tears escaped and dripped down her reddened cheeks. She sank to the floor and sobbed. Jagwynn nuzzled her gently and twisted her tail around her.

"In time child, you will understand how to overcome," Jagwynn said.

32-You Don't Understand What You Think You Do

"Extract of Spoolwood," Luthrous said.

Luthrous pulled the stopper from a glass jar and dripped the contents onto the un-honed steel blade. The thick brown substance oozed over the partially shiny silver. Luthrous set the jar on the table and took a cloth and began rubbing the ointment into the metal in a circular motion. He whispered the ancient words as he rubbed. The brown goo sank into the porous material. Luthrous kept chanting and rubbing until every bit of the substance was absorbed.

"Extract of Night Woodbine," Luthrous said.

He then took another jar and poured the contents onto the blade, and with the same precision, he chanted a new set of ancient words while he worked the substance into the ore. After several more jars,

Luthrous came to the powders. He pulled the string from around the pouch and poured the powder of Mountain Hops into a long trough and returned the pouch. Luthrous took out a pumice stone and grabbed a handful of the powder and spread it over the blade. He gripped the pumice stone and ground the powder over the rough steel. Sweat soon dripped from his brow and he wiped it with his sleeve. With each stroke, he chanted yet another incantation. Each time the grinding stone moved across the metal it became smoother than before, and with each pass the magic of the runes embedded deeper and deeper.

Luthrous turned the blade over and worked the other side in the same manner. This part of the process will take days to ingrain each of the spells into the blade, and Luthrous understood this. Luthrous pulled the blade out of the trough and poured more brown ointment and rubbed it in. Then the next jar of goo and repeated the process until the blade and hilt had been polished and ground to a shine so smooth, he saw his perfect reflection. It surprised him that this body he was now in actually looked like his soul. He studied every bit of the blade to ensure there were absolutely no flaws. After he was satisfied, he rested the blade in a sword cradle. The excitement was fueling his frame, and he had no idea how much time had passed.

Luthrous set the jars aside and pulled another pouch from the edge of the table. He pulled a metal bowl from under the worktable and set it on a hollowed-out stone that was next to the table. He lit the contents of the bowl on fire with a small torch and watched the flames take hold. The orange flames deepened to a blood-red, and he took a flat black onyx stone and put it in the fire. He rubbed his stiff hands over the fire as it heated up the stone. The red of the fire glowed on his face and he felt the tingle from the new magical elements it made as they combined. The black onyx turned red as the Honor Runestone element became infused with the very essence of the Kingdom of the God of Glory stone.

Luthrous waited until the stone was no longer solid and gripped it with long metal tongs. He took a long brown strand of hair and twisted it around the soft ore. He then moved the melted ore onto the hilt of the blade and rested it carefully, making sure it lined up perfectly with the edge of the pommel. A hissing sound spurted out from the hot ore hitting the cold of the steel. He traded the tongs for a very thick cloth and wrapped his hands like gloves. He began to smooth the onyx around the pommel, shaping it into the firm grip for the holder.

Even the pommel had a magical element. In fact, it was one of the most important. This is how the sword determines its purpose. By sensing the intent of the holder, the blade will comply with their demands. This was done on the original sword by adding the birthstone placement. Semis wanted only himself to command the sword so there were no birthstones allowed, but instead, Luthrous was forced to fuse Semias's hair into the hilt. Luthrous understood this is where he would have to be very careful in his word choices. He needed to add a loophole to make the sword accept Semias and do his bidding, but not be limited to only Semias. He was bound by the laws of the Runes, and this was a forbidden rule in which would make a weapon overpowered.

Luthrous remembered he could add an 'exception' rune but struggled with which exception to use. He could use the exception of 'good vs evil' but then that would mean Semias couldn't use it. He could use the exception of 'intent', but that too would exclude Semias, because it was obvious what his intent was. Then he remembered the exception of 'originality'. This would work, it would allow Semias to use the sword on anyone or anything except the 'original' sword, then it would *lose* its power with each hit instead of extracting its powers. Semias's sword would eventually yield to the Honor Blade and become as a normal blade. But when fighting anything else it would be as the original, exacting the unforgiving wound on its opponent.

Luthrous reached into the back of his mind and searched for the correct words. He imagined them come forward in his mind as he smoothed and maneuvered the cooling onyx. He pulled off the mittens and wrapped his worn hands around the hilt. He spoke the words that played out in his mind several times as he caressed and rubbed the new hilt. Over and over and louder and louder he chanted. Energy formed between his hands and the sword, and it grew stronger and stronger. The energy created a level of heat that was almost too much for his skin, and he winced with discomfort. The heat worked up his arms and then into his chest.

A soothing mist carried the power of the ancient words through his body and into the sword. When there was no more room in the blade, he stopped chanting and stood quietly in the dim cavern. His chest heaved with the surge of energy and sweat crested his brows. As the energy dissipated, he peeled his hands from the sword and rested it back in the cradle. He sat on a small chair next to the table and rested his head. He was finished with the blade itself, but now he needed to bond it to the sheath. A sharp pang hit his stomach, and he realized it had been some time since he ate last. He left the cavern and returned to his bed chambers for some food and much-needed rest.

A loud clack echoed and startled Luthrous awake. Luthrous rubbed his eyes and crawled off the bed. The green flames danced around the room as he pulled his cloak tightly around his neck. He yawned and sulked down the hall. The sword was nearly complete. All it needed was the rune to unify it to the sheath and the 'Words of Power" rune. The power of words was the mightiest of forces, even more so than the elements themselves. Fire can be tamed by water, air by earth, earth by fire.

But words can never be taken back, they hurt deeper than any wound can go. Words are complete and can be remembered forever. The power of a few words can bring a nation to its knees. A King to his demise, a lover to become a hater. It was his plan to add the words of power, *Love, Hate, Forgiveness, Appreciation, and Resentment*. This would allow the user to access the desires of their heart. But Semias had learned about this rune and forbade Luthrous from adding it. The words were too strong not to add. He had to come up with another way to add the rune. He had been thinking diligently through every single rune spell he knew. He stood over his notebook and flipped through the pages carefully. A small section of the top corner tucked into the binding caught his eye, and he pushed on the binding to flatten it a little more. He studied the markings and as he went to turn the page, the symbol lined up with the smudges from the other page. A new symbol emerged into his understanding. *Agency-* the power of choice but with the effects of consequence. It would be perfect, it would still allow the user to use the sword based on their choices, like the Power of Words Rune, but it would exact the consequence of that choice on the user, not the victim. *Semias will use it to defeat Gavin, but in doing so it will destroy him.* Luthrous thought.

Luthrous sketched the new symbol onto the page and wrote its definition, uses, and understanding. He practiced several times in his mind how to exact the words with the power of the universe's energy. He rubbed his hands together to warm them up and then stepped to the side of the sword. He drew the new symbol in the air repeatedly several times until a slight glow began to shine where his finger had drawn it. He rolled his hands around the outside of the symbol until the light was solid color on the entire symbol. He lowered the glowing energy while chanting its name until the symbol rested under the last. He continued to chant quietly and then louder, over and over he repeated the repetitions and loudness until the symbol sank into the steel.

Luthrous relaxed as a quiet calm raced through his trembling form. He had done it. He had found a way around the shadow magic. He now fathomed the idea that he could die a second time, and rest in the place of the good, for he had withstood the evils of the shadow once more. He repeated the process for the last rune that united the sword to the sheath. Luthrous softened his chanting as the symbol began to sink into the blade. The symbol, however, wouldn't sink to its core. Luthrous closed his eyes and chanted with more diligence and intensity. He opened his eyes and found that the symbol hadn't changed. He tried three more times, but each time it was the same result. Luthrous returned to his notes and verified that he was using the correct one.

He examined the sword and realized the sapphire stone he used was not the correct one. He frantically searched the collar and couldn't find it. His stomach sank and he almost wretched. The soft whoosh of Semias's cloak rounded the corner and Luthrous gasped. Semias picked up the fine weapon and twisted it around. He admired the shine, the fine edge honed into it, and the smooth dips and peaks of the symbols until he came to the second to the last one. The pit in Luthrous's stomach grew heavy, and he slunk toward the table.

"What is this? I commanded you not to use the Power of Words symbol," Semias sneered.

"And I didn't. That is not the symbol. Here, look for yourself," Luthrous said.

Luthrous pointed to the symbols in the notebook. Semias compared the two and glared.

"Then what is it?" Semias asked.

Luthrous knew the shadow magic would force him to tell anyway, so he explained his new glyph.

"It's the Rune of Agency, it means that you will be given the power to inflict as much harm as you desire," Luthrous said.

"Didn't the Honor Blade have that as well?"

"Well, yes, but that was with the Words of Power rune, which you forbade, so this one will allow you the same without the words of Love and Forgiveness which counter the evil you desire," Luthrous said.

"How can I trust you?" Semias asked.

"I have no power of my own, you have enslaved me to your will, how could you not trust me?" Luthrous asked.

"Then it is complete?" Semias asked.

A jolt in the earth rippled through the cave and jostled them about. Luthrous scurried under the table and Semias steadied himself against the wall.

"What is happening?" Luthrous asked.

"It is time for me to make a change of scenery," Semias said.

"Where will we be going?" Luthrous asked.

Semias slid the new sword into the Honor Blade sheath and then drew it back out. An unsettling scrape wrinkled Luthrous's ears. A realization overcame him, as did a certain peace that his time had come, and he stood up tall. The brand-new blade whipped through the flesh of his body, releasing his spirit from its prison. He floated in front of Semias and waited for him to utter the words that would send him back to the realm of the past.

"You don't understand what you think you do, and it will be to your undoing. The war wizard has more power than you ever will, and you will suffer the pains you inflict on others," Luthrous said.

Semias shouted the last of the words and Luthrous disappeared back into the past where he came from. Another jolt shook the cavern, sending shards crashing to the ground. Semias hurried over the shaking ground, dodging chunks of rock as he ran.

33-Which Is Sunrise Yellow By The Way

The mountain grumbled from the depths below and a sharp jarring sent Amirra stumbling out the cell. The door slammed shut as Amirra fell against the wall. The earth cracked open only a few lengths from Amirra, and a foul gasp of air escaped the cracked and crumbling floor. The few torches on the walls of the corridor blew out with a whoosh. Blackness gripped her senses, and she froze. She fumbled through her cloak and found a flick stick. She felt her surroundings and found a torch. She struck the steel stick against the rough stone, and a few sparks landed on the oil-soaked cloth. She flicked it several more times, getting more and more frustrated that the blasted thing wouldn't light. She moved it several times, trying to shield it from the now constant breeze coming from the depths of the earth. The torch finally lit, and she put the flick stick into her robe. She held out the torch and examined the corridor. A crack separated Amirra from the other side of the hallway. She moved close to the edge and peered over. The crack was dark and Amirra couldn't see the bottom. Her hair blew around her face and she tried to gather it from flipping all around. She tucked it into her hood and turned to face the cell Jagwynn was in. She unlatched the lock and pulled the heavy iron gate, but it was stuck. She heaved several times, but the mountain had settled on the gates frame, locking it permanently.

"Jagwynn, are you in there?" Amirra asked.

Jag opened her eyes and blinked. The brightness of their yellow sent a spike of fear-based adrenaline through Amirra's frame.

"It would seem I will be in here for quite some time," Jagwynn said.

"I'll get you out," Amirra said.

"You will have to find Shaz and have him melt the metal," Jagwynn said.

"I can't," Amirra said.

"Why not?"

"There is a large crack in the corridor, I can't make it across on my own. I was hoping you could leap across it," Amirra said.

Jagwynn sensed her words cracking under hidden tears.

"Well, then I guess we are in a quandary,"

"It's all my fault," Amirra said.

"Yes, it is," Jagwynn said.

"That's lovely that someone else thinks I'm horrible too," Amirra said.

"It doesn't have anything to do with what I think. You have already made up your mind as to who you are. Nothing I say can change that. You will simply have to decide you're something or someone else. What that is, is completely up to you," Jagwynn said.

Amirra slouched to the floor and put her face in her hands. Jagwynn closed her eyes and rested her head on her paws.

"I don't know who I am. I don't know what I like or don't like. I have never even been asked what my favorite color is, which is sunrise yellow, by the way."

"That is a wonderful color. That says a lot about you," Jagwynn said.

"What does it say about me?" Amirra asked.

"That you desire to be free, that if you could overpower the shadow in your heart, you would live with joy and happiness," Jagwynn said.

"You get all that from a color? But how can I, I am a horrible person," Amirra said.

"You are not horrible, have you done horrible things, maybe, but you have also been required to do so. If it were your choice, would you have done them?" Jagwynn asked.

Amirra sagged under her hood and covered her face with her bruised hands.

"I guess I don't have to be a horrible person," Amirra admitted. Jagwynn purred. "But what can I do to change all the horrible things I've done. To good people, to people that didn't deserve anything."

The image of the red-haired woman riding the Wyvern surfaced.

"Now, that is someone you can pattern your life around," Jagwynn said.

"Who?" Amirra asked.

"The red-haired woman in your dreams. Her name is Ada, the queen of the Fire Wyvern's," Jagwynn said.

Amirra jumped up and spun around.

"You know who she is? How? How could you tell she was in my dreams? Who are you? Nitida told me I am her daughter, but I don't believe her," Amirra said.

"Yes, because I have met her, I have been sending you those dreams from the Sun Goddess. She wants you to know who you are, you are precious to her," Jagwynn answered.

"How long ago did she live?" Amirra asked.

"Over three hundred rotations ago. As a descendant of the Fir Bolg, and keepers of the Fire Wyverns. You have been kept hidden by the Velshari to keep you from the Velshari," Jagwynn said.

"That seems a bit risky, but kept me from what?" Amirra asked.

"Gavin Rhill."

"But Semias is one of his closest necromancers. I am sure he knows who I am."

"Semias is so deliriously struck with greed and power he can't even see past his own nose. The Sun Goddess has an extensive task for you, one that will require you to make a very hard decision. One of intense pain and sorrow, but will have an equal reward of joy and happiness. She needed you to see the worst in humanity so that you can also see the best in them," Jagwynn said.

"You're such a silly cat. I have no idea what you mean," Amirra said.

"Let's focus then, on getting us out of here," Jagwynn said.

34-How Bad Is It?

Shaz fought the anger surging in his chest. It wasn't so much that Amirra did what she did, but that he didn't see it coming, after all, it was him that told Serin one didn't have to have magic to be dangerous, and he hadn't figured out what she was so confused about. I guess now he knew. He tightened his belt and slipped the sword into the sheath. Shaz let out a deep breath and watched it create steam in the cold air. He slipped on his cloak but didn't think he would need it. Serin layered several tunics and the special coat the Minca women had made her and rubbed her hands together before slipping her cold hands into her gloves. Serin touched Shaz's arm, and he smiled at her.

"There was no way of knowing she was going to do this," Serin said.

His body was warm, and she wanted to snuggle into his heat.

"It doesn't matter, anyway. What I can't figure out is, how did she get Jag to go with her?" Shaz asked.

"Jagwynn has many secrets, maybe she knows something we don't," Serin said.

"How can you think like that? Always giving everyone the benefit of the doubt," Shaz asked.

"I guess it's because if people judged me by my tattoos, oh wait, they do, then I would feel bad, oh wait, I do," Serin said.

Shaz gazed at the floor.

"I'm sorry, I do understand how that feels, being the only one with blond hair growing up. I guess I forget that it's alright for others to hurt too," Shaz said.

"Come, on, let's just go get Jag and your collar back," Serin said.

Shaz squeezed her hand and kissed her.

"Well, things have definitely changed between you two," Turkill said with half a huff.

"You ready?" Shaz asked.

Shaz took the flap of their hut from Turkill and held it for Serin. They made their way toward the center of the village and watched Riddick nearly fall out of the little hut they put him in.

"I can't believe you even fit in there," Shaz said.

"You and me both," Riddick said.

Riddick straightened his clothes.

"I'm glad to have you here, Riddick," Shaz said.

"Aye, but don't go getting all soft or nothin," Shaz smiled. "So, you two a thing now?" Riddick asked.

Shaz gripped Serin's hand and nodded. Turkill hurumpft. The three laughed.

"I've mapped out the way based on Riddick's description of the faded energy," the Chief said.

"It shouldn't take too long to get there," Shaz said.

"Without Jag, Turkill and Ladtwig won't go as fast," Serin said.

"We'll take up the rear and make sure we're not followed," Turkill said.

"If we don't run into any trouble, we should be there before lunch," Shaz said.

"It's over a day's journey," Riddick said.

"Not the way we travel," Shaz said with a glint in his eye.

Riddick's brows raised, and he studied Shaz. Shaz nodded and Serin threw her arms around herself and cast her air buff on Shaz, Turkill, and Ladtwig. Riddick watched with complete fascination as their bodies lifted from the ground. Serin again called her magic and cast it onto Riddick. The sudden weightlessness made his tall, lean figure off balance. He threw out his arms to steady himself and took several steps backward to keep from falling. His feet didn't touch the ground, and it was like he was stepping on the gooey jungle floor again.

"What in the world is this?" Riddick asked.

"Magic, speed!" Shaz said.

Shaz loved this next part, the part where he digs his toes into the air and shoots out of sight within seconds.

"How does it work?" Riddick asked.

"You just run," Shaz said.

"Like this," Turkill said.

Turkill dug his toes in deep and shoved off the ground. His little frame lurched into a dead run but with no resistance, and Ladtwig followed, Shaz was surprised to see how fast they were and readied himself. Riddick lowered his center of gravity and sucked in a deep breath. He lunged forward and felt the magic shove his body forward. There was no resistance against the earth, and his long strides covered three times their usual length. Shaz shot out after him with Serin right behind him. It wasn't long before Riddick was at ease and moving effortlessly over the rough jungle floor. Riddick slowed a few times to affirm directions. The mountain grew in size the closer they came to it. The wind had blown in and made trenches and drifts of soot, some higher than their heads. They moved through the high trenches, leaving little eddies of soot and disrupting the smoothed walls.

"Stop," Shaz said.

He dug his feet into the air pocket and skidded to a stop.

"What is it?" Serin asked.

Shaz sniffed the air and wrinkled his nose.

"Jaduuk," Shaz said.

"Oh, great. Just great," Turkill said.

"How many?" Serin asked.

"A lot," Shaz said.

"What are Jaduuk?" Riddick asked.

"You'll find out soon enough," Shaz said.

Shaz ripped the sword from the sheath and Serin pulled her bow. Turkill pulled a dart from his pouch and bit it with his front teeth. Riddick pulled his ax from his back and touched the soft dirt with his hand. Ladtwig pulled his dart gun and loaded a dart. The earths' energy transferred into Riddick's mind and gave him a mental picture of what was coming after them. Riddick stood up instantly, his pale face even paler.

"There is no way we are going to take all these on," Riddick said.

"We will have to, we can't let them make it to the Minca," Serin said.

The first beast powered through the soot, sending it soaring through the air like a blizzard. Still enchanted with Serin's wind walk, Shaz stuck his boot into the crook of a broken tree trunk and peeled away. His body soared into the air as he threw the blade over his head.

Yelling at the top of his lungs, he brought the blade down with incredible speed and strength. The blade sliced through the thick skull like a melon. Shaz pulled the blade up and around his body in a side strike and with a twist at his waist, he carried the blade through the chest of another.

Serin found a covered spot and opened her arrow case. She knocked an arrow and aimed at the first beast's eye. She had learned that their skulls were too thick for her arrows to do much damage, and this had played useful in the past. She let the arrow loose and knocked another without waiting to see if the last had hit its mark. Serin was confident that the wind would take her arrows to their exact target. Turkill and Ladtwig also knew they had to be exact in their aim and knew that their poisonous darts did the most damage if they hit the back of their throats. Turkill leaped onto a branch and huddled against the trunk, waiting for the beasts to make their battle cries. Ladtwig ran to the other side and found a stump big enough to hide his body. As soon as one would open its mouth the slightest, they loaded the darts into the shooter and exhaled hard. The dart exited the skinny tubes with a burst and sunk deep into the back of a Jaduuk's throat.

The beast gagged and stammered around, knocking into the creature next to it. The two continued to take several down and Riddick had to leap over the creatures. Riddick swung his ax around, rolling it over the top of his hand and back into his palm. The speed the ax created as it circled gave him extra power. He brought the ax up and sunk it into the chin of a beast and rolled toward the ground. The ax yanked the beast as though caught by a fishhook and slammed into the earth on its back. Riddick gripped the handle and yanked the blade out and buried his dagger into its heart. Shaz rolled under ghastly hooves and sliced the tendons on the back of the legs of another.

The creature hollered in pain and tumbled to the ground. Riddick landed his ax into its skull. The stench of sour blood wreaked havoc on their senses and they found it hard not to feel the need to wretch. Serin now felt the tingle of her air spell dissipate and tucked her bow between her knees. She called the air magic and sent a re-boost to Shaz, Riddick, Turkill, and Ladtwig. A burst of dreaded adrenaline shot through her as she noticed she was running out of arrows. Turkill jumped over an oncoming Jaduuk's blade and grabbed the tree trunk to keep from falling off. He tried to reach a branch above him, but he was too short.

Serin waved her hand, and the air boosted him up. He climbed onto the branch and loaded another dart. He too was running out. He looked out over the distance at the beasts that were as far as he could see. A lump formed in his throat, then sank into his stomach. He whistled and Shaz took the head off a smaller beast and then found Turkill. Turkill tried to yell to him, but the noise of the hooves against the ground was so intense that he hardly heard himself. Shaz turned around in time to put his hand out and, with the heat of his fire element, let out a torch of fire. The beast yelped and howled as the fire consumed its flesh.

Riddick stomped his foot against the ground, and several deep holes opened, swallowing many creatures at once. Shaz sliced through one beast and sent several bursts of fire at one time at another. The flame balls ripped across the darkening sky and drenched the beasts on impact. A massive Jaduuk warrior caught Shaz on the side with his ax, sending a jolt of pain to his brain. Shaz recoiled and gripped his hip. Bright red blood covered his hand. Serin stood out from her hiding spot and sent a burst of healing magic toward Shaz.

The magic tingled his senses and his brain forgot the pain, and the blood crusted up. Shaz grabbed the beast's long fang and yanked himself onto its back. The beast squirmed and tried to throw him off, but Shaz held on tight until he pulled the Honor Blade across its neck. Shaz lifted his legs and leaped off before the beast hit the ground and plowed several lengths of dirt into the air. Riddick grabbed a dead branch and made the wood grow to more than three times its original size with a pointed tip. He slammed the bottom end into the ground and released it. The tip skewered the loins of a beast as it ran full speed toward Riddick.

Riddick grabbed several more broken branches and repeated the spikes until he couldn't find any more. Serin noticed that her air spell didn't only make them run fast, but they moved faster, swung faster, leaped higher and farther. Ladtwig jumped out from the stump as a beast plowed over it. He landed on a splinter of wood and it sunk into his thigh. He called out in pain and Serin waved her hands in his direction. As he hobbled toward a soot bank, the magic pushed the spike out and the blood crusted to make a temporary covering. Turkill loaded his last dart and waited as one of the bigger beasts barreled through the bodies of its fellow warriors. Turkill knew he would have only one chance to take it down. He watched and nervously licked the end of his shooter. The beast's dark eyes caught sight of him, and he turned toward Turkill.

It's lower lip puckered up over its large, sharp fang. Turkill narrowed in on the mouth and watched as several sharp teeth appeared. He sucked in a breath and blew hard and fast. The dart ripped out and whizzed through the air. It barely cleared the teeth in time to sink deep into the back of the throat. The beast gagged but didn't stop as the others had. Turkill had spent time making his poison darts stronger than ever before. By watching the first beasts he knew it stopped them from attacking but it would still take time to kill them.

Turkill leaped from the tree and rolled through the soot. He came to a standing position and darted over toward Serin. Riddick found a vine around a log and pulled it. He remembered the vines in the jungle and imagined this vine just like it. The vine grew in strength and length. He imagined it becoming two vines and then three and more. He threw one of the new vines in his hand around the neck of a Jaduuk and yanked. It tightened around its throat and the beast recoiled and fell to the ground.

Riddick imagined the vines around him attack the Jaduuk and several green twisted vines surged from the earth, pinning the Jaduuk to the ground. Shaz took the idea from Riddick and sent a rolling wall of flames between him and the next wave of Jaduuk. The force of the fire blew Shaz's hair around. Riddick pulled back from the heat and covered his face. Sweat rolled over his soot-covered skin, and he wiped it away before it reached his eyes. Serin sent a burst of healing magic to Riddick, calming the heat in his skin. He smiled with the comfort it gave and waved at her. She smiled and ducked back into her hiding place. She wished she could fight more, but her healing magic was more important, and she needed to conserve her strength. The ground shook and Shaz and Riddick searched around.

"What was that?" Shaz asked.

Riddick touched the earth.

"Very, very, very large creatures," Riddick said.

"What are you saying exactly?" Shaz asked.

"How else can I say very large creatures?" Riddick asked.

A sizzling, popping crackle grew in their ears.

"Duck," yelled Shaz.

Riddick and Shaz leaped out of the way as a ball of explosives careened past them. The ball exploded just on the other side of the firewall. Shaz let down the fire enough to see more than twenty beasts writhing on the ground from the explosion. Shaz searched the direction from where the ball came from and was amazed at one of the Minca's mammoths. A stately platform rested on its back, with several Minca sitting strategically around the little cannons. One Minca held the cannon while two others loaded and aimed them. The wick was lit, and several more exploding balls sizzled through the air. Shaz jumped for joy with a hoot. Tomos from the portal gave him a salute.

Shaz signaled to Riddick to move toward the edges of the firewall. Riddick made his way to one end and Shaz maneuvered toward the other. Turkill and Ladtwig jumped for joy at the sight of their clanmates coming in droves. Turkill slipped out of the tree and hurried to meet up with a group of warriors and refresh his supply of poisonous darts. He led them on little crusades around the battlefield, directing a few other captains on how to take on the Jaduuk. They targeted the leader of each hoard first. Turkill had noticed that they fought in groups and there was always a leader, and the pack would become somewhat disorganized when they were without their leader.

They continued to fight the oncoming hoards with Serin buffing and healing. Babbesh and Fionte had arrived and instructed several other women with Mrs. Bailey's ointment, bandages and Serin's rain cloud and was scurrying around as needed. As more of the mammoths arrived, the Minca pyrotechnics arranged their blasts to take out as many beasts, both in the front and in the middle of hoards. The day had long passed, and the night was in full force. Shaz and Riddick used their magic senses to detect where the beasts were. Shaz sent a blast of fire into the air over the top of a group of Jaduuk, and the Minca aimed and lit the cannons.

The battle raged through the night. Blasts of fire and explosions ripped through the countryside. The earth opened each time Riddick stomped. Even with Serin's magic, they began to tire. The Minca in the front pulled back and let the mammoths from the back move forward while they made more bombs. Even with all the explosives and fire, many of the Jaduuk broke through their stronghold and ran through the Minca warriors. The warriors leaped out of the way, but some didn't get far enough.

Turkill grabbed the end of a long piece of rope and darted in front of two Jaduuk running straight for them. He rounded a stump, and another warrior grabbed hold of the other end. The warrior tied it to a tree and leaped away from the ricochet, the impact of the beast tripping over it gave. Turkill still holding on was jerked backward several lengths. He cried out as a sharp rock sliced his back. The impact tore through the skin and kinked his spine. His body fell with a slump. Serin hurried to him, sliding under a Jaduuk that Shaz was about to impale. She rounded the array of dead trees and slid to a stop next to Turkill. Serin slapped her hands together and rubbed them fiercely.

"Hold still," Serin said.

"I can't even move. My body won't respond," Turkill said.

A bright blue ball of magic formed around her hands and her tattoos glowed a deep silvery purple. She gripped his shoulders and shot a burst into his frame. He sank softly with the sudden release of pain and let Serin roll him onto his side.

"You have to make sure you keep breathing, I need your energy to stay strong," Serin said.

She moved her fingers like she was weaving thread and the magic obeyed. The magic gripped the innermost layers of tissue and pulled them together. Another strand plugged an artery and singed it closed. Serin focused on her fingers, moving the tissues and tendons back into place and singeing the bleeding vessels as briskly as possible. She had gotten so good at stitching up wounds that she hardly had to think about it. With one hand she pulled away from the strings and formed a ball of water that she then dripped over the wound as she stitched.

The bones in his spine were twisted, so she let go of the magic strings and with her magic, gripped the bones and twisted. With a loud pop, the bones rested back in their proper place. Turkill lay there with his eyes closed, trying to keep his breathing constant, not wanting to think about what was going on. He knew that without her he would be dead. His dedication to her was now that of repaying her for his life.

"How are you doing?" Serin asked.

"You tell me," Turkill said.

"You're going to be fine," Serin said.

"How bad is it?" Turkill asked.

"Well, you will have one gnarly scar no one will ever be able to compete with if that makes you feel any better," Serin said.

She leaned over and watched a small smile creep to the corners of his mouth.

"Can you feel your toes?" Serin asked.

Turkill wriggled his toes and smiled. He nodded.

"Good, then you're almost done," Serin said.

Serin smoothed the last layer of skin and slowed her stitches. Being as precise as possible in the middle of a battlefield, she closed the last layer. His tan skin grew together, forming a scar that ran halfway down his back. Serin helped him stand. Turkill wrapped his arms around her neck and gave her a tight squeeze. She kissed his cheek, and he blushed.

"No one, especially Shaz, will ever find out about that," Turkill said.

"Yes, sir," Serin said with a grin.

Turkill garbed his usual scowl and ran back to the warriors. Serin looked for cover and found a boulder with a small lip on the underneath side. She hurried toward the boulder but didn't see a Jaduuk's arm aimed at her gut. It hit her right in the center and sent her flying backward. The impact of her body hitting the ground knocked the wind from her lungs. She coughed and sputtered as she rolled over backward. Her insides were as if on fire and going to burst out of her skin. Tears filled her eyes and drained as instantly as they formed. Her brain tried to interpret what she was going through, but it hit a wall and stopped on intense pain. A series of war howls echoed around her as Turkill and a group of Minca warriors, now armed with swords, raced toward the Jaduuk.

The beast lowered itself onto all fours and ran toward the warriors. One of the warriors, from the northern clans, scurried around another and launched himself. He gripped the fang of the beast and threw all his body weight, which was a bit more sizable than Turkill's people, toward the ground. It was enough weight to knock the Jaduuk off course and sideline it. Another Northman rammed into its side, helping the first bring it to the ground. Several Minca of both clans descended with their swords. The creature fought hard, but there were too many Minca and it surrendered to its injuries. Turkill ran to Serin and helped her to a safe spot. She tried to bring air to her lungs, but they didn't want to respond. Dread filled her mind, and she began to panic. Shaz sensed her distress and slashed the hind legs as he darted around a Jaduuk, bringing it to its knees. Shaz skidded to a stop next to Serin.

"What happened?" Shaz asked.

"She got the wind knocked out of her, but we took the beast down," Turkill said.

"I..I..I can't... breathe," Serin gasped.

Shaz put his hand on her chest and felt the disrupted energy inside her.

"I haven't learned how to heal you," Shaz said.

He cursed to himself, *I need to know how to do this stuff.*

"Ju...st..," Serin tried to speak.

Serin grabbed his hand and said in her mind. *Just send me your energy and I'll heal myself.*

Shaz heard her command and pulled his magic from his core and sent it through his arm and into her. The Northman Minca watched in partial horror and partial amazement as the colors danced around his torso and arm and settled into Serin's body. Her breathing became smooth and regular and she sighed.

"Thank you," Serin said.

"You will have to teach me to heal you when this is all over," Shaz said.

"Just don't let me get hurt and you won't have to," Serin said with a gentle smile.

Shaz knew she wasn't serious, but he took it to heart and declared that he would never let her get hurt again. How he was going to do that he didn't know, but he was going to die trying. Serin watched his face contort through all the emotions of his thoughts.

"You better go kill a few more Jaduuk, just to make you feel better," Serin said.

Shaz smiled.

"Go, we got this," Turkill said.

"I know you do, little warriors," Shaz said.

The men stood with a level of pride they hadn't had in a long time.

35-Try And Take It From Me

The night turned into day and they had finally overtaken enough of the Jaduuk that Shaz, Serin, Riddick, Turkill, and Ladtwig agreed they could leave the Minca to finish the rest and hurried out after Amirra. They followed the original path but had to make a few detours to avoid the Jaduuk. The crew decided on taking a different path up to the entrance in case it was rigged and climbed the backside of the mountain's ragged edges. Serin buffed again with her air-walk, which allowed them to keep a slight buffer between the sharpness of the rocks and their skin, which helped but not entirely.

Riddick was the first to make it to the top, and he carefully scanned with his earth magic while his eyes made a full sweep of the entrance. Even though the sun had been out for half the day, being on the backside of the mountain was still fairly dark. Riddick nodded, it was safe, and they climbed over the ridge. Shaz gripped Ladtwig and Turkill's arms and heaved them over easily. They scurried to the side of the rock face and maneuvered over the uneven surface. It wasn't long before they reached the opening.

A stiff staleness of animal dung, they supposed was from the Jaduuk, met them as they rounded the edge of the opening. Serin created her air bubble around their faces, the same as she had in the dungeons of Ebassia, and they all gave her a thumbs up.

"Do you sense anyone?" Shaz asked.

Riddick shook his head and took several long strides into the corridor. He slipped up against the wall and searched again. The others followed, letting Riddick guide them into the cavern. The once marvelous temple sat in complete ruins. Shaz noted several similarities to the Chantry and decided it was also a temple of magic learning. Several of the markings, however, were different, and he understood them to be the markings of the Velshari. He couldn't decide if it was overtaken or created by the Velshari. Either way, he didn't like what he was seeing.

"I don't see anything," Turkill said.

Shaz threw a fireball into the ceiling of the cave and a flash of light lit it up for several seconds. There was a corridor on the other side and the ancient rune circle engraved in the floor. To the side, they noticed another pathway, but not like the first. It was rough and looked as though it had been carved after the initial creation. A sizable rock blocked most of the entrance.

"I guess we go that way," Riddick said.

Shaz threw another fireball into the ceiling and Serin fed it with air, making it last long enough for them to cross the expansive cave. Shaz found a torch sitting in a sconce on the wall with his forehead and lit it as he rubbed the now bruise on his head. They moved down the corridor, stopping and listening every few steps. Several lengths into the hallway a stifling heat radiated, making it hard to breathe.

Shaz held his arm out and braced Serin against the wall. Riddick hushed the Minca, and they rested up against the warm stone.

"What do you suppose it is?" Serin asked.

"Not sure, but I'm getting a really bad feeling about it," Shaz said.

"How much trouble can that girl be?" Turkill asked.

"It's not her, there's someone else," Shaz said.

"That's comforting," Turkill said.

"Maybe it's that Semias person she referred to," Serin said.

"Probably, but what does that mean, I wonder?" Shaz said.

"Trouble," Riddick said.

Shaz scooted along the wall until he reached the edge of the opening.

"Come, in. Come in," Semias said. Shaz waved to stay where they were and stepped out from the doorway. "The Sheath has brought you here, but it can belong to only one," Semias said.

Semias's long-hallowed face barely showed under the darkness of the red robe. His black eyes reflected the small flame that came from Shaz's torch.

"We haven't been introduced," Shaz said.

"That's true, my name is Semias," Semias said.

"Now that we know each other, I will have my sheath now," Shaz said.

The sheath sat strapped against Semias's leg. His black leather trousers were tight to his form and reflected a hint of the fire.

"Oh, Shaz, son of Reinholt, how I have waited for this. Longer than you could ever know," Semias said.

"And it shows. You should get out more, you look awful," Shaz said.

Serin cringed, she knew this wasn't going to go well, but Riddick snickered. Serin shot him a glare, then Turkill and Ladtwig snickered.

"Tonight, the dreams of the Shadow come to an end," Semias said.

"Shaz, I don't think he's messing around," Serin whispered.

"What does the Shadow dream of?" Shaz asked.

"You know what it dreams of. You have witnessed it for yourself," Semias said.

"I'm only here to get my sheath, so why don't you give it to me, and I'll be on my way," Shaz said.

"Why don't you have your friends come out and try to take it from me," Semias said.

Shaz gulped. He should have known the shadow would know they were there. Riddick stepped passed Serin and stopped next to Shaz.

"And the others," Semias said.

Shaz found it unsettling that the haggard man was finding joy in all this. Serin and the Minca stepped out from the shadows.

"Now, this is a party," Semias said.

He lifted his arm and conjured a ball of fire and shot it across the room. Everyone ducked and leaped out of the way. Shaz leaped into a roll and came to his feet and pulled the sword from the sheath. Riddick reached over his shoulder and grabbed his battle-ax that was secured to his back while the Minca pulled their darts. Serin searched the room for a place to hide but couldn't find anything.

"I need a place to hide," Serin said.

Riddick gripped his mind and yanked the side of the mountain into a hole big enough for her to slip into. Serin smiled and slipped into the darkness. Shaz took the first swing. The Honor Blade collided with Semias' sword, and the ricochet threw Shaz's arm backward. A surge of power ripple into Shaz's arm and into his chest. Semias cackled with excitement at Shaz's seeming loss of strength. Semias swung and Shaz blocked with another recoil of absorbed strength. Semias's eagerness to kill Shaz gleamed in his eyes, but after dishing several blows, Semias's expression turned sour. Shaz started to feel as though his body was not strong enough to contain all the power he was absorbing from Semias. Shaz launched a side strike and Semias's eyes widened with fear as he felt yet another drain of his own magic. Semias blocked Riddick's hit and felt nothing. Riddick rounded through the strike and swung his ax back up and readied for another strike.

Ladtwig and Turkill split in opposite directions and rounded the edges of the room. Turkill loaded his dart gun and sucked in. With his lips tightly around the end, he exhaled quickly. The poisoned needle shot across the room with lightning speed, but Semias sent a blast of fire that consumed it and the ashes fell to the ground. Turkill scowled and rounded a stone and then crouched behind it. Ladtwig had made it almost behind Semias and lowered onto the ground. He slipped from one stone to another until he was close to the sheath.

Shaz parried back and gripped the hilt tightly and threw a rounded side strike. Semias threw his blade out and blocked again. The power raced into Shaz's head, making him woozy. The room swayed slightly, and he stepped back. He steadied himself and scoured his brain for an explanation but couldn't find any. Riddick pulled his hand closed, and a crack echoed around the room. Shards of rocks ripped from the walls and flew over Turkill's head directly at Semias. Semias bent over backward at the waist and allowed the fragments to smash into the wall behind him. Ladtwig covered his head as the debris crashed onto him. Ladtwig shook the dust and rocks off himself. Semias took a step back toward Ladtwig, and Ladtwig reached up and grabbed the leather strap that secured the bottom of the sheath to Semias's leg. The band loosed, and the sheath swung freely. Ladtwig tried to reach for the top strap, but Semias flipped the blade and sliced Ladtwig's arm. Ladtwig recoiled from the pain and scurried back to the wall.

Serin stepped out and threw a burst of healing magic at Ladtwig. The pain eased, but the bleeding only slowed. Serin shot another blast at him, but it did nothing. Fear sank into her chest and her heart beat quickly. Shaz felt her energy shift and found Ladtwig holding his arm.

"Ah, so it does work as Luthrous promised. My new blade bestows the never-ending wound when pulled from the sheath. Which means that your blade is a plain old sword with no powers at all," Semias said.

Riddick slung his ax at Semias, who caught the ax on the hilt and ripped it away from Riddick. Riddick stepped closer to Semias and with his other fist punched Semias square in the face. Semias flew backward, stunned by the sudden feeling of pain rippling across his face. Riddick gripped the handle of the ax before it went flying. Ladtwig lurched forward and grabbed the top strap and yanked. The sheath fell to the ground with a clatter. Semias blinked several times as his eyes adjusted through the pain and tears. Semias kicked the sheath from Ladtwig's reach and used the side of the wall to help him stand.

Turkill jumped from the rock and ran after the sheath that was spinning in the center of the room. Semias threw his arm out and blasted a burst of flame from his hand. Serin shot a burst of air toward the flame, and it consumed the air instead of Turkill. Turkill leaped out of the way but missed the sheath and rolled to a crouch on the other side of the room. Semias thrust an upward strike at Shaz, who sidestepped it and blocked. The Honor blade once again seized a portion of Semias's power. Shaz's heart fire began to swell in his chest. Serin sent a burst of cooling magic that smoldered the heat. Shaz, Riddick, and Semias continued to exchange blows in a rhythmic pattern as though they were taking turns. Turkill carefully made his way to Ladtwig, and they moved around the edges of the room back to where Serin was hiding.

"We have to get that sheath," Turkill said.

"I need to find a way to heal Ladtwig," Serin said.

"Serin, can you send the wind after the sheath?" Ladtwig asked through gritted teeth.

Serin thought a moment and then stepped out of the shadow. She whipped her arms over her head and demanded the wind retrieve the sheath. The sheath shot across the floor with immense speed, and Turkill leaped onto it as it nearly blew past them.

"You will need to fetch me some water. The air in here is so dry I can't summon any, but I think I might be able to use its added strength to heal Ladtwig," Serin said.

Turkill nodded and scurried down the corridor toward the outside. He remembered seeing a small trickle of water near where they had climbed up. The more the two blades collided, the more Shaz inherited Semias's magic. His head became more and more loopy, as though he had too much oxygen. Serin continued to buff him with calming energy, but it was becoming less and less effective.

Serin heard a swooshing noise coming from the dark corridor and pulled Ladtwig tightly into the crevasse. Amirra's red cloak flew passed her hiding spot.

"Oh no, you don't," Serin said.

Serin whipped the air around Amirra and thrust her up against the wall. Amirra yelped in surprise and pain as the realization hit her brain.

"Please, I don't know what I can do, but I want to help," Amirra said.

Amirra's eyes filled with tears, and Serin stepped close and reached for her throat. Amirra squirmed but couldn't move. The air had her pinned against the wall and she felt its strength around her throat. It was very clear that Serin could crush her throat and she would suffocate to death.

"Tell me why I shouldn't just kill you?" Serin said.

"Because you're not a killer," Amirra said.

"I can be, if the right reasons are met and I would say this qualifies," Serin said.

A fire burned behind Serin's eyes and Amirra understood she would, in fact, kill her.

"Then kill me, at least I won't have to fight the shadow anymore," Amirra said.

Serin watched the determination drain from Amirra's face.

"Why did you betray us?" Serin asked.

"Because I had to, I have been a slave to shadow since I was a child. You have no idea the kind of pain it gives when you disobey," Amirra said.

"Actually, I do. But I also know that the shadow can't make you go against your own will. It tries to scare you with pain, but ultimately it has no real power over you," Serin said.

"You sound like Jagwynn," Amirra said.

"So, what are you going to do?" Serin asked.

"If your right, then I do not wish to obey the shadow anymore," Amirra said.

Serin released her wind magic and Amirra plopped to the ground. Serin touched Amirra's temples and sent a surge of healing magic into her core. Amirra felt the coolness ripple through her body and she witnessed the shadow dissipate from her mind.

"I can't believe it!" Amirra said.

"Now, how do we defeat Semias?" Serin asked.

"That I don't know, but I think I know of something that might. Luthrous's rune book," Amirra said.

Amirra gazed into Serin's eyes with a brightness of hope, and Serin nodded. Amirra ran down the corridor and disappeared into the darkness. Serin turned to Ladtwig and found him still bleeding. *I hope Turkill hurries.* She thought. Serin felt Riddick slam into the wall and peeked around the corner. She shot a burst of pain relief into his body and he smiled at her. Riddick jumped up and with two long strides had his ax in his hand ready to attack once again. Serin monitored Shaz's heartfire and felt it increasing in strength. She wasn't sure if it was a good or a bad thing and feared she wouldn't be able to calm it. She had already squashed it three times.

Shaz darted out of the way of Semias's strike and caught the wall with his foot and threw himself into a backward somersault. He landed awkwardly and stumbled. His head was beginning to pound like before he and Serin synergized their magic. He gripped his head and shook it several times. Shaz moved around to the backside of Semias as Riddick grabbed more rock shards and threw them at Semias, who ignited them into melting ore. Riddick leaped out of the way of the scorching liquid while Shaz shot several bursts of flaming balls from behind Semias. Semias's cloak burst into flames and he yelled in pain.

Semias twisted out of the robe and thrust it over his head as it turned to ash. Semias spun on his toes in time to block Shaz's strike. A sudden shift of energy threw Shaz against the wall. It was Shadow magic, but how from where? He felt the bones in his back crack and his legs go numb as he slammed into the jagged wall. Serin came out from the corridor and blasted him with a super-strong surge of healing energy that she even lifted her off the ground. Shaz felt his legs underneath him and his bones pop back into place. Shaz recognized the drain it had left on Serin and was certain she wouldn't last much longer.

He needed to end this and now. Shaz tried to sort through the feelings and thoughts throughout his body. The disorganized energies gave him a nervous feeling. The shadow magic had reached an all-time high, and he feared it was going to overcome him. Amirra dashed back down the corridor and slid to a stop next to the crack Ladtwig was laying in. She threw open the book and started scanning the pages. For what she didn't know exactly, but she did know that the rune symbols had been speaking to her for days.

"Every time the two swords collide, the honor blade takes shadow magic from the other sword. I think it might be overloading Shaz's energy," Serin said.

Amirra flipped through the pages until one of the runes jumped out at her.

"Ah, here, this might help," Amirra said.

"What is it?" Serin asked.

"A runecasting," Amirra said.

"What's that?" Serin asked.

"I don't have magic like you, but I am the new Runecaster, at least that is what Nitida said," Amirra said.

Amirra lifted her hair and showed Serin the newly formed scar.

"Well then do it," Serin said.

Amirra examined the symbols. The meanings suddenly appeared in her mind's eye and she uttered them out loud. A rush of strength she had never felt overcame her frame, and she trembled.

"Are you all right?" Serin asked.

"Better than all right," Amirra said.

Amirra stood up and walked to the edge of the corridor. The words ran off her tongue as though she had been speaking them all her life. She repeated them over and over, growing in strength. Her heart pounded, and she soaked in the strength they gave her. Shaz recognized the words and allowed them to enter his mind. The words swirled around and created a barrier between the shadow and his own thoughts. He shook his head clear and threw out a thumbs up. Amirra turned to Serin with a huge smile. Serin smiled back but a sharp pain hit the back of her head.

36-Why Have You Betrayed Me?

Shaz threw his hand out and let out a long steady stream of fire directly at Semias who threw his own fire magic, in return. The collision created an overwhelming burst of heat around the cavern. The force threw them both backward. Shaz twisted in midair and rolled over backward and landed on his feet. Seimas almost slammed into the floor but Riddick yanked the ground out from under him. Riddick didn't expect the ground to be hollow underneath and Semias fell into the darkness.

"I don't think he could survive that fall," Riddick said peering over the edge.

"Let's hope your right," Shaz said.

"Well don't you exude a ton of confidence," Riddick said.

"I have learned to never doubt the impossible," Shaz said.

"I'm starting to see that," Riddick said.

"Let's get out of here," Shaz said.

Riddick nodded and headed back toward the hallway. The ground under Shaz broke and fell out from under his feet. He fell into the darkness with a holler. Riddick spun on his toe but missed his hand by a few tiny lengths. A dark red glow came into view and Riddick found Shaz sliding unsteadily on the ground like a slide in a downward slope. Riddick launched himself into the expanding earth and grabbed Shaz's wrist as he flew off the edge into the darkened void. Riddick called to the earth and a sturdy platform formed under him, which stopped his own descent. Shaz dangled like a fish over the forever-hole until Riddick pulled him up. They sat on the small ledge and breathed heavily.

"Are you all right, mate?" Riddick asked.

"Yeah, now what?" Shaz asked.

Riddick searched around but found nothing. He reached into his mind and touched the torn earth. A crumbling sound echoed around the massive hole as a narrow ledge formed and spiraled the crevasse back toward the top. Shaz and Riddick carefully, but quickly scaled the ledge. They made it less than a few lengths when the quake shook the ground again. They gripped the edge tightly as the sting of the cold stone ripped through their skin and held on as the earth moved. After several minutes it stopped and Shaz and Riddick let go and winced with the sensation, the blood made as it moved back into their appendages.

"Can you hear that?" Shaz asked as he shook his hands.

"There you go again," Riddick said.

"It's coming from below us," Shaz said.

"See, I knew you were going to say that too," Riddick said.

"Move faster," Shaz said.

Riddick increased his speed, but it didn't help much. The earth shook again, but it wasn't from the ground moving. A blast of steam tore up the hole, scorching Riddick's skin. Riddick tried to shield his face with his hands. The steam bit at the back of his hands and he yelled in pain and shuddered. His body trembled, and he found it very difficult to keep to the wall behind him. Serin peered over the edge and waved her hands. The cooling calm hit Riddick's hands and his body stopped shaking.

"You know, she is truly remarkable," Riddick said.

"You have no idea, mate, but she can't last forever, so let get out of here," Shaz said.

They maneuvered the last several lengths to the top and darted across the remaining floor to the corridor.

"Where is Turkill?" Shaz asked.

Serin examined Riddick's hands and concentrated on pulling the oozing skin together. Soft hues of blue circled his skin, and the skin pulled back together, leaving small lines in its place.

"He went to fetch some water," Serin said.

"I don't serve the shadow anymore, but I also don't know what to do on my own," Amirra blurted.

She gazed at Shaz with pleading in her eyes. Shaz touched her shoulder and nodded, and she breathed out a heavy sigh.

"Ladtwig, how are you feeling?" Shaz asked.

"It won't stop bleeding. Serin keeps the pain down, but it won't heal," Ladtwig said through a shaky voice.

"I even tried a rune chant from this book, but it didn't help," Amirra said.

"I'm hoping I can use water to energize my magic, at least to get the bleeding to stop until we can find another way to heal him," Serin said.

The ground shook again, tussling everyone around.

"Shaz, what neutralizes fire?" Riddick asked.

"Water, I guess, why?" Shaz asked.

Riddick pointed toward the hole. Shaz turned around and stood up slowly. His mind raced to find an explanation of what his eyes were seeing.

"Is that Semias?" Riddick asked.

A set of eyes glared through a shroud of fiery flames. The fire form held the new sword in a grip of flames.

"I think so?" Shaz's perplexed tone sent shivers down Riddick's spine.

Turkill emerged from the darkness carrying the sheath upright. He moved quickly without spilling any water and handed the sheath to Serin, who immediately took several long swallows. A sudden increase consumed her frame. She poured the water onto Ladtwig's arm and witnessed the bleeding come to a complete stop. The wound closed on its own and smoothed into a slightly darker remnant of the injury.

"Did you see that? It healed the wound. Here you have to take a drink. The sheath has some kind of power of its own," Serin said.

Shaz took a swig and passed it to Riddick and then Amirra and the Minca.

"Do you know any marvelous water magic?" Riddick asked.

"Sadly, no. I need to work on that," Shaz said.

"Well, you might want to start practicing because I don't know how we are going to defeat this bastard," Riddick said.

Shaz took the sheath from Serin and strapped it on his hip and secured it to his leg. He slid the Honor Blade into the casing and pulled it out. A sharpening sound sliced through the thick air. Shaz allowed the tickle of raw magic to soak into his fingers and move around his body. He was fully aware of his heartfire and his determination. Shaz nodded at Ladtwig with a deep appreciation for his near-sacrifice in retrieving the sheath. Shaz stepped out from the corridor and studied the flamed figure in the center of the cavern. At first, the flames danced in a chaotic way and Shaz found it hard to make sense of anything.

He slowed his breathing and reached for his own heartfire and observed the chaos transform into a hypnotic pattern of motion. His eyes blurred, and the flames became Semias's human frame. There were several lengths of fire that surrounded his body, but if he could get through them with the sword, it might be enough to dissipate the fire. He explained his plan to Riddick and the others and gripped the hilt. He had grown comfortable with the way the sword fit into his hand, but this time it was smoother, more fluid, elegant, and had a level of its own thinking. The symbols engraved into the hardened steel glowed the same silvery blue as the night he had received it.

Riddick ripped more rock fragments from the walls and thrust them at the burning figure. He noticed Semias was suspended over the hole and wondered how he was floating. Flames reached out like a hand and swallowed the rocks whole. Riddick grabbed more and more and kept throwing with eagerness. Semias blasted a scorching torch of flames, but Riddick pulled up the floor and shielded himself. The flames melted a hole nearly through the thickness, and Riddick shook his head in amazement. Serin gripped the back of her head as another burst of pain hit. Shaz too gripped the back of his head and his knees hit the floor.

"What's wrong?" Amirra asked.

"My head, the pain," Serin said.

Amirra recognized the place where Serin put her hand as the place the shadow uses to control people and wrapped her arms around Serin and chanted the protection spell. She focused hard and smiled when she witnessed her newfound power wrap around Serin, giving her the same mental block she gave Shaz. She repeated the process to protect Riddick and the Minca. Shaz felt the release of the shadow on Serin's mind, and he decided he had had enough. It was one thing to attack him, but to attack Serin was a big mistake.

Serin gripped Amirra's hand and gave her a squeeze and smiled. Amirra smiled, she had finally found her place and was now certain of her new destiny. Shaz moved closer and closer while Riddick was keeping Semias busy. Shaz was steadily growing his heartfire and allowed the anger that he normally kept buried, come to the surface. The one thing he had learned was that he could use anger for good, and right now he wanted to be angry. Serin felt his energy reach its peak and started to send her calming touch, but Shaz blocked her. At first, she was worried and a bit angry herself, but decided that he needed to rely on his own understanding of his magic in order to maximize it. Plus, she knew him now, and she was confident that he would stay under control.

"Do it Shaz!" Serin said, both out loud and in his mind.

Amirra flipped through the book again, hoping to gain more casts. She hadn't realized she was sitting in the opening of the corridor until a shard of stone slammed into her leg as Riddick dodged the onslaught of flames and hit only a length from the hallway opening. Amirra jumped and tried to back out of the way, but not before Semias saw her with the book. An ear-piercing shriek tore through the cave and everyone covered their ears. Amirra grabbed the back of her head and cried out with a sudden jolt of pain. The sensation sucked the breath from her lungs and her body went numb. Serin blasted her with her pain relief magic, and Amirra managed to stand. Serin gave her a nod and Ladtwig smiled at her. She turned and took several steps toward Semias. She tightened her fists and took a deep breath.

"NO, I do not serve the shadow! You have no power over me! I make my own choices!" Amirra shouted.

She repeated the chant she had learned the night she was with Nitida and allowed the power to free herself of the bondage. The flames on the top of Semias's head grew, and he flew toward her, leaving the abyss he came from, but she didn't move. An eerie screech echoed around the room as though Semias was trying to speak, but the flames muffled his words, but Amirra guessed what he was saying.

"You will never have me, you piece of human trash," Amirra sneered.

Large human eyes flashed briefly, long enough for Amirra to see the pain in them, before the flames consumed them once more and he grew to more than twice the size. She smiled with the most exhilarating freedom she had ever felt. Even though she knew this would be her last moments on this planet, she would die a free woman. Semias blasted the fire element toward her. The fire didn't care what it was about to consume, only that it feasted on life's sustenance. Amirra stood with complete peace. The woman from her dreams stood in the distance waiting to welcome her and she was alright with it. Turkill launched himself at her from behind, knocking her over in time for the flames to sizzle above their heads. Shaz had spent the last several moments becoming as the flames himself and was standing nearly inside the shroud of fire.

With a few more steps, he thrust the Honor Blade through Semias's spine. The blade sliced through with ease and Shaz hardly felt the bone or sinew. Semias's face flickered in and out of the flames as the understanding of what had happened overcame him. The fire shroud was sucked from the atmosphere with a pop and left Semias's old and haggard frame half slumped on the floor. Semias lifted the blade up and with the last bit of strength thrust it at Shaz. Shaz pulled the blade from Semias's flesh and whipped it around with such speed that the Honor Blade slashed right through Semias's new blade.

Hardened steel shattered in all directions. Semias yelled as his body failed him and it sank to the ground. He laid on the hot stone with labored breaths, tears streaming down his face. He managed to move his face toward Amirra, who stared in unbelief while pulling herself from the ground. His dark eyes sat deep in the bones of his skull. She remembered him from rotations ago, and the once handsome man he was, and how he used to play with her as a child. The tightness around her throat increased, and she pushed back the tears that now formed. There once was a time she had admired him.

"Why have you betrayed me?" Semias managed.

"I didn't betray you! You were blind to your own greed and desires. It was you that betrayed me, and yourself," Amirra said.

"Why did the sword shatter?" Semias asked, turning to Shaz.

"I figured out that every time the sword struck mine, it gave me power. I assumed it was weakening, and it was only a matter of time before it would be a useless blade," Shaz said.

"Luthrous," muttered Semias.

Semias coughed up blood and then his body fell lifeless.

Amirra wasn't sure how she felt. She wanted to jump for joy at his demise, but there was a source of pain and regret that she didn't expect. Shaz put his arms around her in a hug and gave her a squeeze.

"It will take some time to sort it all out, you don't have to do it all now," Shaz said.

Amirra cleared her throat and wiped the tears, and Serin gave her a hug.

"How can you be so nice to me after everything I have done?" Amirra asked.

"No one is perfect, and we are all we have, we need to stick together now," Riddick said. Amirra smiled and nodded. "Let's get out of here," Riddick said.

"We need to get Jagwynn from the dungeons," Amirra said.

The crew followed Amirra through the tunnels toward the dungeon as she explained her conversation with Jagwynn. The crew wasn't entirely sure if they should believe her, but Jagwynn did seem to have more to her than she had let on. Amirra stopped at the crevasse and started to back up to get a running start.

"Wait, I'll go," Shaz said.

He took a few steps back and ran toward the other side. Serin boosted him with a bit of air that carried him over to the other side.

"She's that way," Amirra said, pointing down another tunnel.

Shaz lit his palm on fire to light his way and found his way to her cell.

"Jag, you in there?" Jagwynn raised her head and yawned. "Well, that's some kind of greeting," Shaz said. He gripped the lock but found it was already unlatched. He gripped the heavy steel bars and yanked, but the door didn't budge. "Humm. It's stuck, looks like the earth settled on it jamming it shut," Shaz said.

He put his hands on the bars and focused his fire element on the metal. A few minutes later, the bars turned shades of orange. Shaz yanked the door, and it popped open as it bent and twisted into a new shape. Jagwynn licked his face and rubbed up against him, nearly knocking him over.

"I know you're a representative of the Sun Goddess and the Dodjen, and you and I are going to have a stiff conversation when we get out of here," Shaz said.

"I love you too," Jagwynn said over a purr.

"I knew it!" Shaz said and wrapped his arms around her thick neck.

She rubbed her large frame into his body and purred loudly, nearly knocking him over. Shaz scratched her ears for a moment, and then they returned to the others.

"There's a way out if you go that way, that way you don't have to jump this again," Amirra said.

Shaz nodded, and they met up in the large room with the rune circle.

37-Is Everyone Alright?

Amirra was the first to exit the mountain. The late evening wind on her skin had a new sensation than it had ever before. The exhilaration of freedom overcame her, and she trembled. Serin gripped her hand and together they navigated the broken terrain. The sun was setting over the ripped and ruined land, and Ladtwig and Turkill gazed in shock at the destruction of their homeland.

"Don't worry, mates. I'll help the earth heal. It won't take long before it will look as brilliant as it did before," Riddick said.

The Minca smiled and followed after Serin and Amirra.

"Any ideas as to how to repair the rip in time?" Riddick asked Shaz.

Shaz shook his head and started down the trail. Once they were off the mountain, Serin buffed them with her wind walk and showed Amirra how to navigate the magic. It didn't take long to get back to the battleground. They found the Minca bandaging their wounded and cleaning as much as they could.

"Where is the Chief?" Turkill asked a warrior.

"He returned to the village not long ago," the warrior said.

"Let's hurry we need to find out if he knows how to fix the barrier," Shaz said.

The sadness in the Minca's postures left little to celebrate. They had defeated Semias and the Jaduuk, but it didn't feel like anything to cheer for. They hurried to the village and found the Chief at the prayer hut. Turkill was the first to enter and then Shaz and Serin, Amirra, Riddick and then Ladtwig. Turkill knelt beside the Chief and waited until he opened his eyes.

"You have returned. I'm so glad," the Chief embraced him.

"Father, do you know how we can mend the time barrier?" Turkill asked.

The Chief shook his head and Turkill sagged.

"I might," Amirra said. She pulled out the heavy book from her satchel. "I don't know all the symbols yet, but I am willing to study as much as I can to find out."

"Shaz might be able to help," Serin said.

Amirra went to the center of the room and placed the book on the floor. Shaz sat on the floor and opened the cover. He scanned over the text and flipped the pages until he came to a parchment that was folded several times. He unfolded it and sat it on the book.

"That's the scroll that Semias used to bring Luthrous here. I saw him study that thing for rotations. I don't think we will ever be able to understand it," Amirra said.

"I can read it, all of it. It's quite complex, however, and it's going to take all of us. Even you Amirra," Shaz said.

But I don't have powers like you," Amirra said.

"That is where you are wrong, my dear. You see, words are some of the most powerful. A simple word can take down an entire kingdom just as one can build one up," the Chief said.

"You sound like Nitida," Amirra said.

"I'm glad you were listening," Nitida said.

They all jumped at the little woman's voice. No one had noticed her sitting in the corner of the hut.

"I'm sorry I did what I did. To ALL of you," Amirra said.

Nitida nodded.

"Now read to me the scroll," Nitida said.

Shaz began reading the ancient language, watching for certain words that had commands in them and substituted them with the general language so that he wouldn't evoke the spell again. Nitida listened carefully and made a mental note of the order of the processes. They spent several hours dissecting the spell, each person adding the pieces of what they understood from their element until they were confident that they knew what to do.

They all agreed that they would return to the mountain cave and evoke the spell from there. The plan would take a bit of time to execute because they had to gather a few things, and Nitida and Amirra would need some time to enchant several items for each person. With all the plans made, they called it a night and retired to their huts. Shaz and Serin walked quietly with Jagwynn through the now dry grass.

"Do you think this is going to work?" Serin asked.

"Aye, why? Don't you?" Shaz asked.

"Yes, but something still doesn't seem right," Serin said.

"Like what?" Shaz asked.

"Well, in the scroll it makes specific mention to the three moons' alignment. The moons aren't even close, and we don't know if that will throw this whole thing off," Serin said.

"True, but we don't know if the spell was originally evoked with the proper alignment either. I don't think it will cause any problems, but we can ask the Chief if he knows when the earth shakes began and have Riddick search it out with his magic in the morning. All right?" Shaz asked.

Serin nodded and pulled her satchel off.

"When this whole thing is over, I'm taking a bath," Serin said.

Shaz chuckled.

"Deal," he said.

Sleep quickly overcame them, but Shaz stirred all night. A mysterious figure standing perfectly still kept coming and going in his dreams. It didn't have a face, but the feeling he got was quite unsettling and he wanted to wake up, but he couldn't. A tightness in his chest gripped his frame, and he was certain fear was going to overtake him.

"Shaz, wake up. Are you alright?" Serin said.

Serin shook Shaz's shoulders and patted his chest, but he didn't wake up. Serin put her hands on the sides of his head and closed her eyes. She imagined herself moving through her magic into his and into his mind. She saw the mysterious figure and Shaz standing there staring at it. She walked up next to Shaz and tried to talk to him, but she found he was in a trance. She searched around his dream and found nothing but mist and darkness.

"Shaz," Serin said softly. "I know you can hear me, and I know that this is someone trying to talk to you, but you have to shut it down for now so we can finish our task. I will help you figure this out, I promise you, but right now I need you. We all need you."

Shaz blinked and looked at her. She smiled and took his hand and started walking away from the figure. Shaz looked back only once and then shook his head clear of the trance.

"Serin, what are you doing here? You're in my head?" Shaz asked.

"I couldn't get you to wake up and you were having a nightmare, so I came to get you. You need to wake up now," Serin said.

Shaz nodded, and Serin quickly faded away. He blinked and stirred, then opened his eyes. Serin's beautiful form was sitting in front of him. He sat up and wrapped her in a tight embrace.

"Are you all right?" Serin asked.

"Were you really in my head?" Shaz asked.

"Yes, do you know who that being was?" Serin asked.

"No, but when this is all done, I will need to figure it out," Shaz said.

"We still have a few hours before we need to get up, try to sleep," Serin said.

Serin started to get up, but Shaz didn't let her go.

"I didn't thank you for healing me and Riddick and the others. You mean so much to me I don't have adequate words to express it to you," Shaz said.

He wasn't the type, but he found his emotions overcome him and tears streamed down his cheeks. Serin found herself feeling the weight of the last several moons escape her, and she sagged into his grip. For several minutes they held each other as their energies realigned and they felt a peace they hadn't in a long time.

"Are you good?" Serin asked.

"Aye, you seem to be able to heal more than just my body," Shaz said.

"You seem to be pretty needy lately too," Serin said.

Shaz blurted a hearty guffaw. Serin chuckled at his laughter and wiped the last bit of tear from the corner of her eye.

"Well, I'm going to have to be a bit needier to finish this off. I have no idea how much shadow magic this is going to take, and even with our synergy, shadow magic still requires a payment of some kind," Shaz said.

"That's what Nitida will be teaching Amirra, how to enchant an item to shield you from the shadows payment, so let's hope it's enough," Serin said.

"Let's hope," Shaz said.

Shaz laid on his pillow and Serin laid next to him. His warmth was comforting. The soot-filled sky had blocked the sun for so long that there was little heat to keep them warm. They laid there listening to the quiet sounds of the early morning. It was much quieter than when they had first arrived. After a while, they heard the Minca village begin to wake and decided to get an early start.

They followed the well-trodden path from their hut into the village and found Ladtwig and Turkill already packed. They knew they didn't have a part in the casting of the spell, but they weren't going to stay back for anything. The Chief and Nitida arrived slightly after Riddick. Shaz rehearsed Serin's concern with them and Nitida re-visited the scroll one more time and discussed it with the Chief quietly over breakfast. Shaz, Serin, and Riddick dished up some hot porridge and found a place to eat while they waited for Amirra.

"Where are Amirra and Jag?" Serin asked.

"I'll go check on her," Riddick said.

"Jag had a few things to take care of for the Sun Goddess," Shaz said.

"Is that weird?" Serin asked.

"I suppose, but she promised she would tell us everything she could when she returned," Shaz said.

Riddick slurped the last bit of mush and returned his dish to the pile of increasing dishes. His long legs carried him quickly through the little people to Amirra's hut.

"Amirra, are you coming?" Riddick asked.

"Be right there," Amirra said.

The flap opened, and she climbed out. Her long cinnamon hair was tied back, leaving a few of the shorter hairs around her face to frame her delicate cheeks. Her sparkling eyes soaked in the murky light.

"You seem different, I like it," Riddick said.

"I feel different. Did you know that last night was the first night of my life as a free woman?" Amirra asked.

Riddick shook his head. "I guess that would make me happy too," he said.

Amirra beamed. Riddick held out his elbow.

"Well, Miss Free, shall we?" Riddick said, his eyes bright.

Amirra laughed and took his elbow, and they returned to the center square.

"Get a load of that," Shaz said, nudging Serin.

"I think it's great," Serin said with a smile.

Shaz nodded.

Their new joy was quickly replaced with sadness and despair as they traveled through the countryside. The devastation was incomprehensible. Little bodies mixed among large beastly frames of the Jaduuk painted an eerie picture of horror. There were far more Jaduuk than Minca, but even one human life lost was one too many. It was hard not to let the anger swell within themselves. The reek of death became almost unbearable. Serin buffed everyone with her air bubble so they could stand to stomach having to find a way through the carnage.

The Chief and Turkill discussed plans for the mass burial services of the lost Minca, and Riddick and Shaz discussed how they were going to discard the Jaduuk. They decided Riddick would open the earth and Serin would use her air magic to move the bodies into the holes.

Then Shaz would burn them, then they would move all the soot over the holes and into the cracks and crevasse that remained. Serin would drench the soot with water and Shaz would heat it up, making a hard covering. It was a good plan, but it all depended on whether they would be able to repair the barrier in the first place.

The late afternoon sun found a tiny hole in the soot-filled sky and broke the dread. They found the trail back to the cave and made a sweep of the caverns to make sure there were no dangers. Amirra pocketed the few things from her old room and found Semias's staff. She didn't fully understand yet how to use the staff, but Nitida assured her she would teach her and urged her to take it. Even though it reminded Amirra of Semias, she found a certain peace knowing that it was hers now and that she would use it for good. She was about to leave his chamber when she noticed the crest of the Velshari that signified his position and rank. She hesitated and wasn't sure she wanted to take it, but she figured it was better in her hands than someone else's' so she stuck it in her pocket.

Shaz stepped on the center rune in the middle of the rune circle. Serin took the East circle with Turkill, Riddick the West and the Chief and Nitida took the south. Amirra gripped the staff and sucked in a deep breath and then stepped onto the North circle. Ladtwig wrapped his arms around Amirra and gave her a squeeze. Riddick slipped his shoes off and allowed the earth's energy to course through his body. Shaz pulled the scroll from his satchel and unfolded the long parchment. The paper draped over his hand and touched the floor. Shaz cleared his throat and began reading the ancient language.

"Ma'rray re mi china charera no'ha, latenta no mevina sanela santo tere. Ano teri nara shento menin shelt me'eari. Ste namari ha'la'tay kina nara. Tay nada' no'halla noch'ari."

His mouth moved clearly and freely through the peculiar sounds. Nitida and Amirra began chanting the rune symbols of the casting circle to evoke the engraved circle's permission to use its powers. Serin focused on Shaz and kept a constant connection with his mind, watching for the Shadow or anything that would distract his focus. She monitored his heart rate and his heartfire.

"Sa nate te narato. Shatyoha re mevina charera, no'ha latenta no novena sanela santo tere. Ano tere nara shento mea'aha teriardi ste namari she'late narata toshchari san ate te narato,"

Riddick searched for every nook and cranny that melted earth could escape from and pictured them closing. A distant rumble echoed through the cavern. The rune circle began to illuminate a soft yellow and then hues of oranges.

"Charlata mo'ha latenta no mevina somella nome' tere. Ano tere nara shento may'ha te narata nochari somatay,"

Shaz carefully read every word. His voice was strong and magnificent. The heat in his chest grew, however, this time there was a delicate string of blue light wrapped around it. He was at total peace knowing Serin's calming presence was there.

Amirra and Nitida shifted to the Runecast of Mind Shield, and between them, they had enough energy to secure the entire group. Shaz became aware of the mysterious being standing on the outer edge of the mind shield. Serin too noted its presence. Turkill wrapped his arms around Serin as she started to sway. He braced his feet against the ground and focused on keeping her from falling.

The hues of yellows and oranges danced around the circle and twisted around each person. Their hair moved and swayed in the breeze the magic created. Riddick gripped his toes into the stone and imagined the earth returning to its previous places. The rumble became louder as it moved closer. Riddick's heart pounded and sweat formed at his hairline. He had pulled his long locks up into a bun at the back of his head. His lightweight leather armor formed around his frame tightly and his muscles flexed as the planet's power came into his frame.

Serin kept a mind's eye on the mysterious figure and noted it didn't show any attempt to harm to Shaz. She reached her arms outstretched and called for the wind to give her strength. A gust of wind circled around her and Turkill. The funnel continued to increase in speed, and she soaked in the power it gave.

The ceiling of the mountain cave cracked, and the blackness faded into a crystal blue. Strings of dancing colors rippled across the opening. The large hole in the middle slowly grew together as one string became two and two became four and so on. Amirra and Nitida then began the ancient apology chant. The need to apologize for the missuse of powers was important to the universal elements and would secure their favor in the future. Amirra read from the parchment that Nitida had written for her, and Nitida held her arms outstretched toward the ceiling. It took Amirra a few tries to get the inflections correct, but soon felt the flow move off the tip of her lips freely.

"Mev'vina charera no'ha latenta no novena sanela santo, mea'aha teriardi ste namari. Anotay re nada' chento ma'ha vi say na marri she'late narata noshari senate."

Shaz finished the last of the ancient words and watched the strings over his head weave back and forth and form a tight surface of magic. A golden string emerged from the fabric and wriggled its way toward Shaz. He sucked in a deep breath, understanding this was the part that was going to hurt. The string entered his chest and his body lifted off the ground. Serin boosted every bit of her energy and thrust it at him. The pain in Shaz's frame wreaked havoc on his senses and he shook. The string followed the course of energy and entered Serin's body. She gasped with pain and tried to suck air into her lungs. The string then moved to Riddick. He closed his eyes, waiting for the pain to hit, and his body arched backward.

Amirra slammed the staff on the ground and the ball at the top glowed a hot red. The string crossed the circle to the staff and entered the ball. A sizzling rage of fiery heat ravaged Amirra's body, and she lifted off the ground. Ladtwig held her tight but closed his eyes. The string returned to Shaz and then a beam of light burst from his body into the time fabric in the ceiling. The string left their forms and secured itself into the last slot of time. The multi-colored strings changed their color to gold, and the barrier was healed. The ground stopped rumbling and a shield of darkness once again covered the time barrier.

Everyone fell to the floor as the lights of the circle faded into blackness. Gasps, sputters, moans and groans from everyone tainted the darkness for several minutes while everyone returned to normal.

"Is everyone alright?" Nitida asked.

Everyone returned their status, and Shaz warmed his hands with firelight. A sconce on the wall opposite him caught his eye, and he commanded the fire element to ignite the torch. Several torches around the room lit and they now saw a beautiful temple. The once black-stone was now soft gray with white speckles. Engravings etched into the stone reflected each of them with their elements, telling the story of how they came together to repair the rip in time.

"This is amazing," Serin said, getting off the ground and taking in all the details.

"Was this a temple before?" Amirra asked.

"It was, but one that belonged to the Velshari. But now it belongs to the four of you." Nitida said.

"For what?" Riddick asked.

"Whatever you may need it for," Nitida said.

"Well, I don't want to stay here, so let's get out of here," Riddick said.

They all chuckled, Riddick and Amirra helped the Minca to the exit, leaving Shaz and Serin in the center of the room.

"There will be a need for this place in the future, but for now, I think we will leave it hidden," Shaz said.

Serin nodded and Turkill turned and nodded from the entrance. Turkill knew it would be his people's new responsibility to keep this new secret and was proud to know why it needed to be that way, why they all needed to be kept secret.

Shaz stopped at the entrance and after everyone was out, he put a shield on the opening. The mountainside grew over the opening covering the corridor.

"Hey look," Serin said.

She pointed at all the stars in the clear night sky. Everyone talked excitedly about all the things they could see from high up on the mountain. The smoke plumes were gone. The crevasses were mended. Soft white clouds speckled the night and two of the three moons peeked out from the purple hazy mist of the skies of Edenocht. Shaz listened to the soft hum of the sword that now rested in its sheath. The calmness it gave his soul was second to the love he had for Serin and his friends.

They were all too excited to make camp, so they traveled through the night back to the village. As they arrived, the sun peeked over the treetops. A warmth covered the land and the little people of the Minca rejoiced. Shouts of joy and celebration rang through the skies. Trumpets blew, drums beat, and laughter echoed. The Chief announced his plans for their celebration but first instructed the Minca on the plans for cleaning up the devastation.

Although their reasons for making the necessary devices were devastating, their singing and music didn't stop. The days were long, and nights were short, and it was days before anyone got any decent kind of sleep. Riddick spent his time opening large holes and Serin brushed the carcasses of the Jaduuk into them then Shaz burned them. Serin tried to keep the ash out of the villages and funneled the smoke into the atmosphere. Riddick grew a plethora of strong-smelling plants around the village to keep the stench of the burning flesh at a minimum. Together they moved as much of the soot piles and compacted them with water and fire, making a thick paste, and then Riddick sealed the holes closed with earth. Riddick walked around with bare feet everywhere he went and focused on growing grass, vegetables, vegetation, and trees. The grass and vegetation was easy, but even with the speed his magic added, the trees would still take much longer to take root and become the once magnificent wonders they used to be.

Riddick tried to show Shaz what he was doing and Shaz tried to walk around barefoot too. Except most of the fresh grass, he walked on melted instead so he gave up and decided that he much preferred the fire element and he would leave the earth stuff to Riddick. Serin instructed Riddick on the types of plants that were needed for Mrs. Bailey's ointment, and then Riddick organized the earth to be able to grow in special gardens. Fionte and Babbesh became the resident healers and when Serin asked the women if she should end her rain cloud they asked if they could keep it, so Riddick constructed a beautiful fountain for the rain-cloud to permanently rest in with the words *Reva-Araceli de Serin,* being translated as, *Rain alter of the Water Mage Serin,* inscribed in the stone. It still had the ability, however, for temporary movement if needed.

The cheerful Minca made the dreaded tasks more bearable, and everyone found a bit of joy in them. Riddick especially loved making pebbles fly around so that the children could try to catch them. Riddick was one of the biggest kids there was, and he found no shortage of activities to entertain himself and Amirra. It became obvious that the two were growing fond of one another.

38-Leave The Adventures To You Two, NO WAY!

The day of celebration finally came and there was so much food, games, activities, and amusement that it would take days to see it all. The Minca from the other clans had set up huts and wagons with all sorts of trinkets and items to trade. Shaz and Serin spent most of the day eating and playing games with the Minca. At one-point, Shaz was part of the amusement with his fire tricks until Serin called down a sudden splash of water and drenched him. Steam billowed from his hot skin and everyone laughed. Riddick and Amirra spent a great deal of time together, and Turkill and his lady friend made special treatment for one another. Ladtwig consumed the most amount of food they had ever seen. It was clear to Shaz and Serin that they wouldn't want to leave and that they would have to part ways.

It had been a long time since their meeting at the castle, and they had grown extremely fond of them. Shaz and Serin discussed quietly how hard it was going to be to say goodbye and all the reasons as to why they should. But it was only a tactic to talk themselves into being alright with the idea.

The day drifted toward evening and Shaz expected things to return to normal, but there was no stopping in sight. He found it quite interesting that the Minca drank so much and didn't even feel woozy or get out of control. He had never touched the stuff at Grandfather's instruction. He didn't then, but understands now, that he can never let his guard down and risk the Shadow to overtake him from a drunken state. The crowds started organizing into smaller groups around enormous bonfires while historians told the events in story form, some to tunes they made up. Shaz watched with wonder and amazement as their little frames exuded so much happiness. It was refreshing, and he wanted to remember it forever.

Shaz found Serin sitting with Amirra and several Minca women discussing a Minca ritual that was meant to attract a man. Serin noticed his presence and looked up. She smiled at him from across the circle. The firelight danced on her features and made his heart swell. Jagwynn had still not returned, and he grew uneasy with the passing of time. Serin understood his worry and gave him a gentle gaze. She excused herself from the group but didn't make it very far when the women saw Shaz. They called to the musicians to play the lover's song and told them to dance. Serin blushed and tried to tell them kindly that maybe another time. Shaz stepped into the circle and took her hands.

She turned to him and he swept her around the fire. Shaz and Serin had been through so much that they had developed a natural rhythm with each other, and their steps were completely in sync. Serin gazed into Shaz's eyes and for the moment felt a joy she would never forget. Shaz and Serin stopped dancing as the music faded and the crowd hesitated as though in their own trance. What Shaz and Serin hadn't noticed was the radiating light of their energies surround them while they danced. The Minca had become accustomed to the presence of magic, and as the hypnotic effects wore off, they cheered. Shaz and Serin excused themselves even with the taunting of more and started back to their hut.

"So, how about this party," Shaz said.

"It's quite amazing, that's for sure," Serin said. Shaz pulled the flap open. "Let's sit under the stars for a bit," Serin said.

Shaz nodded, and they walked to the edge of the river. Shaz moved the sword and sheath out of the way so he could sit. Serin watched as a mixture of emotions came and went from his expression.

"We have to leave soon, don't we?" Serin asked.

Shaz nodded.

"I grow uneasy staying in one place. Plus, I think it would be good to go back to the castle and do more research on the portals and how the travelers used to travel. Riddick was telling me about Yerild and how he used to be a Traveler and in charge of moving artifacts. I don't like that Crolos is still out there and I'm worried about Turob. Plus, we have to get to the Timeless Plains in the Banished Realms," Shaz said.

"When were you going to tell me about that?" Serin asked, a little annoyed.

"I know, I wasn't trying to keep anything from you, it's just been a little crazy with everything going on," Shaz said.

"I know, I'm sorry. What's going on in the Timeless Plains?" Serin asked.

"Gavin Rhill is growing another Jaduuk army, but that's as much as I know. I have a feeling that the mysterious figure from my dreams is connected to it somehow," Shaz said.

"Do you think Inelius will know anything about it?" Serin asked.

"I hope so," Shaz said.

"I don't think Turkill and Ladtwig are going to want to leave again, so I guess it will be you, me and Riddick. Amirra is going to stay with Nitida for a time. She has much to learn and needs time to adjust to her new responsibilities," Serin said.

"I'm not sure where Jag is, so it's going to be just us for now," Shaz said.

"What about Ceros?" Serin asked.

"What about him?" Shaz asked.

"I've been thinking, why did he tell you to destroy the Sev-Rin-Ac-Lavah when others have spoken highly of it. The Whispmother, the Chief, Yerild, Mrs. Bailey, they are all part of the Dodjen, but they all have asked why to destroy it. This Council that the Chief said had it written about Synmagic, and didn't Mrs. Bailey tell you, you were supposed to meet them before rescuing me from the dungeons? I think we need to find out more about this Dodjen and The Council, are they the same, or who are they, and who is actually in charge, or do we tell them *we* are in charge now," Serin said.

"That's a good point. I hadn't thought of that. Maybe Inelius will know about that too. But now you're making me more nervous," Shaz said.

Serin gave him a sideways glare. Shaz smiled.

"So, when do you want to leave?" Serin asked.

"Tomorrow," Shaz said.

"I thought you would say that," Serin said.

"Come on, let's go break the news to the others," Shaz said.

"Let's let them enjoy the party a little longer," Serin said.

She gripped his hand and gave it a squeeze. Serin rested her head on his shoulder and listened to the rushing water. They waited until the noise softened to a gentle hum throughout the village and found each one and told them the plan. Turkill grunted his usual harrumph, and Ladtwig shoved an extra bite of cheese into his mouth. Riddick and Amirra discussed travel arrangements and logistics with Shaz and Serin for several minutes, and then they returned to their huts for the night. Shaz woke before Serin and started gathering his things quietly. He was experiencing a sense of urgency but didn't have an explanation. Serin stirred and rolled over.

"Sorry, I didn't mean to wake you," Shaz said.

"Is everything all right?" Serin asked.

"I guess, we just need to get moving," Shaz said.

"That doesn't sound too sure," Serin said.

"You know me, I'm never too sure about anything," Shaz said.

"Well, that part is true," Serin said.

She got out of bed and started gathering her things. They had received so many gifts from the Minca that they found it hard to move about their hut.

"I hope they won't be upset when we don't take all this with us," Serin said.

"What, you're not going to pack it all?" Shaz asked.

"Nope," Serin said.

Shaz chuckled and threw the last of his clothes into his satchel.

"You're not going to fold those nicely and tuck them in their proper place?" Serin asked.

Shaz looked at her with surprise and then laughed.

"Yeah, I guess there are other things to worry about," Shaz said.

They finished packing and slipped out of the hut they had shared for over a moon cycle. They met up with Riddick in the village square, and then Amirra made her way. Shaz pulled out his map and showed Riddick how it worked. Riddick was as bad as Ladtwig and tried to move the hovering balls around, but with no success. Turkill and Ladtwig showed up a few minutes later dressed, packed and ready to go.

"I didn't expect you two to come," Shaz said.

"Are you kidding? Leave the adventures to you? NO WAY!" Turkill blurted.

"Are you sure? What about your-" Serin started.

"We discussed it, and she agrees, I am too important on this mission to abandon it now," Turkill said.

"Well, then, we are glad you are coming," Serin said.

"Me too," Ladtwig said with a huge smile.

"Aye, you too," Shaz said.

Shaz noticed the Chief and Chieftess coming from their hut and several more Minca clansmen.

"Let's get going before this becomes a major production," Shaz said. Jagwynn padded up behind Shaz and nuzzled into him. "Hey, your back," Shaz said.

"And just in time too," Turkill said.

Turkill gripped a handful of fur and leaped onto her back. Ladtwig tried to get onto her back too, but his overly stuffed backpack, full of food, of course, kept pulling him over. Riddick lifted him up, and he grabbed onto Turkill's waist.

Serin and Amirra hugged each other, and Serin reassured her they would see her again soon. Nitida gave them instructions on how to access the Chantry from Shaz's castle and that they could keep in contact that way. Serin then hugged the Chieftess and Chief and then

Babbesh and Fionte. She choked back the tears that were sitting heavy in her throat and made sure they remembered how to make Mrs. Bailey's ointment. Shaz and Riddick found it hard to say goodbye as well and had to pretend to be discussing the directions they were going to take. The Chief had shown them a different route that wouldn't require them to climb down the cliffs, which brought Serin much relief. The crew started out at a quick pace and soon the village had faded into the background.